GIFTS *of the* PERAMANGK

DEAN MAYES

2012

Central Avenue Publishing Edition

Copyright © 2012 Dean Mayes

This Central Avenue Publishing edition is published by arrangement with Dean Mayes.

www.centralavenuepublishing.com

First print edition published by Central Avenue Publishing,
an imprint of Central Avenue Marketing Ltd.

GIFTS OF THE PERAMANGK

ISBN 978-1-926760-80-3

Published in Canada with international distribution.

Cover Design: Michelle Halket

Cover Photography: Copyright Courtesy of Anne Akiko Meyers Photographed by Lisa Mazzucco

"Prayer Of The Children" lyrics reproduced with the kind permission of Kurt Bestor

In the Adelaide Hills of South Australia lies a triangular wedge of countryside extending from the Barossa Valley in the North to the Southern reaches of the Fleurieu Peninsula. These are the lands of the Peramangk nation and the home of the Peramangk Aborigines - a tribe steeped in a unique culture and held with a mystical reverence.

Aboriginal & Torres Strait Islanders are advised that the following story contains depictions of people who have died.

For Simon...

GIFTS *of the* PERAMANGK

CHAPTER 1

1951

GOLDEN BEAMS OF A MID AFTERNOON SUN knifed down through the canopy of a weeping willow, whose leafy fingers swayed back and forth above a water hole. Silent explosions of light danced across the sun-lit water like glittering fairies until they disappeared on the craggy shore.

This simple ballet regenerated itself, sustaining a hypnotic dance of light and movement which was reflected in the eyes of a child that sat on the bank of the water hole, just forward of the main trunk of the willow tree. Transfixed by the beautiful dance, she tilted her head, allowing the light show to carry her imagination away.

The girl was slight, rake thin, with shining, raven black hair and coffee brown skin. She blinked as the sunlight dazzled her vision and the shimmering light danced across her powdery skin, her flawless cheeks.

She wore a simple cream coloured dress with a lilac flower print. The contrast with her skin was as incongruous as it was pretty. She sat hunched forward slightly, her sinewy legs outstretched, her bare feet exposed to a pocket of sunlight that peeped through the canopy of the willow. Her soles were uncharacteristically tough and leathery in comparison to the rest of her skin—the result of rarely wearing any form of footwear. Not that she was in any way aware of this at her age. For Virginia was only eight years old.

SPLASH.

Virginia's eloquent reverie was suddenly and abruptly broken when something—or someone—hit the water in front of her like a bomb, throwing up glittering cascades of water that drenched not only Virginia, but two of her companions who had been lying beside her, sunning themselves.

"Bloody hell!" Virginia squeaked, as a similarly lithe and dark young figure erupted from the water wearing a huge grin. "You're a menace, Bobby!"

Virginia stood up, arms outstretched, her dress soaked as the shock of the cool water dissipated but was replaced by the awkward feeling of wet clothing stuck to her skin.

She cursed under her breath, inadvertently inhaling some of the water that had splashed across her face. She coughed and spluttered for several moments, wiping furiously at her face.

Virginia had had enough fun in the water for today. Having only recently recovered from a prolonged bout of bronchitis, she had been swimming, jumping and playing in the cool water for the better part of the morning—when the sun's warmth was at its peak. Virginia was exhausted now and thus was happy to relax on the shore and watch the others frolic in the water, swing off the rope and tyre swing that hung from one of the boughs of the willow and sun themselves on the shore.

Stifling her cough, Virginia maintained her steely grimace a moment longer before her facade cracked. Bobby flashed a broad, cheeky smile and she returned it in kind. He then flipped himself into an effortless duck dive and disappeared below the surface. Virginia shook her head then balled her fist to her chest.

There were seven of them in all, a mixture of Aboriginal and Caucasian children: four girls—three of whom sat on the shore, including Virginia, and one in the water—and three boys. They ranged in age from six to thirteen years old. They were as close a group of friends as one could find. The children lived a carefree existence in the Adelaide Hills of South Australia, revelling in the temperate climate of the ubiquitous Australian bush and the rolling green pastures that were defining features of their homeland.

It was an uncharacteristically warm autumn Saturday. The unexpected, extended summer weather gave the children plenty of extra lazy days by the waterhole, their favourite place in the whole world. The boys had built a ramshackle fort here, from pieces of discarded iron and timber that lay nearby. The rope swing that hung out over the water within easy reach was a particularly proud achievement for Bobby who had managed to procure the rope after several failed attempts.

As Bobby surfaced several feet away from where he had executed his dive, Virginia sat down once more, crossing her legs in one effortless motion as she smoothed out her dress before her.

Her companions, who were tying an impressive length of daisy chain, admired her summer dress silently. One of the girls quickly reached out with her hand to billow out the material behind Virginia, to prevent it from crumpling underneath her as she plonked down on the ground.

"Your mum's done such a good job with that dress," one of the girls remarked languidly as Virginia picked up the length of daisy chain before her and assessed her handiwork.

She smiled bashfully, glancing at her friend, Lucy, beside her.

"Mum is a good seamstress. Mrs. Stinson gave her this material months ago and Mum has been working on it, little by little ever since. Mrs. Stinson is good to us."

The Mrs. Stinson Virginia referred to owned the haberdashery in Totness' main street and employed Virginia's mother there as a shop assistant and seamstress. Her mother's work was, in fact, quite well regarded throughout the district.

"Has your father seen it yet? Have you sent him a photograph?"

Virginia bowed her head and shook it meekly.

"We don't know if he got the parcel Mum sent yet," she responded quietly, glancing sideways at her second companion, a slightly chubby Caucasian girl named Rita, on the bank. "We sent him photographs weeks ago but we haven't heard anything."

"Is your mum worried? I heard the men in the pub talking the other day, saying that lots of soldiers are getting hurt in *Karea*."

Rita reached around behind Virginia and poked Lucy in the ribs, causing the younger girl to jump where she sat.

"It's *Korea!*" she scolded disapprovingly. "And don't be so nosey."

Virginia's eyes glazed for just a moment—but it was enough of a moment for the girls to notice that she was worlds away from them. Rita gently placed a hand on Virginia's shoulder and smiled.

"Don't worry Ginnie. He'll be alright. He's a big fella and he knows how to look after himself."

Virginia looked at Rita and managed a wan half smile in return.

"I miss him," she said simply, pausing to stifle another coughing fit from the residual water she had inhaled earlier. "Mum *really* misses him. It's been weeks since we've heard anything. Sometimes I hear her crying at night. I wish he would come home."

Virginia's father was a soldier, an Anzac, serving in the far off country of Korea in a war that Virginia and her mother could barely understand. He had been gone for many months; so long in fact that Virginia feared now that she was struggling to remember him. She desperately missed the sound of his voice, especially his singing voice which was lovely and deep and soft and told the stories of his people—the Peramangk Aborigines of the Adelaide Hills—that had been passed down through generations. She remembered his hands too—large, dark leathery hands that were strong at work but also incredibly tender and soft when he held her own small hand in his. The township of Totness held him in high regard and they were protective of his young family.

From far above the trio, high up in the boughs of the willow tree, an unsettling bird call issued forth suddenly, causing all three of the girls to jump where they sat.

"What was that!?" Lucy exclaimed, startled.

"I don't know," Rita replied, rising to her feet and craning her neck to scan the upper reaches of the willow tree.

Virginia rose with her and together they watched for any movement. The unsettling bird call sounded once more, a deep undulating cry—almost like the sound of a crying baby. The sound was enough to stall the children in the water and all of them stopped their splashing for a moment, treading water in silence.

There was a flash of movement. Then, suddenly, a single small grey bird dove into view, launching itself from the high up bough. It dived down in a graceful arc before peeling away over the water hole toward a eucalyptus on the other side where it had spied a suitable branch upon which to land.

Virginia watched the bird intently, following its flight path as it angled out over the water hole. It cried out a third time, sending a chill through her. She had never heard anything quite like it before.

"It's a Mingka bird," Bobby said evenly, from his vantage point in the water.

"What's that?" Albert, his companion treading water beside him, exclaimed.

"Well…I—um. It's a…I dunno exactly what it is," Bobby stammered. "But my nana told me a story about it once. She said it's a bird that cries whenever somebody is about to die."

Both Lucy and Rita gasped and Rita put her hands on her hips angrily. She flashed Bobby a withering glare from where she stood.

"Bobby!" she hissed. "You can't say things like that!"

Rita nodded her head subtly in the direction of Virginia, so that she couldn't see.

Bobby's expression faltered as he eyed Virginia, who was still staring up at the bird. She gave the impression that she hadn't heard him. The bird cried out once more, its unsettling warble carrying across the water hole.

"Well, I never meant that Ginnie's dad was gonna be…you know…" He paused, sensing that he was digging himself further into a hole. "B-besides…its cry isn't deep enough. It has to be a deep cry if a man is going to die. That cry sounds lighter…more like for a woman. Not a man."

Bobby's words sounded distant to Virginia; her eyes were fixed on the bird far above her. Suddenly, she didn't feel like being here at the water hole any more.

"I think I might go and see Mum," she said flatly. "She should be finished work soon."

Virginia bent down, picked up her towel from the ground and brushed it down with her hand. Both Lucy and Rita were glaring disapprovingly at Bobby while his companions—Albert, Vaughan and Edith—turned away from Bobby and swam to shore. Their splashes caused the bird to take flight once more. It issued one final cry, then disappeared over the canopy of the willow tree and was gone.

"We'll come with you, hey?" Rita offered, nodding firmly at Lucy out of sight of Virginia. "Maybe we could get some ice cream."

Virginia managed a meek smile as the children from the water gathered around her.

THEY SAUNTERED ALONG the path that flanked the main street, heading to the sleepy township of Totness. The girls had managed to coax Virginia back into conversation while Bobby hung back a little, having been stung by their scolding of him earlier. The prospect of an ice cream however, rendered the unpleasant encounter almost forgotten and the group skipped along happily.

Totness' main street was quiet, as it almost always was. The tranquil hamlet, nestled among the patchwork meadows, was by its very nature a sleepy township. It seemed a world away from everything. It served a community of rural folk—farmers, graziers, grain growers, small holders. They were people of the land who knew the land well and worked it with an almost reverential respect.

As the children walked along under the tall plane trees that lined both sides of the street, they chattered and laughed enthusiastically and Virginia joined in, having now forgotten the earlier events. The boys rough-housed with one another while the girls continued their earnest discussion about their impressive daisy chain and what to do with it once they got it safely home. They chattered excitedly about what flavoured ice cream to treat themselves to at the general store. The discussion then drifted back to

Virginia's father.

"My dad says that this war is no good for anyone," Lucy remarked, surprising both Virginia and Rita somewhat since their smaller companion had, until now, remained painfully quiet. "He says it will go on for a long time and lots of men will get hurt."

"Well—it won't be my dad," Virginia declared firmly. "My dad promised me that he will be home as soon as he can. He said it was important for him to do his part—that he serve this country."

"Your dad has always been a hard worker," Edith, one of the Caucasian girls, observed proudly. "I know my dad misses having him working on the farm. No one milks cows like your dad, Ginnie—or fixes fences, or even rides horses! My dad can't round up the cows on his horse. He keeps falling off!"

Virginia smiled warmly at Edith as they approached the general store and stopped before the entrance.

"Now," Bobby said, gathering the children into a circle and fishing around in the pockets of his shorts. "Let's put all of our money together and see what we've got."

Each of the children reached into their pockets and purses to add their own coins to Bobby's. Some of them had less than the others but it didn't matter, for these children looked after one another regardless of who had more or less.

Virginia looked crestfallen as she fidgeted nervously on the spot. Evidently, she didn't have any money of her own to contribute.

"Don't worry Ginnie," Bobby reassured her. "I'll cover for you."

"No!" Virginia retorted firmly. "I won't let you."

Hesitating, Virginia turned to face the small haberdashery directly across the street. She spied an attractive woman in the window, with raven black hair similar to Virginia's, tied back in a bun. Her flawless nut brown skin was lighter than Virginia's. Her facial features were soft, angelic. The woman wore a pretty floral dress underneath a crisp, linen apron. She was arranging some rolls of material in the window display and, upon seeing Virginia she smiled broadly. She waved her in through the glass. Virginia bounded across the street, entered the shop and immediately went to the woman.

"Ginnie!" the woman beamed, leaning down to embrace the child.

"Mum!" Virginia wrapped her arms around her mother's shapely neck.

"Well, look at you. You're all goose pimply from that swimming hole."

Sylvia Crammond brushed down her daughter's summery dress that she herself had made and gently pinched Virginia's arm.

"I hope you've been behaving yourself down there."

Virginia nodded eagerly and gestured through the window at her companions outside the general store across the street.

"Everyone wants to get an ice cream, Mum. I don't have any money to get one."

Virginia eyed her mother plaintively as Sylvia regarded her daughter with mock scepticism.

"Well…I don't know if you should be having such things so close to dinner, young lady. You'll ruin your appetite."

"Aww, Mum," Virginia pleaded. "I promise I'll eat my dinner—all of it—even my vegetables."

Sylvia cocked her head, levelling her suspicious glare before smiling once more. Reaching into the pouch of her apron, Sylvia drew out a single silver coin, proffering it to Virginia.

Virginia's eyes went wide and she gasped with delight. Sylvia dropped the coin into her daughter's hand as Virginia planted a kiss on Sylvia's cheek.

"Thank you, Mum!" she beamed.

Sylvia drew her daughter away and held Virginia out before her. She lovingly smoothed down Virginia's dress, frowning only half seriously at a couple of dirty stains from the water hole.

They were extremely close. The absence of her husband had taken a toll on Sylvia though outwardly, she had never revealed it. Sylvia had become accustomed to maintaining her stoic demeanour for the sake of her daughter whom she knew missed her father terribly. They carried on as best they could with the support of a select group of towns-folk who watched out for Sylvia and Virginia.

"I'll be finished here soon," Sylvia assured her daughter. "Go and get your treat and hang about until I finish. Then we'll go home and make our dinner."

Virginia nodded then diverted her eyes over her mother's shoulder as a tall and stately woman breezed into the room from the back of the shop. She was armed with a cup of tea.

Mrs. Stinson stood nearly six feet tall. She was reed thin with piercing, owl-like eyes and a prominent nose that was turned upward slightly. She wore a dark dress under her own apron, her greying hair was pulled back in a severe bun and she looked, for all the world, like a very harsh person. But when Mrs. Stinson smiled, all trace of rancour disappeared and her face lit up.

"Well good afternoon, dear child!" Mrs. Stinson greeted in a perfectly clipped accent. "You do look as though you've had a most wonderful time."

Setting her cup down on the counter top, Mrs. Stinson rounded it gracefully and swept over to Virginia and her mother, cupping Virginia's cheek in her hand in a motherly gesture.

"We made a much longer daisy chain today," Virginia reported proudly. "There were plenty near the water hole."

"Well I hope you didn't stay out in the sun for too long my dear," Mrs. Stinson continued. "We don't want you burnt to a crisp."

"No, ma'am," Virginia nodded respectfully. "We were really good. Made sure we stayed under the willow."

"Ahhh—*that* willow. Do you know that willow tree has been by that water hole since I was your age?"

Virginia nodded, having heard that story from Mrs. Stinson countless times before. She fidgeted for a moment as silence fell between them, then she looked up at her mother.

"Go on," Sylvia smiled. "Go and get your ice cream. I'll be along soon."

Mrs. Stinson nodded in understanding and winked at the child. Virginia turned and darted out of the shop, across the street to where the other children were still waiting.

Mrs. Stinson watched as the children disappeared into the general store one by one.

"She's growing up so fast," Mrs. Stinson mused cheerily as she picked up her tea and sipped quietly from the fine bone china. "Have you heard anything at all from Artie?"

Sylvia hung her head slightly and shook it.

"Beryl keeps a close eye on the telegraph for me but there's been nothing for three weeks," Sylvia's quiet voice cracked with emotion. "The wireless news talked about rumours of a major push soon but…I don't know if he's involved in it or not."

Sylvia stifled her emotions as Mrs. Stinson set her cup down and put an arm around Sylvia's shoulder.

News from the battlefield was often sporadic at best, but at least Sylvia had previously been able to get *something* from her husband. Now, it had trailed away to nothing and Sylvia had been plagued with many a sleepless night.

"There, there child," Mrs. Stinson soothed. "Look, why don't you finish early today. I'll close up here and call on you both a little later."

Sylvia looked across at her employer through swollen eyes.

"No, no—I'll finish. There's not much left to do."

Mrs. Stinson held up her hand and silenced Sylvia.

"*I* can finish that for you. I'll not have another word from you on the matter. Go and spend time with your daughter."

Sylvia nodded gratefully and bowed her head, wiping away a single tear from her eye.

"Thank you," she whispered.

ARMED WITH A single-scoop ice cream each, the seven children sat themselves down on the curbside outside the general store. They immediately went to work, enjoying their treats in the warm afternoon sun, licking furiously as the ice cream began to melt and drip down over their fingers.

Sylvia emerged from the haberdashery and crossed the street armed with a kerchief in one hand, having spied her daughter the moment Virginia sat down.

Sylvia knelt down beside her daughter and wiped her cheeks. All of the children giggled at one another as they observed each others' handiwork.

The breeze rustled through the tops of the plane trees lining the street and the eucalyptus behind the buildings. The strong scent from the eucalyptus wafted through the main street catching Virginia's attention and she stopped for a moment to appreciate it. It was her favourite smell of all. It was clean and crisp. It was home.

"Hey!"

The children turned almost simultaneously at the sound of Bobby's voice and followed his outstretched finger as a trio of vehicles came into view from the far end of the township. As they approached, the children could make out the familiar black and white colours of a police sedan leading the convoy of three, followed by a grey sedan which was in turn shepherded by a rickety looking truck.

They glanced at each other with a hint of nervousness.

Mrs. Stinson appeared at the entrance to her shop, having heard the approaching vehicles and she crossed over the street to stand next to Sylvia.

The vehicles slowed to a stop, drawing close to the curb on the opposite side of the street. The children watched as the engines were silenced and the three cars sat for a moment. Bobby stood, growing suspicious of the new arrivals.

The doors to both the police sedan and the grey sedan snapped open.

Two constables stepped out, as did two suited men after them. They inspected their surroundings with a barely concealed distaste.

Virginia's attention was drawn to the two suited men who stood directly across from her.

The first man—the driver—was tall, possibly the tallest man Virginia had ever seen. Dressed in a drab, grey tweed suit and colourless bow tie, he sported spiky, thinning hair that was perfectly manicured into an impeccable short back and sides. His features were sinister, with long sallow cheeks that gave his thin lips the appearance of being permanently pursed. His eyes were distorted behind thick, black rimmed glasses that sat, perched precariously, on the tip of his nose. He held a clipboard in one arm as he swiped his free hand down his jacket absently.

His colleague, who emerged from the far side of the sedan, rounding the vehicle to stand next to him, was an equally dour presence. This man was barely half his colleague's size, his head reaching to just past the top of the first man's chest. Dressed similarly in uninspiring grey tweed, his slick, brown hair was combed severely to one side with *Bryll Cream*. It did not move at all in the afternoon breeze. This man wore a pair of gold rimmed glasses over small eyes and large, bushy eye brows and sported a short, thick moustache that gave him a perpetual scowl.

Sylvia glanced at Mrs. Stinson, then placed her hand protectively on Virginia's shoulders, drawing Virginia close to her as the tall man set his eyes upon the group. She glanced to the old tray truck from which two more men had stepped. She recognised one of them right away—the township's kindly local doctor, Dr. Flaherty, a man who usually wore a smile, no matter what his disposition might be. Today, however, he appeared particularly troubled. He was accompanied by a second man, unfamiliar to Virginia and her mother. He carried a battered leather Gladstone bag which was partly opened and revealed the end of a stethoscope that hung lazily down one side.

When Virginia looked up at her mother, the worry etched into her features was palpable and Virginia felt that worry seep into her pores, into her blood and it coursed through her.

The tall man adjusted the clipboard he held in his arm and gestured wordlessly to the two medicos, approaching the two women who had now been joined by the proprietor of the general store, the butcher immediately next door and the postmistress. The children, who had retreated a little further under the verandah of the store, watched as the man nodded to the police constables on his left.

Mrs. Stinson stepped forward through the group, puffing her chest out boldly, setting her expression like steel as the men approached.

"What seems to be the trouble, Wally?" she queried Dr. Flaherty malevolently. "This is all a little theatrical, even for you."

Dr. Flaherty was unable to make his jaw move immediately and he looked down awkwardly at the bitumen.

"Routine inspection, Grace," the doctor grumbled, gesturing to the two suited men. "This is Bytes of the Aborigines Protection Board. He's here to…"

"There have been reports from this District," the tall man, Bytes, interjected abruptly, eye balling Mrs. Stinson. "…of malnourishment and serious illness among the *blacks*. It is our job under the Act to investigate any reported cases of *neglect* and intervene accordingly."

Sylvia visibly stiffened at the way Bytes cast a pejorative edge on the word black then, but she remained silent, her fear far outweighing her anger at this point.

"*Mal-nourishment,*" Mrs. Stinson exclaimed incredulously. "Whatever in the world gave you that idea?"

Dr. Flaherty fidgeted where he stood, rubbed the back of his neck and tried to make himself as small as possible in the formidable presence of Mrs. Stinson. However, it wasn't too long before the austere business woman levelled her glare on the medico once more.

"Wally? Do you want to explain this?"

She stepped forward until she was standing before Dr. Flaherty. The doctor seemed to wither where he stood.

"L…look, it's mandatory, Grace," he whispered fearfully to her. "If I get a call from the Board requesting information, I've got to give it—under the law. They could toss me in jail otherwise."

Bytes stepped toward the children and inspected them cursorily, before signalling to his counterpart behind him. The second bureaucrat stepped forward and for several moments, they whispered between themselves, occasionally pointing to the children and gesturing with a nod to the doctor accompanying Dr. Flaherty.

Bytes extended a finger toward the group, causing all of them to flinch and withdraw further. He gestured with a nod to the two police constables on his left.

"You will all step forward!" he snapped chillingly. "Now!"

Both Sylvia and Mrs. Stinson moved to stand in front of the children. Mrs. Stinson flicked her eyes at one of the police constables.

"Barry. Don't be ridiculous. You're scaring the children."

The constable named Barry seemed to falter slightly, indicating that he had some sympathy for her opinion, but he quickly regained his composure when Bytes whipped his head around and glared menacingly at him.

"Look here ma'am. I am here on the authority of the South Australian government and I *don't* have all day."

The bureaucrat, Bytes, was now standing so close to Mrs. Stinson that she could smell his breath when he spoke. Not surprisingly, it was foul, a mixture of tobacco and halitosis, and she wrinkled her nose accordingly. Sylvia, standing slightly behind her, tightened her grip on Virginia.

"We are going to examine the Aborigines and determine whether or not they need to be treated further down in Adelaide!"

Bytes jutted out his lower jaw until he was mere inches from Mrs. Stinson's face.

"I *will* have you arrested if you interfere in our work."

Hesitating, Mrs. Stinson looked over at a worried Sylvia. She proffered her hand, palm down in a gesture of reassurance.

Bobby, Lucy and Albert all lined up side by side on the curb while Virginia, petrified now, clung to her mother's leg. One by one, the children were examined by both doctors right there in the street. They were given what amounted to as thorough a physical as could be administered outdoors. Dr. Flaherty was more gentle with his charges, Bobby and Lucy, than his counterpart who wrestled with a fidgeting Albert, who refused to comply.

The owner of the general store stepped out onto the pavement and stood, observing silently while several other passers-by stopped a little way off.

Stethoscopes were placed all over the children's chests and backs, their temperatures were taken and noted, tongue depressors were slapped firmly down and throats examined, their heights recorded. When it came to Virginia's turn, she squeaked, terrified, and hid even further behind her mother. The government doctor was not at all impressed and grabbed at her angrily. Sylvia stood her ground.

"Listen you! I will examine this child," the doctor hissed as Bytes stepped forward to assist.

He grabbed Virginia's arm and wrenched it, whipping Virginia's body like a rag doll out from behind her mother. Dr. Flaherty flinched, clearly uncomfortable. Bytes deposited Virginia roughly in a standing position in front of him on the road way.

Paralysed with fear, Virginia remained frozen.

"Now bloody well stand still!" he barked, gesturing for the doctor to continue.

He listened to her chest, examined her throat, felt under her chin and neck.

"Cough," he barked at her soullessly.

Virginia gave a pathetic little hiccup that barely resembled anything like a cough.

"Properly!" the doctor hissed, growing increasingly frustrated. Sylvia stepped forward anxiously but was warned off by the constable nearest her.

When Virginia coughed, properly this time, flecks of blood hit the roadway between her and the doctor.

Immediately, he looked up at Bytes who had his folder opened and was writing something down in it.

"Mmm-hmm," he mused caustically.

A feeling of dread flooded through Sylvia and she tried to go to her daughter. This time the constable stepped into her path and grabbed her arm.

"No," she hissed.

"Right!" Bytes announced dispassionately. "This one and…"

He looked at the doctor beside Flaherty, waiting for his suggestion.

The doctor pointed at Albert, who was trembling beside Bobby.

Without even hearing the words, Sylvia knew instinctively what was about to happen. She had heard stories of others further afield who had come to the attention of the Aborigines Protection Board.

Her heart was in her mouth as time seemed to slow to a crawl.

"You can't!" Sylvia screamed as Bytes grabbed Virginia's arm once more and delivered her into the hands of the second constable—Barry.

"What are you doing?!" Mrs. Stinson implored furiously as the constable lead Virginia to Bytes' car.

"Mum!" Virginia squealed, petrified as she was led away.

"I'm taking these children into protective custody so we can examine them further down in Adelaide. Clearly there is evidence here of illness and neglect. We will decide whether they will be returned or not."

As Bytes' colleague moved to round up Albert, Bobby stepped forward, shielding him from the bureaucrat.

"Don't be a bloody black fool," the bureaucrat spat, pushing Bobby out of the way.

Bobby retaliated, balling his hand into a fist and whipping it up viciously, catching the bureaucrat with a blow to his chest.

Immediately, the second constable launched into action and he pounced on Bobby while the stricken man collapsed to the road, the wind having been sucked from his lungs. Bytes himself lurched forward and grabbed Albert with the help of the government doctor and Flaherty.

Sylvia launched herself at the car, where Virginia had been deposited into the back seat.

Her heart pounded noisily in her head.

This can't be happening. This can't be happening!

The terrified child screamed and bashed at the window with her fist while the police constable subdued Sylvia and prevented her from getting any closer to the car.

Bytes and the two doctors, who all had a firm grip on the kicking and screaming Albert, quickly carried him to the vehicle and tossed him inside on the opposite side.

Mrs. Stinson was impotent with rage.

"How can you do this!? That child's father is serving this country!"

Bytes simply shook his head as he rounded the rear of the car and went over to check on his winded colleague.

"He'll be notified…if we decide to do so."

The pair of police constables shielded the car while Mrs. Stinson rushed to Sylvia's side, gathering her in her arms as Sylvia's legs went to jelly and she collapsed to the roadway, wailing hysterically. Mrs. Stinson cradled her as she glared at Constable Barry with disgust.

"What have you done!?"

Bytes assisted his colleague to the car, set him inside then quickly got into the driver's side and started the engine. The constables fell back to their own vehicle while the doctor signalled to Flaherty, who was standing off to one side and appeared shell shocked.

Inside the car, Virginia continued to scream and punch at the glass while Albert sobbed and sobbed, kicking at the passenger door. As the car pulled away from the curb, both children huddled together, wrapping their arms around each other. All at once they fell strangely silent.

Sylvia desperately, frantically reached out with her hand toward the car as it pulled away from her.

"Noooo!" she wailed.

All three vehicles executed a full turn in the middle of the township then accelerated away from where they had come.

Though she was too young to comprehend the full gravity of what had just happened, Virginia Crammond knew in the depths of her soul that she would never see her mother again.

CHAPTER 2

PRESENT DAY

A BITUMEN STREET, POCKED WITH CRATERS. A road-way neglected. Nature strips adorned with yellowing and dying vegetation. Gardens drab and straggly. There are trees and bushes but they are dark—lacking flowers, lacking colour. Lawns are either overgrown or non-existent. The hulk of a car sits on blocks in one yard—it has not seen a road in years. Stinking refuse piles up in another yard, a cornucopia of household rubbish, food scraps, an abandoned mattress, pieces of furniture. It is a haven for feral cats who rifle through it looking for mice or rats which exist in plentiful supply. Death metal music blasts from a window somewhere nearby; an oppressive, depressing maelstrom that could hardly be described as music. Not that anyone here would care. No one is prepared to confront the owner of it.

Red brick, semi detached commission houses stand in various states of disrepair. They lack any individuality; well, save for one or two…which strangely enough, appear to be reasonably well cared for. In the main, however, none of these houses are owned – they are tenanted, and no one here has any particular predilection toward pride of place.

This place…

Commission housing. Government accommodation provided to those who could least afford it. This place could best be described as a ghetto but no one would dare utter that term aloud. It was hard to think of it as anything else.

Here, in the northern suburban fringe of Adelaide, South Australia, the poky little houses lining the street were, at their most basic, a roof over one's head, but little more. Where the red brick housing of the older design and build provided a little more warmth and comfort, the newer cinder block homes were draughty, cold and chronically damp. Again though, no one cared much. At the very least, it was shelter. Gratitude was expected in such circumstances.

It wasn't always this way. In the post war boom, when the suburb was conceived and built, heavy industry was the epicentre of the community. It was a place of modest prosperity. Everyone had a job, a car, a family, a measure of security. There was a sense of pride and optimism.

The houses boasted perfectly manicured gardens, clipped nature strips, lush green lawns. A local legend told of a competition that was conducted amongst the residents where they would prepare and present their gardens as enthusiastically as anything put on at the Chelsea Flower Show. Judges assessed the gardens accordingly and awarded prizes for the best. Neighbours looked out for neighbours. Community spirit was bountiful.

With the passing of time, the decline in industry, the disappearance of jobs, the economic rationalism of the modern era, a new paradigm was created. Creeping unemployment was imperceptible at first but slowly and surely, as one generation birthed another, it became so entrenched that now children knew nothing of the notion of work because their parents—if they had any—had themselves never worked. Welfare spread like a cancer. Social dysfunction replaced the nuclear family, crime and drugs and despair seeped in to accompany the decay.

The misfits, the poor, the down trodden.

All of them living here. All of them existing.

But barely…

"Kick it long!"

The scuffed, red leather football sailed high through the air, reverse spinning slowly as it completed a beautiful, parabolic arc. At one end of the street stood a motley band of children, boys and girls all rough housing with one another, jockeying for a position to receive the lofty projectile as it floated toward them, while at the other end, a similar group watched the football on its journey down the street.

The children were a mixture of boys and girls, Caucasian and Aborigines, teens and children. They had been playing on the street for hours, kicking the football back and forth as they sought to emulate their Australian Rules heroes. The group waiting to receive the ball was laughing and chattering excitedly, preparing themselves to launch into the air once the football came within their reach.

Their clothing was as motley as the children themselves. Some of the boys wore the familiar jerseys of their favourite football teams. In Adelaide, there were only two national football teams and they were well represented here. The teal, black and white of Port Adelaide and the red, yellow and blue of the Adelaide Crows. Some of the children wore jerseys of both teams while the others wore a mixture of T-shirts bearing the images of the current crop of pop stars like Beyonce, Jay-Z, Eminem, Lady Gaga and Pink.

The leather ball reached the zenith of its arc and then whistled downward. The taller children drew closer together, pushing and shoving more forcefully in readiness to receive it. The ball plunged through a gap—none of the outstretched hands came even close to touching it—and landed in the waiting arms of a girl whose eyes were shut fast until she felt the impact of leather on skin.

There was a moment of silence as every eye turned toward the small scrap of a child who had seemingly emerged from nowhere and snatched the football into her grasp.

Then the group erupted into enthusiastic cheers and claps, slapping her back in congratulation and grabbing her free hand, shaking it vigorously.

The girl gazed down upon the football in her arm. Her jaw fell open in shock. Her face morphed into an expression of utter amazement. She was barely able to comprehend her sudden and unexpected achievement. One of the teen-aged boys lifted her up off the ground and, holding her aloft on his shoulder, turned several circles, bouncing her small frame up and down, before setting her down again.

Eight year old Ruby Delfey beamed proudly and she hand passed the ball to that teen-aged boy who took it, stepped forward a few paces then dropped it onto his foot, punting it high and long toward the second group of children some twenty yards or so down the street.

As she watched it sail high, Ruby spied a strapping, athletic teen-aged boy in amongst that group. He was shirtless, his rippling muscles and coffee brown skin glistening with sweat and he stood apart from the others, clapping his hands slowly and nodding admiringly in her direction. Her eyes met his and she directed her smile toward him now, a moment of silent affection between herself and her cousin, Jeremy.

"Good mark, Ruby," Jeremy complimented softly.

Her wind-blasted, shoulder length hair, seemingly frozen in a dozen different directions was loosely tied back with a simple elastic band. Her large, dark eyes were worldly, expressing an intelligence and wisdom far beyond her tender years. She stood no more than perhaps four feet tall – not especially unusual for a child her age – but considering that she was only half a head taller than her five year old cousin beside her, she was, perhaps, a little on the petite side. Her delicate light brown skin was her most striking feature. It was flawless – unusually so. It was a talking point among her circle of family and friends. Though, unbeknownst to many of those very same people her skin was not completely without blemish.

As Ruby watched the ball sail back down the street, she discreetly took the opportunity to step away from the group. As plucky as she was and outwardly equal in stamina to the older children, Ruby did her best to conceal her exhaustion. They had, after all, been out here on the street all day, playing in the warm sun with little respite. She took a moment to catch her breath, putting her hand to her chest to slow her breathing and her heartbeat. She could feel under the T-shirt she wore, that single blemish to her otherwise perfect skin—a singular, thin scar over her sternum – the remnant of a surgeon's cut from when she was an infant to repair a hole in her heart.

Before the others noticed her absence, Ruby quickly rejoined them as the ball came barrelling back down the street, bouncing crazily along the bitumen. The game continued on, back and forth, the children blissfully ignorant of anything else other than the favoured activity. Ignorant of the death metal blasting from the front window of number 27. Unaware of the stinking refuse pile in number 18, its wafting odour of rotting food and cat urine. Blind to a drunken duo—a father and son—bickering over a car hulk at number 24, all tools and beer and bad language.

Ruby lived with her cousins, fifteen year old Jeremy, his eleven year old sister Asher—whom she stood beside now—and their five year old brother who they called "Minty" on account of his obsession with the sweet of the same name.

On the porch of the red brick house at number 22, quietly watching over the children, sat an elderly woman on a battered kitchen chair with ripped upholstery on the seat back and rusted patches on the chrome legs.

She watched, occasionally flicking ash from the end of a cigarette that she held in her nicotine stained fingers. Bringing it to her lips, she gave life to the freshly exposed ember and coughed, a hacking gag that forced her to hunch over. Her ill-fitting cotton dress hugged her larger frame up top and hung down over her legs, ending at the knees. The flip flops she wore on her cracked and dry feet were far too small—but she seemed oblivious. Her wild grey hair was messy and ungroomed and it framed a dark, leathery face that was heavily lined. Her eyes—one of which was a glass prosthetic—were sunken into the shadows under a prominent brow. A faded but mighty scar traversed over her left eye socket from her cheek to just below her brow. When she looked up, her left eye looked out at an odd angle. Her nose was at once typical of an Aboriginal woman, yet it was slightly thinner and more delicate than one would expect.

She had been sitting on the porch for as long as the children had been playing in the street, content to watch them and smoke her cigarettes. A small can with a label for pear slices peeling away from it sat near her right foot, half filled with extinguished cigarette butts she added throughout the morning. Beside that sat a chipped china tea cup, half filled with milky tea, the tea bag string hanging over the side. Leaning up against the red brick of the house, was a worn and gnarled walking stick with a brass inlay on its handle.

Occasionally she stood to get a better view of the children over the top of the pomegranate tree at the edge of the driveway. Her attention was drawn to two of the children in particular, her grandchildren Asher and Ruby. She watched them competing ferociously, occasionally wincing when either of them took a tumble on the unforgiving pavement. Then, as the football was kicked long back to the other end of the street out of view, she would settle back on her rickety kitchen chair once more and doze in the afternoon sun.

Though Virginia was now in her 67th year, she looked and felt much older. Time had not been kind to her. Her hands, once nimble and dexterous, were swollen now. They were slowly being consumed by arthritis. Her spine was similarly deteriorating and because of this, Virginia could no longer move as freely as she once did. Without the aid of the walking stick, Virginia was unsteady on her feet. Transient memory lapses, which she had previously dismissed, were now becoming more frequent and she was grappling with a recent diagnosis of mild dementia.

Virginia lived here at her son's home, with his wife and three children, along with Ruby—for whom Virginia was legal guardian. She and Ruby had moved out of the house Virginia owned and had lived in for most of her adult life, after an incident where she had put a saucepan to heat on the gas stove top and forgotten it. The resulting fire had gutted the entire kitchen and would have extended much further, had it not been for Ruby's quick intervention. Ruby had single-handedly stopped the fire before it could spread.

Though the house here was patently inadequate in size to accommodate this extended family, somehow they made it work.

Both her son Rex and her daughter in law Belle were presently at work. Outwardly, Virginia was charged with looking after the children though, for most of the time, it was more the case that the children were caring for Virginia.

The football floated high and came into view from the far end of the street on a trajectory that would have it land right at Virginia's feet. As the children in the street watched it hawk-like, honing in on its target, all of them shouted out in their loudest voices.

"Mark it, Nana!!"

Virginia flinched and she lifted her head skyward as the ball dropped like a stone and bounced at her feet.

"Bloody hell," she grumbled under her breath, jumping in her seat once more as the football bounced crazily in front of her while she fumbled impotently where she sat in a vain attempt to lay a hand on the crazed projectile.

Ruby skipped up the driveway and made a bee-line for the football, securing it in her grasp. She went over to her grandmother who was still collecting her frayed nerves. Ruby smiled broadly and reached out, placing a steadying hand on her grandmother's arm.

"Sorry, Nana. We thought you were watching."

Virginia looked at her granddaughter blankly for a moment. Then a grizzled smile spread across her lips.

"Daydreaming again," she answered softly, her aged voice barely cracking above a whisper.

Virginia noticed beads of sweat glistening on Ruby's brow and she lifted a hand to wipe them away.

"I hope you're bein' careful out there. You know you gotta watch yourself with that heart of yours."

Ruby rolled her eyes discreetly in a 'how many times have I heard this before' expression.

"I'm fine Nana," Ruby stressed as she backed down from the porch and prepared to turn away back to the street.

"Hmm…" Virginia grumbled disapprovingly. She pointed a gnarled finger at her granddaughter. "Don't forget you've got a lesson this evening. We can't have you exhausted for that, now can we. And I certainly don't want you to damage those fingers of yours with that dashed football."

At the mention of 'a lesson' Ruby's eyes brightened and she smiled broadly once more.

"Oh don't worry Nana. I'll be fully up for it."

Ruby's infectious grin soon cracked the disapproving facade of Virginia's own expression and, eventually, the elderly woman smiled warmly in return.

With that, Ruby turned away and trotted out onto the road, passing the ball over to one of the older boys as she rejoined them.

On the porch, a still smiling Virginia leaned back in her chair and began humming the first notes of *Spring* from Vivaldi's *The Four Seasons*.

THAT EVENING, THE children sat at the kitchen table eagerly awaiting their dinner, watching Asher who stood on a wooden stool at the battered stove, tending to a large pan on the gas cook top. Asher was a willowy girl with two precisely fashioned plaited tails that hung down either side of her face so that they just brushed the tops of her shoulders. She possessed jewel-like green eyes that were ensconced behind a pair of glasses—a hand me down from Virginia who had discovered, quite by accident, that Asher's poor eye sight was vastly improved with her own prescription. Thus, no one had actually gotten around to taking her to an eye doctor to have her eyesight assessed properly—not that they could afford it anyway.

Asher stirred the beef stroganoff with a wooden spoon while Virginia prepared plates beside her, spooning out dollops of piping hot mashed potato from a larger saucepan, depositing fluffy white mounds onto each plate. Virginia hummed a tune as she served up the meal, occasionally glancing across at her granddaughter, inspecting her handiwork and smiling approvingly. Asher's cooking had really come along of late and, though the recipes that she and her grandmother attempted were becoming increasingly challenging, Asher was proving herself more than capable every time. Virginia often said of Asher that she could go far as a chef, if she wanted to.

Asher, for her part, smiled bashfully as she listened to the quaint little ditty from her grandmother. Asher often observed her grandmother humming like that for no reason at all and on the most random occasions. She had no idea what the tunes were, but they were light and happy tunes that made her feel safe—especially during those times when she didn't feel safe at all.

Virginia studied her family. Ruby and Minty were giggling at one another as they stole glances at Belle—the children's mother, Ruby's aunt—who sat at the end of the table, nodding off to sleep. A single tear-drop of saliva hung precariously from the corner of her lips and the children were wagering as to how long it was going to stay there before it broke free. Virginia frowned at the children momentarily then her attention drifted through the doorway where an audible racket spewed forth from the TV in the living room. Evidently, Jeremy was in there now lounging on the sofa, watching American wrestling.

"Jeremy!" Virginia called out authoritatively. "Get yourself in here to the dinner table now. And turn that bloody racket off."

Belle shuddered in her chair at the old woman's bellowing voice, disturbing the bead of saliva as she instinctively wiped at her face.

Belle was still in her nurse's aid uniform—a striped blue blouse, gold fob watch on the breast pocket, navy culottes. Though she was in her mid thirties, Belle appeared much older. Her dark hair was greying such at the temples, that it almost rivalled her elderly mother in law. She was thin, gaunt almost, with high cheek bones but leathery, tanned skin.

Belle had worked her seventh straight shift at a local nursing home and the relentless hours were taking their toll. As an Enrolled Nurse, Belle was usually at the coalface of hard work. But recently she had been called upon to work additional overtime hours because of a staff shortage at the home and it was clear that she was struggling. She had barely spoken to the children this week. Usually, she would come home from work, stumble through a few mouthfuls of food before collapsing into bed in order to steal as much sleep as she could before having to get up early to do it all over again.

Virginia leaned over to take a closer view of the stroganoff in the pot and she nodded approvingly once more.

"Now—take that pepper and toss a couple more pinches into it. I reckon she'll be just about ready."

Asher did so. Then, proudly, she and her grandmother delivered the dinner plates to the table, setting them down in front of Belle, Ruby and Minty then placing their own plates down along with Jeremy's.

Belle sat up straight in her chair and rubbed her nose with her hand. Both Ruby's and Minty's eyes went wide as they admired the hearty dish before them, licking their lips and arming themselves with mismatched cutlery.

Virginia gave the children a warning glower, signalling for them to wait while she looked through the doorway to the living room again.

"Jeremy!" she thundered. "Get your bum in here now!"

She waited, listening for movement in the other room and was rewarded when the noise from the television abruptly silenced and Jeremy appeared in the doorway. Virginia swatted the air with her hand near his right ear as he passed and cursed under her breath. Jeremy flashed her a dopey grin and took his place at the dinner table.

Once they were all seated, Virginia glanced at Ruby and Minty and gave a subtle nod of her head. They instantly dove into their meal with gusto and Virginia chuckled softly. She nudged Asher beside her and smiled warmly.

"You've done a marvellous job, dear," she praised.

Asher returned her smile.

This was, perhaps, the best meal they had eaten all week. Fresh vegetables and quality meat were commodities the family could rarely afford. To eat such a salubrious meal as this was a treat indeed.

Belle absently nudged a few morsels of meat around her plate but didn't immediately eat any. Not until she realised that Asher was looking at her hopefully.

Sensing her daughter's eagerness for her opinion, Belle caught herself and quickly took in a mouthful.

Finally she spoke.

"I'm sorry love," she offered apologetically. "I'm a million miles away. This is real good."

Virginia considered Belle disapprovingly.

"How many more shifts is that place gonna make you work before you drop dead where you sit?"

Belle rolled her eyes almost imperceptibly. She'd evidently heard this question before.

"Only one more, Virgie. Then I've got a day off."

"A day!? Then what? Another seven day stretch to contend with? That's not working—it's bloody slavery."

Belle didn't respond. She was too exhausted. But Virginia continued without missing a beat.

"These children need you here, Belle. They can't keep coming home to a broken down old bullock like me."

Belle snapped her head up and glared at Virginia then. Her fork clattered to the plate.

"Well, what am I supposed to do Virgie—tell me? Rex can't get any decent work right now can he? I'm the only one who can bring in any sort of income. If I don't work, this household will fall apart!"

The children stopped eating and gawked at the two women. Even Jeremy shared an awkward expression with Ruby. Virginia was stuck for a response and Belle knew, with a measure of bitter satisfaction, that she'd made her point—not that it made her feel any better.

Collecting herself, she reached across and squeezed Virginia's hand fleetingly.

"Look Mum," she offered, more softly this time. "It won't last. The home says they'll be taking on new staff soon, so I won't need to work so many overtime hours. It'll be fine."

Virginia's own expression softened though her concern remained.

"Have you heard from him today?"

Belle shook her head, knowing immediately to which "him" Virginia was referring to.

"Davo managed to get him a few hours at that building site over at the Corner, but I haven't heard from him since this morning. I thought he would have been home by now."

Immediately, an unspoken feeling of dread passed between the two women and both of them glanced at the clock above the stove.

It was almost seven PM—well past the end of the working day.

Virginia and Belle looked at each other knowingly but said nothing. There was no need.

"How did you kids go at school?" Belle queried, changing the subject as swiftly as she could. She looked to Jeremy, who sat hunched over his food, head down, chewing in silence. He shrugged his shoulders without speaking.

"Well," Belle pressed, nudging her son. "You're not in trouble with that bloody teacher again are you?"

Now it was Jeremy's turn to roll his eyes. Stubbornly, he refused to respond.

Belle gauged him with suspicion as well as sympathy and touched her hand to his arm.

"It's just that I worry about you love," Belle implored softly. "You've gotta do well at school, if you're gonna make a go of it."

Jeremy's shoulders relaxed slightly and he offered her a single nod. Belle then diverted her eyes slowly toward the others.

Minty sat upright in his chair, beaming proudly through a mouthful of food. He twisted in his seat and pointed at the refrigerator where a bright piece of artwork had been pinned to the door. The centre piece of the work was a rainbow that curved across the page in a slightly crooked, but charming arc that featured all of the correct colours. Surrounding this were several birds whose bodies were no less than scrunched up "Minties" wrappers, neatly arranged so that the tails, wings and feet of each bird were clearly discernible. There were pieces of multicoloured wool for trees and cellophane flowers arranged along the bottom.

It was in fact, quite an accomplished piece for someone so young.

For the first time this evening, Belle smiled and clucked.

"Well! Isn't that impressive. And of course, you didn't leave out your favourite things with those "Minty" birds did you?"

Virginia blinked at the sound of Belle's descriptor and a shiver passed through her as a long dormant memory flashed inside her and was gone before it could take root.

The memory of a bird.

Virginia turned to Ruby who ate quietly, whilst watching her older cousin Jeremy with concern.

"You've had a good day today too, haven't you?"

Ruby blinked and looked at her grandmother. She smiled wanly and nodded.

"I got a good mark on my music project," she said, turning toward her aunt.

Belle studied her niece with an expression that was completely devoid of emotion.

"Is that right," she said flatly.

"Oh come now Ruby," Virginia interjected. "It wasn't just a good mark—it was a great mark! 9 out of 10! The teacher was very pleased."

Ruby blushed as Asher dug her in the ribs playfully. Belle remained unmoving.

"Humph," she muttered under her breath as she ate a mouthful from her plate. "Don't understand what use music is. Just a waste of time if you ask me."

She offered nothing more, which didn't escape Virginia's notice while Ruby felt an acute twinge of embarrassment and she shrank in her seat.

"I reckon it's real good, Ruby," Jeremy said, through a mouthful of food, coming to her defence with a subtle smile from the corner of his mouth. He offered her an encouraging wink.

Their dinnertime conversation was interrupted, as the sound of a car screeching to a stop in the driveway outside caused Ruby, Asher and Minty to jump in their seats. Belle stiffened where she sat and listened intently for the sounds of activity outside.

There was a gap of several seconds as the car idled in the driveway, before the engine was extinguished.

A car door snapped open. A man could be heard shouting at the top of his voice, a mouthful of expletives spilling forth as the crash and clang of a rubbish bin on the concrete made everyone jump again.

The children shared worried glances, hesitating with their food.

"Ginnie, why don't you run the children a bath," Belle suggested evenly, keeping her ear attuned to the commotion outside.

Virginia didn't hesitate. She was too old for a confrontation right now, even if it was her son. In the past, she had been able to get him to listen to her when she stood her ground. But his recent behaviour where alcohol was involved was too unpredictable.

A single gesture from Virginia and the three younger children rose from their seats and filed quickly out of the kitchen. Belle shot a quick glance at Jeremy.

"Stay with me," she said firmly. "I might need you."

Virginia took Minty by the hand and led him straight to the bathroom while the others followed close behind. Asher paused beside Jeremy and she looked up at him through eyes that were filled with dread. He simply nodded as encouragingly as he could and brushed her away.

Asher retreated to the bathroom and shut the door behind her. Looking at both Ruby and Minty, it was clear that they were as frightened as she was.

In the living room, Belle and Jeremy approached the front door and cautiously opened it, just in time to see the silhouette of two men standing in the headlights of the vehicle which sat at a crazy angle in the driveway.

Both men were drunk—very drunk.

One of them was being supported by the other as they limped up onto the porch. Belle flicked the porch light switch and squinted in the blazing head lamps.

Just as she suspected, it was her husband who was the worse for wear, although his companion, their friend—Davo Thompson—clearly wasn't far behind him.

Davo was a tall, lanky Aborigine with a wild and curly shock of hair and a thick beard. He wore dusty work clothes—a flannelette shirt, dark jeans and solid steel capped boots.

He looked up as the porch light came on and he squinted at the shadow of Belle standing behind the wire screen door. Rex lifted his head slowly, as though it weighed a tonne, and he gurgled something incomprehensible, before slumping further into the grip of his friend.

Belle shook her head in disgust as she opened the door. Both men reeked. She stepped out to face them, crossing her arms over her chest defiantly.

Davo fixed her with a stupid grin.

"G'day love. How are ya?"

Belle's eyes narrowed and she shook her head slowly.

"Where have you two been?"

Davo worked his lower jaw impotently, unable to produce a response.

Extricating Rex from his grip, Davo steadied his drunken friend on the porch, gently slapping Rex's cheek in an effort to snap him awake. He was cautious in doing so however, for fear of how Rex might react.

Rex Delfey stood nearly six feet tall and had an exceptionally muscular build underneath a dusty, blue workman's singlet. His dark, rippling arms were adorned with several tattoos. His face, though contorted into a chemically impaired expression, was hard but handsome. He had intense eyes and a closely shaven head which revealed yet another tattoo haloing his right ear.

Any sense of his innate intensity was completely buried underneath untold pints of beer.

"W-we finished on the build early today. Problems with supply," Davo finally spluttered. "We had a few beers at the t-tavern…just a few."

Belle hissed disgustedly and stepped forward to take Rex's arm. She was less fearful of her husband, knowing that he was completely incapacitated.

She made a critical mistake. As soon as she tightened her grip on his arm, Rex spasmed and wrenched his arm away before whipping it around, fist balled, and she was forced to duck. The stinging blow glanced off the side of her cheek and ear as she baulked and though she didn't absorb its full impact, the blow was enough to make her yelp in pain.

All of a sudden, Rex was bouncing around like a crazed boxer, arms raised in preparation for a repeat assault.

Inside the bathroom, Virginia and Asher tended to Ruby and Minty as they splashed in the bath, encouraging the kids to make as much noise as possible. Virginia began to hum a tune and she eyed Asher, encouraging both her and the littler ones to join in.

Asher took off her glasses and set them on the edge of the bathroom sink behind her. Ruby watched as she wiped at her reddened eyes and tried to hold her composure. For Asher, it was a long suffering ordeal—her father's drunkenness. Ruby hadn't lived here long enough to experience it with the frequency that she and Minty had.

Upon hearing Belle's cry, Virginia looked at the bathroom door and began fidgeting where she sat.

She turned to Asher and gripped her shoulder.

"Stay here sweetie. Keep the girls safe."

Asher and Ruby's eyes went wide and they both gasped as Virginia stood and opened the bathroom door.

Out on the porch, Belle steadied herself and shook her head to rid herself of the pain. With one hand to her stinging ear, she looked up at Davo.

"Help me get him inside," she hissed shakily.

Signalling to Jeremy, who stood inside the door, Belle turned and stepped back from her husband. Though she gave nothing away, her heart was racing, the white hot pain from her ear fed into her fear of him. It took all of her resolve to keep herself composed.

"Come inside the house now Rex. Come on, before you hurt yourself."

"Bugger off!" Rex slurred, spitting saliva in all directions, which captured the light from the globe of the porch light and glittered in the space between himself and his wife.

Davo was not so out of it that he didn't feel a terrible awkwardness at what he was witnessing. He stepped forward and gingerly put his hands out, placing them cautiously on his friend's outstretched arms.

"Come on Rex, let's get you in the house, mate."

Rex lurched his head in Davo's direction and steeled himself against his friend's hands. But this time, he did not protest. He lowered his arms slowly as Davo moved in closer and guided him toward the front door.

"There you are, mate. That's it," Davo said evenly.

Belle stood fast, her expression stony as her husband passed her.

Jeremy held the door open for his father and Davo. When Davo looked at Jeremy, he nodded and smiled bashfully.

"How are ya, fella?" he greeted encouragingly. Jeremy nodded respectfully but said nothing. He was watching his father with a mixture of revulsion and fear.

Rex snapped his head up abruptly and glared maniacally at his son, through bloodshot eyes that were suddenly filled with a frightening focus. His face came to within mere inches of Jeremy's.

"He asked you a question boy," Rex hissed malevolently. "Answer him!"

Jeremy stifled his sense of smell against his father's putrid breath and gulped.

He looked sideways at Davo and cleared his throat.

"Good, Davo," he whispered.

Without warning, Rex exploded from Davo's grip and clasped one hand firmly around Jeremy's neck, locking it like a vice. He shoved his son up against the wall beside the door so hard that Jeremy's head hit the plaster, causing him to see stars. Filled with an incomprehensible rage, Rex tightened his grip on Jeremy, choking him mercilessly, lifting him fully off the floor. Despite Jeremy's considerable biceps, which were flexed like stone, he was powerless to overcome his father's grip. All he could do was flail impotently.

"You show him some fucking respect boy! You useless little shit."

Belle was still following them in and screamed when Rex erupted. Davo reacted immediately and pushing a flailing Belle aside, he bull-rushed his drunken friend, knocking him off balance and forcing Rex to release his son from his grip. He crashed to the floor in the hallway roaring in pain.

The children in the bathroom huddled together with tears streaming down their faces while Asher did her best to cuddle them close to her. Upon hearing the sound of Rex crashing to the floor, they jumped, fairly paralysed with fear.

Without warning, Virginia appeared, as if from nowhere and shrieked at her drunken son. Grabbing a folded umbrella from just inside the doorway, she wielded it like a club.

"You miserable bastard!" she screamed as she thwacked him hard in the side of the head, over and over again. All Rex could do was scramble impotently along the floor, tripping and falling over himself through the kitchen and toward the back door of the house, desperate now to escape his rampaging mother.

Anywhere she could get in a good strike, Virginia found it easily. She seemed determined to beat him senseless, drawing blood with the metal frame of the umbrella as it began to disintegrate under the strength of her blows.

Rex collapsed against the screen door and tumbled down the back stoop. Virginia finally stopped and flung the ruined umbrella at him.

Lying spread-eagled on the lawn, Rex finally lost all momentum and promptly vomited all over himself. Out of breath and smarting all over, he finally lapsed into unconsciousness.

Giving a satisfied nod, Virginia turned on her heel and slammed the back door shut locking it behind her.

Returning to the lounge room, Virginia found Davo standing in the doorway behind Belle, who was rocking back and forth, tears falling down her cheeks and looking out into the night. Virginia knew instantly that Jeremy was no longer there and she felt a pall of dread in the pit of her stomach.

"He j…just ran off," Davo spluttered worriedly. "I turned ba…"

"Go home Davo," Virginia ordered malevolently. "Hopefully Cherie will kill you."

Davo didn't linger. Without another word he stumbled out of the house and swaggered wildly toward the car, leaving Virginia and Belle standing on the porch, a relative peace having returned to her home.

Virginia placed a hand on her daughter in law's shoulder, but Belle brushed it away.

Fighting to prevent herself from breaking down completely, Belle pushed the threatening sobs down and stood holding the door, looking for her son in the darkness.

CHAPTER 3

VIRGINIA SAT AT THE EDGE OF HER bed in the converted garage at the back of the house—her granny-flat—cradling the same china cup she'd drank from earlier in the day. Her eyes were closed. She swayed from side to side as she listened to the soft sound of a violin. The light from the lamp on her bedside table cast a soft glow across her features. Both Asher and Minty were huddled beside her on the bed in their pyjamas. Asher cuddled Minty in her lap and she held a picture book which she read quietly to him. Minty, however, was distracted by his grandmother and he kept watching her curiously, clutching his teddy bear as Virginia, seemingly lost in the music, allowed herself to be carried away by its melody.

Ruby stood before her now, armed with that very violin, drawing the bow slowly and expertly across the bridge of the instrument, re-creating the beautiful sounds of Vivaldi in Virginia's small bedroom.

Ruby herself had her eyes closed and she moved slowly in a similar fashion to her grandmother, negotiating a set of complex fingerings that she knew by heart, with a skill that one would associate with someone much older. The battered instrument—an antique—was nestled securely against Ruby's collar bone. Her chin was positioned on the rest. She did not choke the instrument. Rather she held it in a way that was relaxed yet firm—a well practised method.

The children had become so accustomed to hearing Ruby play that none of them really understood just how talented she was. In the aftermath of the earlier violence, the violin was a soothing, calming distraction and they were appreciative of it as a means to put the terrible confrontation out of their minds.

As Virginia and Asher listened, Minty had begun drifting off to sleep and he nestled further into his sister's lap, resting his head on her chest. Asher gently lay the picture book down and picked up her own book from the bed beside her—C.S. Lewis' *The Lion, The Witch & The Wardrobe.* Having Ruby play allowed her to delve into the wonderment of that story and focus her mind and her emotions there, forgetting for a moment all the violence and the anger here in her real world. Asher was a voracious reader, courtesy of her grandmother. Virginia often spoke of the importance of being able to read because, without it, one could not hope to make it in this modern world.

This was her gift to Asher.

Virginia looked across at her peaceful grandchildren and smiled softly. It was an indication of just how special Ruby's talent was—that she was able to bring peace to them through her music and Virginia took a special pride in that, for it was she who had taught Ruby to play.

This was her gift to Ruby.

Approaching the end of the piece, Ruby lifted the instrument sharply and fumbled on the last few notes. Virginia screwed her expression into a disapproving frown, without immediately opening her eyes. She blinked in the half light and then looked up at Ruby quizzically.

"What happened there?" Virginia scolded questioningly.

Ruby lowered the instrument and blew a puff of air up over her nose in frustration.

"It's those last notes, Nana. I always trip myself up on them."

Virginia smiled whimsically and she glanced at Asher and Minty who had drawn his legs up and cuddled the teddy bear closer to him, yawning behind the ears of the stuffed toy.

"That's because you're impatient," Virginia said gruffly, pointing a gnarled finger at Ruby. "Always rushing to get to where you're going rather than taking your time to experience the journey. I keep telling you—you must be patient with the song—*the palti*—for that is what the violin is all about."

Ruby pursed her lips awkwardly and nodded.

The palti.

Her grandmother often used curious words and phrases to make her point or to explain herself and though they were mostly unfamiliar to her, Ruby knew what palti meant. Virginia always referred to the violin's song as its palti. Ruby had never heard the phrase spoken by anyone else and she had assumed it was some sort of made up language known only by her grandmother.

Virginia raised the china cup to her lips and sipped noisily from it while Ruby regarded her instrument, stifling her frustration. In the four years since she had first picked up this violin, she had received that scolding from her grandmother dozens of times. And it was no less frustrating every time.

She lifted the violin and held it in both hands momentarily, calming herself, then she brought it to the ready position once more.

Virginia nodded.

"Let's hear it again."

Ruby lifted the bow and gently lowered it over the bridge, eliciting a soft first note that she held expertly for a moment before delving into the heart of the piece.

This violin…

The instrument had once belonged to Virginia, though Virginia herself had never spoken of its origins. Ruby had found it amongst her belongings at Virginia's house, before they came here.

That shed at the back of Virginia's old home had been locked up for years, ever since her husband had died. It was once a well ordered workshop, a carpenter's workshop but since his death it had become little more than storage space for furniture, clothing and a myriad of other items that were no longer required.

Ruby had been warned not to go near that shed. Virginia had made up some story about it being riddled with snakes and spiders—a ruse that had been effective to ward off any inquisitive children…or so she thought.

Ruby, Jeremy, Asher and an infant Minty, had inevitably found a way in, and had made the shed their ultimate adventure playground—the centrepiece of which was an ancient car, a Ford Anglia that was almost completely buried under boxes and cases and paraphernalia.

Usually led by Jeremy, Asher, Ruby and Minty snuck inside the dormant motor vehicle. There in the cluttered interior, they would make room amongst more boxes and bags, books and clothing and pretend to drive away on some fantastic motoring holiday—like the ones their grandmother used to talk about going on with their grandfather.

They would go wherever their imaginations led them, far away from the grime and the grey of their life here at home.

It was Ruby who was the most reluctant. She didn't feel comfortable disobeying her grandmother's warning especially since it would be her that would incur her wrath if they were ever caught.

But, on one occasion, her curiosity drew her toward the belongings, the clothes and books, the furniture pieces, items of crockery, old shoe boxes—all the things that represented the life her grandmother and grandfather had shared. Of particular note were the books printed in French that belonged to her grandfather, a native of France.

The day Ruby found the violin sitting on the shelf behind the back seat of the car remained particularly vivid in her memory. She had never seen the case before and, upon dragging it from its resting place, Ruby became immediately intrigued by its strange form.

Extricating herself from the vehicle while the others continued to play inside, Ruby carefully set the case down on the concrete floor. She brushed her hands over its dusty surface, revealing a small brass plate upon which a name was inscribed.

"Virginia Crammond"

Her curiosity aroused, Ruby flipped the latches of the case, lifted the lid and gazed down upon a seemingly ancient violin sitting snugly in the plush lining.

The surface wood was scratched and had lost much of the gloss that once characterised the instrument. The handle and scroll work at the end were equally weathered and looked as though they hadn't been cared for in decades. But the strings of the violin were all present as well as the accompanying bow whose horse hair fibres were still taut and intact.

Ruby had never seen anything quite like it. She was utterly fascinated.

"What are you looking at?" Jeremy called out from inside the car.

Ruby whipped her head around and shushed him, fearing her grandmother would hear them.

Lifting the violin from the case, Ruby carefully held it in both hands, noting the chin rest, the rusted metal work that held the strings in place on the face of the violin. She took out the bow then and considered it.

What am I supposed to do with it? she wondered.

Instinctively, Ruby nestled the end of it in the crook of her neck, so that her chin sat perfectly on the rest. She held it like that for a long moment. Something about it felt very comfortable, very natural. Whatever this thing was, Ruby thought it was very pretty.

Lifting the bow, Ruby balanced it in her grip and gently lowered it onto the bridge, drawing it slowly across the strings. The action was true, delicate and the resulting note was crisp and pure.

Without warning, the garage door swung noisily up on its rusting hinges, screeching in the darkness of the shed, causing the children to jump clear out of their skins. The piercing racket drowned out the sound from the violin.

Silhouetted in the blinding day light that had suddenly flooded in, Virginia stood, an expression of clear anger on her face. Her eyes drilled into Ruby, who sat frozen on the concrete. Her jaw opened but she was too scared to speak.

"I…I," she stammered.

When Virginia spoke, Ruby was completely unprepared for what she said.

"Do that again," Virginia snapped.

Ruby fumbled with the instrument, as Virginia stepped forward into the darkness. Ruby dropped the bow and winced as it clattered to the floor beside her.

"Slowly," Virginia hissed.

Picking up the bow again, Ruby desperately tried to slow her breathing while the other three children, huddled in the car, peeked over the dashboard.

Ruby drew the bow smoothly across the violin again, producing an almost identical sound to the first one. She held it for several moments, failing to notice that Virginia had closed her eyes and was listening intently.

Ruby drew the bow up and away and sat there expectantly, waiting for Virginia's countenance to erupt.

But it never did.

She simply opened her eyes, stepped toward Ruby and knelt before her granddaughter.

Taking Ruby's free hand, she placed her fingers around the end of the bridge and gently manipulated them into position on the strings.

Ruby, her fear now replaced by curiosity, watched as she held her fingers in place, where Virginia had set them. The others in the car had slowly exited and stood a little way off watching the interaction.

Satisfied, Virginia nodded firmly at Ruby and stood again, folding her arms.

"Again," she instructed.

Ruby steadied herself, and adjusted her grip on the bow. She brought it down and glanced the strings, this time producing a soft and languid note that was pure as silk.

Virginia stood silent. But her expression was unmistakable. It was one of approval, of satisfaction.

It was the beginning of a new relationship—that of teacher and student. Virginia's expertise was considerable—that much was clear. But where she had come to acquire such expertise was a mystery.

Standing in Virginia's bedroom now, Ruby's skill had grown and matured into something far beyond her years. She played with a technique that was refined, if a little brash.

Approaching the challenging end of the piece once again, Ruby intensified her concentration as she lifted the end of the violin slightly and rode down the fingers required to finish the piece.

This time she did not falter, though her execution remained a little stilted.

She looked expectantly to her grandmother who sat there with a blank expression for a moment.

Finally, she nodded.

"Better…but it needs work."

Belle appeared in the doorway then, looking half asleep.

"Come on you lot," she croaked in a gravelly voice. "Time to give up that racket and get to bed. You'll never get up in the morning."

Ruby screwed up her face and gripped her violin tightly.

"Awww…do we have to stop now? I'm so close to getting this part right."

With a wan smile, Virginia shook her head.

"Come now, child. Listen to your aunty. You need to get a good night's sleep."

Ruby reluctantly set the violin down into its case and closed the lid, then shuffled across to her grandmother, planting a kiss on her cheek.

"Can we do this again tomorrow?"

Virginia nodded as Belle lifted a sleeping Minty up into her arms and carried him out of the bedroom while Asher trailed wearily behind.

"Of course," Virginia assured her. "We'll get it right, don't you worry."

Ruby smiled faintly and left the bedroom, leaving Virginia alone.

Virginia regarded the violin case on the chair adjacent to her and allowed her mind to drift. A procession of images flashed before her mind's eye, memories from another time—another life.

Her life.

She let them hover, then she shut them out before they could linger too long.

LATE INTO THE night, Ruby sat huddled in her bed, her sheets and blankets drawn over her head like a makeshift tent. Underneath, she sat cross legged, the light from a torch illuminating her little cavern as she held a fence paling in her arms—a crudely fashioned imitation of a violin without the body or scroll work or neck rest. On the face of the timber, Ruby had attached four lengths of woollen yarn that represented the strings, while at one end, she had painted strategic dots with nail polish she had borrowed from her aunt. Completing the simulacrum was the disused handle of a feather duster, which Ruby now used as her bow.

She was oblivious to the sounds around her. Her aunty Belle and uncle Rex were screaming at one another out on the back lawn as her aunt tried in vain to get him inside the house. Distorted death metal music continued to blare out from the neighbour's house across the street. A police siren wailed somewhere nearby. All of the violence, all of the chaos—Ruby heard none of it.

Closing her eyes, Ruby practised the fingerings of the piece of music she and her grandmother had been working on earlier. She imagined the music in her mind and performed her part silently. She was at one with her imaginary orchestra. The despair of the street could not touch her here.

Ruby employed this technique when she was restless or challenged by a composition. It was also a way to improve her dexterity, a way of remembering her scales and tweaking them. The method was one Virginia had once described to Ruby as useful and so, Ruby had procured a fence paling in order to construct her own practise model.

Her need to practise bordered on the obsessive. Ruby loved the violin so much and she was driven to become the best that she could be, that she kept practising whenever she could. For it was her dream to play and perform on a real stage one day, to become a true artist. And the only way to do that, was to keep practising, practising, practising.

Eventually tiredness overcame her and she did finally settle down to sleep. In doing so, Ruby's concentration drifted back to the present, the sounds around her, and it was then that she heard a quiet weeping across from her.

It was Asher and she was crying.

Ruby immediately felt awful that she hadn't heard her cousin before now. With Aunty Belle and Uncle Rex continuing to rage outside their window, it was almost impossible to hear something as quiet as Asher's crying.

Ruby slipped from her bed and crept across to Asher's, climbing in beside her and holding her in her arms.

Ruby knew how much her aunt and uncle's behaviour affected Asher and it made her feel sick with worry. Right now, Asher was shaking like a leaf. All they could do was wait until both Belle and Rex gave up their useless battle.

He was aware of a wet, sticky sensation on the side of his face, along with an accompanying smell that he could not put his finger on. It was something akin to cooked meat, though it had a slightly putrid quality.

Rex's eyes fluttered open and he found himself lying on the dewy grass at the bottom on the steps leading up to the house.

"What the…?"

The swirling fog in his head, the furry taste in his mouth slowly gave way to the realisation that one side of his face was stuck fast to a pile of dog shit on the lawn. Rex recoiled in disgust and sprang up into a sitting position, swatting angrily at his face in a desperate effort to remove the faeces that was caked there.

"Jesus!" he growled.

The disgust Rex felt quickly gave way to an intense throbbing in his head. He realised then, that he was hung over—*severely* hung over.

Staggering to his feet, Rex went over to a nearby garden tap and washed the offensive excrement away. The perpetrator of the dog shit, an elderly mutt, appeared from behind Virginia's granny flat, its ears flattened down, sad eyes angling toward Rex. Rex, who was now washing his mouth out, spied the mutt out of the corner of his eye and flicked his head in its direction, growling malevolently at it.

He spun awkwardly on his heel and stomped away as the dog backed up from where it had first appeared, whimpering softly.

The back door to the house was locked and he cursed under his breath. Despite his hung over state, Rex had enough smarts to work out what had happened last night. When he and Davo got together, the result was usually the same.

Banging the door with a fist he listened, hoping someone was inside. He had no idea what the time was beyond the fact that it was morning.

Several moments passed. He heard nothing.

Growling in frustration, Rex lifted his fist again and prepared to bang once more when the door abruptly swung open to reveal Virginia standing there with Minty peeking out from behind her legs.

Rex blinked stupidly and almost over balanced on the step.

His mother's expression was ice cold.

She turned away and led Minty into the house, leaving Rex standing in the doorway. Eventually, he followed her inside.

In the kitchen, Asher turned as her father entered and she froze, not quite knowing where to look. Virginia patted her shoulder gently and whispered something into her ear. Slowly Asher turned from the kitchen sink and rounded the table on the opposite side from where her father stood. She kept her eyes down as she scooted past.

"Asher?" Rex said, pleading for her attention before she disappeared. "Asher!?"

His daughter didn't respond and she was gone from the house a few seconds later.

Virginia stood at the bench pouring boiling water into a cup and following that with a splash of milk.

A cursory glance at the clock told Rex that it was after nine in the morning. Immediately, the dark pall in the pit of his stomach amplified. He'd missed the opportunity for another day's work.

He slumped down at the dining table just as Virginia placed the coffee cup down in front of him and stood, hands on hips. He reached across for the sugar—a glass 'Vegemite' jar that served as a sugar bowl.

As if reading his thoughts, Virginia nodded in acknowledgement of his unspoken realisation.

"Davo called by this morning to pick you up. We couldn't wake you though. We actually thought *you were dead.*"

The way she said that last sentence, sounded almost as if she were disappointed that he wasn't.

"You know," Virginia began. "I should have put salt in that bloody coffee."

Minty, who was sitting across from his father, buried his face in his teddy bear, trying to conceal a broad smirk.

For his part, Rex just sat there, stirring his coffee sullenly.

"You were a disgrace last night," Virginia continued, turning her back. "God knows what damage you've done to your kids."

Rex brooded as Virginia paced back and forth on the other side of the table.

"Poor Asher was beside herself for hours. So were Minty and Ruby. As for Jeremy—well he didn't come home. We haven't heard from him at all."

"Off with those dip shits he hangs around with probably," Rex finally mumbled through a mouthful of coffee.

Virginia stepped forward deftly and slapped Rex hard across his cheek, causing Minty to jump.

"That's enough!" Virginia thundered, as Rex sat bolt upright, the stinging in his cheek shocking him rather than hurting him.

"You're a miserable bastard," Virginia continued, standing over Rex, her white hot anger palpable. "The children don't deserve this. You going off half cocked, wiping yourself out when you should be setting an example. They need you—Jeremy especially. He's struggling. You should be bloody ashamed of yourself."

Rex glared at his mother but she remained steadfast, unmoving.

"The boy needs to toughen up," he retorted. "Instead of behaving like an idiot—following the pack."

Virginia leaned in close then, and Rex flinched, thinking she was going to slap him again.

"Maybe if his father stopped getting blind drunk, throwing him up against the wall every other night, he might listen more. At this rate, you're going to ruin him, Rex, not to mention Asher and Minty and Ruby. Then what?"

"That child's not mine," Rex countered with bitter sarcasm.

Virginia's nostrils flared and she gripped the back of the chair she was standing next to.

"Ruby is a part of this family, whether you like it or not and you are responsible for the effect your behaviour has on her—just as much as you are for your own children."

"Right," Rex leered bitterly, covering his face in his hands. "Except, I didn't ask to look after somebody else's *mongrel.*"

Virginia gripped the chair so hard that her arthritic knuckles turned white. It was all she could do to keep from throttling her son. That last barb pierced so viciously, that it took her breath away.

"No. Nobody did ask you—but you're bloody well expected to," she hissed malevolently. "And, if you ever breathe a word of that to Ruby, so help me God, I will kill you in your sleep."

With that, Virginia turned from the room and disappeared out through the back door, slamming it behind her.

Rex watched his mother leave the room then gazed blankly at the cup in front of him, dark thoughts rushing through his mind.

Father and son sat across from one another in silence. Rex closed his eyes and rubbed his temples with his fingers, trying to stymie his head-ache. Plumes of acid blossomed in his gut, rising up his gullet to break like waves against the back of his throat. The metallic taste in his mouth almost made him vomit.

The memories of last night came to him in flashes—fragments that skipped like film on a poorly aligned reel. He recalled the violence he had wrought against his son but it was distant, disjointed—almost as if they were the actions of someone else. He felt nothing—no shame, no concern—just pity for his predicament now.

Resting his forehead against his hands, his elbows on the table, he slowly rocked back and forth, trying to expunge the awful hangover. As he blinked sleep from his eyes, Rex caught Minty out of the corner of them. The boy sat across from him, his hands steepled in a perfect imitation of his father, slowly rocking back and forth on the balls of his elbows, grimacing just like Rex.

Without betraying his knowledge of Minty's actions, Rex stopped rocking and drew his hands away from his forehead, stretching his fingers out, keeping his hands intertwined.

Minty followed suit…exactly.

His headache forgotten momentarily, Rex took an interest in this sudden little game. He lifted both arms up; stretching them high above his head, balling his hands into fists, then released them.

Minty, with a mischievous smile, imitated his father perfectly.

Rex, now smiling, also lowered his arms, drew his hands to his cheeks and hooked his fingers into each corner of his mouth, pulling his lips back and poking out his tongue. Minty, trying not to giggle, did exactly the same thing, until he could take it no longer. He giggled, while Rex's visage broke out into a broad grin and he held his arms out toward Minty.

"Come here," he said gruffly.

Minty shook his head furiously, grinning.

"Come here now," Rex repeated playfully.

Minty leaped into his father's lap but flinched as he landed, screwing up his face.

"What's the matter?" Rex protested mock seriously.

Minty wrinkled up his button nose and screwed up his mouth.

"You smell like dog shit."

The boy's candour stopped Rex cold and he couldn't respond immediately.

He had a point.

Rex silently reached into his pocket and drew out two white wrapped objects that caused Minty's eyes to go wide.

They were a pair of "Minties"—his favourite treat.

Rex placed them into Minty's outstretched hand and nudged him off his lap.

"I better clean myself up," Rex declared wearily, rising to his feet.

Minty was already unwrapping one of the sweets and beaming proudly. He looked up at his father.

"Don't you let your grandmother catch you using that sort of language," Rex warned Minty solemnly. "She'll kick me in the bloody arse."

CHAPTER 4

THE CLASSROOM WAS STIFLING; THE WINDOWS ALONG one side of the room were shut against the blistering heat outside. Despite the fact that it was autumn, it was not uncommon for the traditional Australian summer to continue well into the following season. So it was, here and now, at the end of March that the extended summer sun beat down with a ferocity more suited to mid December.

A pedestal fan stood in the corner of the room. It was idle—as was the air conditioning unit above the backboard at the front of the room. Jeremy was sitting at the rear of the classroom, gazing absently at the room full of students who sat in silence as their teacher, Mr. Baxter, stood before the blackboard writing an elaborate algebraic equation.

Stephen Baxter was tall, athletic, dressed in a tight fitting polo shirt that revealed a muscular upper body, sporting shorts and running shoes. Evidently, mathematics was not his primary teaching area. As he wrote on the board, Jeremy noticed a number of the female students sitting at the front were eyeing him off admiringly, whispering to one another—probably commenting on his tight arse. Sweat beaded on Baxter's brow, on his upper lip, it stained his under arms, but he ignored it. In fact, he seemed oblivious to it.

Eventually, Baxter completed his equation and turned to face the class whereupon he was confronted by a group of faces that were clearly uncomfortable. Jeremy shook his head as Baxter scanned the classroom dopily. Students were slouching in their chairs, using pieces of paper to fan their faces. One student blew a puff of air up over her face, another daubed at the sweat on his brow. As though he needed to examine each and every occupant in the room, the teacher scanned his students slowly, painfully so.

Baxter's lip quivered slightly and he turned to his desk, picking up the remote to the air conditioning unit there. An audible sigh rippled through the room as he pointed it at the unit above the blackboard. Within moments, cool air began to fill the room, much to everyone's relief. Mr. Baxter grinned slightly, then he tapped the desk with his piece of chalk.

"Okay, okay you lot," he said with a soft hint of authority. "Sorry about that. Let's try and focus on this formula now, shall we?"

There was momentary shuffling in the room as the students refocused.

Scowling, Jeremy returned to engraving something into the surface of his desktop with a pocket knife, oblivious to the commotion around him. His text book and writing folder were open before him, his pen lay on the desk, but he was disinterested in the algebra class. The intricate formulas and myriad numbers on the page were complete gibberish to him. They may as well have been another language. This was a double period—an hour in length. But he had zoned out long ago.

Across from him sat Wayne, a friend of sorts. Well, Jeremy didn't consider Wayne so much a friend as he did a class mate who he often sat next to. But he didn't completely dislike him. An Aboriginal boy, like Jeremy, Wayne lived near the Delfey house and they often walked to school together, played football at school with a group of boys from the other forms. But Jeremy preferred to keep his distance from most people, including Wayne. Such was his quiet nature.

Wayne watched out of the corner of his eye as Jeremy continued to etch graffiti into the top of the desk. He leaned across and clicked his tongue against the back of his teeth to get Jeremy's attention.

Jeremy didn't respond. He was lost in defacing the desk top.

Scanning the front of the classroom to ensure the teacher wasn't watching, Wayne reached out and nudged Jeremy in the ribs.

It had the desired effect, although Jeremy flinched, dropping the knife onto his desk.

He glowered at Wayne.

"I saw Mickey and his crew earlier, scoping out the school ground," Wayne whispered out of the corner of his mouth. "They were looking for you."

Jeremy narrowed his eyes in annoyance.

"So," he hissed quietly. "What's it to you?"

"They're hanging around a lot. Chad says they want you on their crew. They're grooming you."

Jeremy shifted uncomfortably and looked away, trying instead to focus on his school books. The mishmash of attempted equations and scribble taunted him from the page.

Wayne knew he had guessed correctly. He'd struck a nerve.

"Chad says you guys pulled a job last Saturday night," Wayne persisted with increasing enthusiasm. "He says he saw you riding with them."

Jeremy flicked his head at Wayne and shushed him as quietly as he could.

"Delfey!" Baxter called out from the front of the classroom.

Every head in the room turned to face Baxter.

"Perhaps you could explain the second step in the equation using the method we've just discussed."

Wayne retreated back to his desk as Baxter approached both boys, hands on hips.

Jeremy sat with his mouth open but was unable to respond. He was barely able to conceal the pocket knife before Baxter was close enough to see it.

"No?" Baxter queried as he stopped before the two boys, folding his arms across his chest. "Surely you *have* been following this whole time, haven't you?"

Baxter looked down Jeremy's notepad on the desk, the mess of scribble over the top of several vain attempts at following the equation Baxter had written on the board. The teacher reached down and rotated the folder on the desk, examining Jeremy's work—or lack thereof.

Wayne glanced across discreetly as Baxter turned the pad around, inspected it, then turned it back to Jeremy, shaking his head slowly, sarcastically. The teacher's hand brushed over the graffiti Jeremy had etched into the desk and brushed a few splinters of plastic and chip board away.

All at once, Baxter's mocking expression darkened.

"I must have been mistaken, Delfey. Here I was thinking that, because you appeared so relaxed and comfortable, you were miles ahead in your understanding of the task."

Baxter lifted the notepad in his hand and proffered it in front of him, so that everyone could see the page.

"Obviously I was wrong. It's obvious that you are far from having *any* understanding."

Jeremy's cheeks flushed and he shrank down in his seat.

Abruptly, Baxter tossed the notepad at Jeremy where it slapped down harshly on the desk. Baxter stepped forward, placing a finger down on the graffiti.

"This is mathematics Mr. Delfey, not Mrs. Hewson's art class."

Without warning, Baxter shoved his finger into Jeremy's chest before turning abruptly and walking toward the front of the classroom.

Jeremy massaged the spot on his chest, smarting from Baxter's unexpected action.

"If you aren't prepared to even try and count to ten—*like most of your kind*—then I don't want you in my class at all."

Jeremy's eyes hardened into a glare at Baxter's callous jibe and he felt his embarrassment at being laid bare in front of the entire class quickly coalesce into anger.

Baxter stood there, eyeing Jeremy sanctimoniously, crossing his arms over his chest again.

"Fuck you," Jeremy spat venomously, causing his classmates to gasp in shock.

Baxter's arms fell slackly to his sides and his expression fluctuated from disbelief to barely concealed rage.

"What did you say to me?" Baxter retorted angrily.

"You heard me," Jeremy shot back. His hand shot out and shoved the notepad and text books off his desk. "Fuck-wit."

Baxter stepped forward and with an outstretched arm, pointed a finger at Jeremy.

"Get out of my class right now!" he spat, so forcefully that he launched visible spittle from his mouth.

Jeremy sat in his seat defiantly. He crossed his arms, clasping his hands into fists.

The veins in Baxter's neck popped out as he marched up to Jeremy's desk. With a single, abrupt motion, Baxter swept his arm down and tossed the desk aside as though it were made of match sticks. Jeremy barely scuttled back on his chair to avoid being struck.

"Get out NOW!" Baxter bellowed, leaning in so close that Jeremy could smell his breath.

His defiance faltered while the words of his teacher still echoed in his mind—*"like most of your kind."*

Jeremy finally stood. His eyes remained locked on Baxter as he slowly stooped to pick up his scattered belongings from the floor.

"Just leave them and get out," Baxter shouted. "Principal's office—now!"

Wayne, sitting in silent fear across from Jeremy, watched as his friend slowly walked from the classroom and exited.

In the hall, Jeremy nearly crashed into a woman who was coming from the direction in which Jeremy was heading.

"Jeremy!" she exclaimed, her voice tinged with concern more than fright. Evidently, she had heard the shouting from down the hall and had come to see what all the commotion was about.

Jeremy deftly side-stepped her and marched on down the hall.

Miss Glasson, a svelte woman with a kind and pretty face, turned and hurriedly followed him.

"Jeremy. What on earth is wrong, mate? Please stop."

"Leave me alone Miss!" Jeremy shouted. "Just fucking leave me alone!"

Miss Glasson slowed to a stop in the hall and watched helplessly as Jeremy barged through the exit to the building, and was gone.

Inside the classroom, Baxter stood before the upturned desk. The students around him sat in stunned silence. Though this was not the first time they had locked horns, this confrontation was particularly shocking. No one would dare to cross Baxter in the way Jeremy had.

Turning to Wayne, Baxter signalled to him brusquely with that same accusatory finger.

"Redmond!" he barked, before turning toward the front of the class-room. "Pick up that bloody desk."

Wayne scrambled to his feet and set about complying with Baxter's orders. As he put his hands to the desk itself, his fingers brushed across the graffiti that Jeremy had scratched into the surface and he looked down at it as he righted the desk.

It was a small but perfectly constructed etching of a violin.

Jeremy sat with his head bowed, his back leaning against a fence at the front of the school complex. His arms rested on his knees and he rubbed his palms together absently. Despite the heat from the afternoon sun, he was oblivious. So much so, that when the school bell chimed distantly in his ears, it was several moments before he heard students filing out from the building, signalling the end of the school day.

His anger swirled inside him and he allowed it to fester. He wanted to smash Baxter's teeth in, knock him to the ground and kick him in the stomach. His words continued to reverberate inside Jeremy's mind.

'...*like most of your kind.*'

The dark thoughts threatened to run away from him, but Jeremy was interrupted when Wayne approached him, brandishing his books and stationery.

Jeremy looked up, squinting in the daylight as Wayne plonked down on the grass beside him.

"What did the principal say? Are you suspended again?" Wayne asked almost too enthusiastically.

Jeremy flashed him a glare as he began stuffing his books into his backpack.

"I didn't go to the principal. Are you stupid?"

Wayne seemed to pale considerably.

"Well Mr. Baxt…"

"He can *bite me!*" Jeremy retorted, cutting him off viciously. "I'm not gonna do anything that prick says. He doesn't give a shit about me or you or any one of us."

Jeremy pointed harshly at his own chest, emphasising the bare patch of dark skin there.

"He won't help us try to understand any of that *bullshit* maths. He only cares about the *good* students in the class. I'm done with him."

Wayne tried to think of something to salve his friend's anger but he couldn't. He decided to remain silent.

From behind both boys, through the sounds of various cars arriving and pulling up to the curbside behind school buses, the low grumbling of one particular vehicle rose out of the background hum, accompanied by the booming sound of hip hop music.

Immediately, Jeremy snapped his head up, recognising the sound of the approaching vehicle. He stood as a menacing looking Holden Monaro coupe slowed to a stop before him. Decked out with wide rimmed alloys, fat tyres and spoilers both front and back, the dusty, burgundy vehicle stood out like a sore thumb.

A trio of young males sat inside the car, all of them laughing and bouncing around to the music. They were dressed in varying styles of street wear—garish and expensive looking. Upon seeing the two boys, the male in the front seat dropped the volume on the car's stereo just enough so that he could make himself heard.

Lifting his sunglasses away from his eyes, he flashed an unnerving smile at Jeremy, revealing several gaps in his teeth.

"G'day, bro," he greeted, chilling Wayne but causing Jeremy to smile faintly in return.

He immediately jumped the fence and stepped up to the car.

"What's happening? You coming with us?"

Jeremy's smile faded instantly and he scratched his head.

"I can't Mickey," he responded cautiously. "I…I've got other things on tonight."

The youth, Mickey, flattened his expression and he studied Jeremy with intimidating arrogance. His companions peered through the open passenger window.

"Other things…" Mickey echoed in a monotone voice. He rubbed his chin thoughtfully for a moment then nodded.

"Gavin won't be happy to hear that, you know."

Jeremy fidgeted on the spot where he stood, unconsciously backing away, just a little.

"I've gotta look out for my sister and cousin," he explained weakly. "I-I've gotta see them home, wait for my folks. There's no one else to do it."

Mickey made a face, screwing his nose up as though an awful smell had pervaded his nostrils. He glanced across the school grounds where one of the teachers was standing, hands on hips, watching the car suspiciously.

Mickey rolled a piece of gum around in his mouth and patted the outside of the car door with his hand in time to the music.

Finally he nodded.

"Gavin *will* be disappointed…" he began, then he shrugged and signalled wordlessly to the driver. "Oh well…it'll be on your head."

Mickey jabbed his finger at Jeremy threateningly. The driver gunned the engine and the vehicle sped away from the two boys.

Wayne looked worriedly at Jeremy then at the rapidly disappearing muscle car.

"What are you gonna do?"

Jeremy himself watched the car until he could no longer see it then shook his head.

He turned and walked away from Wayne without answering.

THE SUBURBAN TRAIN trundled along the tracks through the inner northern suburbs of Adelaide on its way to the city's central station. A blurry stream of houses, buildings, trees and parks rushed by Ruby's field of view as she sat with her forehead leaning against the glass, lost in thought.

Her school bag lay across her lap, containing her violin case. Ruby held it close to her chest protectively. Beside her, Jeremy sat bent forward, elbows resting on his knees, absently scanning the various passengers as they entered the cabin and left again. He had done this trip enough times now, that many of the faces were familiar to him. He was interested in people's faces, their expressions and he often wondered what was going on in the minds of those passengers. What secrets did they hold, what struggles did they endure in the lives they led? It was a curiosity Jeremy had, though he didn't fully understand why he had it. Perhaps it was because of these trips accompanying Ruby—his sense of duty to watch out for her on these trips.

These trips.

Every Tuesday, Ruby and Jeremy would sneak away to the city after school under the pretense that Jeremy was going to football training at a local sporting ground and Ruby wanted to watch him. Instead they would catch the afternoon express service into the city.

Asher was in on the ruse while Minty was not yet old enough to see through the deception. So far as her aunty Belle or uncle Rex were concerned, Ruby knew they had no idea—not that they would have cared much anyhow. As for her grandmother and her increasingly frequent lapses in memory, Ruby was confident that Virginia was as blissfully unaware as Minty was.

All Ruby really knew about the Elder Conservatorium of Music was what she had discovered from an old newspaper Arts supplement. Ruby had retrieved it from the art and craft box in her classroom when her burgeoning interest in the violin began. A feature article, spread across two pages of the supplement, profiled the world renowned school of music in the heart of Adelaide, its history, and its prestige. It described in detail how the school had become the home for many ensembles and orchestras.

But it was less the descriptions of the school itself than it was the images of musicians playing that drew Ruby to the Conservatory. In particular, it was a quartet—a string quartet—that really captured her imagination. Ruby was fascinated by the picture of a beautiful woman, dressed in a flowing evening gown, playing the violin in one image. She imagined herself, dressed similarly one day perhaps, performing just like that woman.

Ruby marvelled at another shot of the quartet performing on a stage in front of a capacity audience. She'd pinned these pictures to her bed head and looked at them every night before going to sleep.

Ruby knew then, that she had to find this place and experience its music first hand. When Ruby began making her trips and she found the Conservatorium, she discovered a place in the gardens just outside a window where she could listen to the quartet rehearse. It turned out to be the ideal vantage point, hidden away from view of passersby.

After listening each week, Ruby went home to practise and incorporate elements of what she'd heard into her own performance. Before too long, Ruby had begun to bring her violin with her so that she could practise as though she were a part of the quartet inside.

That curiosity had blossomed into an insatiable love for their music, for their performance. And over time that love evolved into ambition—an ambition to become just like these musicians and to play on a stage for an audience.

It was her dream—a dream that she wanted more than anything else.

Ruby blinked, snapping out of her trance and she turned toward Jeremy who remained lost in his own world. Slowly lifting one hand off her school bag, Ruby extended her finger and jabbed him in the ribs. Jeremy jumped in his seat and cursed her. Ruby giggled and raised her bag in front of her as Jeremy turned to attack her playfully.

"You little bugger," he growled jokingly as he poked at her around the bulk of the bag.

"I was just trying to wake you up," Ruby squeaked as she batted his arms away ineffectually. "You've said nothing since we got on the train."

Jeremy ceased his attack and slumped back in his seat.

"I'm alright," he said simply. "Just—thinking about stuff."

"What stuff?" Ruby asked absently, gazing out the window once more. When Jeremy didn't answer, Ruby turned her head in his direction.

"*What stuff?*" she repeated, studying his features more attentively.

"Nothing," Jeremy answered quietly. "It's nothing."

Ruby frowned, knowing right away that Jeremy wasn't being truthful.

"C'mon," she pressed, her smile fading. "You're hopeless at fibbing. Tell me."

Jeremy retreated further into his seat and he shifted uncomfortably. "Really, it's nothing to worry about."

"Are you having trouble with that teacher again?"

"Rube…" Jeremy flashed his cousin an icy glare and added a warning tone to his voice.

"You're gonna get suspended if you keep having run-ins with tha—"

"Rube, shut up! It's none of your business alright!"

Ruby shuddered at the forcefulness of Jeremy's voice and she shuffled away from him, pressing herself up against the window of the train.

"Sorry," she retorted quietly, screwing up her face at him, while Jeremy shook his head and folded his arms over his chest, annoyed.

"Aunty Belle's gonna kick your ar—" she began to mutter under her breath until Jeremy whipped his head around and glared at her.

They rode the remainder of the trip in silence.

The late afternoon traffic snaked along busy North Terrace as Jeremy and Ruby walked silently side by side, making their way toward the university precinct. A breeze had struck up, blowing the leaves from the plane trees across the pavement and up onto the steps of the Roman inspired art gallery building.

Ruby eyed Jeremy as they walked along but she wasn't game to speak. She sensed something must have happened to him at school today. It had been an ongoing problem and Jeremy seemed to be willfully exacerbating whatever conflict there was.

As she thought about it now though, Ruby felt guilty for having pressed him on the train. But she didn't know quite what to say to make it better.

They approached a large stone structure upon which sat an imposing bronze statue of a man reclining in a chair. The man's face was stern, etched into a foreboding frown. His hair and beard were thick and bushy; his mighty hands rested on the arms of the chair, looking as though they could pound the chair itself into splinters.

The memorial was a depiction of Sir Walter Watson Hughes, one of the founding benefactors of the Adelaide University and, perhaps one of the strongest advocates for the genesis of Elder Conservatory.

Ruby slowed to regard the statue and Jeremy wordlessly rolled his eyes, watching her stop at the foot of the stone, where she raised her head up to regard the bronzed figure.

'*Here we go again,*' Jeremy thought as he distanced himself from his cousin just enough so that he was still in close proximity, without looking like he was with her.

Ruby shifted on the spot as she regarded the statue reverentially.

"Hello, Wally!" she greeted aloud, squinting her eyes so she could focus more clearly.

"How many times have I told you not to call me that, child!?"

A deep, rumbling voice boomed in Ruby's ears and she flinched, causing a group of nearby pigeons to scatter.

Ruby looked up into the piercing eyes of Sir Walter Hughes.

"Sorry, sir," she replied awkwardly, clutching her bag in front of her.

She waited for what seemed like an eternity.

"How is your practise coming along this week?" he asked. "Have you managed to master the ending of that Vivaldi piece yet?"

"No," Ruby answered, downcast. "I've gotten better at it, but Nana says I'm still too impatient. That's why I keep stuffing it up."

Sir Walter clicked his tongue noisily and peered down upon Ruby, leaning his great forearm on the arm of his chair.

"Patience is the most important skill a violinist can covet on their journey. It is indeed a gift—the patience to listen, the patience to find each note. You *must* learn to attain it and savour it. That is how you will succeed, my child."

Ruby looked down at her feet and nodded.

"I understand," she said simply.

She glanced over her shoulder at Jeremy who stood, hands in pocket across the plaza from them.

"He seems troubled," Sir Walter observed with a note of concern.

Ruby wrinkled her nose worriedly.

"He's still having problems at school. I tried to talk to him about it today but he got angry with me again."

"Hmm," Sir Walter mused thoughtfully. "You cannot force a person to speak if they're not ready to. He may be struggling with the situation."

"But I just want him to talk to me," Ruby pressed. "Not, like, about his troubles but…just, about anything. I don't like it when Jeremy doesn't talk."

"Well," Sir Walter ventured. "Maybe you should surrender what it is you need from him and think about what he might need from you instead."

Ruby's brow furrowed in confusion.

"I don't understand," she grumbled.

Sir Walter's great form seemed to recline further back in the chair and he chuckled low in his throat.

"Patience, child…"

Frustration welled inside her and she wheeled away from Sir Walter.

'What kind of answer is that?' she thought angrily as she began to walk away. A few steps from the stone monolith, Ruby swiftly turned back to protest further. But all she found was the imposing bronzed figure sitting silently, reverently underneath the boughs of a Moreton Bay fig.

"Patience," she hissed. "Everybody wants me to be patient! Well, I can't be patient! I've got places to go—things I have to do!"

Shaking her head, she gave up on Sir Walter and made her way angrily over to Jeremy, who was pacing back and forth, a figurative storm cloud of his own over his head.

As she approached, Ruby noticed his dark expression, his tensed shoulders. Clearly, Jeremy was grappling with something big. In that moment, Ruby's own frustration and annoyance with him gradually melted away, was replaced by concern and then by sympathy, then sorrow. She knew then, what the legendary professor had meant.

Jeremy flicked his eyes toward her and spat absently out of the corner of his mouth onto the pavement.

"You done going crazy at statues?" he grumbled darkly.

Ruby met his eyes with hers and she nodded, her cheeks flushing with embarrassment.

"I'm sorry," she said softly. "For…you know…"

Jeremy's shoulders relaxed and his anger seemed to dissipate all at once. He managed a wan smile.

Jeremy nodded toward a stately building across a lush, green lawn.

"Come on," he said, flicking his head in the direction of the Elder Conservatory. "We'll miss your practise."

Jeremy sat on a large boulder underneath a leafy tree watching as Ruby perched herself on a stone ledge adjacent to a window. The window was open several inches, allowing the music from the string quartet to filter through it. As one of her legs dangled down off the ledge, Ruby held her violin. Her eyes were closed, her concentration focused. She matched, note for note, the violin inside that lead the quartet. Jeremy kept a close watch, but he was distracted by Ruby's performance, carried away by her skill and the harmonic unison she achieved with the quartet. Eventually, he let his guard down completely, moved by the plaintive beauty of Ruby's violin. His troubled mind was awash with the sound of her music and everything else—his teacher, the gang, his father—was swept aside. He was peaceful, serene.

Ruby listened intently to the piece as she played it, drawing the music from her memory in the way her grandmother had taught it to her. She heard her grandmother's voice in her head, guiding Ruby with her gentle instruction. And, as she often did when playing, Ruby wondered about her grandmother's gift. Where had it come from? How had she been able to impart it to Ruby?

It was a mystery that Ruby had pondered for much of her life.

CHAPTER 5

1951

A SINGLE RATTLE TRAP UTILITY BUMPED ALONG an outback road, heading toward an unseen destination. It kicked up plumes of dust behind it that were caught up and carried away by a languid breeze, disappearing into an overcast sky above a field of yellow pasture. Clouds had gathered on the near horizon behind the truck and tendrils of rain fell from them but it was unlikely that rain would catch the truck any time soon. The fields around the truck and the sparse population of sheep and cattle that grazed within them had not seen rain for a long time.

A small figure sat huddled in the tray of the truck, holding onto the wooden sides with a vice-like grip every time the truck shuddered over a pot hole in the track. Virginia winced as she bounced on the wooden surface, her tail bone hitting it harshly. She did not dare protest to the driver inside the cabin. It was likely to fall on deaf ears anyway.

Virginia sat downcast, her knees drawn up against her tiny frame, her bony arms wrapped around her knees. She appeared emaciated; her hair was stringy and limp. The plain dress she wore was made of a harsh material that had been plied with so much starch that it felt abrasive against her skin.

She felt sick. It seemed as though she always felt sick nowadays. Not since she had been taken from her mother did she remember feeling anything but sick. The food that she had been served up, day after day at the hospital where she had lived for the past few months was little more than gruel. Eventually, and unbeknownst to the Sisters there, Virginia had stopped eating the food altogether. In her mind, it was patently inedible.

It felt as though a lifetime had passed since she had seen her mother. The very thought of her and not being with her weighed so heavily upon Virginia that it threatened to crush her. Even now, the memory of her mother caused tears to well up and Virginia could not hold them back. She couldn't understand why her mother never came to get her and take her home, nor could she understand why her questions about seeing her mother again were dismissed by those who had taken her. No one had told Virginia anything, except that she was sick and that her mother could no longer look after her.

She had been separated from Albert not long after they had been brought to the hospital in the city. Though she had seen him once or twice some time after they arrived, Albert was eventually taken away from there and he disappeared altogether. They wouldn't tell Virginia where he had gone.

Initially, she had persisted with her questioning, drawing the ire of the Sisters and Aboriginal Protection Officers. She had been punished many times for defying their instructions whilst in the hospital, for refusing to eat her meals, for trying to escape, for crying for hours on end. Eventually, Virginia stopped fighting them, defying them. A deep depression set in. She grieved for her mother and father. She grieved for Albert and the other children. She grieved for home. In the depths of the night, in the cold hospital ward, she lay curled up in her bed, weeping softly, singing the Peramangk lullaby her father had sung to her about the Wild Dog Rainbow whose colours could be seen in the waters of an ancient creek. Over and over again, she whispered it into the darkness, desperate to cling to something that reminded her of her home. After a time, Virginia stopped interacting or speaking. She experienced night after night of sleeplessness. Her memories became as fractured as her health. The lullaby left her entirely. Her resolve left her and she allowed her captors to do with her whatever they desired.

Now, inexplicably, she was here. They had bundled her up into this rickety truck without explanation, driven her out of the hospital and away from the city on a road that seemed endless, its destination uncertain. She had sat for hours, passing through rain and wind and the blistering sun with nothing but a canvas sheet to protect her. They had told her nothing.

The truck passed by a tall, gnarled, dead tree standing solitary near the road. Virginia glanced up at it, spying two crows sitting side by side on a twisted branch. One of them issued a long, mournful caw as the truck passed by. She stared blankly at them until they were out of sight and the road angled around to the right. The tree shrank to a speck behind her, swallowed up by the vastness of the landscape.

A line of bald hills flanked the road to the north on her left while, to the south, the fields stretched away into infinity. There was so much space that Virginia felt threatened by its vastness.

Suddenly, Virginia heard the sound of a dog barking and she turned slightly to peer out over the tray. A lean black and white cattle dog galloped along beside the truck at a cracking pace, its tongue flapping along side in the breeze. The dog jumped deftly over the uneven ground beside the road, flanking the vehicle, yapping enthusiastically up at Virginia who just stared dumbfounded at the mutt.

Overcoming inertia, Virginia turned herself around and looked through the rear window of the cabin. Out through the windshield, sitting on a slight rise above the road, she saw a farm house. It was an austere sandstone homestead with a wide verandah that wrapped all the way around it. Several smaller buildings stood off to one side. Palms bordered the property near a fence that stretched along the front of the grounds.

For the first time in what seemed an eternity, her curiosity was piqued.

The truck slowed as it approached the property, allowing the enthusiastic dog to leap across in front of it. It passed through an entrance and over a steel cattle grate, scattering a group of chickens just beyond, before it turned in a wide arc around a lush circle of lawn in front of the farm house. The driver brought the vehicle to a stop and extinguished the engine.

Virginia slumped back against the cabin of the truck and drew her legs up even closer, gripping the single bag she held in her hands. Though she felt too tired to be frightened at this point, her heart was pumping quickly in her chest.

At the foot of the stairs leading up to the verandah of the house, a tall man stood in wait. He was wearing a flannel shirt, dusty brown pants with suspenders and an aging leather belt. A wide brimmed pastoralist's hat sat low on his head, concealing his eyes and much of his face in shadow. A cob pipe jutted from one corner of his mouth; curling wisps of blue smoke drifted up into the air from it. The man stood, his huge arms bent at the elbows, his hands in his pockets, silent. Waiting.

The driver stepped out of the cabin of the truck and strode around to the rear. Once there, he signalled with a sharp gesture of his hand and a shrill whistle.

"Come on," he snapped.

Virginia didn't respond. She didn't look up. She didn't move.

Hoisting himself up into the tray, the driver snatched the bag out of Virginia's hands and angrily tossed it over the side. Before she knew what was happening, he grabbed her arm roughly and jerked her forward, dragging her like a rag doll off the back of the truck. Once off the ground, he leaned close to her.

"Pick up your bag, you little grub."

He let her go and immediately stood tall, flashing a syrupy smile as he adjusted his Stetson on his head and walked up to the man at the foot of the verandah.

The dog, who had sat itself down on the ground several feet away, watched the crumpled form of the girl beside the truck. Slowly, she got to her feet and stepped over to her up ended bag. The dog, its tall ears pricked up and forward, whimpered softly, its long tongue lolling.

The driver offered his hand to the silent man who remained frozen where he stood. He did not return the gesture.

"Good afternoon," the driver greeted drippingly, withdrawing his hand quickly in a pathetic attempt to pretend that he had meant to swat an insect from in front of his face. "I'm Whitchester, from the Aborigines Protection Office."

The Pastoralist's eyes were focused beyond Whitchester, upon the child who stepped gingerly toward them, her bare feet flinching on the hot, dusty ground. Her dress was dirty, plain and torn in a couple of places. She looked sick and pasty, despite her dark skin.

Virginia stopped a few feet behind Whitchester and looked up at the Pastoralist. He was a huge man, with a broad pair of shoulders, a stubbly jaw that appeared as hard as granite. She could not see his eyes under the brim of his hat.

Whitchester turned and subtly dragged Virginia by her arm around to stand in front of him. He placed his hands down on her shoulders, causing her to wince.

"This is the black you asked for," Whitchester said.

The Pastoralist tilted his head, examining the child from head to toe. His expression remained as flat as Virginia's. After a few moments, he spoke.

"Bit small. She got the mange or something?"

"No, no—not at all," Whitchester answered hastily. "It's perhaps just the drive up. We passed through some weather on the way. I can assure you, the Office has given this black a clean bill of health. It'll be…*productive.*"

The Pastoralist took a meaty hand out of his pocket and rubbed his chin thoughtfully allowing several more moments of silence to pass. On the verandah behind him, two figures huddled at the corner of the house, watching the exchange.

He cocked his head and issued a shrill dog whistle that echoed across the compound. The two figures, two young Aboriginal girls several years older than Virginia skittered quickly along the verandah and stopped at the top of the stairs.

Without turning, the Pastoralist spoke.

"Clean her up. Get her out of those rags."

One of the young girls skipped down the stairs and went across to Virginia.

The barefoot teen-aged girl wore a crisp, white linen dress with an apron. Her hair was shiny and combed neatly to one side. When she reached Virginia she flashed her a warm, encouraging smile and took her hand. The girl's skin felt soft and velvety against Virginia's own. Quite inexplicably, Virginia felt a sharp jolt of something she had not experienced in a while.

It was warmth.

She had no idea what to expect. No idea where she was being taken to, but she submitted to the girl's leading hand without protest.

From a window of the farm house, Virginia caught a fleeting glimpse of a pair of eyes that peered out from behind a curtain. As Virginia climbed the steps, she noticed the curtain being held back by a petite and feminine hand. It lingered for a time, then it released the curtain and was gone.

As the child stepped up onto the verandah, the dog sitting across the compound tracked them both with its eyes until they disappeared around the side of the house.

The Pastoralist waited until the girls were out of sight then he turned on his heel and ascended the stairs silently, leaving Whitchester to stand there alone, awkwardly.

Eventually, hesitantly, he turned and climbed into the truck. He started the engine and drove away from the farm house, disappearing over the horizon as though he had never existed.

Virginia sat in a large metal tub filled with hot, soapy water as the two girls washed and scrubbed her tiny frame.

It was the first bath she'd had in days and though she didn't say it, Virginia felt indescribably good to be clean again.

One of the girls, whose name was Deliah, fussed over Virginia's hair, massaging it with the ends of her fingers, ridding it of all the dust and the grime that had accumulated. The second girl, the one who had first greeted Virginia, was perched on her haunches in front of Virginia, armed with a cloth and was cleaning her face. This girl, Marjorie, chatted away happily as she washed, telling Virginia all about the farm, the chickens in the yard, the wood they used for the fire, the shearing sheds for the sheep, the horse stables and the farm house with its beautiful furniture, its large kitchen with a big, old, cast iron stove and the ginger cat that flopped around lazily on the table there.

Virginia remained silent, not daring to utter a word. Squinting through the soap, she surveyed her surroundings. They were inside one of the stone buildings outside the main house. It was a sparse single room with a fireplace at one end, a table and chairs in the middle, a sink and cabinets along one wall behind and a pair of bunks, standing along each side wall at the other end.

Finally, Virginia was extricated from her bath and was dried off with fluffy white towels. They dressed her in a brand new white cotton dress, similar to the ones they wore, and an apron.

Deliah combed Virginia's hair, parting it carefully to one side until she was satisfied, then she nodded to herself.

"There you are," she said proudly. "Good as new."

Virginia didn't say anything. She just blinked up at Deliah.

"You don't say much do you," Deliah noted. "Can't you talk?"

Virginia remained silent.

"Well, that's no good," Marjorie observed dryly. "We love to talk around here. We always talk—especially to the animals. They're the best ones to talk to. All the time! Talk, talk, ta—"

"*You* love to talk Marjy," Deliah cut in gruffly. "You'd talk the leg off a horse if you were given the chance."

Marjorie appeared hurt for a fraction of a second before she smiled and winked at Virginia.

Deliah appraised Virginia with her hands on her hips.

"You don't have to talk if you don't want to—but it would help if we knew your name."

She cocked her head slightly, waiting for an answer.

Virginia didn't respond.

Unperturbed, Deliah turned and went over to the bag Virginia had brought with her, which lay on the bed.

Deliah opened the flap and rifled through it casually, looking for anything that might be labelled. Sure enough, she lifted one of the hospital dresses out of the bag and inspected its collar.

"V. Crammond." Deliah announced. "V. What is that—Violet?"

Virginia remained still where she stood.

"Hmm," Deliah mused. "Viole…What about Veronica?"

Still, Virginia didn't move, didn't speak.

Deliah frowned then looked down into the bag once more. She reached in and pulled out a rather squashed and wrinkly rag doll—a bear—with patches all over and one missing button eye.

She turned it over in her hands and looked closely at some text written on a tag that jutted out from one hip.

"Virginia," Deliah said. "It's Virginia."

Marjorie grinned broadly and clapped her hands together.

"Oooh—that is a lovely name," she gushed.

Deliah carefully returned the items to her bag and closed the flap once more. She stepped toward Virginia again.

"Well, Virginia it is then. We'll look after you here, Virginia. This place isn't like the hospital. It's—*different.*"

Virginia noted Deliah's pause, and fleetingly wondered at its significance. But she said nothing.

"We have lots of things to do and we're always bus—"

The door to the out building flung open and the huge figure of the Pastoralist stepped through the entrance, ducking his head to avoid hitting it on the door frame.

Both Deliah and Marjorie snapped to attention as he rose to his full height once more, while Virginia froze where she stood, blinking up at the Pastoralist, dumbfounded.

He eyeballed all three girls.

"You got her clean yet!?" his voice boomed in the confines of the room, causing both girls to shudder where they stood, while Virginia remained deathly still.

The Pastoralist inspected Virginia up and down. He reached out and grabbed her hands in his own, seemingly monstrous palms. He turned them over in his, checking to make sure they were clean. He inspected her nails to ensure there was no dirt trapped underneath.

Virginia watched him, too frightened to move or to protest.

Once he was satisfied, he let them go and stood back.

"Put her to work!" he snapped malevolently. "There's chores to be done!"

The Pastoralist scowled at them, before backing out of the room and leaving without shutting the door.

Once he was gone, Deliah and Marjorie looked at each other with barely contained relief.

Marjorie crept cautiously over to the entrance and peeked around the door frame to make sure he was gone.

Deliah put her hand on Virginia's shoulder.

"Come on kiddo," she said flatly. "We'll start you out on the verandah."

And it was on the verandah, where it began—this new life that Virginia had been foisted into. She had no idea what was expected of her, no idea why she was here. Deliah fetched a wide broom that was leaning up against the stone work of the house and placed it into Virginia's hands. She gestured to the dusty wooden boards of the verandah.

"Start," she said simply.

While Deliah assigned herself to an axe handle and Marjorie spirited herself away to the kitchen, Virginia stood on the front porch of the house, armed with the broom that was almost twice as tall as she was. Slowly, steadily, Virginia extended the broom outward in her hands and began sweeping.

With a methodical rhythm, Virginia quietly swept away the vestiges of her old life.

SHE AWOKE BEFORE dawn, when the night sky still twinkled with a billion stars and began with the twice daily routine of sweeping the verandah of dust and grit. She was then directed to the chicken coop, down behind the out house where she slept, where she collected the eggs then cleaned out the coop—a constant battle she undertook with birds flying about her head and defecating on her. After that, Virginia was put to work in the horse stables, feeding the Pastoralist's horses hay, ensuring they had fresh water and that their stalls were mucked out. She chopped wood in the darkness of the pre-dawn and long after dusk, regardless of the weather, wearing nothing but her linen dress. Chopping the firewood was the one task that frightened her. She struggled with the heavy axe and could barely wield it. She constantly feared that she would break it. She had already witnessed the consequences of breaking one of the Pastoralist's tools.

Once, Deliah had done just that whilst attempting to split a particularly knotted piece of timber. Deliah had brought the axe handle down, striking the wood awkwardly and the handle had cleaved clean in two. She stood there, blinking at the broken end of the handle. As if from nowhere, the Pastoralist materialised and stormed up to Deliah like a monstrous wraith. He snatched the broken handle from Deliah, grabbed her throat with his huge hand and smashed the splintered axe handle across her face, over and over, drawing blood through gaping lacerations. His ferocity wasn't assuaged until she lapsed into unconsciousness. Then, calmly, he threw her to the ground and walked away, the bloodied axe handle still in his hand.

Stunned by the horror she had witnessed, Virginia turned away and continued with her own work, too frightened to go to Deliah's aid. She withdrew even further, making her work her refuge, her protection. Day after day, she would toil without stopping, without protest. All the while, watching from a short distance away was the black and white cattle dog with the pointed ears and mottled socks on its front legs. Virginia knew he was watching her, but she didn't respond to him.

Virginia fell into her bed each night and lay in the darkness, weeping softly until she fell asleep, tormented by her longing for home. Above Virginia, recovering from her grievous injuries, Deliah listened to her quiet sobs, whilst holding back her own, but she made no move to comfort Virginia.

Virginia lost all concept of time. One day melded into another. She saw the sun rise and set. She made every effort to avoid the attention of the Pastoralist. She quickly grew to fear him—to hate him and she made sure she kept as far away and out of his view as possible.

One evening, just on dusk, when the shrill song of crickets floated across the fields, Virginia moved along the verandah in one direction, sweeping the wooden boards clean, quietly proud of her work. She was careful to ensure that she had covered each part of the verandah twice, making sure that no area was missed or that a rogue collection of dust had accumulated behind her. The Pastoralist would skin her alive if the boards were not perfect.

The dog sat beside a rocking chair while she worked, watching her. The dog had become a constant companion, even though Virginia continued to ignore his presence.

As Virginia progressed, her mind filled with images of home. Memories of sweeping the small verandah of her parents' cottage. Virginia would look up to see her mother's smiling face as she watched Virginia with gratitude. Other memories rose up. Of riding tall on her father's shoulders, laughing and singing as together, they walked along a track under the boughs of eucalyptus.

She struggled against the grief as she stood here alone, on this vast porch that could, for all the world, have swallowed her whole. Tears spilled from Virginia's eyes and dropped onto the boards under her feet. Panicked, she swept them away with her broom, fearing that the Pastoralist would see her and punish her.

Why am I here? Why can't I go home?

The questions echoed, reverberating off corners and around bends inside her mind, tormenting her.

She looked across the compound, out through gates of the farm, along the road that disappeared into the vast distance—an all consuming nothingness. Her desolation was complete.

Suddenly, from behind Virginia, a sound issued forth from the closed window. It was a sound that Virginia had never heard before—a long, crisp refrain that seemed to go on forever. It wavered melodically then dissipated into nothingness.

Virginia wiped furiously at her eyes and turned around as the sound came again, slightly louder this time, as pure as the one before it. She was struck. What on Earth could it be? Carefully scanning the verandah, ensuring there was no one else around, Virginia crept slowly up to the window. She leaned the broom handle against the stone work beside it and carefully placed her hands on the sill. As gently as she could, Virginia leaned in, craning her neck and peered through the glass.

In the parlour beyond, a woman sat in a plush chair, her back to the window. A gramophone with a large brass horn stood on a pedestal in front of the woman. She was perched slightly forward and was holding something in her hands, up against her neck. Virginia squinted in the soft light from the parlour, trying to make out what it was. The woman drew a long, thin stick with a string tied to it across the object, eliciting a sound— the sound that Virginia had heard.

Her grief had been completely usurped now, by fascination.

The woman played, stringing several of these long notes together into a coherent stream of sound that sounded all at once somewhat mournful but also very pretty.

Virginia was entranced.

She watched, as the woman played some sort of music with the object in her hands. To Virginia, at first glance, it resembled something akin to a guitar. But she had never seen a guitar quite that small.

Her attention was so focused, Virginia failed to notice that the broom handle beside her started to slide downward from its position, the head losing purchase on the wooden boards. Inevitably, it clattered noisily to the floor.

Virginia squeaked in alarm and jumped. Inside, the woman—startled by the noise—lowered her instrument and wheeled around in her seat, just as Virginia ducked out of view.

Crouching low, below the window sill, Virginia could feel her heart pounding with panic. She was unsure if the woman inside had spotted her. The dog got to his feet and gingerly stepped forward toward Virginia, whimpering softly.

Several moments passed before Virginia plucked up the courage to creep on her haunches to the fallen broom and picked it up as quietly as she could. She did not dare look around. Virginia quickly skittered away to the other end of the verandah and furiously began sweeping once more—stealing worried glances at the window at the far end of the house.

The woman inside the parlour stood at the window, looking out upon the spot where, just a few moments before, the child had been. She turned to one side and lingered for a moment, a smile tugging at the corners of her lips.

Then she turned away.

CHAPTER 6

RUBY REHEARSED BEFORE HER GRANDMOTHER'S BATTERED MUSIC stand, upon which sat an aged and worn book, bursting with additional pages and pieces of paper that had been taped and stapled to it. It represented the wealth of Virginia's accumulated musical knowledge.

She studied and performed the scales on the page, occasionally glancing at her grandmother for confirmation that she was playing them correctly. Virginia rarely verbalised her satisfaction or dissatisfaction with Ruby's performance. Rather, Ruby took her cues from Virginia's subtle nods, her facial expressions when she had gotten it right or wrong.

They were a well worn method Virginia employed to ensure Ruby was focused for each lesson. Through them, Virginia could sense the most minute distraction in Ruby's performance. So attuned was Virginia's ear that any inattention on Ruby's part would translate clearly through the sound of the bow across the strings. When this happened, Virginia would bow her head low and immediately halt the lesson. They wouldn't resume until they had talked through whatever distraction Ruby might be holding on to that was affecting her technique.

So it was disconcerting to Ruby that, despite her unspoken concern for her grandmother—which was affecting her performance—Virginia gave no indication that she disapproved of what she was hearing now. In fact, as her practise wore on, Ruby deliberately flubbed some notes, just so she could elicit some sort of reaction from her grandmother. Virginia remained unaffected. Her one functioning eye remained as distant as her glass one. A curious smile tugged at the corner of her lips. Moments passed by before Virginia eventually blinked, as though returning from somewhere far away and she continued listening without so much as a hiccup.

It began to rankle Ruby.

Her grandmother seemed more frail this evening. The lines on her face were etched deeper into her skin and she appeared pale and tired. Ruby noticed this more frequently and it filled her with worry. She sensed

Virginia's health was failing—that her grandmother was becoming more forgetful and the stoicism that was such a hallmark of Virginia's character was crumbling ever so slowly.

Uncle Rex's increasingly erratic behaviour was surely weighing heavily. Ruby felt frustrated and powerless. She would never dare cross her Uncle Rex for fear of receiving the same sort of punishment he often meted out to Jeremy and Asher. Jeremy was able to defend himself but Asher was completely impotent in the presence of her father's drunken tirades and she often bore the brunt of them.

As far Ruby was concerned, she sensed that her uncle Rex hated her—her aunt Belle as well for that matter. Belle never uttered more than a few sentences to Ruby and when she did, it was only to criticise her. Uncle Rex was another proposition entirely. He harboured a dark dislike of Ruby and precluded her from anything related to the family. She did not understand what it was nor why, but he filled Ruby with dread. Virginia would inevitably become too frail to protect Ruby and once she was gone, what would become of Ruby then?

Ruby shuddered and pushed the dark possibilities deep down inside her.

"Ruby!" Virginia snapped unexpectedly, causing Ruby to jump and completely dislocate her bow.

Virginia clucked disapprovingly and folded her arms.

"Where were you then?"

"I don't know," Ruby confessed, shaking off the dark thoughts.

She looked at her grandmother and, without thinking, her eyes narrowed. Ruby shot back with "Where were you?"

Virginia blinked, not expecting Ruby's probing countenance. She feigned protest and indignation but then Virginia finally frowned, accepting that she had been pegged by her eight year old granddaughter.

"I don't know," Virginia admitted wistfully.

Ruby lowered her violin and rested it on the chair beside her.

"Nana, are you alright?"

Virginia blinked again, this time regarding Ruby with a defensiveness that wasn't entirely convincing.

"Of course I am," she retorted. "What kind of question is that?"

"I dunno," Ruby responded, bowing her head. "You seem—tired."

Virginia clucked at the irony of Ruby's suggestion. She patted the bed beside her, gesturing for Ruby to come and sit.

"I *am* tired," she admitted as she placed a protective arm around Ruby's shoulder. "I don't run around the way you kids do any more—full of beans and biscuits. My bones are old and creaky and my heart doesn't tick like it used to."

"I didn't mean it like that, Nana," Ruby said solemnly.

The way Ruby looked firmly and directly into Virginia's eyes caught her by surprise and she fumbled for a response.

"I—I think you should spend less time worrying about me and more time concentrating on your school work—if you want to make a go of it out there in the world."

"*Nana*," Ruby countered. She wasn't going to be deterred.

Virginia sat up straighter and her chin jutted forward. But after mere seconds, she let her shoulders relax. The defiance seemed to dissipate and she patted Ruby's shoulder reassuringly.

"I'll be fine, my *pilta*," she said, leaning in closer to her granddaughter.

There it was again, Ruby mused. Her grandmother's funny words.

She smiled awkwardly at Virginia and blushed. Virginia lifted her finger silently as if in question.

"Possum," Ruby answered, translating the curious phrase.

Virginia smiled and nodded sagely, before patting her.

"It just takes me a little longer to think things through. Doesn't mean that I'm going to drop off the twig tomorrow."

"But what if something *does* happen, Nana?" Ruby pressed. "I'm worried what will happen to me."

This time Virginia drew back and eyed her granddaughter with gentle incredulity.

"What do you mean by that?"

"I mean—what will Aunty Belle and Uncle Rex do with me. I *know* they don't like me. They won't want to look after me if you're not here. They definitely wouldn't let me play violin if you weren't here."

Ruby stabbed a finger at the violin laying on the chair opposite.

Virginia shook her head swiftly.

"That is not true, child. Both your aunt and uncle love you as much as their own children. They just don't show their affection very often is all—even to the others."

Ruby wasn't convinced by her grandmother's contrivance and Virginia knew it.

"That's not true Nana—and you know it."

"Look," Virginia continued firmly. "Your uncle Rex is going through… a bad patch at the moment, is all. And when he has too much to drink your aunty Belle and I have to make sure he doesn't hurt himself or any one of you children."

"But he's hurt us, Nana," Ruby countered. "Jeremy especially…and Asher."

Virginia took a deep breath and nodded slowly. She knew there was no deceiving her granddaughter. Virginia had raised her too well.

"Let's just…" she began cautiously. "Let's just worry about tomorrow when tomorrow happens alright. We need to find you a teacher who'll be able to help you more than I can. I can only take you so far, Ruby. Eventually, if the violin is what you want to do, then we'll need someone who can continue your journey."

Ruby grew downcast and she fidgeted with both hands in her lap.

"How's that ever gonna happen, Nana? You can't afford the kind of lessons I'll need. Aunty Belle and Uncle Rex won't help. Let's face it—I'm stuffed."

"Watch your language, young lady," Virginia scolded her sternly.

Ruby looked up at her grandmother apologetically and was relieved to find a little of the mischievous spark had returned to Virginia's eyes.

Virginia hugged Ruby close and pointed toward the violin.

"Come on. Let's get back to it okay? It's almost your bedtime."

THE FOLLOWING MORNING, the children rushed about ahead of Virginia, preparing themselves for school. As was usual, despite her faltering memory, Virginia's adherence to routine was unfailing. She ensured they were awake early, dressed and their tummies full with breakfast, taking the reins from Belle who had retired to bed not long after coming home from her night shift. Rex, thankfully, had gotten away early, having secured several days worth of labouring work on a building site with Davo. As much as the children fussed and fidgeted—as they often did—Virginia's relentless badgering of them ensured that they would leave the house on time.

The value she placed on education was of paramount importance to her and she constantly drove that point home to each of the children. If they were ever to break out of the chains that bound them to their lives here, a good education was critical. And though they often protested, Asher and Ruby at least knew deep down she had a point.

Jeremy was another proposition entirely.

Ruby's worry lingered long into the night and she had slept poorly after her lesson. As such, she was the worst of the three this morning, stumbling aimlessly to get herself prepared with Virginia constantly poking and prodding at her to get ready.

Standing at the bathroom sink brushing her teeth, Ruby was struggling to keep her eyes open as a thick soup of random thoughts and worries passed through her mind.

"Ruby," Virginia snapped from the living room. "Hurry it up in there. You're going to be late for school."

'*School*,' she thought darkly. '*That's the last place I want to be right now.*'

"I'm coming, Nana!" she called.

Though she enjoyed her classes, Ruby often saw them as a distraction that prevented her from concentrating on her music. The music program at school was mediocre at best, designed for students who were nowhere near the level Ruby was. As such, Ruby often became disruptive in the class and was routinely being sent home with notes from her teacher requesting that Virginia or Belle meet to discuss Ruby's behaviour.

Today was, very likely, going to be no different.

Ruby leaned forward and spat into the basin, then rinsed her mouth with water. As she set the glass back on the window sill and put away her tooth brush, an object on the floor caught Ruby's attention.

Looking down, Ruby saw a black leather wallet lying on the tiled floor.

She frowned and bent down to pick it up.

Almost immediately, she realised it was her uncle Rex's wallet. He must have dropped it.

Holding it in her hand, Ruby's curiosity teased at her. Checking to see that nobody was nearby, she opened the wallet.

Inside, she found the usual paraphernalia: credit card, driver's license— which she noted was currently suspended—and scraps of paper. Poking out from behind one of those scraps, Ruby caught sight of the edge of a photograph. Gently pulling the photograph out, Ruby gazed down upon the image of a young Aboriginal woman, posing beside a car.

Ruby frowned. She didn't recognise the woman in the photograph, although there was something familiar about her. She wondered who it was.

The screen door at the front of the house slapped noisily shut and Ruby shook herself back to the present, realising that she had to get moving, otherwise Virginia would have a fit.

Stuffing the photograph back in its place and folding over the wallet, Ruby quickly wiped her hands on a towel and prepared to dash from the bathroom.

She threw open the door and ran headlong into her uncle who was standing right in the middle of the doorway.

Ruby staggered back and fell in a heap on the floor.

Rex immediately saw the wallet in her hand.

"What are you doing with that!?" he growled angrily, his eyes going wide.

"I'm sorry…I just…foun—" Ruby stammered.

Rex snatched the wallet out of her hand and began checking through it.

"Did you take anything from this?" he snapped, thumbing through the notes inside. "Did you!?"

"N-no," Ruby shook her head desperately. "I promise."

Rex stood over her, eye balling Ruby malevolently.

"I'll know if you're lying."

Virginia appeared in the hallway then, brushing up past Rex with an exasperated look on her face.

"For goodness sake, Ruby, what are you doing?" she probed in a harassed tone. "You're going to be late."

Helping Ruby up off the floor in complete ignorance of her son, Virginia collected Ruby's back pack from the lounge room and hustled her out the door where Jeremy and Asher were waiting by the gate, talking to Davo who was waiting in his utility truck.

Rex stood in the hallway still checking to see if any of the contents of his wallet were missing. Virginia came back into the hallway as Rex turned around.

"That little mongr—" Rex began angrily, before he was cut off by Virginia's raised palm.

"Don't even think about it, Rex," she warned. "You know full well she would never take anything."

Rex considered his mother for a moment. Then, without another word, he strode from the house and out the door.

Ruby paced back and forth underneath the watchful presence of the Sir Walter Hughes statue on North Terrace.

After another frustrating day, Ruby was as tired as she had been this morning when she'd left home. While the mysterious photograph in her uncle's wallet had nagged at her consciousness, the greater concerns about her grandmother overtook her and she'd remained troubled by them. She had even considered skipping this trip into the city, but the pull of the hall and the music of the string quartet was enough to keep her in its grasp.

As usual, Jeremy stood a little way off under the steps of the art gallery building, while he waited for Ruby to have her "talk" with the statue. As embarrassing as it might have been for him and as weirded out as he was by Ruby's quirky little ritual, he had kind of become accustomed to it.

Ruby stepped to the end of the stone platform upon which the statue's column sat then turned, hesitating. She didn't know what to say this afternoon, how to begin the conversation. There was so much swirling around inside of her that she felt impotent.

"What is it, child?" the voice of Sir Walter asked voluminously.

Ruby pursed her lips and twisted them into an odd angle.

"I'm worried," she said. "About all sorts of stuff."

"You're carrying the weight of the world on your shoulders, my child. How could this be?"

Ruby nodded, then squinted up at the face of the legendary figure.

"I'm worried about my music—my violin—I'm worried about my nana."

"Mmm. Age catches us all eventually…" There was a pause as the breeze picked up around the base of the statue, like a weary sigh. "For some, its grip is much harsher than most."

Hughes' sombre words hung in the air between them.

"It's getting harder for Nana to remember things," Ruby continued. "Like when she is teaching me. She always makes sure I'm concentrating but lately, *she's* not concentrating. It's like, she's not even in the room with me at all any more. I'm scared that soon, she won't even be able to remember how to teach me."

"You love the violin very much, don't you?"

Ruby nodded earnestly and clutched her bag closer to her chest.

"I love to play more than anything in the world. Nana says that we need to find a teacher who can take me on. But she can't afford the kind of tuition I need. I don't even know if there is anyone out there who would teach me—not where I live anyway."

"Surely it's not as dire as that?"

Ruby shrugged meekly. In her heart though, she knew that the odds were stacked against her.

"No one is beyond suitability for learning, my child – no matter who you are or where you come from. If you have the desire to learn—a fire in your belly that drives you—then…you can prevail in your search."

"What's *that* supposed to mean?" Ruby questioned a little too forcefully. The expression on the imposing features of Sir Walter Hughes' visage gave nothing away.

"Merely this…" Ruby waited expectantly for half a heartbeat longer.

Sir Walter always liked to draw his explanations out. "That which you seek may well be closer than you think."

CHAPTER 7

THE CROWDED BAR OF THE PUB WAS raucous with conversation. A bank of TV screens hung in a row along one wall, spewing various sporting events—horse racing, greyhounds, Australian Rules Football, and rugby. Every available space seemed to be taken up with patrons. It was dark, save from the lights from the bar itself and the glow from the screens. The air was thick with a mixture of beer, cigarettes and perspiration.

Its patrons ranged from working men, dusty tradesmen, factory workers and—though it was rare for this place—a smattering of business shirts and ties. In amongst these were groupings of unemployed bar flies in barely presentable clothing, gambling addicts who would leave their machines only to refill their glasses at the bar before returning to sink more coins into the slot, punters with one eye on TV broadcasts of horse races and the other on a crinkled newspaper turf guide. There were hard drinkers for whom beer was a daily constitution, if not an addiction itself. All of them mingled here in the soupy atmosphere of their 'local.'

In one corner of the main bar stood a pool table underneath a smoky, fluorescent light. A game was in progress and a sizable audience was gathered around it watching the progress intensely.

Rex was armed with a cue, standing at one end of the table beside Davo, watching as another player leaned over the edge of the table at the opposite corner preparing to take his shot. Both Rex and Davo had been here for several hours, after a long and productive day on the building site.

Davo had managed to talk to the foreman on the site about giving Rex another chance and after some consideration, the foreman relented. For whatever faults Rex might have had off the site, the foreman agreed he was a hard worker and a good labourer. Thus, he had given Rex the benefit of the doubt.

Rex had lost count of the number of games they'd played. What had started out as a couple of casual rounds of eight ball, turned into a serious contest with an increasing pool of cash thrown into the mix. So far, Rex and Davo had proven to be an indomitable pair and had racked up an impressive kitty between them—most of which had gone into more beer and upping the stakes.

Rex watched the player opposite as he targeted the white ball, then struck it smoothly and swiftly, sending it into a yellow ball that was perched at the corner pocket, right in front of Rex. The white ball clinked true and sent the yellow into the pocket. Applause and cheers went up from the audience.

The player, a tall and lanky man with curly, sandy hair and piercing blue eyes, smiled cheekily at Rex as he rose to his full height and nodded.

That single shot had turned the tide of this current game and, for the first time this evening, Rex and Davo were on the proverbial back foot.

Taking a gulp from his beer glass, Rex stepped up to the table and assessed their situation. Davo sidled up to him.

"They're turning the screws on us, Rexy," he commented worriedly. "I hope you've got something up your sleeve, mate. The pool has just tipped over a thousand dollars."

Rex felt his stomach drop. A thousand dollars was more money than he had seen in a long time. It would certainly come in handy right now, given that he had wagered not only his week's income from the labouring job, but also his unemployment benefit cheque. To lose now would be a disaster. He tried to shut out the distraction around him as he approached the table and assessed his options.

Their opponents hadn't given them much room to move, having flanked most of Rex and Davo's "bigs" with their "smalls" around the table. The eight ball sat in a precarious position at the central side pocket to Rex's left. One of their balls—a green—sat next to it. It seemed to him, the only viable shot at this point. He could try and pocket that ball, but the risk of pocketing the eight ball along with it was substantial and, given how much alcohol Rex had consumed, the chances of that happening were better than average.

Davo observed Rex sizing up that very shot and his eyes went wide.

"Mate, don't try it," he whispered as subtly as he could. "You're good— but you're not that good."

Rex glared at Davo darkly and clicked his tongue against his teeth.

"I can make the shot," he retorted. "I'm not that drunk."

Davo raised one eyebrow at his friend and shook his head slowly.

"You won't make it. Go the safer option and set up the red further down."

Davo's suggestion only annoyed Rex more and he gripped the cue tighter.

"Stand back, smart arse."

Rex approached the table, positioning the cue behind the white ball which was sitting at an angle that would challenge the most skilful of players. Another of the opposition's balls sat in the path of where Rex wanted to send the white ball and it would take a considerable amount of dexterity to round it successfully on the path to that green ball that sat snugly beside the eight ball.

He lowered the cue to the table and softly lined up the ball in his sight. The level of tumult rose in pitch as whoops and whistles and shouts of derision and encouragement assailed Rex all at once. Squeezing his eyes shut, Rex tried to block out the noise, steadying himself on the lumpy sea of his inebriation. Behind him, Davo watched on, silently willing Rex to make the shot, hoping against hope that he would prevail.

With a twitch of his elbow, Rex launched the cue and tapped the white ball on its way. It shot forward gracefully, with a subtle arc and it deftly rounded the ball in its path before straightening up once more. Every eye around the pool table was fixed upon the white ball. The whoops and shouts all coalesced into a singular rising hum.

The white ball glanced off the eight ball without even touching its target and the crucial black and white orb disappeared into the pocket.

The crowd erupted into applause, cheers and jeers as money changed hands and congratulatory back slaps were foisted onto Rex and Davo's opponents.

Davo leaned back against the wall and drank from his glass, shaking his head in bitter resignation while Rex stood before the table, his shoulders slumped, mouth open in disbelief as his opponent plucked up the pot of cash that included the entirety of Rex's income for the next fortnight. Money that he needed to support his family. The dawning realisation of his failure struck him at once.

His opponent beamed sarcastically at Rex.

"Cheer up, Delfey," he sneered. "At least you've still got the shirt on your back eh? Mind you, the missus might have a hard time washing it this week without any laundry powder."

A cold sweat broke out on Rex's brow. He couldn't respond. He was completely flummoxed.

Davo stepped into the breech and held out his open palm.

"Steady on Barry. Just take your dough and leave him be."

"You c-can't take that money," Rex muttered shakily.

Barry frowned theatrically then and turned back toward Rex.

"What was that? You're telling *me* that we can't take our winnings?"

Barry put his tongue between his lips and blew a raspberry at Rex, peppering him with spittle.

"Go home Rexy-boy. You've humiliated yourself enough for one day."

Rex stiffened and through the swirling panic, a rush of anger surged and he stepped in front of Barry. A few watchers had begun to take an interest in the escalating tension and turned in their direction.

Barry dismissed Rex out of hand, and he simply stepped back in the other direction, handing his pool cue to a friend.

"What are you doing?" he said dismissively, deflecting Rex with a shove to the shoulder. "You're a bloody piss pot. Go home and dry out. Surely you can hold out 'til dole day anyway. The government is giving you a fair cheque surely. You've got the right coloured skin, haven't ya?"

A ripple of "Ooo"s from several of the onlookers circled the two men as Rex's visage set like stone.

Barry simply shook his head, turned his back on Rex and walked away from him. As he did so, he muttered something under his breath, just loud enough that Rex could hear.

"Yer fucken coconut."

Rex's rage became white hot. The words were unmistakable. It was the worst insult one could inflict upon an Aborigine. Before anyone knew what was happening, Rex exploded. Slapping a hand on Barry's shoulder, Rex spun him around and pitched a fist at his unsuspecting opponent. It smashed into his cheek and nose simultaneously, shattering bone and cartilage. Blood spattered over both Barry and Rex.

The bar erupted in whoops and whistles as a stunned Barry reeled backward like a spinning top. He swung his arms reflexively, balling his fists in a vain attempt to protect himself and return fire until he could steady himself. Several blows connected with Rex and he staggered; a high pitched ringing pierced his ears and knocked him off balance.

Barry came back, slamming precise blows into Rex's face and body, forcing him back with the power of a freight train. Rex seemed powerless to stop him. Davo desperately tried to get in between the two men but he was caught by several of Barry's blows and knocked to the floor.

Several patrons intervened to try and break up the two men but they were blocked by yet more men until several clashes broke out around the pool table.

It had degenerated into a full blown bar fight.

Rex and Barry locked arms and were now desperately trying to up-end one another in a vicious parody of wrestling until they both collapsed to the floor. Rex pounced, pinning Barry to the floor and pummelling him with a relentless barrage that further reduced his face to a bloodied pulp. But it was not without cost. Barry returned fire, opening a vicious cut above Rex's left eye and caused ruddy bruising to blossom all over his face.

Rex was impotent with fury, unable to focus or reason. He simply reacted, allowing the words that clanged around in his head as loud as church bells to feed his rage and his appetite to destroy.

Yer fucken coconut.

A number of patrons and staff finally managed to overpower the scrum of brawlers and break up the skirmishes. A pair of burly bouncers pounced upon the two men, breaking them apart and pulling them away from each other.

"You're a fucking fraud Delfey!" a bloodied Barry spat as he struggled in the grip of the bouncers. "You're nothing! You're worse than a mongrel!"

It took a trio of men to secure Rex and frog march him from the bar. He howled like an animal as they dragged him through the front entrance and tossed him outside on the bitumen of the car park. A steady rain was falling, though it wasn't cold.

"Bloody give it up, Delfey!" one of the men snarled at Rex as he swung his arms spastically.

The patrons, still reveling in the unexpected entertainment, followed them out as several police cars pulled into the car park of the pub with lights and sirens flashing and wailing.

Spent now, Rex was overcome by exhaustion. His arms became heavy and all he could do was use them to support his weight as he looked down at the bitumen. In the blinding beams from the headlights of the police car, he watched as his blood dripped from his cut and mixed with the falling rain on the pavement and, for a moment—through the fog of his defeat—he was fascinated by the swirling patterns he saw there.

Davo emerged from out of the throng of patrons and came to Rex's side, dropping to his haunches immediately.

"Come on, mate," he urged sympathetically. "We gotta get you out of here before the coppers ping you."

Rex looked up drunkenly at his friend but did not answer. He was too spent.

The sound of heavy footsteps approaching caused the two men to look toward the stationary police vehicle. Shadowed in the glare of the headlights, the shining black leather of a policeman's shoes was unmistakable.

BELLE SAT ON a bench in a waiting area of the police station, her arms folded across her chest, her feet tapping incessantly on the floor. The tension in her face and body was palpable. She held her jaw tightly and she was grinding her teeth. It was a little after four AM and she was wearing her nurse's aid uniform, having been called at work and advised of her husband's whereabouts. She hadn't so much as been asked to come in as she had been instructed to do so. Evidently, this particular police station's cell block was over capacity and they needed to empty it of some of the lesser offenders.

Asher and Ruby sat beside her dressed in their pyjamas. Ruby was dozing, her head leaning on Asher's shoulder, while Asher sat quietly, afraid to speak to or even look at her mother for fear she might explode.

Asher knew why her mother had dragged the two girls out of bed at four in the morning. She sensed raw anger from her but she had also sensed fear. It was etched into Belle's tired face. Asher knew that her father's violent outbursts were becoming more unpredictable and God only knew what state he was in now. While being an outwardly strong woman—particularly when it came to managing the children—Belle struggled to manage Rex or defend herself against him. The one hope she had in bringing the girls along with her, was that Rex would be less likely to act out violently in their presence.

Asher stifled a yawn and gazed, bleary eyed at the police constable who was standing at the front counter, apparently looking at some important papers in front of him. The only problem with that was, he kept nodding off to sleep and would startle himself by over balancing where he stood.

Belle fidgeted and looked over the front counter, hoping to see if there was any activity going on behind. She had waited a full half an hour already and her patience was ragged.

Rex's drinking was getting worse and as such, he was getting worse. Belle feared her husband but it was a fear tempered by her own anger toward him. He was capable of physical violence and had beaten her many times during their marriage. Now that pattern had extended to the elder of their three children. The recent deterioration in his relationship with Jeremy had seen him develop a nastiness to his demeanour that fuelled Belle's anger and it was beginning to manifest within her, as a protective mechanism.

Belle abruptly launched off the bench and paced back and forth in front of the counter, causing both Asher and Ruby to jump where they sat. Belle stifled the urge to fish a cigarette out of her bag and instead turned to her daughter.

"I need to pee," she snapped. "Don't move from that seat."

Asher nodded almost too quickly, watching her mother disappear into the nearby toilet as Ruby rubbed the sleep from her eyes beside her.

"Wha…" she mumbled reflexively, sitting up straight.

"It's okay," Asher reassured her. "Mum's just gone to the toilet."

Ruby blinked vaguely and rubbed her eyes again.

"Is she still mad?" she asked.

Asher nodded and bit her lip nervously.

"She's fuming. I think she wants to kick the toilet bowl or something."

Ruby smiled wanly at her cousin's joke and leaned back slightly.

"She's scared too," Asher added worriedly. "Scared of Dad."

"He's angry lots more," Ruby observed. "I reckon it's because of Nana and me living with you. We're taking up too much space and he doesn't like it."

Asher frowned.

"I don't believe that. You and Nana take up no room at all—and you help out around the house. Mum definitely appreciates that."

"Aunty Belle doesn't like me," Ruby said, bowing her head sadly.

"That's not true," Asher shot back. "Mum loves you just as much as she loves me and Jeremy and Minty. She just doesn't show it much, is all. She has a lot of worry with work—and Dad."

Ruby wasn't convinced but she didn't say anything in answer to her cousin.

It was now Asher's turn to bow her head and Ruby watched her cousin clench her fists in her lap, a bitter expression flashed across her face.

"I hate him," Asher whispered through clenched teeth.

"Don't say that," Ruby chided gently. "He's your father."

"He's selfish and angry and I hate what he does to Mum, to Jeremy— and to me."

Ruby didn't know how to respond. All she could remember was her uncle's violent outburst toward Jeremy the other night and the memory of his last attack on Asher. It filled Ruby with dread but there was something else.

"At least you have parents," Ruby said softly.

That single comment caught Asher off guard and she gasped silently, forgetting, for just a moment, her anger toward her father. She looked at Ruby with barely concealed shame.

"You…have my mum and da—"

"No I don't," Ruby countered swiftly. "They're not my *real* parents."

"No," Asher admitted. She placed a supportive hand on Ruby's shoulder. "But you did have parents who loved you. Mum says the car accident that…"

"I know the truth," Ruby cut her off abruptly. "There was never a car accident. That's just a story Nana made up to make sure I never knew what really happened…"

Ruby paused and looked down sadly at her hands which she had cupped delicately in her lap.

"My father raped my mother and I was the result. He wanted my mum to get rid of me and she wouldn't so he strangled her with me still inside of her."

Asher was so shocked by Ruby's frankness, it was she now, who was unable to find words.

"I've heard them talk," Ruby said, referring to Belle and Rex. "I heard them when they thought I wasn't able to hear. I've heard them say not to tell me anything about the truth. That's why Uncle Rex can't stand the sight of me. I'm his bastard niece—that's what he's called me to Nana."

The door to the toilet opened and Belle appeared, looking tired. There was some commotion behind the counter where the constable was standing as a door opened and a second uniformed officer appeared along with a downcast Rex, who shuffled into view. The constable walked him over to a concealed gate that appeared to be a part of the counter and lifted a portion of the desk above it. He ushered Rex through.

Belle appraised her husband with barely concealed disgust. He reeked of alcohol. His face was swollen, one eye was closed over and dried blood caked his upper lip. His clothing was crumpled and stained with vomit. Rex did not return her look. He merely hung his head.

"He's had a few hours to dry out," the police officer said, causing Rex to flinch as though the sound of his voice was as piercing as a fire siren right next to his ears. "Luckily for him, the other party has elected not to press charges. I would suggest that Mr. Delfey consider laying particularly low for a while."

Belle signalled wordlessly to the girls who were watching Rex fearfully. They quickly launched to their feet and scurried out of the reception area, then Belle abruptly turned on her heel and stormed from the police station. Rex stood there in the company of the officer, dumbfounded and swaying back and forth.

The officer slapped Rex roughly on the back of his shoulder.

"On your way Rex," he said. "Don't fancy your chances with her. Stay out of trouble for Christ's sake."

Moving as if on autopilot, Rex stumbled through the entrance and down the path to the car park of the police station where he found Belle standing beside her small hatchback.

"What?" he mumbled sullenly as he went to step past Belle and open the passenger door.

Belle calmly stepped in front of the car door and steeled herself where she stood, preventing him from going any further. Rex blinked and stumbled backward. Inside the car, the two girls peered out, watching Rex and Belle fearfully.

"What did you do?" Belle asked softly, her voice shaking with anger.

Again Rex tried to step forward toward the car. This time, Belle shoved him in the chest with flat of her palm.

Rex glared impotently at her as he swayed back and forth.

"I've been slaving Rex," she said shakily. "Working twelve hour days, seven days a week trying to keep this family together and what are you doing? Wiping yourself out night after night at that bloody pub."

"Don't speak to me like that woman or I'll fucking smash you," Rex spat threateningly, waving his arms about. "I work too. I take whatever shit job I can get. I've been back and forth, back and forth Belle. Nobody wants a *half caste coon* working for them!"

Though she wanted to lash out at him, Belle held her tongue, less at his threat of violence and more at the mention of that particular pejorative.

"Don't you stand there and wallow in self-pity! You don't have that luxury."

Belle stepped to one side and gestured through the car's window at the two frightened girls huddled inside.

"These children are supposed to look up to you! And look at what you're doing."

Rex glared through the window at Asher and Ruby. His eyes flicked between the two girls until they settled on Ruby.

She retreated back as his glare seemed to drill into her—a mixture of hatred and revulsion. Ruby knew instinctively what he was thinking.

Belle noticed her husband's expression and shook her head.

"D…don't Rex," was all she could manage as she wheeled away from him and climbed into the car. Belle started the engine and put the car into gear.

Rex shook himself back to the present, realising that he was standing alone before the car.

"Belle!" he shouted.

"Get in!" Belle shouted at him.

He stumbled and fell to the ground, completely missing the handle of the car door. Rex cursed into the night and shook his fist as he kicked and waved his arms like an upturned beetle on the ground.

Belle shook her head and lowered it, closing her eyes and sighing wearily as Rex finally struggled to his feet and managed to get inside the car.

She didn't wait for him to close the door. Gunning the engine, she took off with a screech of tyres on bitumen as he fumbled with the seatbelt for several moments before giving up and lapsing into unconsciousness once more.

In the back seat, Asher and Ruby huddled together as far away from Rex as they possibly could.

Once home, Belle ordered the girls back to bed quickly, then struggled to get her semi conscious husband inside. All the while, he struck out at Belle, resisting her and cursing at her.

Asher and Ruby huddled together in their bedroom, listening to Rex's abusive shouting and hitting until Belle closed her bedroom door as well as the hallway door, where it continued on in muffled tones for another hour or more.

Both girls quivered with fear but as Ruby held her cousin closer, she looked into Asher's eyes and saw something there that frightened her even more than her uncle.

A pure and burgeoning rage.

CHAPTER 8

JEREMY APPROACHED THE BURGUNDY HOLDEN COUPE FROM the opposite side of the street. It sat in the car park of a shopping mall, bathed in the orange glow of the mall's lighting. A misty halo of light seemed to surround the vehicle, in part due to the steady rain that continued to fall from the night sky. Jeremy drew up the collar of his rain coat and looked up and down the street before crossing over.

He was on edge, nervous and he felt a knot of tension in the pit of his stomach.

He was about to participate in his first active run with the gang. He had no idea what they had planned. He hadn't been told anything other than where to show up. Since Jeremy was the newest member, having been recruited into it by Mickey, he was rarely included in any of their discussions. Jeremy understood the hierarchy of the group and his place in it. He had to prove his worth and tonight was just a first step.

Crossing over a verge that divided the car park from the pavement, Jeremy heard the click of a car door and a figure stepped out from the passenger side. It was Mickey. He acknowledged Jeremy with a simple nod.

He had a cordial enough relationship with Mickey, but Jeremy did not regard him as a friend. He knew he had to be on his guard with Mickey as the older youth was unpredictable, likely to turn on him in an instant.

Also athletic, Mickey stepped around the open door and shut it, standing in the rain, unaffected by it. He wore a similar black rain jacket to Jeremy, and a woollen beanie.

He looked Jeremy up and down.

"You ready?" Mickey asked bluntly, his expression blank.

Jeremy nodded hurriedly, wiping the rain from his face.

"Don't speak. Don't ask questions. Just do as you're told," Mickey ordered, ushering Jeremy toward the car.

Jeremy approached hesitantly as Mickey pulled the passenger seat forward, allowing Jeremy access to the rear of the coupe.

Inside, Jeremy was confronted by the same two individuals who had accompanied Mickey the other day.

An obese teen shuffled into the middle of the seat, glaring malevolently at Jeremy. So large was he, the boy had been given the nickname "Jabba" after the character from the Star Wars movies. He was roughly the same age as Jeremy, but he had been in the gang for at least two years. Jabba's role in the group was unmistakable. He was their heavy hitter. He wore his black hair long and curly and it was parted almost perfectly in the middle.

Next to Jabba, sitting directly behind the driver's seat, was a similarly dour looking individual who was the complete antithesis of his huge companion. Dubbed Spider, the Caucasian teen was thin, with sinewy arms and long legs which were drawn up in the cramped confines. He chewed on a wad of gum, working his jaw angrily and rolling his tongue around.

Finally, sitting in the driver's seat was Gavin, the leader of the group. In his early twenties, he was the oldest of all of them and the most malevolent. He commanded attention with a silent authority that few ever questioned. Tall, muscular and brooding, Gavin possessed piercing eyes and he wore a cleanly shaven beard and moustache on his chiselled visage.

Jeremy settled into his seat, hoping that Gavin would acknowledge him but the leader did not look around. His gaze remained fixed straight ahead, out into the inky night.

As Mickey himself sat down, Gavin started the car and gunned the engine. The car took off, its rear wheels spinning on the slick pavement of the car park.

They coasted down the thoroughfare of the inner suburbs, heavy metal music blasting from the stereo. Jeremy watched Gavin in silence, was fascinated by the older youth who rarely, if ever, said anything. He never showed emotion but he commanded complete obedience from those who ran with him. He had a charisma that drew others toward him. Gavin had never so much as acknowledged Jeremy's existence—other than when he instructed others, like Mickey, to demand his presence when it was called for.

Reminded of his decision not to go with them the other day, Jeremy had no idea whether Gavin was angry with him for instead accompanying Ruby to the Conservatory. Nothing had been said then or since, when Mickey had contacted him about tonight.

Maybe Gavin had decided to let it go, Jeremy thought. He hoped that was the case.

Beside Jeremy, Jabba shuffled uncomfortably, annoyed at being flanked on both sides by Jeremy and Spider, neither of whom could prevent coming into contact with Jabba's huge bulk. He flashed another glare at Jeremy, making clear his distaste for him. For his part, Jeremy had to stifle his sense of smell against Jabba's appalling body odour, which was a pungent mix of fast food and faeces. It was rumoured that Jabba rarely wiped himself properly after using the toilet. Spider, beside him, was unaffected. His eyes were closed as he napped.

After about twenty minutes, Gavin slowed the coupe and flicked a switch on the dashboard, shutting down the car's headlights. Jeremy forgot about Jabba and the others and he craned his neck to see where they were. They turned off the main road and motored slowly down a side street flanking a strip mall that was populated by a variety of shops including a butcher, a hair dresser and a take away outlet. It also housed a larger liquor store. Despite some of the shops being lit from inside in addition to a trio of street lights that illuminated the parking space in front, at this late hour, none of them were open.

Gavin circled the complex once, making a mental note of certain land marks. He pointed silently to a grey transmission box that stood on the opposite corner of the street and Mickey nodded in acknowledgement. Mickey put his gloved hands on a menacing pair of bolt cutters that sat between his legs and steeled himself as Gavin crossed over the street, slowing as he approached the box. Without stopping the vehicle, he nodded once at Mickey, who opened the door and leaped out onto the street, shutting the door behind him.

Instantly dropping to his haunches, Mickey surveyed his surroundings, ensuring no one was in his vicinity, then he crept around to the front of the transmission box. He destroyed the padlock with the bolt cutters and threw open the door. Reaching into his pocket, Mickey revealed a pair of wire cutters and immediately went to work on the complex circuit boards inside the box, cutting through wires indiscriminately.

Inside the car, the others watched the strip mall expectantly. Mickey's actions had their desired effect as the lights in the car park as well as the shops flickered and died, enveloping the mall in darkness.

This was Gavin's cue to move. He gunned the engine and turned down the side street, looking for the narrow entrance to the rear of the strip mall. He found it and turned in, motoring up a short laneway that opened out into a compound-like parking area and loading zone.

Both Jabba and Spider reacted, reaching into their clothing and pulling out a ski mask each. Jabba slapped Jeremy's shoulder and pointed roughly at a rear pocket of the front passenger seat where a similar ski mask poked out. Jeremy took it out hesitantly and held it in his hands, the realisation of what they were about to do dawning on him.

Skidding to a stop in the centre of the darkened car park, Gavin and the others exited the vehicle. The rain fell heavier now as Jeremy watched Spider lift the boot door of the car and take out two sheets of black plastic as well as a roll of electrical tape. He went to work on the license plates of the car, wrapping them in the plastic and securing them with the tape.

Jabba, meanwhile, lifted a large object out of the boot which Jeremy identified as a sledge hammer. Wielding the heavy hammer effortlessly, Jabba swung it over his shoulder and walked over to Gavin, who was appraising the liquor store. There was a set of double glass doors in the centre of the building and off to one side, a large roller door—the loading dock for the liquor store. It was this roller door that commanded Gavin's attention.

Gavin gestured discreetly at the glass doors.

"Get in there and make sure we're clear. Their security system runs on a back up power source. Cops probably know already," he muttered to Jabba, who nodded obediently. Jeremy realised that it was the first time he had heard Gavin speak tonight.

Gavin turned to Mickey, who appeared from the laneway.

"Keep watch. The minute you see anyone, buzz me."

Mickey nodded, feeling inside his jeans for the familiar bulk of his mobile phone. He trotted back off down the lane while Gavin looked across at Spider. Jeremy watched as they wordlessly acknowledged one another, then Gavin climbed into the vehicle and started the engine, while Spider walked up to Jeremy and grabbed his arm.

"C'mon. Follow my lead and do exactly as I do."

Jabba sauntered toward the darkened entrance, his ski mask pulled down over his features, while Gavin turned the Holden coupe in a full circle until its rear lined up with the roller door of the loading dock. Jabba stepped up to the glass doors and, without any effort at all, he swung the heavy sledge hammer off his shoulder and gripped it in two hands like a baseball bat. Using all the force he could muster behind his huge frame, Jabba began counting out loud as the steel head of the hammer struck home, smashing dead centre into the double set of glass doors and completely obliterating them. The force of his swing was in fact, so powerful that it tore one of the doors completely off its hinges and catapulted it a full six feet inward. Glass rained everywhere but Jabba ignored it, stepping through the ruined entrance and into the darkness beyond.

Dropping the sledge hammer, he instantly drew the can of spray paint out of his track pants and casually strode toward the tell-tale red light of a security camera, mounted high up on the ceiling inside the door. Still counting out loud—a methodical "Eight…Nine…Ten"—Jabba pointed the can at the camera and sprayed until it was covered in a thick coating of black paint. Then he turned to his right, toward the loading dock interior where he walked up to two more winking red lights and did the same.

"Fifteen…sixteen…seventeen…"

Outside Jeremy watched, his heart racing. He glanced over at Gavin inside the car and frowned, puzzled as he noticed that Gavin was mouthing numbers silently, evidently counting the seconds from the time Jabba had destroyed the door.

Unbeknownst to Jeremy, the gang had mapped this hit out well before its execution. A full week prior, Gavin and Mickey had made several trips to the liquor store—ostensibly as customers—and had managed to "reccy" the building, its layout, its security system, power supply, loading dock and access points. They knew Mickey's sabotage of the lights and main power would not extend to the store's security system and silent alarm—but that didn't matter. All they needed to do was to ensure their concealment here and now and the timing of their raid. They had garnered intelligence on when a significant stock delivery was to be made to this particular store, a delivery that would include top shelf liquor, worthy of a hit. That very delivery had been made earlier this very day.

Gavin kept watch in the rear view mirror, looking toward the destroyed entrance, waiting for a sign from Jabba. As his count approached twenty seconds, Jabba had still not appeared at the entrance and Gavin smiled. He dropped the gear shift into reverse and, balancing his feet on the brake and the accelerator simultaneously, he revved the rumbling engine.

"Twenty one…twenty two…twenty three…"

Outside, Spider nudged Jeremy and pulled both his and Jeremy's ski masks down over their faces.

"Get ready."

At last, Gavin said aloud, "Twenty five," and he planted his foot. The Holden's tyres squealed on the slick pavement and it leaped backward, angling straight at the roller door. The flimsy metal of the roller door whined in protest and crumpled inward as the Holden punched through it, opening a gaping hole and revealing the loading dock to the elements.

Gavin leaped from the driver's seat and pounced up a set of stairs where Jabba was waiting at the top beside a pallet of boxes that contained bottles of spirits.

"This is gonna be *too* easy," Gavin grinned, surveying the pallet.

Spider and Jeremy sprinted into the dock and positioned themselves just below Gavin and Jabba, who began handing them boxes of clinking bottles. Following Spider's lead, Jeremy took a crate of whiskey, deposited it into the boot of the car then turned to receive another. He struggled to keep pace with Spider who moved swiftly and effortlessly, but Jeremy worked as hard as he could, receiving another and another, lining them up inside the boot space as carefully as he could. Sweat broke out on his brow underneath the thick wool of the ski mask.

From somewhere in the distance, the wail of a police siren became audible. Jeremy felt his stomach lurch. He glanced sideways at Spider

"C'mon!" Jabba snarled as he dropped a box at Jeremy, who wheeled around too late to catch it. It dropped straight through his arms and smashed on the floor—pungent whiskey leaking out from inside the ruined box.

Jeremy looked up at Jabba startled.

"Fucking forget about it!" Jabba hissed as he grabbed another box and dropped it at Jeremy. This time he caught it—but only barely—and deposited it roughly into the car boot, hearing glass clinking inside the box. He winced underneath his mask, knowing Gavin would be livid.

The siren drew closer now. The four youths ramped up the pace, a silent desperation growing. After several minutes, they had lined the boot with two full layers of boxes. Suddenly, Mickey appeared in the ruined opening.

"We've gotta split!" he hissed. "An old fart is standing on the porch of his house across the street and the coppers are coming hard."

Both Gavin and Jabba leaped from the upper level of the dock and threw open the car doors. Spider slammed the car boot closed and signalled to Jeremy to retreat.

Jeremy backed up from the car and started forward when he slipped on the whiskey covered concrete. Reflexively, he shot out his arm to break his fall, his palm crashing through the ruined box of whiskey bottles on the floor and he cried out in pain, feeling shards of broken glass cut deeply into his skin. Dizzy with nausea and pain, Jeremy tried to ignore it as he yanked his hand free.

Within seconds they had all piled into the Holden. Mickey, now in the driver's seat, wasted no time. He ignited the engine, threw it into gear. The

Holden burst from the building, careened down the laneway and onto the street, its tyres squealing. Spying the figure of an elderly man waving his arms in the front yard of a house immediately opposite, Mickey spun the steering wheel hard left, directing the car away from the highway and instead into the dense residential area behind the strip mall.

At the same moment, a single patrol car sped into view of the darkened strip mall from the highway. It veered over the intersection, through a red light and swung into the car park in front of the liquor store, just as the Holden disappeared from view.

The youths in the coupe whooped victoriously as they sped away from the scene, satisfied that they had escaped without being seen. Jeremy watched the others distantly, cradling his injured hand which was bleeding profusely underneath the sleeve of his hoodie. He had pulled the sleeve down and gripped it with his hand to try and stem the blood.

"That entrance was so fucken clean, man!" Spider leered at Jabba, who had crossed his hands over his bulging stomach and wore a satisfied grin. "You carved through it like it was paper."

Gavin turned in his seat and acknowledged Jabba admiringly.

"It was nearly perfect. You had the timing down just like we practised."

"*Near* perfect?" Jabba retorted. "Fuck that bro, it *was* perfect. I moved like a ghost."

Spider cackled maniacally beside Jabba while Mickey kept checking the rear vision mirror for any sign of followers. Fortunately, there were none.

They drove on through the night, until Mickey finally brought the car to a stop at the football oval where he and Jeremy trained.

Once there, they emptied out of the car and both Spider and Jabba immediately went to the boot to inspect their considerable haul. Gavin went up to them and stepped in between them and the car.

"Come on fellas, you gotta clear off. We don't want to risk getting caught up together. I'll get this stuff organised as soon as possible."

Jeremy stepped back from the vehicle and watched the others as though through a fog. He wanted desperately to get away before he vomited in front of them. Mickey came over to him.

"You better get your arse home too," he said flatly. "Don't speak to no one."

Jeremy nodded and was about to turn away when Gavin came up to them both.

Jeremy stiffened, trying to ignore the pain. This was the first time Gavin had acknowledged him all night.

The older youth appraised Jeremy dispassionately.

"If you're told I want to see you," he began, pausing midway for effect. "You bloody well better come. I don't want to hear of you saying no to me again."

Abruptly, Gavin wheeled away from Jeremy and went over to the others.

Jeremy's heart sank, his shoulders visibly slumped.

Mickey regarded him a moment longer and then he too, turned away.

A dark cloud settled inside of Jeremy. He felt sick, embarrassed and he wanted to get as far way from here as he could. He wiped the rain from his face and turned to leave.

Gavin called out to him.

"Jeremy."

Jeremy stopped and looked back over his shoulder.

Gavin was looking at him and he nodded at Jeremy.

"You did alright," he said simply.

CHAPTER 9

1951

IN TIME, HER YOUNG LIFE BECAME OCCUPIED solely by working on the Pastoralist's farm.

Day after day, week after week, Virginia toiled away with little respite from her servitude. It was repetitive and mundane and there was nothing else to occupy her mind—nothing else to think of than her oppressive life here. All of the colour and life, the warmth and happiness of her childhood home was replaced by the ruddy yellows and browns of this harsh and unforgiving place. Virginia doubted if it had ever been green here. The dust and the heat and the flies were all-consuming—omnipresent.

Worse still, was the effect it had on her emotions—what it took from her.

Hope.

Virginia remained mute, despite the best efforts of the older girls to get her to talk. All she wanted to focus on was getting through each day without drawing attention to herself. There were a number of people who worked for the Pastoralist and it was clear she was considered the lowest form of worker. She took refuge in her work. Her once delicate hands were now calloused and tough. She struggled with constantly itching skin due to the soaps and detergents she was forced to use in the outhouse toilets. If it wasn't that, the grime and the shit of the stables and yards had gifted her with a number of ailments: eczema, infections and lice. But she dared not complain.

The consequences of speaking up were dire.

Virginia had come to know the Pastoralist as a brutal and unforgiving man who accepted nothing less than complete obedience. The consequences of failing him were severe. Virginia learned early on never to question him and, up until now, she had avoided his wrath. But she had witnessed it, through the misfortunes of Deliah and Marjorie. He routinely meted out punishment to them, either for innocuous infractions or just because he felt like it. They were never without the physical scars, to say nothing of the mental scars. Virginia lived in constant fear, knowing that her turn would surely come.

When it did, Virginia was totally unprepared for it.

It followed a particularly awful day on the wood heap in early winter. Long before dawn, Virginia had been summoned from her bed and ordered by one of the Pastoralist's nameless lackeys to chop up an entire truck load of firewood for the homestead. Quite unexpectedly, Virginia was greeted by the first rains of the season and they arrived with a vengeance. There was a sense of urgency over this task because the homestead was running low on dry wood for the fireplaces and the kitchen stove. The wood had to be chopped and stacked safely away before the inclement weather rendered it useless.

The three girls were forced to work on a roster based system, rotating through the various chores around the farm and so it was Virginia's turn to chop the wood. She dreaded it because she was the worst at it. The axe was heavy in her small hands and she could barely lift it. Thus, it took her twice as long to chop and stack the wood as it did Deliah and Marjorie.

Stepping out into the darkness of the pre-dawn, the rain was already coming in hard. It peppered her skin like needles, it carried with it an interminable chill and it soaked everything. The sky above crackled with lightning, forks of electricity licked the pasture all around. However unnerved Virginia might have been, she didn't dare protest or abandon her task; the memory of witnessing the Pastoralist taking the broken axe handle to Deliah was still fresh in her mind and it frightened her into action.

Virginia toiled away in the mud and the wet, wielding the axe that stood almost half her own height. The only respite she could get from the storm was the skeletal remains of a burnt out shed that stood next to the wood pile. Though its stone and brick walls were largely gone, parts of the iron roof were still intact so she was able to gain some protection from the elements. Virginia retrieved some discarded sheets of iron that lay on the ground nearby to erect a makeshift wall on two sides so she could shield herself from the worst of the rain. It worked—but only partially.

With a painstaking effort she began to master the axe and her output increased accordingly. She loaded pile after pile of soaked firewood blocks into a rusted wheelbarrow, then she transported them through the driving rain along the long path to the shed behind the homestead. Over and over again she did this. By midday, Virginia was shivering from the damp, but she tried to ignore it.

At some point, Deliah appeared with a plastic garbage bag she had spirited to Virginia from inside the house and that did provide Virginia some protection. Deliah had also brought her a chicken sandwich and an apple, having taken them from the kitchen when no one was looking. Together they stuffed the food items under some more iron inside the ruined shed where they would stay dry. As much as she wanted to, Deliah didn't stay—she couldn't—for her work inside the house went on and the Pastoralist was, reportedly, in a foul mood because of the weather. If he caught Deliah out here, she would surely suffer.

By mid-afternoon Virginia was numb—physically and emotionally. She struggled to move in her sodden clothing. It had stuck to her skin, despite the plastic garbage bag she wore. Occasionally, she paused to gather her strength under the shelter of the iron, making sure that no one was watching. Sitting down on a dry patch of earth, she took out the sandwich and nibbled on it.

There was someone however—more specifically—*something* watching her.

The black and white cattle dog had snuck into view from the shelter of the out houses and had been surveying Virginia from afar. When Virginia disappeared from view, the dog whimpered from his vantage point, trying to see where she had gone. Eventually, his curiosity prompted him to brave the weather and he made a dash for the wood pile where, upon rounding the corner of the shed, he found the little girl huddled up under the iron.

Virginia looked up and regarded the dog absently. She was shivering too much to acknowledge him. The dog stopped before her, his eyes falling across the morsel of food Virginia held in her hand.

"Well?" Virginia croaked, her voice gravelly from months of silence. "D-don't just stand there."

The dog needed no further prompting. He trotted in under the shelter and sat down on his haunches, wagging his tail as Virginia handed him a small corner of her sandwich. He gobbled it down eagerly and then whimpered expectantly for more.

"I got no more," Virginia held out her empty hands, but the dog wasn't looking at her hands. Rather, they were focused on the apple that sat in her lap.

Virginia glanced down and the shining red fruit and frowned quizzically at the dog.

"*Fruit?*" she questioned incredulously. "How silly. What sort of dog eats fruit?"

Taking the apple in her shaking hands, Virginia bit off a piece of flesh and tossed it to the dog who snapped it up effortlessly in his jaws.

That single action both surprised and delighted Virginia who, for the first time in what seemed an eternity, did something that felt completely foreign to her.

She smiled.

Taking another bite of the apple, Virginia reached out for the dog's collar and thumbed a silver disc that hung from it. She read the inscription that was engraved on its surface.

Again she frowned.

"*Simon?*" she croaked. "What kind of name is that for a dog?"

The dog, Simon, just sat there, quivering with excitement rather than cold.

Virginia shared another piece of the apple with Simon, then another, until all that was left was the core.

She appraised the drab sky.

"Is it always so miserable here Simon?"

The dog barked and wagged his bushy tail enthusiastically.

Her hunger assuaged, Virginia got to her feet, brushed down the plastic of her make shift poncho, then took the axe handle from its resting place.

"You stay here," she ordered as earnestly as she could. "No sense in two of us getting soaked through."

As she was about to return to her work, Virginia stopped when, from across the compound, the sound of music drifted through the rain and the storm and into her ears. Virginia whipped her head in the direction of the homestead and stood perfectly still, listening to the beautiful, plaintive sonnet.

It captivated Virginia.

She had begun to look forward to hearing the music every day when she was working. In fact, she made sure that her other chores were completed and she was out on the verandah, sweeping and dusting. It always began at the same time each day and it stopped her dead in her tracks and the more she listened, the more she was drawn to its beauty.

Virginia knew now what it was and who was playing. It was the Pastoralist's wife and the instrument was called a violin. Virginia had only ever glimpsed this woman from a distance and she had never actually seen her instrument. She was never in a position to see the woman play but Virginia always knew by her music that she was there.

In that moment, there on the wood heap, a thousand miles from any-where, Virginia closed her eyes and drifted away from the farm on the sounds of the violin music. Time melted and was gone. She felt as light as a feather. There was nothing but peace.

Her reverie was suddenly and violently broken when a sharp, stinging blow crashed into the side of her head—so powerful that it lifted Virginia off her feet and propelled her small body across the muddy ground where she crashed into the wood pile.

Immediately overcome by nausea, Virginia scrambled desperately where she lay. Struggling to focus, Virginia blinked furiously and looked up to see the towering figure of the Pastoralist standing over her.

"What are you doing?!" he bellowed satanically.

Virginia stifled the urge to vomit from the stinging pain and an ac-companying, high pitched ringing that had assailed her hearing. Her heart raced and her lungs heaved as though she had forgotten to breathe. Gain-ing a precarious hold on her senses, Virginia became aware of a snake like object the Pastoralist gripped in his right hand.

It was a bull whip.

"Answer me!" the Pastoralist roared, reaching down with his free hand and grabbing Virginia by the throat, yanking her to her feet.

"I don't give you shelter here so you can do what you like, when you like…" he paused as he reached into his pocket and pulled out the half eaten apple. "And I won't have thieving in my home!"

Virginia blinked dumbfounded as the Pastoralist threw the apple at her as hard as he could, striking her square in her belly and winding her. He grabbed at the plastic and the fabric of her dress, tearing them from her in one swift motion. Then he stepped back several paces, unspooling the bull whip.

Standing completely naked, Virginia stood paralysed. Her disorienta-tion had coalesced into blinding fear. The Pastoralist raised the thick handle of the whip above his head and he parted his legs.

"Turn around!" he screamed.

Virginia stared blankly up at him, his stony features shaded by the brim of his hat. She couldn't move.

The Pastoralist spat on her and brought the handle of the whip down with a flick of his wrist. The length of plaited leather whistled through the air, snapped back loudly and Virginia yelped in pain as the whip's end cut a deep crimson gash into her skin. Intense pain blossomed across her chest and she began to shake uncontrollably. The music from inside the house stopped and all Virginia heard now was the crack of the whip echoing in her head.

The Pastoralist brought the handle back over his head and cracked the bull whip again, the end striking her identical to the first. She bit her lip. Tears streamed down her face and she felt her legs buckle.

Quite unexpectedly, a single thought passed across her failing consciousness.

'Where has the music gone?'

As the Pastoralist whirled the bull whip around for a third time, Virginia crumpled to the ground, vomiting into the mud. Her consciousness fading, the Pastoralist's whip struck across her shoulders. She made no sound as her blood trickled down over her skin and was washed away by the rain. The pain overwhelmed her and she succumbed to the darkness.

The Pastoralist glared at the unconscious child, his anger boiling like a furnace. He closed his eyes and tried to calm his nerves; to slow his breath. Then, he turned on his heel and strode away, leaving the child on the ground.

Simon, who had been cowering under the shelter of the ruined shed, waited until his master was gone from view, then he slunk cautiously over to Virginia's still form.

The darkness seemed to envelop everything…but not quite.

A blanket was draped across her still form, protecting her from the rain. She could sense a pair of delicate, feminine hands on her skin—then more hands underneath her, lifting her. And then she was no longer out of doors. In her darkness, she could hear the echoing whispers of a woman's voice, issuing instructions to someone unseen. "Bring the disinfectant and towels. I need boiling water, bandages." She could sense the urgency around her but she couldn't open her eyes to see. Then the blackness prevailed again. There was nothing.

Virginia awoke in her bed and blinked her eyes. Sitting herself up, she winced as burning daggers of pain arched across her back, her shoulders and her chest, almost taking her breath away.

Waiting until the pain settled, Virginia looked around her darkened quarters noticing Simon laying curled up at the end of her bed, fast asleep. For a moment, she was disoriented and felt herself begin to panic but she managed to slow her heart beat and force her mind to think.

She had lost days.

For over a week, she had been confined to her bed where she'd battled a rampant fever and excruciating pain. She hadn't been able to keep any food down nor fluids. She hadn't so much as slept as she'd writhed in the fog of infection, night after night. Deliah and Marjorie were sent a fresh supply of bandages and antiseptic twice a day to tend to her wounds. Food was brought from the kitchen by the head housekeeper each day— more food than they were ever allowed before. The girls were ordered to keep quiet and make no mention of this in front of the Pastoralist. Clearly, someone else was ensuring the girls had what they needed to care for Virginia.

Eventually, her fever broke. She began to recover, and now, she found herself here.

The previous night, Virginia had been inspected by the chief house-keeper. She had been declared fit for duties once more. But this time, she was summoned to the kitchen—much to her shock and surprise.

Working inside the house was considered a significant step up for a domestic servant and it only ever came after a significant period of proving oneself in performing the more menial and less desirable chores.

Virginia had encountered the Pastoralist's head housekeeper in passing and she had learned to fear this imposing barrel of a woman who always wore a scarf around her head and only seemed to bellow orders to the other girls.

Virginia gingerly stepped from her bed and dressed while Simon stirred and woke, watching her from his vantage point on the bed.

"Come on fella," Virginia said. "Let's go and see what we've got to do."

It was clear from the moment that Virginia stepped into the kitchen, that the housekeeper was not at all impressed with her. Mrs. Finchner examined Virginia with the eye of a drill sergeant, grabbing her ear lobes roughly and checking behind them. She held Virginia's hands, turning them over, picking at her eczema-afflicted skin. Finally the housekeeper inspected Virginia's finger nails, noting specks of ingrained dirt in some of them which she tried to loosen with her own claw-like nail. Virginia just stood there and quivered like a jittery field mouse, jumping at shadows and the softest of noises.

The housekeeper shook her head.

"You're too scrappy to be inside here," she appraised her dourly. "But I've been...*encouraged*...to make use of you."

The housekeeper turned to a cupboard on the far wall of the kitchen and fetched a bucket, an apron and some cleaning cloths.

"You'll start in the bathroom. Mop the floors, buff and polish them.

Make sure those tiles glimmer. Then you'll attend to the toilets and the laundry. Understand?"

Virginia blinked and nodded obediently as the housekeeper deposited the equipment in front of her.

The housekeeper pointed toward a doorway that led through to the inner house.

"Go," she ordered. "I'll be in to check on your work."

Gingerly, Virginia gathered up the bucket and mop and slowly made her way through the doorway. A long hall greeted her and she was immediately struck by the grandness of it. Plush carpets under foot, large paintings hanging from the walls on either side of her, large and imposing items of furniture standing silent, their contents visible through shining glass. She imagined that this was what a castle might be like.

Her work began again but, this time, Virginia felt strangely calm and protected in the confines of the homestead. She mopped and scrubbed the tile work and the floors of the laundry and bathroom, removing every trace of mould and dirt from the grout in the spaces between each tile. She buffed and polished the brass taps and fittings until she could glimpse her own reflection. She took special care with the tile work in the bathroom which had pretty patterns and shapes that Virginia found herself drawn to.

Time blurred once more and Virginia became lost in her tasks.

That was until the bathroom door swung open abruptly and the housekeeper appeared just as Virginia was making one final pass of the bath tub.

The housekeeper glared at Virginia kneeling before the tub. The child fairly jumped out of her skin and froze where she knelt.

The housekeeper inspected the bathroom with a keen eye and opened her mouth as if to point out some flaw in Virginia's work. But she held her tongue. She couldn't say anything. The child had done her job well… very well.

"Come with me," she snapped, turning on her heel from the doorway, forcing Virginia to clumsily gather up her things and follow hastily.

She caught up to the housekeeper just as she disappeared into a large dining room, the centrepiece of which was a long, shining, mahogany table with seating for twelve. It was quite possibly the largest table Virginia had ever seen.

The housekeeper turned to Virginia and snatched the bucket and mop from her grasp, replacing them with a feather duster, a bottle of furniture polish.

"Every surface needs to be dusted and polished until it shines," the housekeeper instructed. "There will be not one speck of dust on them when I return."

She swept from the room leaving Virginia to marvel at the beauty of the formal dining room. A huge clock stood in the corner immediately to her left and she approached it serenely, gazing at the shining brass pendulum that swung back and forth inside it.

Adjacent to the clock stood an imposing display cabinet which housed the most beautiful collection of crockery and glassware Virginia had ever seen. Hesitantly, she knelt before the glass doors of the cabinet and cast her eyes over the wondrous treasures inside.

All at once, Virginia felt panicky and she stood bolt upright, flicking her head in one direction then the other. She couldn't understand why she was here after the brutal punishment she had received from the Pastoralist. Why had she been assigned to such a privileged position in the homestead when surely the older girls—Deliah and Marjorie—were more entitled than she?

The need to work to distract her thoughts from anxiety flooded her and she rushed over to the entrance, picked up her equipment and furiously began dusting the furniture in an effort to calm herself. The clock behind her suddenly came to life, its internal mechanism clicking and whirring until the chime inside sounded noisily in her ears.

Virginia yelped, scrambling underneath the table where she cowered until the clock finished chiming, loudly and methodically, eleven times. Then, the quiet tick-tock returned to the dining room.

Virginia hesitated as she scanned the room, looking for any sign of somebody coming to punish her for making such a racket. After several minutes, with no sign of anyone, Virginia cautiously crawled out from underneath the table.

From somewhere nearby—another room in the house—Virginia heard the sound of a curious crackling issue forth. She cocked her ear to listen. The crackling lasted mere seconds before it was replaced by the tinny sound of a piano being played. A lovely melody filtered through into the dining room.

It was the music.

Setting her feather duster down, Virginia carefully tiptoed across to the doorway and peeked around the frame of the entrance. The music was coming from directly across the hall, from the parlour—the very parlour that she knew from lingering outside on the verandah. Virginia positioned herself so that she could watch without being seen. A woman was visible through the doorway, sitting on a soft high backed chair, holding a violin in her hands.

It was her.

The Pastoralist's wife was tall and stately, even when seated. Her hair was a rich chestnut, swept up on one side and clipped into place with an ornate hair pin. Her skin was as fine as porcelain. Virginia had never seen skin so soft. Her large eyes were a deep, jade green. Curiously, Virginia sensed something in those eyes—a hint of sadness—although she couldn't be sure. The woman's fingers were long and delicate, yet they held the instrument confidently. She wore moleskins, leather riding boots and a checked shirt.

Just in front of the woman, Virginia could see the conical brass shape of a gramophone's horn—the source of the music. As the piano accompaniment lilted toward a pause, the Pastoralist's wife lifted the violin to her neck and began to play, drawing the strange bow across the long end of the instrument and harmonising beautifully with the piano.

Virginia was mesmerised.

Each stroke of the bow made the violin sing in long, languid notes and rapid stanzas like a stone skipping across a pond.

Unconsciously, Virginia moved further into view until her head was now visible in the doorway. So engrossed in the music was she, she had failed to notice that the woman had detected Virginia out of the corner of her eye. One corner of her ruby red lips turned upward but she gave no hint that she had seen Virginia.

The sonata continued and though the gramophone record featured both the piano and the violin, the Pastoralist's wife played so expertly that Virginia could hear only her violin as she played it.

It was more beautiful here and now, at such close quarters, than she could have imagined.

Standing in full view in the doorway now, Virginia remained unaware that the woman's playing had drawn her out from her hiding spot.

The sonata rose to its finish and the woman lifted the bow away from the instrument with a theatrical flourish. Then, she looked directly at Virginia. The woman's deep green eyes drilled into Virginia's own and Virginia shivered.

She was paralysed where she stood.

The Pastoralist's wife rested the violin on her lap and regarded Virginia with a flat expression. Then, she tilted her head to one side.

"Come," she said softly, beckoning with a gesture of her hand.

Virginia shook her head reflexively.

The woman's expression coalesced into an unexpected smile.

"It's alright. I won't bite. Come and let me see you."

Something in the woman's voice relaxed Virginia and her fear melted away all at once. Slowly, she stepped forward, through the entrance and across the hall into the parlour until she was mere feet from the woman.

Once there, the Pastoralist's wife leaned forward and rested her elbows on her crossed legs, still balancing the violin in her lap.

"I've been watching you," she said. "I know you've been listening to my music."

Virginia held her hands behind her back and tried to look everywhere but at the Pastoralist's wife, unsure as to whether the woman was about to be angry or otherwise. Her demeanour didn't suggest anger but Virginia nonetheless remained guarded.

"What's your name?" the woman queried with an intrigued lilt to her voice.

Virginia hesitated, trying to quell the noise of her heartbeat in her ears. She opened her mouth to speak but she bit her lip at the last moment, as though trying to prevent her voice from escaping.

"V...Virginia," she whispered scratchily.

"Virginia," the Pastoralist's wife echoed softly, smiling warmly. "That is a pretty name. My name is Mrs. Penschey."

"Pen..." Virginia began, struggling to pronounce the name. "...*shay?*"

"That's right," the woman praised brightly. "You *do* have a good voice."

Virginia fidgeted nervously and stifled a wince when she arched one of her shoulders back causing a dagger of pain to knife through her.

Through a gap in the neck of her dress, Mrs. Penschey could see the top edge of a dressing that covered the wounds on Virginia's chest. A small spot of fresh blood was visible. Mrs. Penschey's expression quickly melted into concern and, quite unexpectedly, her eyes registered guilt. She reached out toward Virginia and placed a gentle hand upon her shoulder.

"They still hurt, yes?" she observed quietly.

This time, Virginia nodded. She did not pull away.

Shame flashed across Mrs. Penschey's eyes and as she looked away from Virginia fleetingly, her bottom lip quivered.

Virginia's eyes fell across the instrument in Mrs. Penschey's lap.

Mrs. Penschey's own gaze return to Virginia's face—then to the violin. She sat back in her chair, placed her hands on it and lifted the instrument toward Virginia.

"Would you like to hold it?"

Virginia blinked and hesitated a moment, looking over her shoulder.

"Oh, don't worry about Mrs. Finchner," Mrs. Penschey assured her softly, holding the violin out closer. "Here."

Slowly, Virginia held out both her hands and allowed Mrs. Penschey to place the violin gently into them.

Virginia was immediately struck by just how light the instrument felt. It was as if it were hardly there at all. But, more than that, she was transfixed by its beauty—its richly grained wood surface, its intricately scrolled neck.

"What do you think?" Mrs. Penschey asked.

Virginia's expression was one of reverence and unbeknownst to her, she bore a fascinated half smile.

"It's…b-beautiful Missus."

Gently, she raised the violin up and turned it over in her hands, nestling it gently into the crook of her neck in an attempt to replicate the way she had observed Mrs. Penschey hold it. Instinctively, she rested her chin onto the rest at the foot of the violin and held it there.

When she looked up at Mrs. Penschey, she was met with an approving smile and a nod.

"It feels natural…doesn't it?" Mrs. Penschey questioned.

Virginia nodded.

Mrs. Penschey picked up the bow and placed it into Virginia's free hand. Then she gently manipulated Virginia's fingers into position on the fretboard of the violin.

"Now…see if you can produce a note."

Virginia looked up at Mrs. Penschey nervously.

"Go on. You can do it."

Slowly, Virginia raised the bow, trying to keep the fingers of her other hand in position on the fret board. She adjusted her grip and closed her eyes, lowering it toward the centre of the violin's strings. As she touched the surface, Virginia instinctively drew the bow across the strings, eliciting a perfect note that lingered softly until she halted her stroke at the end of the bow's length.

Snapping them open, she glanced across at Mrs. Penschey who sat there nodding slowly.

"That was beautiful," she praised. "How did that feel?"

Virginia stood with a curious smile, holding the violin in position. She felt a reluctance to let go. It felt comfortable in her grasp. Standing there in the parlour of the homestead, Virginia felt something inside of her that she had not felt in many months.

It was hope.

CHAPTER 10

RUBY APPROACHED THE BATHROOM DOOR AND ATTEMPTED to open it, but she found it locked. Annoyed, she rapped loudly on the door.

"Asher! Are you in there? C'mon—we're gonna be late."

Receiving no response, Ruby put her ear up to the door and heard the sound of water running from the basin tap. Someone was definitely in there. Her eyes narrowed and her annoyance grew.

"Come on Asher! I need to brush my teeth."

Abruptly the door unlatched and swung open revealing Jeremy standing there, wearing only his pyjama bottoms and an angry look on his face. Instantly, Ruby was struck by how pale and sweaty he looked but she was given little opportunity to react because Jeremy reached out with his hand, grabbed her and yanked her into the bathroom, shutting and locking the door behind them.

An angry Ruby was about to retaliate when she noticed Jeremy's traumatised left hand as he immersed it under the running water.

Her eyes went wide.

"What did you do?" Ruby whispered breathlessly. She stepped up to the sink so she could get a better look and she gasped.

The deep, ragged gash crossed over nearly half the width of Jeremy's palm. The skin surrounding it was pale and raised and it looked awful.

"I just hurt myself on—the back fence—last night," Jeremy responded.

Ruby rolled her eyes at his pathetic explanation.

"Jeremy," she chided. "The back fence is wooden. There is no way that happened on a wooden fence."

Jeremy scowled, turning off the tap and holding his hand over the sink, letting the bloodied water drip away from his skin.

He was clearly in a great deal of pain.

"You've gotta go to the hospital," Ruby urged him. "That looks like it needs stitches."

Jeremy shook his head and lifted his arm up. His hand was throbbing; the pain threatened to overwhelm him.

"I can't go to the hospital," he said through gritted teeth. "They'll ask questions."

Ruby stepped back, took a blood-stained towel from the edge of the bath tub and handed it gingerly to Jeremy.

"Questions about what?" she pressed cautiously.

Jeremy glared at Ruby, a flash of knowing passed between them, but neither of them were willing to acknowledge it aloud.

He snatched the towel from her and wrapped his hand in it, patting it dry, hissing through clenched teeth as he did so. He sat down on the edge of the bath and cradled his hand in his lap, rocking back and forth.

"Well. W-what are you going to do?" Ruby asked with increasing worry. "You can't just leave it like that."

Jeremy looked up at the window sill above the basin where he had placed several first aid items he'd raided from a supply that Belle kept in the house.

Ruby immediately gathered up the items there, placing them down on a clean towel on the floor. Rummaging through the dressings, Ruby glanced up at Jeremy, signalling wordlessly to him for what to use. He pointed to a packet of small butterfly tapes and she picked them out, tore open the packaging and carefully peeled back the individual tapes.

Jeremy unwrapped his hand and gently presented it to Ruby. With as much care as she could, Ruby secured the tapes to his hand, one by one until she had covered the entire length of the wound. She plucked out a combine pad and placed that over his palm. Then she slowly and securely wrapped his hand in a bandage until the wound was completely concealed.

For the first time, Jeremy managed a wan smile.

"You should be a nurse like Mum," he observed softly.

Ruby scowled at her cousin.

"Yeah—well…" she said grumpily. "You've gotta stop running around with that gang. You're gonna get caught out."

Jeremy stiffened.

"Don't you say a word," he whispered harshly, leaning in close. "*To anyone.*"

"But…"

"I mean it, Rube. If you breathe a word to anyone – especially Mum… I'll do *you* in. I'll tell them where you go every Tuesday."

Ruby retreated from him then and she registered a flash of panic.

"Y…you wouldn't," she stammered.

Jeremy stood up, balling the blood-stained towel in his uninjured hand then proceeded to the bathroom door. Looking back at Ruby, his shoulders relaxed slightly and the tension went out of his jaw.

"Come on," he hurried her. "We're gonna be late for school."

Ruby followed him hesitantly out of the bathroom and down the hall to his bedroom.

"Jeremy?" she began hopefully. "You're still gonna come into town with me today, aren't you? You *did* promise."

Jeremy fished a T-shirt out of a pile of clothing on the floor of his room and turned toward Ruby. The expression on his face was utterly blank and gave nothing away.

Jeremy sat with Miss Glasson in the empty classroom, quietly working away on a maths problem. Having been banished from Mr. Baxter's class, Jeremy had narrowly avoided suspension on the proviso that he work one on one with Miss Glasson, who was the special needs teacher at the high school.

Of all his teachers, Jeremy liked Miss Glasson the best, though he would never openly admit it. Louisa Glasson was popular among many of the students; regarded as a friend and mentor to even the most hardened of troubled teens. She never lost her patience or got angry. Miss Glasson worked with a number of struggling students, offering them an educational program that assisted them in areas where they were falling down. Jeremy wasn't enrolled in it currently, although she had been gently encouraging him to consider it. So far, he'd baulked at it.

Right now, despite her best efforts, Jeremy was struggling to understand the current algebra problem they were working on. She could tell his frustration was building. Discreetly checking the clock on the wall above the white board at the front of the classroom, Miss Glasson noted that they'd been at it nearly thirty minutes.

Jeremy scribbled on the notepad beside him angrily, destroying a mosaic of numbers and figures that represented his working out so far. He gritted his teeth.

"Look," Miss Glasson said gently, placing her hand over his and taking the pencil from his fingers. "Why don't we take a break—before you stab me in the eye with that pencil."

Jeremy looked up and blinked, seeing her lopsided smile. He managed a sheepish grin in return, then slumped back in his chair.

Suddenly, his mobile phone vibrated in his pocket, loud enough that Miss Glasson could hear it. She levelled her eyes at him.

Jeremy felt for the bulk of his phone, then stopped himself short, realising he'd been caught out.

He looked at her apologetically.

"Sorry, miss," he said softly. "I forgot I had it on."

Again Miss Glasson smiled disarmingly. Glancing over her shoulder to check that no one was looking, she nodded sneakily.

"Go on," she nudged him. "Just this once while we're taking a break but you turn it off once you're done."

Jeremy grinned bashfully and took out his phone.

His smile faded as he scanned the single text message that was waiting for him on the screen. Miss Glasson noticed the sudden change in his demeanour.

"Are you okay Jeremy? You look like you've seen a ghost."

Jeremy's eyes flicked from the phone's screen to her and back again. He shifted uncomfortably in his seat.

The message was from Mickey.

'Meet after school. Gavin expects you.'

Jeremy shut the phone off and shoved it in his pocket.

"Jeremy?"

Jeremy shook his head dismissively.

"It's nothing, miss," he said. "Nothing…"

"It didn't look like nothing," she said evenly, unconvinced. "You *can* talk to me you know."

Sensing the tension in Jeremy rising, she sat back in her chair, adopting a less confronting posture and diverted her attention away from him for a moment.

She pointed at his work book and algebra text in the centre of the table.

"Have you given any further thought to my program?"

Jeremy felt an instant circuit breaker of relief at her change of subject, even though it pertained to something he had also been trying to avoid talking about.

"What—*vege maths*?" he scowled.

"No—not *vege* maths," she fired back with just the right amount of sarcasm in her voice that he smiled bashfully.

"Come on Jeremy. My program will help you in the areas you've been struggling with. It doesn't mean that you're dumb and no one else should think of you that way. You've seen the difference it's made with some of your friends. They're doing really well now and their grades reflect that."

Jeremy nodded slowly.

"Put it this way," Miss Glasson quipped. "Do you want to keep butting heads with Baxter or would you rather score a kick in the pants from me?"

Jeremy couldn't help but grin this time and he brought a hand up to his face to cover the fact that she had made him blush.

"Between you and me," she continued, leaning in close. "I think he's a jerk—but you never heard me say that. Alright? So—what have you got to lose?"

Miss Glasson held her arms out in a kind of victory gesture but Jeremy remained quiet, as if he was considering her offer.

"Who are you worried about Jeremy? Surely not your mates who are already doing it. They wouldn't be wise in lining up to pay you out. So who could..."

Miss Glasson's voice trailed off and Jeremy's expression became downcast. His jaw set. Miss Glasson sensed where his mind was focused.

"Is it your dad?" she ventured.

Jeremy looked up at Miss Glasson and held her gaze momentarily before retreating into his chair. He knew that Miss Glasson had some knowledge of his family background.

Still, Miss Glasson feared she had crossed the line. So she was surprised when Jeremy nodded in the affirmative whilst looking down at his hands.

"He's getting worse..." he said quietly. "Angrier."

Miss Glasson listened, allowing him as much time as he needed to offer whatever information he felt he could.

"He...fights," he continued. "With Mum...with me. He gets so violent."

"Tell me more about that," Miss Glasson probed carefully.

Jeremy looked at her awkwardly.

"It's like...he hates everything when he gets drunk. Especially me. He...thinks I'm stupid."

"And how does that make you feel?"

Jeremy shrugged his shoulders, trying to find the right word to describe his feelings.

"Angry...and useless."

Miss Glasson tilted her head slightly, her expression offered sympathy and understanding.

"Don't let anyone—*anyone*—make you feel useless Jeremy," she said firmly. "You're not useless and you're most certainly not an idiot. You're bright and you have plenty to offer."

Jeremy raised an eyebrow, considering her words.

"Look…what about your mum? Your nan? What if I met with them and talked about the program. Would that be better? I'm sure your mum would have no problem at all with you joining my class."

"Maybe. Mum's got too much on her own plate to be worried about me. Probably wouldn't care one way or the other."

"Well then…what do you think about it?"

Jeremy laughed quietly in spite of himself, picked up a pen and started doodling on the page in front of him.

"You're pushy, miss," he quipped. "That's what I think."

Miss Glasson watched Jeremy absently sketching something and she leaned in slightly to see what it was.

Her own eyebrow rose up this time.

"That's rather…abstract…isn't it?" she remarked.

Jeremy looked down at the page, as though he'd just realised what he had been doing.

"A guitar?" Miss Glasson queried, craning her neck to see the upside down image from her side of the table.

"A violin," Jeremy corrected her, almost grabbing the page as if to screw it up but then he stopped and turned it around for her to see.

"Ahhh," Miss Glasson mused. "This would be your…cousin's?"

Jeremy nodded, a wistful smile tugging at the corners of his mouth.

"Yeah. She plays. She plays it really well…although nobody knows it. I'm supposed to take her to the city tonight so she can play but Gavi…"

His voice cut off abruptly, as though he had just remembered something unpleasant. It was an almost identical reaction to the one he'd displayed earlier and Miss Glasson's eyes narrowed accordingly.

"What, Jeremy?" she pressed, sensing he had revealed something he hadn't meant to.

The school bell rang then. Both of them sat for several seconds, then Jeremy began gathering up his books and stuffing them into his school bag.

"Talk to me, Jeremy," Miss Glasson pleaded. "I can help, but only if you'll let me."

"No one can help me, miss," he said dismissively. "Can I go now?"

Jeremy didn't wait for her to answer. He turned from the classroom and exited before he could hear her response.

Miss Glasson sat there, her teeth clenched in frustration, knowing that she had gotten closer than ever before to uncovering the truth behind the rumours that Jeremy was involved with some kind of criminal gang.

On the piece of paper he'd left behind, beside his doodle of the violin, she wrote down a single name.

'*Gavin.*'

CHAPTER 11

RUBY AND ASHER SAT BEHIND THE FENCE of the football oval watching a group of boys, including Jeremy, as they trained out in the centre of the ground.

Asher noted that Ruby seemed impatient. She was checking her watch repeatedly and looking out toward the group on the field.

This wasn't unusual behaviour for her, Asher observed with amusement.

Ruby often had one eye on her watch whenever she and Jeremy were to catch the train to the city. The particular train they took delivered them into Adelaide in time for her to make it to the Conservatory and the string quartet's rehearsal session. It was known to be occasionally early and more than once in the past, they had missed it.

Asher smiled knowingly and prodded Ruby gently.

"It'll be alright, Rube. You know he likes to leave it 'til the last minute just to give you a stir."

Ruby managed a half smile and clasped her watch arm awkwardly between her knees.

"It's just that…I know that the quartet is practising for the Lord Mayor's Town Hall Recital and I don't want to miss it. It might be the only chance I get to hear them completely from beginning to end."

The girls were distracted then, their eyes drawn out across the field to the group of teens. Jeremy had clasped the ovular ball in both hands and was now sprinting down the ground, breaking away from a pack. While he moved effortlessly, on close observation, one could see that his hand still hurt him. He dropped the ball onto his foot and he punted it onwards, its spin and trajectory true. The entire group including the coach applauded his display enthusiastically.

Asher returned her focus to Ruby and regarded her cousin with a lop-sided grin.

"Where *do* you find out all this stuff?" she asked, with a hint of wonderment.

"On the computer at the school," Ruby shot back swiftly with a hurt expression. "The quartet has all their information up on their website. I can look at it whenever I want."

"That's a little obsessive, don't you think?" Asher remarked.

"Nooo-uh!" Ruby countered overly dramatically.

There was a pause between the two girls before they both burst into a fit of giggles and Asher punched Ruby playfully on the arm.

Regaining their composure, Ruby's eyes brightened when she saw Jeremy jogging over to them. Asher handed him a drink bottle from her bag and he took a long and generous swig from it, causing liquid to stream down his neck. Once his thirst was quenched, he handed Asher the bottle and wiped his arm across his mouth. He stood up and curiously scanned the car park beyond the two girls. He couldn't see any sign of Gavin's car anywhere.

"Who are you looking for?" Asher asked, looking over her shoulder herself.

"N…no one," Jeremy responded hastily.

"C'mon then," Ruby quipped, jumping down from the bench and grabbing her back pack. "We've gotta go, otherwise we'll be late."

Jeremy scratched at the back of his head awkwardly and hesitated, checking his own watch and scanning the car park once more.

"Ahh…"

Ruby flashed him a suspicious glare.

"What is it?" she questioned reflexively.

Jeremy didn't answer.

There was still no sign of the vehicle and a quick check of his cell phone revealed that there were no new messages waiting for him.

Maybe they had forgotten, he wondered, with a confusing mixture of worry and relief. Maybe they had decided to do something else without him today.

Slowly he reached into his own back pack and took out his fleece lined wind breaker.

Ruby still hadn't taken her eyes off him and she had now folded her arms protectively across her chest, clearly concerned. Asher was also watching her brother in a similar fashion.

"Jeremy?" Ruby pressed forcefully, anxiety blossoming inside her.

"Nothing," he said finally. To himself, he thought, *'They aren't coming.'*

"Come on," he said, feeling a sense of urgency to leave. "We better go."

Ruby quickly slung her back pack on her shoulders and smiled with relief at Asher.

Jeremy turned and flipped a jaunty wave at a couple of his teammates on the oval then followed after the girls who were already at the gates.

As he caught up to them and they prepared to cross the street, Jeremy suddenly heard a familiar metallic rumble approaching them. He turned to see the burgundy Holden coupe motoring toward them. Instantly, Jeremy felt an uncomfortable knot tighten inside him.

Gavin's car stopped in front of the trio. The darkened driver's side window lowered, revealing Mickey at the wheel.

His malevolent grin sent a chill through all three children.

"Where are you off to, mate?" Mickey quipped with a threatening hint to his voice. "Did you forget something?"

Ruby looked up at her cousin with an expression of confusion. Asher too, regarded her brother, while keeping one eye on the vehicle in front of them. The hairs on the back of her neck bristled.

"Jeremy? What is this?" Ruby hissed under her breath.

"I know you got my message," Mickey said icily. "You ready to go?"

That last sentence was less a question than it was a statement—an instruction.

Ruby felt her heart pound, as though it had risen up into the back of her throat. The realisation of what was happening was beginning to dawn upon her and with that realisation came the painful feeling of betrayal.

"Jeremy. You promised me," she whispered angrily.

Jeremy looked down, unable to meet her eyes directly. His expression was a mixture of guilt and disappointment. The knot inside him migrated to his temples and he began to feel sick.

"I…I know I did Ruby," Jeremy began. "But I…"

Ruby's eyes began to glaze with tears. She gripped the straps of her back pack tightly and ground her teeth together, to prevent herself from crying in front of both Asher and Jeremy as well as the strangers in the car. She heard a callous snicker emanate from inside, which cut through her like a knife.

"Jeremy!" Mickey snapped warningly.

"I'm sorry Ruby…I've got no choice. We can go another time, another day."

Abruptly, he turned from Ruby and Asher and strode toward the vehicle, leaving them standing on the curb, staring after him with disbelief.

"Go straight home," he instructed pathetically.

"No!" Ruby spat with a venom that surprised even her.

She took off down the street, running as fast as she could so that she could get away from the others without them seeing her sobbing openly.

Jeremy hesitated at the open door of the car, watching impotently as Asher started after her. She stopped on the other side of the street and wheeled back toward Jeremy.

"You are a selfish pig!" she yelled. "Look what you've done!"

Gavin reached across, pressed his hand to the horn on the steering wheel and shouted, "Get in the car!"

Jeremy flinched where he stood, his guilt palpable. Slowly he lowered himself into the vehicle, disappearing from view.

Ruby sprinted as fast as her legs would carry her through a busy shopping mall near the train station. Without pausing for breath, she skipped through a gaggle of people coming down a wide thoroughfare from the station platform and she skidded to a stop beside the very train she needed to catch.

Wiping her angry tears, cursing herself for showing weakness in front of those boys, Ruby felt the betrayal boil inside her.

How could he leave her like that, knowing that this was always *their* day?

Jeremy knew how important this was. He must have known how she looked forward to these Tuesday afternoons. It was her only chance to dream of what playing with a quartet was like. He promised her this was how it would always be. Now, he had broken that promise.

Ruby had no time to wallow further. The train's horn sounded, signalling its departure. The last passengers were clearing the platform. Suddenly, Ruby realised that she had no money for a ticket. She had left her money with Jeremy.

"Ruby!"

Ruby wheeled around to see Asher coming toward her from the exit ramp. The train's horn sounded once more and its engine began to throttle up.

Ruby turned toward the carriage door that was closing and made her decision.

She sprinted toward the train and leaped—her lithe frame whistling through the closing gap. The doors closed behind her and the train began to move.

Asher stood alone on the platform, watching the train trundle away from her, gathering speed as it rounded a bend and was gone.

IT WAS TWILIGHT by the time the train pulled into Adelaide's central station and Ruby knew that she was running late. In order to evade the fare collector, she'd spent the journey locked in the carriage's toilet.

She ran along North Terrace toward the Conservatory, single minded in her purpose. Anger continued to gnaw at her. Fresh tears streamed down over her cheeks and she bit the inside of her lip as hard as she could to keep herself from crying. All she wanted was to immerse herself in the sounds of the quartet, to disappear into the world of music to forget the wretchedness of her existence. It took all of her resolve to push her anger away so that it wouldn't poison her. She would not allow it. Her violin was the only pure gift she owned, untainted by her circumstance.

Ruby ran past the statue of Sir Walter Hughes, kicking up a stream of crackling leaves in her wake, completely ignoring the statesman.

"Ruby?"

"I haven't got time!" Ruby shouted angrily at the statue, causing several passersby to turn their heads in her direction. "I'm late!"

She skipped deftly over a garden bed and skirted the path until finally, she stopped outside the open window of the auditorium where she could hear rehearsal taking place inside. They were beginning their practise performance.

Thankfully, Ruby's little corner was shrouded in darkness and the last pedestrians leaving the university were petering out. Concealed by the bush, no one could see her. The single nearby lamp cast just enough light so that Ruby could see to unload her backpack. She set it down carefully, taking out her violin case from inside.

Ruby allowed the music from inside the hall to calm her and she focused on a peaceful centre in her mind. Moving her fingers across the latches of the case, she lifted her instrument out. In her mind, Ruby listened, seeking the rhythm of the piece being played and she found it, mentally joining with it and nodding her head slowly as she sat cross legged on the ground, raising her violin into position.

Closing her eyes, Ruby fell into step with the lead violin and played with flawless synchronicity.

The cool night air descended, though Ruby did not feel the cold. The sky above twinkled with a billion stars but she was oblivious to their beauty. The thrum of the nearby traffic was so distant that it did not register in her ears.

All that mattered was the music.

"Hey!"

Ruby was jolted from her reverie by the sharpness of the voice nearby. Her eyes snapped open and she flinched into the blinding white of a torchlight that was directed straight at her.

She froze as the hulking silhouetted figure holding the torch moved toward her.

"What are you doing there!?"

Ruby didn't respond. She was frozen on the spot.

Forcing herself to think, Ruby sprang to her feet and hugged the violin close to her chest. The torch light remained trained on her, disorienting her and feeding her panic.

The figure lumbered forward. Ruby abandoned her school bag and she turned to bolt, but she immediately crashed into a second person who was wielding his own torchlight. She was sent sprawling and her violin was pitched from her arms.

Ruby scrambled across the ground in an effort to escape but the second security guard was on her in a flash, clasping her shoulder with a vice-like hand.

"Not so fast!" the guard growled, signalling to his colleague. Evidently, Ruby had inadvertently butted her head into the guard's groin and had knocked the wind out of him. As soon as his colleague took the child from him, he subtly bent over and drew a long breath, trying to overcome the pain.

"What have we got here?" the first guard questioned ominously, holding Ruby's arm tightly, shining the torch into her face.

Ruby struggled impotently, trying to break free. The man towered above her.

"What's a little *abbo* doing, hanging around a university campus?" he barked, ignoring her attempts at punching his hand free.

"Looks to me like we've got a bit of thieving going on, Russ," his colleague wheezed, nodding toward the fallen violin on the ground.

The guard named Russ, who was holding Ruby, shone his torch over the instrument then back at her. He leaned down.

"Is that right?" Russ ventured malevolently. "Now why would you be wanting to steal a fiddle from the school, huh? Got someone who can sell it? Were you planning on making a little money for yourself?"

Ruby flinched at the pungent smell of garlic on Russ's breath. She pulled away from the guard as hard as she could. But it was no use.

"It's mine!" she spat angrily, catching both guards by surprise.

The second guard walked gingerly over to the fallen instrument and bent down to pick it up.

"Yeah—I call bullshit," Russ dismissed. "Looks to me like one of the instruments from inside."

Turning the violin over in his hands, the guard's eyes wandered over it to the fallen case and the bow nearby.

"What would you know about playing a fiddle?"

"I think we better call the police, Mick," Russ declared, clearly trying to frighten his young captive further. "Let them deal with it."

Ruby eyes bulged. Her breath caught in her throat.

"I didn't steal anything!" she protested angrily. "That violin belongs to me!"

Both guards eyeballed her dispassionately.

"You'll have to do better than that," Russ dismissed her. He nodded to his colleague, Mick.

Mick nodded back and together, the two men dragged Ruby from her hiding place.

CHAPTER 12

THE SECURITY GUARDS MARCHED RUBY INTO THE Conservatory building, ignoring her screaming protestations, scratching and kicking. She did everything she could to break free of them until they entered into Elder Hall itself. Ruby fell quiet, realising that this was the first time she'd actually been inside. And it was a most beautiful building at that, with high, ornate ceilings and grand arches. Ruby was simultaneously afraid and captivated.

Her momentary reverence passed and she struggled in the grip of the security guard, kicking angrily at his ankles as he strode through a hallway, holding her in one hand and the violin in the other, ignoring her. His counterpart walked a few steps behind, barely concealing a smirk.

The guards entered into a small office where Ruby was deposited into a chair. Her captor immediately turned to whisper something to his colleague and he picked up the receiver of a telephone on a messy desk beside him.

The significance of what was was happening didn't register with Ruby because the sound of the string quartet rehearsing floated clearly and voluminously through a window that looked out onto the hall's auditorium. Turning cautiously in her seat, Ruby peeked around and for the first time could actually see not only the auditorium—which she had only been able to imagine until now—but the very quartet that she had listened to and performed alongside for so long from her hiding place outside.

She was captivated.

At the bottom of the auditorium, four stately women of the string quartet sat and stood in the middle of the stage performing a light and breezy sonata. An audience composed of students and teachers sat randomly around them, both on the stage and in the first few rows of sumptuous, plush red seating, watching in respectful silence. The quartet held them enthralled.

Ruby noticed an elderly man pacing back and forth around the perimeter of the quartet, listening intently, bobbing his head at particular junctures of the piece. He held out a hand, waving it subtly in the air, keeping time with the music. Ruby frowned curiously as he removed a pair of gold rimmed glasses and rubbed the bridge of his nose between thumb and forefinger. Then he dragged the hand upward through his thick, curly hair that looked wild and frizzy. The delicate way he moved his fingers through the air seemed at odds with his masculine arms. And though his frame was diminutive, the presence he commanded from the audience and the quartet was all-consuming. Figuratively at least, he towered above everyone else in the room.

From a distant corner of her mind, the voice of Sir Walter echoed. *'That which you seek may be closer than you think…'*

Suddenly, the guard named Russ spun Ruby's swivel chair around and he leaned in close.

"Now! I'm gonna give you once last chance. Tell me your name and the *real* reason why you stole the fiddle. Otherwise I *will* call the police"

Ruby quivered in her seat. Her eyes flicked between Russ and her violin which lay on the desk beside them both.

"No answer then?" he barked.

Ruby's expression hardened.

"That is my violin!" she shouted defiantly. "I didn't steal nothing!"

The second guard, Mick, grunted, trying not to laugh, causing Russ to look over his shoulder incredulously.

"Are you right there?" he asked angrily, before pointing at the telephone. "Get on the blower, will ya? Get a copper out here now."

Ruby unexpectedly stood up on the seat and squealed.

"NO!!" she bellowed. "No one is going to take my violin from me!"

Her outburst drew the attention of the audience in the auditorium including the elderly man, all of whom turned in the direction of the office.

Without warning, Ruby leaped to the floor, making a beeline for her violin. Snatching it up from the desk she whirled around as both security guards scrambled after her.

Ruby dropped and scurried through Russ' legs before spying the exit. She sprang to her feet and prepared to escape.

Just when she thought she was home free, a thick hand slapped down on her shoulder, wrenching her back as Russ captured her once more.

The violin went flying and clattered to the floor.

Ruby willed herself into a frenzy, slapping and kicking at her captor, screaming at the top of her lungs. She no longer cared who heard her. The quartet stopped playing this time, and everyone looked in the direction of the office.

Russ was having no more of this little shit.

"Mick! Get on that bloody phone will ya!"

Restraining Ruby in a powerful hold, securing her arms behind her, Russ prepared to march her from the office.

In the auditorium, the man scowled incredulously and marched up the aisle toward the office just as the guard emerged from inside.

"Could you kindly refrain from this inconsiderate racket!" he shouted in a heavy accent.

Russ regarded the man with contempt and shoved Ruby out in front of him. Mick, who was holding the receiver to his ear, had to block out his colleague's exchange with the new arrival.

"What is the meaning of this?!" the man demanded, glancing fleetingly at Ruby before fixing his glare on the guard.

"Nothing you need to worry about Mr. Khalili," Russ grumbled. "Just a little thief that we've gotta deal with. You can go back to your musicians."

The sarcastic inflection Russ added to 'musicians' was enough to make the man named Khalili bristle. His jaw set hard and he ground his teeth together.

"Nothing to worry about?" Khalili echoed incredulously. "You bluster your way into *my* auditorium in the middle of an important rehearsal, making all sorts of racket and you expect me to ignore it?"

Mick blushed sympathetically as his colleague brushed past Khalili and began marching down the hall.

Gathering up the violin, case and bow, Mick sidled past Khalili and hurried after his colleague, turning back briefly to apologise.

Khalili shook his head, bewildered by the rudeness of the brutish pair, the former of the two continuing to struggle with the child in his grip.

Shaking his head, Khalili turned back to the auditorium where a low murmur was rippling through the audience. He prepared to step forward when an almost involuntary expression of confusion creased his brow. All at once, he stiffened and gasped.

As the guards prepared to disappear around a corner, Khalili's voice boomed down the hall.

"STOP!"

Both guards reacted, skidding to a halt in the middle of the hallway. Ruby stopped struggling and went limp.

They turned as Khalili rushed toward them, the hard soles of his shoes clip-clopping noisily on the polished floor.

He stopped before Mick, his bespectacled eyes focused not on Mick's face but on the contents he held in his arms.

"Let me see that violin," he ordered, holding out his hands.

The confused Mick relented, clumsily offering the violin to Khalili who plucked it from him.

Khalili stepped back and held the instrument gently in his hands, turning it over, inspecting it with a practised eye. The expression on his face slowly began to dissolve—first into one of dawning realisation and then utter amazement. A beatific smile spread across his lips, as though he had discovered a precious jewel.

He looked over at the child.

"Where did this come from?" he quizzed Ruby with an almost child-like wonderment.

Ruby hesitated and actually withdrew behind Russ's leg.

Khalili waved at the guard and clicked his fingers.

"Let her go, let her go," he whispered sharply.

"Professor…" Russ protested.

"Do it!" Khalili snapped angrily.

His grip on Ruby's hand slackened and he released her. In that moment, she flirted with the opportunity of bolting once more, but something in the man's vivid green eyes told her to wait.

She rubbed at her sore wrists.

Professor Khalili returned his attention to Ruby and nodded.

"Go on," he said, the level of tension in his voice dropping.

Ruby gulped softly and looked directly at the professor for the first time.

"It was my nana's," she whispered croakily. "She gave it to me."

Ruby pointed up at Mick and the case he held.

"Her name is Delfey. It's on the label inside the case."

Mick prepared to open the case but Khalili shook his head silently.

"Whatever on Earth were you doing that caused you to come to the attention of these…*guards*?"

Khalili took fleeting pleasure in adding his own sarcastic inflection to the word 'guards.'

Ruby fidgeted, unable or perhaps unwilling to speak.

"We found her outside…in the fore court," Mick offered gingerly.

Khalili flashed him an angry glower, making it clear that he expected Ruby to answer.

Turning back to Ruby, Khalili nodded expectantly.

"Well?"

Ruby jumped. The man's voice cut through her like a knife.

"I…I was playing," she responded. "Rehearsing."

Both Russ and Mick slowly turned and stared incredulously at her.

"Playing?" Khalili echoed quizzically.

"Look, can we drop the Q and A session?" Russ barked angrily. "The police will be here shortly."

"This child will not be going anywhere," Khalili shot back instantly, glaring at the security guard over the tops of his spectacles.

Before Russ could protest, Khalili stepped toward him. He held out the violin, turning it over in his hands and pointed to a small plaque positioned high upon the back side of the body, near the neck.

"See that? It's a maker's mark—for a Vrassidaun violin. This instrument was made in Austria and…"

"But we…" Russ cut in with increasing annoyance.

Khalili's hand shot up between them, commanding immediate silence. Ruby shuddered, trying to make sense of what was happening. Unbeknown to them, several people in the auditorium had filtered into the hall to find out what all the fuss was about.

Khalili continued.

"…And there has not been a Vrassidaun produced anywhere in the world in over one hundred years."

"Meaning what?" the guard questioned dismissively.

"Meaning that this child could not have possibly *stolen* this instrument from this school or any other school. The violin is a rarity. She speaks the truth."

For the first time Russ was completely flummoxed.

Khalili turned his head toward Mick.

"Call off the police now. They will not be required."

Khalili signalled to Mick to hand over the violin case and bow while he snatched Ruby's school back pack from Russ.

He looked directly at Ruby and motioned with a clinical snap of his head.

"You will come with me at once," he ordered, before adding an uncharacteristically mischievous wink.

Ruby felt her frail heart tumble over inside her chest and she slowly stepped away from her captors. She wanted to run. She wanted to stay right here in the hall. She wanted to follow.

Khalili turned and marched from the security guards, forcing Ruby into making a decision—an almost involuntary decision.

She followed.

She had to run to catch up with the professor but she fell in behind him as she entered the auditorium. Almost immediately, Ruby gasped, stopping at the top of the aisle where she faced not only the audience but also the string quartet, all of whom were staring at her.

Khalili signalled to the members of the quartet.

"I apologise ladies. Kindly take a moment longer and we will resume shortly."

Khalili turned and gestured to Ruby who was trying to take in the environment she now found herself in. The huge, ornate hardwood beams supporting the roof above her seemed to hang in defiance of gravity, curving over her head like silent leviathans. Arched windows, high up on the white walls on either side of her cast ethereal light into the hall from outside, melding with the glow of the lights hanging down from the rafters. The stage stretched across the breadth of the building and was dominated by the pipes of a massive organ that watched over it like soldiers standing in formation.

She could barely comprehend this world within a world and she stepped reverentially down the aisle toward the stage, her mouth agape, her neck twisting upward and around her in wonderment, while the eyes of those around her watched her as she approached the stage.

Khalili ushered Ruby up some steps and over to a quiet corner of the stage where he pulled together a pair of chairs and motioned for her to sit down. He sat before her and rested the violin in his his lap, placing both hands on its polished surface.

"Now," he began curtly. "May I ask your name?"

Ruby's brow furrowed and she shuffled nervously where she sat.

"It's...Ruby," she said, so quietly that she, herself could barely hear her own voice.

"Ruby," the professor echoed melodically. "Ahhh...from the Latin *ruber* meaning 'red.' You were born in the month of July, yes?"

Ruby blinked in surprise and the professor smiled knowingly.

"How did you guess that?" she blurted reflexively.

Khalili shrugged his shoulders with a hint of mischief as he turned the violin over in his hands, inspecting it closely.

"The precious stone ruby is the birth stone for the month of July in our Gregorian calendar. It is an—*appropriate*—name for a child born in that month."

Ruby was struck by the professor's explanation and sat awkwardly on the edge of the chair.

"So…you can play this instrument?" Khalili ventured, swiftly changing the subject. "How long have you been playing?"

"Since I was four," Ruby answered. "…Four years."

Khalili raised one of his eye brows and nodded.

"Interesting…" he mused. "And who is your teacher?"

"My nana teaches me. We practise every day."

"Ohhh," Khalili said with a lengthiness to his 'ohhh' that Ruby found grating. She sat up straighter in her chair and jutted her chin forward.

Khalili patted the violin softly.

"The Vrassidaun violin was hand crafted, you know—in a little village high in the Austrian Alps near the border with Germany. The Vrassidaun family produced only a few of these instruments each year, from a type of maple that grew sparsely on the mountain tops."

The professor was becoming increasingly animated now, which made Ruby uneasy. He continued.

"It has been said that, unlike the Stradivari, the Vrassidaun timber required no additional preservatives, no chemicals. So dense and so *unique* is this wood that these violins produce a sound that is quite unlike any other. It has an unmatched purity."

Khalili leaned forward in his seat, his green eyes alive and larger than any eyes Ruby had ever seen.

"Do you know that there may only be a dozen of these Vrassidaun violins left in existence?"

Ruby didn't respond. She was unsure of what to say or do.

Khalili studied Ruby quizzically through the scratched lenses of his spectacles, his curious smile giving little away.

"Do you expect me to believe that you can play a Vrassidaun after only four years of tuition?"

Ruby's expression flickered between confusion and annoyance—evidently, she was unfamiliar with the word tuition—but she felt an indignant twang in her stomach and she arched her shoulders back accordingly.

"Yes," she said defiantly. "I do. I mean…I can."

The professor's eyebrows arched and he leaned back in his chair, measuring up the child sitting before him.

He held the violin out toward her, nodding his head and making his intention clear.

Ruby took the violin from Khalili and cradled it awkwardly in her lap.

Her eyes darted between the professor and the audience behind him, some of whom were now looking in their direction, their curiosity piqued at the interaction between the professor and the child. A lump formed in Ruby's throat. Her tongue dried up and beads of sweat formed on her brow.

Overcoming inertia, Ruby stood and held both violin and bow in her left hand while she reflexively pumped her right hand open and closed, limbering up her fingers. She fought to quell her nervousness.

She had never played like this before—on a real stage, in front of a real audience.

Remembering her grandmother's instruction, Ruby began her breathing exercise, closing her eyes and drawing herself inward to her centre. Then, she drew the violin up, testing its position under her neck.

Khalili watched her with a curious expression. The way she held her violin, the way she positioned her head and neck to become one with instrument. There was something immediately familiar about it that captured the professor's attention. His eyes narrowed unconsciously.

Ruby hurriedly searched through her catalogue of music. Once she decided upon a piece, Ruby nodded to herself.

Khalili noticed that the expression on her face had subtly switched over from an intense focus to an almost reverent calm. He sat forward slightly, expectantly.

The bow came down and Ruby launched into the plucky beginnings of a famed composition by Max Bruch known as his Violin Concerto No. 1 – a romantic piece of music that she knew by heart.

She began deftly, negotiating the dance of the violin solo and infusing her performance with a passion and a power that defied her youth. Opening her eyes fleetingly, she noticed that everyone in the auditorium was caught completely by surprise. A tangible electricity passed through her.

The cellist, sitting in conversation with one of the violinists from the quartet turned her head swiftly and her jaw fell open. The cellist's bow slipped from her hand and clattered to the floor. The reaction to the tiny performer was replicated right throughout the hall as every head turned toward Ruby.

Ruby closed her eyes again as the fluid and captivating melody flowed from her mind into her fingers and her brow furrowed in concentration. She rode on the back of the music perfectly balanced, meeting each chord progression with her agile fingers and confident sweeps of the bow.

Professor Khalili sat, his expression giving nothing away. But as Ruby progressed, a curious smile passed across his lips. Almost unconsciously, he began tapping the fingers of his left hand on his knee, matching Ruby's fingers on the fret board whilst mimicking the subtle nods of her head with his own.

Rising up on the balls of her feet, Ruby approached the finale and gripped her violin tighter, anticipating the challenge of that final flourish that had tripped her so many times before. She entered it, held her poise, imagined time slowing down and met each final stroke. She faltered yet again but it was too subtle to derail all that had come before.

And then it was over.

Her head remained tucked close to her violin. Her eyes stayed closed as she was greeted by silence and, for a moment, she felt panicked. Then, a single pair of hands began to clap. Slowly, another pair joined in—then another and another until the entire auditorium erupted into a round of applause. Ruby opened her eyes and looked out across the stage and blushed. A smile creased her lips as the quartet clapped enthusiastically.

Khalili simply nodded but his curious smile remained.

CHAPTER 13

1952

Mrs. Penschey began to teach Virginia the violin. Once a week on a Tuesday, the Pastoralist would leave the station for several hours to attend to business in town and it was rare for him to be home before dusk. Agreeing to a rather clandestine domestic ritual, Virginia worked furiously in the morning, making sure that all her chores in the homestead were completed well in advance of him leaving the homestead. She scrubbed and dusted to her usual high standard, working herself into a sweat in order to get the work done in time.

Mrs. Penschey would enter the homestead just before two PM. She would collect a cup of tea from Mrs. Finchner in the same fine bone china cup and saucer. She would then proceed to the front door of the house and stand sipping her tea quietly, watching through the window until her husband's truck drove into view and rolled through the front gate. Waiting until it was just a speck on the horizon, she would hurriedly signal to Virginia, who made sure she was dusting in the dining room at just the right time, and together they would disappear into the parlour.

For two clear hours on that and each subsequent Tuesday afternoon, under the pretense that Virginia was finishing her house work in that very room, Mrs. Penschey began teaching Virginia the very same method that she herself had been taught as a young girl in a far away place called Vienna.

Their initial encounters were hesitant. Virginia was overcome by nerves and they often threatened to overwhelm her. Thus, she remained painfully reserved in Mrs. Penschey's presence. Virginia was unsure of this woman's motivation for taking such an interest in her. Virginia regarded all the adults she had encountered on the station with distrust and suspicion and, despite her curiosity in this stately woman who played the alien instrument, Virginia couldn't help but feel skittish.

She never dared to ask why Mrs. Penschey was giving her this unexpected respite from her bleak existence in this place. Though Virginia outwardly feigned ambivalence, she secretly began looking forward to the lessons.

They were arduous in the beginning. Having never encountered a musical instrument like this in her life, Virginia firstly had to understand the very basics of how to hold the violin in her embrace and how to place her fingers on the strings. Neither were easy propositions given that the violin itself was clearly designed for somebody much bigger than Virginia. She spent the majority of those early lessons focusing just on how to hold it, struggling to come to grips with the unwieldy bulk. She felt clumsy and accident prone and several times she almost dropped the violin—much to her panic. Mrs. Penschey however, never scolded Virginia or lost her patience – although she did often steal worried glances at the door, fearing that the housekeeper and kitchen hands would hear those strangled first attempts at producing sound and come running to see what all the commotion was about.

Slowly, Mrs. Penschey introduced Virginia to a set of basic scales that would exercise her fingers and foster a familiarity with correct positioning in order to produce a set of notes. To this exercise, Mrs. Penschey taught Virginia how to shift her fingers across the fingerboard whilst drawing the bow across the bridge of the violin. How the heaviness or lightness of her draw affected the sound she produced. She began to make sounds with the violin but her first efforts were hesitant and choking. She raked the bow across the bridge far too heavily or she dropped the bow entirely or created noise that was akin to somebody running their fingernails down a blackboard.

Virginia felt frustrated and discouraged and feared that the Pastoralist's wife had set her a goal that she was manifestly unable to achieve. But Mrs. Penschey remained quietly determined, never indicating that she was losing faith. The lessons soon became the one thing—the only thing—that Virginia looked forward to and from somewhere deep inside her burned her own determined flame, telling her to press on.

It was during a particularly drab day whilst working away in the vegetable garden at the rear of the homestead that Virginia struck upon a novel idea. She found an old fence paling that had fallen to the ground beside the tomatoes along with a thin, wooden stake that was used to support the tomato vines. Spiriting the contraband into her out house, Virginia marked the position of the strings on the paling with a pencil she'd procured from inside the homestead. She then whittled some small gouges into the wood, representing the finger positions that Mrs. Penschey had taught her.

Each night, after the older girls were sound asleep, Virginia lit a candle and huddled up on her bed with Simon the dog nestled next to her. Using the makeshift simulacrum, Virginia practised those fingerings she'd learned, imagining the notes in her head and playing them in silence, while Simon watched her with wide-eyed curiosity. She spent hours repeating the exercises over and over, much to the silent chagrin of the dog who often fell asleep in her lap while Virginia continued long into the night. She imagined the pieces of music she'd heard in her mind, playing her violin part as though she herself were a part of the orchestra. Virginia lost herself in the music.

And, slowly but surely, Virginia's unwieldy fingers began to stretch and strengthen. They became nimble and confident and they began to skip effortlessly across both the imaginary strings of her makeshift instrument and the real strings of Mrs. Penschey's violin. They found their mark effortlessly and, not only did Virginia begin to play competently, she unlocked a graceful and precise technique that was as individual as Virginia herself.

From then on Virginia learned quickly. She felt the real instrument become a natural extension of her arms and hands. Her confidence grew, her technique flourished. Together, Mrs. Penschey and Virginia drew from within her a purity of sound that felt complex yet light. It was fully formed and confident.

Mrs. Penschey's lessons evolved from routine instruction and became conversations about the instrument itself, its distant origins; its most famed practitioners and the body of compositions that had been solely devoted to it.

Every Tuesday, teacher and student listened to the gramophone in the parlour, exploring the sizable collection of recordings Mrs. Penschey had amassed over a number of years. Virginia chose pieces that she found appealing and with Mrs. Penschey's guidance she mastered them with intense concentration and determination.

Eventually, the ever curious pup, Simon, managed to sneak inside the house and join Virginia and Mrs. Penschey in the parlour. Simon had already begun to stick close to Virginia whilst she was cleaning the bathroom and laundry but during her lessons he would curl up underneath the chaise lounge while Virginia played. Both Deliah and Marjorie too, made sure they were in the vicinity of the parlour so that they could listen to the weekly performances by Virginia.

During the times when Virginia sat on the window sill listening to the gramophone, Simon found his way into her lap and stayed there while she gazed out across the fields beyond, absorbing the music of the moment. Mrs. Penschey often chose recordings that suited the mood of what Virginia saw through the window – be it rain or wind, dust or sunshine. Virginia curiously found herself drawn to the music that best suited the rain, though she wasn't sure why. Mrs. Penschey encouraged Virginia to revel in the emotion and the imagery the music evoked in her. Through it, Virginia unlocked a door to a world that, even before she came here, she never knew existed.

From those tenuous and hesitant beginnings, a bond was fostered between Virginia and Mrs. Penschey and with time, it became a friendship. They began to converse more and more, not only about music but also about life both on the farm and beyond its confines. Mrs. Penschey talked about travelling through her native Europe and she showed Virginia albums of photographs that she had put together herself, having taken many of the images therein.

They read books together and Virginia surprised the Pastoralist's wife with her ability to read and write. At Mrs. Penschey's suggestion, they spent time nurturing Virginia's reading and writing skills so that she would not lose them to the drudgery and the unforgiving domestic work that was Virginia's first priority.

All of these activities blunted the sense of isolation Virginia felt being in this place. But it was the music that lifted Virginia up and carried her, giving her a sense of freedom. It nurtured her soul more than anything else could and she threw herself into the violin with more vigour and dedication than anything else.

She progressed from learning the compositions Mrs. Penschey had introduced her to purely by ear from listening to the gramophone to reading sheet music that Mrs. Penschey provided. At first it was a challenge, co-ordinating her playing whilst constantly training her eyes across the notes and bars on the page. But, as with her first tentative steps with the violin itself, Virginia displayed a remarkable ability to adapt quickly and, not only that, she developed an uncanny ability to recall whatever music she was introduced to once she committed it to memory.

Agatha Penschey knew that Virginia's talent was prodigious—unprecedented. And yet she was unable to reveal Virginia's gift to anyone beyond the confines of the house.

Agatha began to wonder at the origins of her young protégé and whether this gift was a characteristic trait common to Virginia's native people. She knew of accounts of Aboriginal tribes which had existed in large numbers in the South Australian bush and coastal hinterlands and knew that many of these tribes had a strong musical culture amongst them.

Her curiosity grew and grew until one day, Agatha could ignore it no longer. During a break in one of their sessions, while she poured both herself and Virginia a cup of tea, Agatha finally braved the question.

"Where is your country, child? Where does your heart belong?"

Virginia blinked, as though unable to comprehend the question.

"The Aboriginal people believe that we all belong to a place—a country that is a part of our soul—it is a part of who we are," Mrs Penschey explained, tilting her head slightly. Her gaze drifted away from Virginia.

"I don't know," Virginia replied sadly. "I-I can't remember any more. It was a hilly place…green and there were lots of farms."

"That sounds very pretty," Agatha suggested. "I'm…sorry that you have no family any more."

"My family is still there," Virginia said softly. "My parents…my friends."

Agatha's eyes flicked back to Virginia and her expression became one of shock.

"Your family…?"

"I *have* a family," Virginia said, her voice tinged with annoyance at Agatha's vacant question.

She shifted uncomfortably as Agatha sat down opposite her and held her cup.

"I don't know where they are," Virginia continued, turning her face away from Mrs. Penschey. "Dad was away a lot. Mum and I lived in a cottage in the town where she worked. But…"

Her voice trailed off and she bowed her head down, looking at the sleeping dog whose head lay in her lap.

"What, Virginia?" Agatha probed gently. "What happened?"

"No one told me anything, missus." Virginia looked up, her eyes filled with a withering heartache. "The people who came. They just took me from my mum without even asking. They didn't explain why—they took me away and that was the end of it."

A sickening knot had begun to twist inside Agatha Penschey. She had never questioned her husband about the domestic help that had come to work on the station over the years. Agatha had assumed that they were either orphans without a home or any family whatsoever or they were from poor families who couldn't afford to care for them and had thus sent them away to work on farms like this in the hope that the child would have a better life.

"D-did your parents not give the authorities permission? Did they not know that you would be given a better life?"

Virginia shook her head and, inexplicably, she began to feel a rising anger.

"*A better life?*" she echoed defiantly. "I was happy before. I had a home, ice cream on hot days, friends to play with, tea with my mum at night, and I was loved. That was my life. Now…there's *this!*"

Agatha was stunned. She sat across from Virginia in silence, the guilt she felt coursing deep inside of her.

Without warning, Virginia pushed back on her chair and stood, summoning Simon with a click of her fingers. Her emotions were overwhelming her and she suddenly felt claustrophobic in this spacious parlour. She stumbled across the room and opened the door.

"W-wait," Agatha Penschey implored after the child. But she stopped once Virginia and the dog had disappeared and she stood in the centre of the parlour, unable to move.

She remained there for a long time after Virginia left the room.

CHAPTER 14

THE SLEEK BLUE MERCEDES BENZ COUPE MOTORED slowly along the inner-city arterial. Rain fell steadily all around it and was getting heavier, as evidenced by the thickening haze haloing the car. Thick droplets were reflected in the beams of the headlights that stabbed into the night-time and splashed onto the glistening bitumen. The car seemed oblivious to the traffic passing by it on the busy road. While they were in a hurry to get to their destinations, the Mercedes instead cruised along, as though it were out for a leisurely Sunday drive.

Ruby sat silently in the passenger seat, gripping the violin case tightly on her lap. She kept her eyes ahead, concentrating on the pattering of the rain on the windshield, the wipers that swayed back and forth across the glass. They almost lulled her into a trance.

The passenger seat was particularly uncomfortable. The aging leather of the back rest was split in several places, exposing a couple of the inner springs which poked Ruby in the small of her back. The moth eaten bath towel Khalili had placed there to protect her from getting jabbed provided no respite at all, so she had to remember to keep moving away from the niggling foreign object.

She had barely spoken since they had left the city. Neither of them had for that matter. Khalili seemed content with his own counsel as he concentrated on the road ahead and he barely even looked at Ruby from the time they had set off for the northern suburbs. For her part, Ruby was unsure whether she should be scared of the professor or not. Though she was well aware of the whole stranger danger message that had been constantly drilled into her at school, the police officers who eventually showed up at Elder Hall—despite Khalili's instructions to the two inept guards not to call them—were happy for him to drive Ruby home. They had initially offered to drive her themselves, but Khalili wouldn't have it—reasoning that they had more important duties to attend to in the city. Thus, the officers were content in trusting Khalili and had given their blessing. Ruby didn't protest it at the time. But now, sitting here, she wasn't so sure.

Unknown to Ruby, Khalili did occasionally steal a glance at the child beside him, aware that she was retreating further and further to the right of the passenger seat. Therein lay another reason for his insistence upon driving Ruby home—not that Khalili was prepared to reveal it just yet. He just smiled to himself, gently reaching over to the knob of the Mercedes' ancient radio and turned it until it clicked on. A soft orange light illuminated the station display and soft chamber music filtered into the cabin.

The effect was immediate, Khalili observed. Ruby glanced hesitantly at the radio then at the professor but looked away before he could meet her eyes with his own. She seemed to relax and, unconsciously, she began tapping her finger on the side of her violin case.

"Mozart," she identified correctly, her voice so soft that Khalili almost didn't hear her.

"Very good," he nodded approvingly. "One of his more refined pieces."

Ruby shrugged her shoulders.

"Mmmm…Nana thinks he is too showy…that he was a bit of a wanker."

Khalili turned his head toward Ruby and studied her with surprise.

"That's rather colourful language, don't you think?"

Again Ruby shrugged her shoulders, as if it were of no consequence.

"Maybe…what sort of car is this?" Ruby asked, changing the subject.

Khalili sat straighter in his seat and nodded proudly.

"It's a '67 Mercedes Benz 250 SL—a very rare automobile. Are you impressed?"

"It looks like a big turtle," Ruby responded, totally deadpan. "And it's got awful seats."

Khalili chuckled at this and rubbed at the back of his neck.

"And let me tell you, my young friend, it drives like a big turtle sometimes," he quipped, patting the steering wheel with his left hand. "But she rarely complains so I give her a little credit because she is getting on in years…rather like myself. These days, I don't push her any harder than I have to."

Khalili chuckled as he clicked the indicator lever up. Turning the steering wheel down hard, he accelerated down a residential street, heading toward her house.

Ruby felt an uncomfortable knot twist inside her. She could only imagine the trouble she was in—especially if her uncle was home. Khalili saw her stiffen and he smirked.

"So how long have you been getting away with these clandestine visits?"

"Months…a year maybe," Ruby replied through clenched teeth. "My cousin Jeremy and I come to the city by train each week…I know when the quartet rehearses."

"Ho-ho," Khalili crowed. "Well, you are well and truly—how do you say—*busted now.*"

He paused and then winked mischievously at her over the top of his spectacles.

"Let me do the talking, huh? Let us see if an old firebrand can get you out of this mess."

Ruby nervously pointed out her approaching house. Khalili slowed the Mercedes and turned into the driveway. Almost immediately, the single light globe above the front door burst into life and the door itself snapped open. Khalili stopped the car and extinguished the engine, watching as the wire door was flung open and Belle stormed out onto the stoop, followed closely by Asher, Minty and Virginia. Virginia immediately placed her hands on both Asher and Minty's shoulders holding them back under the verandah from the rain, which had now tapered off to a light drizzle.

Ruby could tell right away that she was furious.

"Where have you been?" Belle screeched at Ruby, ignoring the professor who had stepped out of the car and was putting his hat on. He watched in silent alarm as Belle grabbed Ruby's arm and yanked her like a rag doll around in front of the car. She staggered on the path as Ruby pulled against her aunt and in that moment, Ruby caught the scent of alcohol on Belle's breath.

Belle glowered down at Ruby, her eyes aflame.

"Where's Jeremy?" she barked drunkenly. "What the fuck have you two been getting up to?"

Ruby was too frightened to answer.

Inside the house, Rex yelled drunkenly from the lounge room.

"Keep that *fucken* noise down out there, will ya!?"

Minty clung to his grandmother's leg and began wailing at the scene of his mother attacking Ruby while the family dog started barking from behind the house, adding to the cacophony of noise that had suddenly assailed the professor from all quarters.

On the porch, seemingly oblivious to the chaos around her, Virginia was studying the stranger standing beside his flashy car. He was slight but he stood tall and confident. He was well dressed, in the kind of clothes that one just didn't see around these parts. There was something about him.

"Ruby!" Belle echoed warningly. "Answer me!"

"Ma'am," Khalili stepped in finally. "If you'll let me explai—"

Belle whipped her head up and flashed Khalili with a menacing glare.

"Who the bloody hell are you?!" she snarled.

"Mrs. Delfey—my name is Khalili. I am a music professor. Your daughter was found outside my concert hall in the city. She was...*rehearsing*...with my quartet."

Virginia's ears pricked up at the mention of a concert hall and she immediately stepped around Asher and Minty and off the porch. She shuffled across the lawn as Belle turned to Khalili, while still holding onto Ruby's arm.

"Who do you think you are that you can drive around with a girl in your car late at night? What are you—some kind of *pedo* or something?"

"Aunty!" Ruby protested shakily.

"Belle!" Virginia shouted immediately after her.

Suddenly, Virginia pitched herself forward, causing Minty to break his grip and immediately rush to Asher. Catching everyone off guard, Virginia stormed up to Belle, violently slapping her hand away from Ruby and immediately shepherded Ruby behind her.

"Take the children inside!" Virginia ordered, her eyes ablaze. "Now!"

She pushed Belle hard in the ribs, almost knocking her off balance.

"Now!!"

Belle blinked at Virginia and hesitated, switching her gaze between Virginia and the stranger. Slowly, Belle backed away and turned toward the house.

Virginia waited until she had gone inside, then she turned back toward the professor.

Ruby, who had retreated back behind the front of the car watched her grandmother, unsure of what she was about to do or say. Was she angry with her? Was she angry with the professor?

Khalili stood there, watching the elderly woman, waiting for her to speak.

Virginia appraised him, maintaining a shield of defensiveness that only added to Khalili's uncertainty—so much so that he was wavering between remaining where he stood or backing away altogether.

He hesitated, turned slowly, preparing to retreat to the driver's side door, then he stopped.

He looked back at Virginia, through earnest and open eyes and spoke softly.

"Where does your heart belong…ma'am?"

Almost imperceptibly, Virginia's breath caught in the back of her throat, causing an audible squeak. A long forgotten memory coalesced in her mind's eye.

A woman in a parlour room, a teacher—*her teacher*—posing that very same question.

Virginia's posture faltered as she focused on Khalili. His question, while direct, was a traditional greeting for an Aboriginal person—a respectful opening that struck Virginia like a lightning bolt.

"I come…from the Peramangk," she responded ever so quietly. "My heart belongs to the hills and the valleys of Peramangk country."

Virginia raised a finger and pointed back over Khalili's head, toward the line of the Adelaide Hills known as the Mount Lofty Ranges. Ruby followed the line of her finger toward its destination, toward the distant hills and she repeated the word *Peramangk* in her mind. She hadn't heard her grandmother mention it before and it intrigued her.

"Ooh-ahh," Khalili responded, again softly, with a common Aboriginal turn of phrase indicating respect. "And it is a beautiful country. I have spent many wonderful hours amongst the people of the Adelaide Hills."

Virginia felt her emotional armour crumbling and she managed a half smile.

Ruby, standing nervously over by the front of the car, watched the exchange with increasing curiosity, her previous fear melting away.

"And you…?" Virginia ventured after several moments, "Where does your heart belong?"

"Oh," Khalili mused with an impish smile. He turned his head upward to the night sky, old memories washing through him and causing his eyes to widen with child like affection.

"I grew up on the shores of Beirut, far, far from here. I cherish the sea there and the music that it brought to me."

He nodded wistfully, a glint in his eye.

"Mmmm," Virginia nodded thoughtfully. "I know it—from books—and TV. Never been there though."

Khalili's eyes wandered across to Ruby, who jumped where she stood as he spoke.

"Your granddaughter *apparently* has not been completely honest with you or her parents."

"Those aren't her parents," Virginia quipped dismissively.

Virginia turned and gestured toward Ruby hurriedly, signalling for her to come out of hiding. Ruby gingerly stepped around the vehicle and sidled cautiously up to stand beside her grandmother.

"I see," Khalili continued. "It is you who has taught her the Vrassidaun—yes?"

Virginia nodded, glancing down at Ruby affirmatively.

"I have…since she was four."

"Hmm," Khalili mused. "It seems she has not been wasting her time away from your tutelage. Ruby was…discovered…in the courtyard outside my Conservatory building. She tells us she has been…attending my rehearsal sessions for some time."

Again Virginia nodded.

"I know."

Ruby gasped and looked up at Virginia, her eyes nearly bulging out of their sockets. She could not believe what her grandmother had just said.

Khalili raised an eyebrow and rocked back and forth on the balls of his feet, his hands in his pockets.

"Usually, she catches the train into the city with her cousin Jeremy," Virginia explained, completely unravelling the supposedly secret sorties Ruby and Jeremy had been engaging in for months. "Jeremy told me a long time ago what they were up to. I gave him my blessing, so long as he looked out for her. It's the only way that Ruby gets to practise beyond our lessons—the only way she can perform."

"But she was found alone this evening," Khalili noted.

Virginia eyed Ruby conspiratorially and pointed an arthritic finger at her chest.

"She and her cousin came to blows this evening," Virginia said. "Ruby took off one way and he the other."

Khalili *tsked-tsked* under his breath and shook his head slowly.

"I hope the boy is alright."

Virginia shrugged.

"He'll be home soon."

Quiet settled between them once more and neither seemed to know what to say next. Khalili lifted a hand to his head, adjusting his hat.

"It has been a long time since I've encountered a soloist such as your granddaughter. She has…*a particular technique*…I've not seen in a very long time. Does she receive any additional instruction aside from your own?"

Virginia's shoulders slumped ever so slightly and she frowned.

"I can't afford the kind of teaching she needs."

Khalili pursed his lips subtly.

"You a teacher?" Virginia's question sounded more like a statement of fact than a question.

"I am," he confirmed. "I have taught many over the years."

"You can teach my Ruby," Virginia said suddenly, causing the professor to stiffen and rub his brow nervously.

"W-well…I…not so much any more," he lied weakly. "I am scaling back my commitments at the Conservatory. Soon, I will be retiring."

Virginia's eyes narrowed and she titled her head slightly to one side.

"Yet, you drove all the way out here with my granddaughter just so you could meet me and talk about how '*gifted*' Ruby is."

Virginia kept her stare firmly focused on Khalili and allowed the import of her words to penetrate him for several seconds. She stepped forward.

"She has a photographic memory," Virginia said with a gentle urgency. "She can recall a piece of music she's never seen before."

Virginia held up her hand and clicked her arthritic fingers theatrically.

Khalili stayed silent, but Virginia could see that his mind was working. He looked across at Ruby, down at her violin and then back to Virginia.

"And she's got a keen ear," Virginia continued. "She can play a note without ever having heard it before. It's her gift."

Khalili pursed his lips and shifted back and forth, sizing Ruby up.

Virginia stepped forward even closer to the professor.

"My health is failing," she whispered solemnly. "My mind and my sight are no good any more and I can't give her the kind of instruction she needs. Ruby is a one-off, mister. She just needs a chance to prove herself."

A curious smile tugged at the corners of Khalili's lips and slowly, he reached into his pocket and took out his wallet. He plucked a small rectangle of card from inside and handed it to Virginia.

"Have Ruby come by my office on Wednesday after school," he said simply with a just a hint of coyness.

Ruby's jaw dropped open and her eyes nearly bugged out but Virginia squeezed her hand to stifle her excitement.

Khalili reached out and shook Virginia's hand slowly, then he stepped back, climbing into his Mercedes and starting the engine.

As the rain began to fall once more, Virginia and Ruby stood and watched until Khalili's car disappeared from view down the street.

Ruby jumped into the air and squealed with delight, turning several circles in front of her grandmother. Virginia's countenance, however, remained stony and Ruby eventually stopped, looking up at her grandmother – a feeling of dread coming over her.

Folding her arms, Virginia fixed Ruby with a withering glare.

"I am *not* at all happy with you, young lady."

Ruby counted several agonising seconds by, watching her grandmother worriedly before Virginia could no longer keep herself from smiling broadly.

"Come on," she ordered mock seriously. "Let's get you inside and out of those clothes. You'll catch your death of cold."

Just as they turned to go inside the house, Jeremy came into view from out of the darkness of the street.

Both Virginia and Ruby glowered at him as he approached.

"You better head around the back – unless you want another row with your father."

Jeremy opened his mouth to speak, but Virginia hushed him with the outstretched flat of her hand.

"Don't say anything, boy. I'll deal with you later."

JEREMY SKULKED INTO his bedroom and tossed his jacket on top of a pile of clothes on the floor. Flicking his bedside light on, he turned to swipe the bedroom door closed but stopped when he saw Virginia standing in the doorway, her hands on her hips, her expression dark.

Jeremy just rolled his eyes and lifted his head away as he flopped down on the bed.

"Go away, Nana," he grumbled, turning away from her. "I don't wanna talk right now."

In one deft movement, Virginia plucked one of Jeremy's football boots off the floor in front of her and pitched it at him, hitting him squarely in the back of the head.

"Ow!" he yelped, scrambling like an upturned beetle on the bed.

Wheeling around into a sitting position, Jeremy blinked painfully at Virginia who had stepped right up to his bed.

"Well, we're gonna talk right now, young man," she retorted, her nostrils flaring. "And don't you dare back-chat me unless you want a good kick in the pants. I can still lift my leg if I need to."

Jeremy scowled half heartedly into his lap and drew his knees up as Virginia sat down on the end of his bed.

All at once, the tension in her features faded and was replaced by concern. She gazed upon her grandson.

"Now," Virginia began softly. "I want you to cut out all the bullshit and tell me what is really going on with you."

Jeremy shrugged his shoulders weakly, refusing to meet her eyes.

"Nothin'," he mumbled.

"Don't make me pick up that football boot and clock you a second time," Virginia warned, arching her back straighter. She glanced over toward the door, hearing Rex yelling drunkenly at the TV in the living room. "I know you're mixing with those Reid Street boys. I got it out of Asher tonight."

Jeremy blinked, his expression taking on a mixture of surprise and exasperation. How could his grandmother have any knowledge of the Reid Street crowd given that she routinely struggled to remember routine things around the home?

He whistled air between his clenched teeth and shook his head angrily.

"It's got nothin' to do with her, Nan. It's my business, no one else's."

Virginia turned her head away from him and nodded slowly.

"When the girls are affected by what you get up to with those hooligans," she said, "then it becomes other people's business. It becomes this family's business. It becomes my business."

Virginia fixed Jeremy with an intense look that unbalanced him and his defiant posture sagged just a little.

"When you made that commitment to Ruby, to look out for her, she depended on you. She trusted you."

Jeremy rolled his eyes again and, this time, Virginia lurched across and slapped his cheek briskly. She pointed her finger at him.

"They're no good for you Jeremy—those thugs," she growled. "Believe you me, I've been around my fair share of those characters and they are nothing but parasites. They will suck you in and spit you out just as quickly and they won't give it a second thought."

"It's n-not like that, Nana," Jeremy snapped defensively.

"Oh—really?" Virginia challenged him defiantly. "I'll bet you think that by hanging around them, you feel as though you belong to something, don't you—that you're worth something to them. Well…it's a charade boy. They don't give a damn about you."

Virginia paused, letting the impact of her words reach him.

"But I'm telling you this. There are people who do give a damn about you, Jeremy, and they love you. Asher and Ruby and Minty—they adore you and they would do anything for you. Your mother and I love you… even your fath…"

"No!" Jeremy snarled, cutting her off in mid sentence. "Don't tell me that."

He didn't want to think about his father or even acknowledge him right then. He shook his head defiantly as his eyes welled with tears. He brushed at his face, trying not to lose his composure.

Virginia waited for a moment, sensing the turmoil within her grandson, then she lowered her voice.

"You do belong to something. And although it's far from perfect, there's a lot of good in this family. I and your Mum and the girls and Minty—we depend on you to do the right thing, even when…"

Her voice caught in the back of her throat then and Jeremy saw flashes of regret and shame plague her eyes.

"…especially when your father can't."

Virginia looked down at her hands resting in her lap and sighed. She knew that she shouldn't burden Jeremy with the kind of responsibility that should be his father's but, they both knew that in the absence of a strong male figure in this household, the girls and Minty looked to Jeremy.

Jeremy saw her shoulders droop as if a great weight had descended on them.

"You are the *kuyeta*—the first-born son of this family," Virginia said earnestly, emphasising the ancient Peramangk word. "And soon, you'll be a man. So long as you belong, Jeremy—you don't ever have to feel alone."

Sitting straighter once more, Virginia balled her fist and tapped it to her chest, over her heart.

Jeremy looked away and covered his eyes with one of his hands.

Virginia could sense the turmoil within him. She gently patted his knee, then stood and shuffled slowly across to the door. She turned back to him.

"You're a good person, Jeremy," Virginia said. "Don't throw your life away on those who don't show you respect."

CHAPTER 15

GAVIN'S HOLDEN COUPE WAS PARKED IN A busy beachside car park over-looking the azure waters of Adelaide's Gulf of St. Vincent. The car stood next to a second vehicle, a beat up orange panel van whose occupants—a mixture of Caucasian and Aboriginal males and females—were mixing and mingling with the members of Gavin's gang.

Jeremy watched the nubile young women, whose bikinis left little to the imagination, from his vantage point on a grassy hillock up above the two vehicles. He wished he was down there in amongst them but he had been made a point guard of sorts, keeping a lookout for the local police, while the others drank beer from a cooler in the back of the panel van. Evidently, the car park was a designated dry area and the fines for getting caught with alcohol here were considerable—especially given that it was a family friendly part of the coast. The gang certainly didn't need any additional attention from the authorities right now.

Jeremy felt more than a slight twinge of jealousy as the girls in the group squirmed suggestively in amongst the others—Gavin, Mickey, even Jabba was getting some attention. He was largely ignored by them, except for the occasional questioning nod from Mickey to ensure that he was still keeping a close watch on the esplanade behind them.

The sunny Saturday afternoon had brought many to the seaside. Families were out and about, flying kites on the beach, playing games and swimming in the sea. Children were riding their bikes along the path that divided the car park from the dunes. People were walking their dogs. Teens were laughing, chatting and sunning themselves on the sand or were mingling around parked cars nearby.

Jeremy found himself detached from it all. His orders had been made clear from the time they'd arrived at the beach. Keep a careful look out and don't bother the others—especially Gavin. Jeremy once again felt the uncomfortable awkwardness that came with being relegated to the outside. It made him feel isolated. He was beginning to question whether he would ever be brought into the fold of the gang…or if it was worth the trouble.

He was also distracted by the conflict at home. Virginia's talk with him the other night played on his mind. As much as he might have tried to deny it, her words had affected him. Given her failing state of mind, his grandmother's clarity and her strength of conviction was something he had not expected from her. He'd found himself thinking about her words constantly and it only fuelled the conflict within him.

Jeremy shook his head and scratched at the grass between his legs. There was a kind of twisted irony in that—of all the people in his life— his grandmother was the one person he thought he understood the least. The other night brought home to him the fact that she was, perhaps, his staunchest ally.

Every so often, Jeremy's eyes wandered back to Gavin, who was engaged in an animated discussion with the owner of the panel van, a young man of a similar age. Jeremy hadn't met this man before, nor had the others spoken of him but he guessed he was a close associate of Gavin's—someone with whom he had collaborated in the past. There was a definite tension between the two presently. They were disagreeing about something but, from his vantage point, Jeremy couldn't hear them above the music that was blaring from the car stereo.

Eventually, two of the girls began pulling their respective boyfriends in the direction of the beach itself, indicating that they wanted to take a dip in the sea. The girlfriend of Gavin's associate got in between him and Gavin and began kissing him on his cheeks until he relented and stepped back from Gavin. It was clear that they were all headed to the beach but Jeremy wasn't sure if that meant he was invited to join them as well.

Mickey turned toward him, grabbed a beer from one of the others then trotted in between the cars and up the hillside toward Jeremy.

"Take a break, Delfey," Mickey said, sitting down beside Jeremy and handing him the beer with an uncharacteristically friendly smile. "The girls wanna have a swim…should be a good *perv.*"

He nudged Jeremy conspiratorially and Jeremy smiled bashfully.

"Who is that?" Jeremy asked hesitantly, setting the beer can down beside him without opening it. He gestured with a nod at the stranger walking alongside Gavin.

"Baner?" Mickey responded. "He's a sort of rival of Gavin's but they've tended to work with each other more than against one another…so it's sort of hard to say that they're truly in competition."

"He—Baner—seems intense," Jeremy observed, recalling the heated exchange.

Mickey dismissed it with a shake of his head.

"Nah. Baner's trying to get Gav—*and us*—to help him out with a little problem he's having. See, Baner's in the car business but stock—good stock—has been scarce lately. Vehicle owners are more cautious, there's outside competition from rival gangs who've moved in on Baner's turf and the police have been more vigilant. They've taken down a few of the bigger gangs recently which has made it harder to get good cars. Baner's looking for a smaller crew, one that isn't as visible.

"A crew like us," Jeremy ventured.

"Well…*us*," Mickey corrected, pointing at his own chest with his thumb. "Not necessarily *you*."

Jeremy's shoulders sagged visibly and he looked down and away from Mickey.

"Why not me?" he said, a little pathetically.

"Gav doesn't feel you're up to the task. He's not convinced you're capable."

"*But I am*," Jeremy protested. "I did my part on that last job and we got away clean. I'm doing everything Gavin is asking."

Mickey fixed him with a look that hovered somewhere between mock sympathy and sarcasm.

"But you're sloppy, mate," Mickey pointed out. "Gav's not sure that you're dedicated enough—that you'd go all out for this crew."

"What's that supposed to mean?" Jeremy retorted churlishly.

"It means that if you wanna be a part of our crew, then you're gonna have to prove yourself, like *really prove yourself*. You're gonna have to put this crew before everyone else…even your family."

Jeremy looked up at Mickey then and held his stare. Mickey smiled knowingly and nodded slowly.

"You need to quit bullshitting around with that little cousin of yours and her *poofy* little violin. Stop pretending that your dad is gonna get his shit together and be good to all of you. He's never gonna be the kind of dad you want him to be. If you wanna real family Delfey, then we can be that family. But you're gonna need to earn your place here."

Mickey allowed Jeremy time for those words to sink in.

Jeremy fidgeted absently with a few blades of grass between his legs. His longing to be accepted, his frustration at being kept at an arms length, the conflict he felt—all of it swirled around inside him and made him feel nauseous.

"Well…wh-what do I have to do?" he asked, his voice cracking, barely above a whisper.

"Don't worry. An opportunity will come," Mickey said knowingly. "Gav is watching. We're looking for the right—moment—to test you."

He got to his feet then and stood beside Jeremy a moment.

"When it does come…you'll have your chance to prove yourself. You'll *need* to prove yourself. Otherwise, you're an impediment to the crew and a danger to it."

Mickey started off down the hill to the car park and the beach. He stopped at the bottom and turned back, gesturing to Jeremy with an almost laconic wink.

"Come on…let's walk. There's some nice tits to look at over there."

Jeremy hesitated, feeling even less sure about himself and his place than he did before. Forcing a smile, he got to his feet and followed Mickey across the bitumen and toward the beach.

Ruby meekly stepped through the doorway to the main auditorium of the Elder Conservatory and paused at the top of the stairs, once again taking in the grand and lofty hall before her.

Despite the knowledge that she was now here as a legitimately invited guest, Ruby remained overwhelmingly nervous and still harboured the feeling that she didn't belong—that she was an intruder. She had passed one of the guards from the other night outside—the nicer of the two—and he'd smiled at her, but his gesture didn't make her feel any more at ease. She'd merely clutched the handle of her violin case tighter, lowered her head and kept walking.

The lavender cardigan she wore chafed the back of her neck and the floral print dress she wore seemed ill-fitting, alien and uncomfortable. The ensemble only added to her feelings of awkwardness. But her grandmother had insisted Ruby wear them today. They were the only dressy clothes she owned. Thankfully, Virginia hadn't protested when Ruby chose her sandals over a stifling pair of leather shoes.

Ruby could see Khalili now, down on the stage under the mighty pipes of the organ, instructing a group of musicians who sat in a semi circle around him. They appeared to be some sort of smaller orchestra. A few people occupied the seating closest to the stage, in much the same way as they had the other night, chatting amongst themselves or practising their own music.

A couple of the students in Khalili's group glanced up at Ruby as she entered, prompting Khalili himself to turn around. He smiled upon seeing her and motioned her hurriedly to come down.

"Now, I want you to run through the first and second movements before we meet again on Friday," he instructed, turning back to the group. "Are there any questions?"

Receiving no responses, Khalili nodded.

"That is all for today."

The group stood and began gathering their belongings while Khalili turned toward Ruby once more as she approached the stage, hesitating at the bottom of the stairs.

"Come, come," he smiled warmly, holding an outstretched arm.

As the members of the group he had been instructing dispersed and filed off the stage, Khalili took a pair of chairs and set them down facing one another. He then retrieved a music stand from the semi circle and set it next to the chairs.

Ruby ascended onto the stage and stepped cautiously over to the chairs as Khalili sat down and patted the seat opposite.

"Have a seat," he said. "How are you today?"

Ruby nodded almost too quickly, causing the professor to chuckle.

"It's alright, child. Remember—you are here with my invitation."

Ruby shifted in her seat, her eyes darted from Khalili to the people around them, to the rafters high above.

"How was your journey?" Khalili asked. "You took the train, yes?"

Ruby nodded again and opened her mouth to speak.

"Nana gave me the fare this time," she answered, her voice a whisper.

"Good, good…" he responded before adding a mischievous grin. "You *must relax*. Breathe, my child."

Khalili nodded, then patted the top of the violin case.

"Now—let us see the Vrassidaun once more. I have been so eager to hear it again since our last meeting."

Ruby looked down and brushed her hand across the case. Flipping the latches, she opened it, taking the aged violin and bow out carefully then setting the case to one side. She lifted the violin in her well practised method of finding her best positioning under her neck and adjusted her grip on both the bow and fingerboard.

Khalili watched on, his demeanour immediately slipping into that of an instructor with a keen eye and Ruby sensed that he was assessing her. Khalili sat forward in his seat and placed his hands at Ruby's sides, gently pivoting her hips and straightening her spine. He tut-tutted as he did so and shook his head slowly.

"Always neglected is the posture," he mumbled, proceeding to lift her elbows then press down on the tops of her shoulders.

At first Ruby didn't know what to make of his fussiness and she was more than a little perturbed by it. But once he sat back and studied her, she relaxed into her new posture and smiled faintly.

"How does that feel?" Khalili asked.

Ruby took a moment to gauge how she felt, adjusting her grip on her instrument before nodding affirmatively.

"It feels…good…different."

"Hmm," Khalili mused. "You should always remember that posture is everything to a musician. Without it, you cannot hope to project the strength of your sound nor give your audience a fully realised performance."

He stood and retrieved a battered brown leather bag from the centre of the semi circle where he had been teaching earlier.

"Now," he began, returning to his seat and rifling through the bulging bag. "Your grandmother says that you can read music very well."

Thumbing though a thick sheaf of disorganised paper, Khalili squinted and blinked, searching and searching until he stopped, his eyes widened and a grin creased his lips.

"Ahh—here we are—Franz Liszt. I doubt you would have seen this piece before. Correct?"

Ruby sat forward and inspected the sheet music in front of her. She shook her head slowly.

"I know that," she said.

Khalili frowned slightly and delved into his collection of sheet music, searching again.

"What about…" he said, thumbing through the pages. "Ahh, what about Rhychner? You wouldn't have played Rhychner."

Ruby met his eyes with a flat stare.

"Played it."

Khalili sat back in his seat and gauged the young girl before him with a probing look.

"Okay…" he ventured, appraising his leather bag once more.

Khalili took hold of a folder therein and pulled at it, struggling as the folder seemed to be stuck between other such folders and papers. With an effort, he yanked harder until it came free, causing several other papers to pitch from the bag and into the air.

"Damn," he cursed.

As the sheets of paper floated down, Ruby's eyes fell across a tattered and yellowing sheet of music that stood out. It settled to the stage floor, slightly away from the others.

She stood and retrieved the sheet of paper—a hand written sheet of music.

Khalili saw her with it and reached out with his hand toward her.

"Y-you don't want to read that," he mumbled dismissively.

Ruby retracted her hand and fixed him with a conspiratorial glower.

"Why not?" she probed, examining the page.

"*Laaa…Chaimm?*" she intoned slowly, reading title of the piece at the top.

Khalili withdrew his own hand and clasped the leather case close to his chest.

"*L'Chaim*," he repeated for her, adding his subtle accent to the word.

"*L'Chaim*," Ruby repeated. "What does it mean?"

Khalili sighed, rubbing his brow in mild frustration.

"It is a Hebrew word," he said brusquely. "Meaning *'to life.'* It is a kind of praise to—or a celebration of life."

"I don't know this piece," Ruby said as she carefully studied the notes, beginning the process of committing them to her memory. She frowned and glanced around the page at Khalili. "I could play this."

Khalili folded his arms and reclined in his seat.

"I-I don't know," he ventured worriedly. "It is very rough."

"W-well…who wrote it?" Ruby probed, undeterred.

"It was written long ago, long before you were born," he said. "Perhaps…even before your grandmother was born. A young man first conceived of it in a very dark room where he spent many days and nights all alone."

That last sentence made Ruby shiver.

"That sounds awful. Why was he alone?" she asked with alarm.

"Because," Khalili sighed. "He had little choice. He was forced to stay in that room along with many others who were held there against their will. They were prisoners you see."

Ruby studied him with a puzzled frown.

"I thought you said he was all alone."

A wan smiled passed over Khalili and he cocked his head to one side.

"He *was* all alone…in his heart and his mind…" he corrected subtly. "As were all of those who were with him. But, he discovered a way to conquer the loneliness. He used his imagination and lessons he'd received in music. And this…" he paused, leaning forward to tap the sheet music in front of Ruby. "…was what his imagination produced."

Ruby began to hear the music in her mind. She saw within the notes on the page, a stark underlying emotion—a darkness that unnerved her and intrigued her simultaneously.

"Let me play this," she said confidently.

Khalili's eyes narrowed and he set his leather bag down on the stage floor.

"I-I don't know…"

Ruby ignored him.

Setting the sheet music on the stand in front of her, she settled back in her seat, lifted her violin. Her uncanny ability switched on like a light bulb and she closed her eyes. She breathed softly.

Khalili's hesitation gave way to curiosity then. He entwined his fingers together and rested them on his knees in wait.

Ruby positioned herself as Khalili had shown her just a few minutes before and she raised the violin to her chin.

She drew her bow across the strings, eliciting a long and plaintive note with just enough quiver on it to give it a satisfying vibrato. She knew she had attained the note perfectly. A familiar feeling, akin to a buzz, rippled in her temples and slowly she opened her eyes.

In her mind's eye, the darkness and the dank cold of a cramped bunk house coalesced, filled with the sad faces of people. They were huddled together for warmth around a pair of candles that were seated in the middle of the room. A large and heavy steel door at one end of the building was fastened shut. In the flickering light that played upon their anguished features, Ruby could see them clearly—their sunken eyes, their prominent cheek bones, their lips—chapped and cracked from the cold, faces pocked with sores. Men, women and children coughed and spluttered under the weight of chronic illness. They wore tattered clothing over emaciated frames. Ruby played their circumstance upon her violin.

Tendrils of fear weaved their way through the group as they sat on the earthen floor, each of them afraid to move or speak. Outside the brick walls of the bunk house, guttural sounds, inhuman sounds swirled all around, taunting them. The sounds of machinery, belching smoke and fire melded with anguished voices that cried out in pain. Ruby's violin traversed the huddle of people, translating these sounds with a chaotic progression of notes, a chilling representation of dread. That dread germinated in the pit of her stomach as she played which, in turn fed through her fingers onto the strings. The piece returned to those poor souls trapped in the bunk house and Ruby descended into ominous plucking of low notes. Something was happening that changed the dynamic of the piece. Ruby was heralding the arrival of a foreboding presence somewhere nearby—a presence that was coming.

Several in the group began crying, weeping; their tear-filled eyes held a long suffering fear—as though they had been crying for all of their lives. Ruby played long, lingering high notes; suggestive of their grief, suggestive of their wearied panic before she plunged back down into the lower registers again as the unseen presence outside grew closer and more threatening. It amplified their fear, causing many of them to scramble backward across the floor to the corner of the room that was farthest from the direction of presence.

The room was suddenly rocked by a powerful explosion which seemed to strike just outside the bunk house. Like an earthquake, the explosion caused the entire bunk house to shake. The flickering light from the candle flame threatened to burn out. The panic that surged through everyone was all-consuming. They were paralysed where they sat or stood.

A second explosion, even louder than the first struck with a deafening boom, causing the brick wall at one end of the bunk house to visibly shake. Mortar dust collapsed from the spaces between. The prisoners huddled closer. Ruby translated their terror with rapid, punctuated strokes of her bow.

And then, from the centre of the huddle, a lone figure stands. A child, a boy, wearing a moth eaten woollen pullover and tattered shorts steps forth and peers through the darkness toward the precarious brickwork. His companions gasp in horror and desperately try to coax him back, but he ignores them. Something has piqued his curiosity. He shuffles cautiously across the earthen floor on shoeless feet that are hardened and calloused.

A third explosion rocks the bunk house with such force that the brick wall and part of the roof crumble and collapse with a cacophony of noise and dust and iron. A gaping hole is revealed through which the boy gazes up into a night sky ablaze with fire.

A monstrous shadow falls across the gaping maw of the ruined building. Its form is suggestive of a beast-like figure with huge hands and a powerful jaw, but there is no physical accompaniment to it. It exists— wraith-like in the darkness. Two great limbs plant themselves upon the ragged edges of the hole and the presence glares down into the bunk house. The boy stands solitary, returning the glare of the presence with an innocent curiosity. He has no fear, despite the violence that rages all around.

And with that innocence, the boy reaches up with an outstretched hand toward the presence and he smiles warmly.

There is surprise. There is confusion. There is hesitation.

The presence reaches down into the ruined building and takes the boy's hand gently in its own. All at once, the violence, the chaos and the terror fall away. The screams subside. The machinery throttles down to a low thrum. Ruby's own strokes slow as she holds several high notes with a delicate hand.

His hand still entwined in that of the presence, the boy gingerly steps forward and over the pile of ruined bricks, led by the shadow, out and away from the bunk house.

The boy turns back to his companions inside, as the dawn begins to break. The presence too has dissipated with the violence and, with a warm glow playing across the boy's dirty face, he smiles, urging them to follow him.

Through the gap they file – slowly, hesitantly. None of them are sure of what to expect. But, as a dawning sun rises to meet them, they step out of the bunk house. Each and every one of the prisoners is touched by a comforting warmth that splashes across their faces—a light that has eluded them for what seemed like a lifetime.

The concentration camp crumbles all around them. Buildings collapse inward and plumes of smoke rise in their wake. Other gaunt, emaciated prisoners file out of similar structures.

The boy leads the way toward a brilliant green meadow, beyond a ruined barbed wire fence. Wild flowers bloom as the prisoners cross over from the coarse, grey stone of the prison to the soft, lush pasture of the field beyond.

Some fall to their knees in gratitude of the splendour to which they have been delivered. Others just stand, unsure of what to make of their circumstance now. But in time, they look around at each other and, slowly, they greet each other with beatific smiles.

In the centre of the meadow stands the boy, free of the shackles that have been his bondage. His eyes meet those of an elderly woman who kneels on the ground nearby, unable to support her own frame. In that moment, her eyes are as vibrant and alive as his very own.

In that final moment, Ruby drew the bow away from the violin, allowing the last note to trail away. Then she lowered her instrument and gingerly looked up at Khalili. She was surprised to find him sitting there, his eyes reddened with evidence of tears.

Ruby shifted uncomfortably and fidgeted with her violin.

"W-was that okay?" she asked hesitantly.

Khalili nodded slowly and gestured silently to the auditorium behind Ruby.

Slowly, she turned to see a number of people who'd been watching her. They appeared visibly moved. Some of them, like Khalili himself, were wiping away tears.

"I have not heard that piece played in a very long time," Khalili said, his voice thick with emotion. "And I don't think I have heard it played so… *beautifully.*"

Ruby smiled awkwardly, not quite knowing what to say next.

"How did you do it?" Khalili asked, after several moments. "How did you play so…completely…having never seen that piece before?"

Ruby shrugged her shoulders.

"I just…read it…I see all of the music on the page and I bring it inside of me. It's how Nana taught me."

Khalili seemed to slump back in his chair and he whistled air through his teeth absently.

"There are perhaps only a handful of individuals in the entire world who can do what you did just now, child. I have no doubt that you are indeed gifted."

Ruby's eyes widened then and she sat up straight.

"Does that mean you want to take me on?"

Khalili indulged in a thoughtful pause that seemed to last for an eternity. Then he nodded.

"We will work together—you and I—and we will refine your technique. You could go far, young Ruby. Farther than anyone I have encountered in a long time."

Ruby nearly launched off her seat and into the air, letting out a squeal of delight, causing some in the hall to jump in their seats. She stifled her voice almost immediately and regained her composure.

"Will you come to see me again next week? Same time?"

Ruby nodded eagerly, but then hesitated, frowning.

"I don't know if I can pay you, Mr. Khalili."

The professor brushed her concern away with a wave of his hand.

"Do not worry about that, young Ruby. Money is the least of our concerns. Just you make sure that you arrive here safely."

He lifted the sheet of music from the stand and closed it, handing it to Ruby.

"Take this. Put it in your case and take it home to your grandmother."

Ruby gently took the aged piece of paper from Khalili and laid it in the violin case before placing her instrument in after it.

"No one has given me a chance like this before Mr. Khalili."

Khalili nodded and smiled as he stood and gestured toward one of the side doors of the hall.

"Well, maybe we can do something about that."

Unknown to Khalili, Ruby or anyone else near the stage, far up in the rear seats at the back of the hall, a lone figure stood, watching quietly. Dressed in a pair of denim jeans and wearing a grey suit jacket, he was tall, handsome and though quite a lot younger than Khalili had a stylish greying at the temples of his neat, short hair. Charlie Lynch was a fellow teacher of music in the school and a close colleague of the professor. He'd slipped in part way through Ruby's performance and watched her play and he remained there now, studying Khalili and the young girl curiously as they walked toward the exit.

Once the child stepped through the door and was gone from view, Lynch maintained a thoughtful expression, as though he was mulling something over. Then, he turned and left the hall as silently as he had entered.

RUBY RETURNED THE following week and the week after that at the same time and via the same train she'd caught previously, only now she and Jeremy did so without having to dodge the ticketing officer. Each time they dutifully presented their tickets to the officer who fixed them both with suspicious looks before moving on without so much as a word.

Together, with Jeremy watching from his seat in the front row of the hall, Khalili and Ruby conducted her lesson over the course of a couple of hours, refining her technique, introducing new exercises to her repertoire, challenging her with new compositions that were previously unknown to her. Ruby's approach was the same every time. No matter what it was that Khalili put in front of her, Ruby devoured the music on the page, committing it to memory and reproducing it with meticulous attention to detail and an emotional investment that drew an increasing audience to the auditorium whenever Ruby was there to play. Jeremy himself could see the effect that Ruby was having on the people around him. They were transported by her skill through every single note and, all the while, Khalili was gentle in his instruction, modifying her technique only subtly in order to extract the very best from her.

For Jeremy, those two hours took him away from his own turmoil, the problems at home and at school, his obligations to Gavin and Mickey. Ruby's music nurtured something unspoken inside of him—something pure and untainted. It was something he was sure was reaching the others in the audience. It was, quite simply, beautiful.

Ruby brought her music home and played it for Virginia who seemed equally nourished by it and Jeremy noticed a glint in his grandmother's eyes whenever Ruby performed for her and the children. It was as though Virginia was remembering a time long ago, when she herself was young and was filled with a happiness and contentment.

And, all the while, Charlie Lynch, who'd appeared previously at the very top of the seats far back in the hall, returned each time – even if it was only for a few minutes – to watch the young Aboriginal girl and her uncanny gift and his colleague, Khalili who seemed to be relishing his role as a one on one tutor more than he ever had before.

But Lynch did not know who this child was. She wasn't on the books as a student officially, nor had Khalili introduced her to anyone in any official capacity. Each week, she came, she performed and learned and then she disappeared as if she had never been.

It was creating mutterings among the music students, the faculty and the school more widely.

Lynch remained silent. He merely watched with quiet poise each week and left the auditorium before he could be seen by Khalili or the child.

CHAPTER 16

1959

Simon the dog was no longer the gangly pup Virginia had encountered by the wood pile all those years ago. He was now a handsome adult with a shining black and white coat, a proud face and a lean body. Despite the indeterminate mixture of his breeding, Simon was the finest working dog on the farm, the most active. He was also fiercely loyal to Virginia and had become her protector of sorts.

Virginia was now sixteen and she too, had come to be regarded as the hardest working 'employee' on the Penschey farm. No longer was she the sickly child who had first arrived here. She had grown into an attractive and athletic young woman, whose quiet and unwavering commitment to her work had made her physically strong and often, as capable as her male counterparts. Strange as it might have seemed, Virginia had earned the grudging respect of the staff on the farm, particularly among the horsemen that worked for the Pastoralist. Virginia was often called upon to prepare their horses before they headed out each day. She knew how each of them liked their saddles and bridles applied to their mounts. One horseman, in particular, often slipped her a piece of fruit or a portion of his sandwich on his way out each day. It was a kindness that Virginia cherished.

There were, however, individuals on the farm who regarded Virginia with contempt. One in particular, a pimply young stable hand with a nasty air about him, constantly harassed Virginia whenever she was working in the stables, feeding the horses or mucking out the stalls. He would hang about whenever she was working there, sit on the railings above her and spit at her or make cruel jibes about her skin colour. At other times, he would interrupt her with a couple of the other young farm hands by tracking mud and manure through her freshly cleaned stalls and try and get a rise out of her by getting close to her and taunting her.

Virginia kept her head down and tried her best to ignore him but he remained unrelenting.

And then the taunting took a sinister turn.

The young stable hand and his colleagues would push her into the darkest corners of the stables where no one could see. Then, each would take turns, pushing themselves on top of Virginia, forcing themselves inside of her while the others held her down, covering her mouth with their hands so that no one could hear.

In the beginning she screamed at the top of her lungs, terrified and desperate to get away from the boys. They beat her, scratched at her body and struck her face. And then the threats came. They threatened to tell the Pastoralist that she was the instigator of their advances—that he would send her away and she would be put into an institution. The only way she could prevent this from happening was to remain silent. And so, Virginia endured their behaviour—the fear of what the Pastoralist might do to her far out weighed anything that the young men did. Likewise, she felt could never tell Mrs. Penschey; for fear that she might confront her husband about their behaviour and place Virginia in the same peril as a result.

But then, almost by accident, Virginia discovered a way to deter them. The young stable hand, as it turned out, had a fear of dogs and he came to be particularly terrified of Simon.

This she discovered one day when she brought Simon with her to the stables, which she didn't normally do, for fear that the dog would unsettle a couple of the newer horses.

On this occasion, the stable hand turned up as usual and, without warning, Simon attacked him—launching at him like an enraged lion, growling and snarling at him before taking a large chunk of skin out of the young man's rump.

From then on, Virginia kept Simon with her at all times—especially, whenever she was working in the stables. His presence and, more importantly, his growls and snarls whenever the stable hand came within range ensured that she was protected from him.

Simon and Virginia became a ubiquitous partnership. They were rarely seen around the farm without one another. He was beside her at the wood pile, overseeing her daily routine of chopping the firewood for the homestead, at the stables, tending to the horses and he was there beside her when she was sweeping the verandah, washing the windows and scrubbing the timbers.

As far as everyone was concerned, it was an unspoken expectation that wherever one was, the other would be close by.

Despite the hidden abuse she endured, Virginia had become a popular part of the domestic staff. She had even broken through the once impenetrable exterior of the head housekeeper, Mrs. Finchner, and had become quite friendly with her. But while Virginia valued these friendships, she remained the painfully quiet young girl she had always been and rarely spoke unless prompted. She also remained a solitary figure, preferring her own company – or that of her canine counterpart.

It was a protective measure, because she had come to recognise that people came and went with increasing frequency and she learned that getting close to people was emotionally painful. She felt this most acutely when Deliah left the farm once she had turned eighteen and had moved away from district entirely. No one knew where Deliah had gone – not even Agatha Penschey. It was information known only to the Pastoralist himself. The Pastoralist hadn't replaced her either. Marjorie had been moved to other quarters and thus Virginia found herself living in the out house alone. There, she continued to eat, sleep, live and contemplate her circumstance, to despair the life she had lost and endure the life she had now.

That life, for Virginia at least, had been made less arduous and more meaningful – thanks to her continued friendship with Agatha Penschey.

On Agatha's instructions, the out house was given a fresh coat of paint; a timber floor had been installed inside by a couple of the farm hands as well as a larger window which allowed generous sunlight into the once dark and dingy room. Agatha supplied Virginia with some material with which to sew some curtains and she brought in some additional furniture for the out house—a small table and chairs, a wardrobe for her clothes and a desk so she could continue studying under Agatha's guidance.

All of this – apart from the external renovations to the out house—was achieved without the Pastoralist's knowledge. He remained as cold and unfeeling toward Virginia as he had from the moment she had been dragged from the trailer of the utility as an eight year old. He continued to mete out occasional punishment for trifling infractions, though these episodes were fewer and farther between as she'd grown older – mainly because she had learned to avoid them through her disciplined approach to her work but also because she was largely protected from him by Agatha, Mrs. Finchner and a handful of the staff who were brave enough to stand up to him.

Within the confines of the parlour, Virginia's violin lessons with Agatha Penschey continued.

Virginia had progressed from the hesitant, struggling student to a violinist of exquisite skill and poise. Together, Agatha and Virginia journeyed through the entirety of Agatha's musical collection and her years of experience, to which Virginia became expert and they sought out new compositions to sustain Virginia's skill. There was little that Virginia could not master. Her ability to grasp a piece of music was now far advanced beyond even Agatha herself and Agatha marvelled at the prodigious talent of her student. Virginia's memory was photographic and she could expertly play a sheet of music she had never encountered before within an hour of studying it through.

Agatha Penschey began to talk about the ramifications of Virginia's talent and she wondered whether there was a way that she could release Virginia from her life as a domestic servant so that she could be introduced to the most prestigious music schools in the country – the Sydney Conservatory Of Music, The Melbourne Conservatorium, even Adelaide's Elder Conservatorium. Agatha's enthusiasm in the possibilities and her belief in Virginia appeared absolute. But the concept was more than Virginia could ever hope to attain and she baulked at the suggestion.

Virginia was astute enough to know that none of these institutions would ever consider an Aboriginal student and she also knew that the Pastoralist would never release her from her servitude before she was 18. Virginia felt uncomfortable whenever Agatha began talking about it.

The station was the only place Virginia knew. She hadn't left its confines in nearly a decade, so the very thought of leaving it was too much for her to bear. Despite her circumstance, Virginia felt a sense of comfort in her service, the accompaniment and companionship of Simon the dog and, most importantly, in the secret lessons with Agatha Penschey and the gift of the violin she had given to Virginia. The thought of jeopardising that by way of revealing the true nature of their friendship to the Pastoralist was too much for Virginia to consider.

It was perhaps the only significant disagreement between Agatha and Virginia. Though she despaired privately that she could not change things, Agatha came to understand Virginia's point of view.

Their Tuesday lessons continued and for those precious hours each week, Virginia and Agatha revelled in the beauty of music. It nurtured their friendship. Agatha introduced Virginia to one of her other favoured pursuits – that of photography—and whenever they could, under the guise of Virginia's work, Agatha took Virginia out on horseback to take photographs of the farm, the wild life that lived in abundance there and she encouraged Virginia to master the 'box brownie' camera herself. It was another skill that Virginia took to readily and before long, she was taking her own, impressive images of the world in which she lived.

It was the conversations with Agatha Penschey that Virginia most enjoyed. They conversed about all manner of subjects and, despite Virginia's own fears about the world outside, Agatha maintained an open window upon it, stimulating Virginia's interest in life beyond her confines. Agatha was fond of talking about the faraway places where she had been raised and lived and visited before settling in Australia and coming to the station. She spoke of how she had embraced learning from a very young age and how music had inspired her to learn as it had done with Virginia. The violin, it was clear, had been such a strong influence in Agatha Penschey's life.

And within those conversations, Virginia became aware of something about Agatha Penschey that she hadn't previously considered.

It was an acute sadness.

Aside from the time they spent together here in the parlour, Agatha Penschey's happiness only occasionally flickered whenever she was speaking of her life before coming to the station. The realisation dawned upon Virginia that she'd rarely seen Agatha Penschey smile at any other time.

Of the few occasions that Virginia had witnessed the Pastoralist and his wife together, Virginia couldn't remember ever seeing them talking to one another or interacting in the way a husband and wife were supposed to. In fact, there seemed to be a coldness between them whenever they were in each other's presence. Virginia reasoned that it was appropriate for the Pastoralist to maintain such a demeanour with the workers on his farm, including herself—but not with his own wife.

It began to play on Virginia for some time until one afternoon, Virginia surprised herself by asking the question of Agatha Penschey.

"How did you and Boss meet?"

Agatha blinked, surprised by the question, not necessarily because of the nature of the question itself but more for the fact that Virginia had ventured to ask a question of her at all.

Agatha Penschey raised the delicate china cup by the handle toward her lips and sipped quietly, considering her answer.

"It was…during the war," Mrs. Penschey responded in her softly accented voice. "He was stationed in Paris toward the end of the conflict in Europe, after Hitler had been defeated. He was an officer…such a dashing one at that. I had been studying in Paris and had met him at a club where I was working."

She paused, recalling the memory with a wistful but sad smile.

"He caught my attention from the moment we met," she recalled. "And very soon, we fell in love. We were married by the sea at a place called Cherbourg. He brought me here after we were married and—well—here we are."

Agatha Penschey faltered on that last sentence and her expression faded, which didn't escape Virginia's notice but she didn't respond to it.

Instead, Virginia reclined on the sofa by the window; her gaze was drawn outward and over the fields beyond. A tractor meandered lazily through the paddock where two men unloaded bales of hay from a trailer to an eager flock of sheep who followed after the tractor.

"My dad was a soldier," Virginia said simply.

She instantly bit the inside of her lip hard as an unexpected font of emotion bubbled up.

Agatha Penschey sat up straighter in her chair. Virginia had rarely spoken about her life before coming here – not since that first occasion where she had revealed that her family was still very much alive. Agatha had since avoided raising it with Virginia nor giving it any consideration.

"I…y-you," she stammered, searching for her voice. Agatha stopped herself after several moments and cleared her throat as a single question coalesced in her mind.

"Where?" she asked, setting her tea cup down.

"Korea," Virginia answered with equal simplicity. She sipped her tea from her own cup and scratched Simon behind his ear, before continuing. "He had been serving since the first troops went across. He wrote my mother and I as often as he could up until just before I was taken from her. His letters stopped just as his unit were about to participate in a big fight there."

Agatha quickly searched her mind for the year that Virginia arrived, recalling that it was early in 1951.

"Was it the Battle of Kapyong?" Agatha asked.

Virginia shrugged.

"Don't know. I was too young to know anything much then and…I've never been able to find out since. I don't even know if he's alive or dead."

The familiar pangs of guilt gouged Agatha Penschey and she gazed at Virginia with profound and unspoken sorrow. Virginia's young life had been so disrupted and Agatha knew that there was little information that had been given to her husband about Virginia when she first came here. The Aborigines Protectorate Office rarely supplied any information beyond a child's vital statistics. But, Agatha surmised, that wasn't to say that there wasn't a means of finding out.

Virginia cradled Simon's head in her lap and stroked his ear gently as she continued to sip her tea.

"What if I could find out for you?"

Virginia turned her head toward Agatha; her eyes going wide.

"How?" she asked. "I don't think they even keep any records on Aboriginal soldiers. They're not considered—*people*—in the eyes of the Forces."

Agatha lifted her own cup once more and sipped thoughtfully.

"There are means of finding information—if you know where to begin looking."

"I don't know," Virginia hesitated, biting the inside of her lip nervously.

This was the first time anyone ever broached the subject of finding out information about Virginia's past. It wasn't something she herself could ever achieve on her own.

"What about Boss?" Virginia asked.

Agatha straightened herself and flashed a defiant smile.

"He doesn't have to know. I can make some inquiries without his permission."

Virginia shifted uncomfortably and sat forward, her tea cup rattling precariously on the saucer. She could see that Agatha's mind was working furiously.

"I don't want to get into any trouble," Virginia said.

Agatha held up her hand and waved her concerns away.

"Look, don't you worry about my husband. Virginia—I have wrestled with the notion of you girls coming here in the capacity that you have for years. Deliah was an orphan and Marjorie, like you, was taken from her family and forbidden to have any contact with them ever again. I have hated knowing that you were torn from your mother and I have been powerless to do anything about it. Well, no more."

Agatha stood from her chair and paced with her hands on her hips.

"I am going to find out about your family, your mother and your father and—*if I can*—I am going to make contact with them. Let them know where you are."

Virginia couldn't believe what she was hearing and she gazed up at Agatha with a look of surprise. Unbeknown to her, her lips had curled upward in a faint smile.

Agatha nodded confidently.

"I will do this, Virginia – no matter how long it takes. I will do it. And I will give you back your past."

CHAPTER 17

KHALILI AND RUBY DEVELOPED A PARTNERSHIP AS teacher and student that was unlike anything either one had experienced before.

For Ruby, Khalili's teaching method, though not too dissimilar to her grandmother's, was far and away more intensive and focused. Where Virginia had begun to falter with her declining health and memory, Khalili was able to tap into the style of her teaching method through watching how Ruby performed and take it forward in such a way that, for Ruby, felt new and vibrant.

Khalili, who had lived and breathed the violin for over half a century, had never encountered a soloist with such raw talent as Ruby. It seemed there was nothing she could not do, no challenge she could not overcome. He believed without a doubt that Ruby was a prodigy, possessed of an incredible gift that deserved to be nurtured. But he had to be careful in doing so.

As their lessons continued, Ruby's talent was attracting increasing numbers of people to the hall who had heard about this young Aboriginal prodigy and were keen to see her play.

Though it wasn't uncommon for people to watch rehearsals and lessons in the hall—and he tolerated it in the beginning—Khalili became concerned by the growing interest and began taking steps to protect her from it. He was shrewd enough to realise that there was a certain novelty factor in Ruby that could be construed in an unfavourable light by the faculty who, to date, remained unaware of her.

Or so he thought.

In a quiet corner of the grounds just outside the hall, Russ—the security guard who had originally found Ruby in the garden by the window—was pacing back and forth impatiently, holding a cigarette down low beside him, stealing puffs from it as he waited. Frequently, he checked his watch and cast a scanning eye across the grounds toward the street, then cursed.

He didn't see the person he was looking for.

As he turned and began pacing back in the other direction, Russ looked ahead of him to see a pretty young blonde hurrying toward him. She was accompanied by a young man carrying a compact digital video camera in one hand and balancing an equipment bag that hung off one shoulder.

The television reporter approached with an apologetic look on her face and Russ immediately shepherded them into an alcove flanking the hall.

"Christ, you took long enough, Dimity," he complained.

"We got held up in traffic and Blake couldn't find a park," the reporter, Dimity explained in a harassed voice, glancing over Russ' shoulder to the door behind him. "Is she in there?"

Russ nodded then gestured toward the rear of the hall.

"I'll take you in the rear entrance and you can blend in up the back of the seats."

Dimity nodded and looked to her cameraman, Blake.

"Good. Are you set?"

Blake nodded once and held up his camera, which was switched on and ready to go.

"Right. Let's do this."

Adjusting her tight fitting skirt, Dimity was about to walk in the direction Russ had indicated when he tapped her on the shoulder.

"Hang on," he said then gestured with his hand in a 'hand it over' sign.

Dimity flashed Russ a lop-sided frown then reached into her handbag, taking out a crisp hundred dollar bill.

"You're a prick, you know that?" she scowled half seriously as Russ eagerly snatched the bill from her outstretched hand.

"Yep," he quipped with a sardonic grin as she turned away from him and headed in the direction he had previously indicated.

Russ took a moment to appreciate Dimity's taut behind and her curvy hips before following.

At the entrance, Russ opened the door for them and ushered them through.

"Now remember," he whispered in a warning tone. "We never spoke about this. You're on your own from here—okay?"

Dimity flashed him a sarcastic look as she passed him.

"Thank you," she said in a syrupy voice. "I'll be in touch."

"Yeah, righto."

Russ closed the door behind them, shaking his head as he walked away.

DIMITY AND BLAKE scanned the auditorium and, upon finding a row of seating about half way down, they discreetly made for a pair of empty seats spaced just away from a group of people, where Blake had a clear line of sight to the stage.

The girl was there, just as Russ had confirmed and she was in the middle of discussing something with an older man.

The teacher, Dimity supposed.

As Dimity settled into her seat, she nudged Blake with a barely contained look of excitement.

"This is gonna be golden," she whispered.

"Yeah," Blake replied with a scowl as he prepared his camera. "So long as we don't get caught."

Apparently her little crack about him not being able to find a park earlier had stung him.

"Oh there, there," Dimity needled him relentlessly. "I'll buy you a beer after."

Blake got his camera ready, signalling for Dimity to be quiet, then he began filming.

Ruby raised her violin and began playing the composition she and Khalili been discussing—a portion of Mendelssohn's *Concerto for Violin and Piano in E Minor*. Khalili sat at a grand piano, accompanying Ruby while she effortlessly kept pace with him, bobbing her head in time with the music. Khalili would stop in mid performance and lean across to make several subtle adjustments to her positioning of the instrument in her hand, to which Ruby rolled her eyes but she smiled, maintaining the position he had manoeuvred her into.

Dimity and Blake watched on, absorbed by what they were witnessing on the stage. The child played like a professional, like somebody much older, her teacher playing the piano beautifully. She was indeed just as Russ had told her—a wunderkind, a prodigy.

"We've struck gold," Dimity whispered to Blake excitedly. Blake nodded, continuing to film for a few minutes until he was satisfied that he had gotten enough footage. Then he closed down the camera.

"I reckon we should approach them," he said, leaning back in his seat. "At least give them an opportunity to speak."

Dimity shook her head hesitantly.

"Russ told me the old man has kept her out of the spotlight—doesn't want anyone to know that she's even here. I don't think even the school knows she's here."

"Yeah, but can we run with this story without even giving her the chance to speak to the camera? She might even go for it."

Dimity sat back, considering his suggestion.

"I dunno…it's risky."

Blake nudged her arm with his elbow. "Well, you haven't let that stop you before."

Dimity considered Blake for a moment, then a thin smile parted her lips.

Suddenly, she was on her feet and stepping down the aisle toward the stage.

Ruby was in full concentration, her eyes closed as she negotiated the complex piece of music, therefore she didn't notice the woman approaching the stage. Neither did Khalili as he, too was watching Ruby's finger technique. Thus, the young woman was almost on top of them before either of them registered that she was there.

"Excuse me?"

Khalili and Ruby jumped at the same time and their eyes shot in the direction of the voice that had interrupted them.

"Hi," the woman greeted softly. "Um, sorry to bother you but I was hoping I might have a word. I was just sitting up in the middle rows watching. I must say, you are an amazing young musician."

Ruby smiled bashfully at the woman and looked to Khalili who, by contrast, studied the woman suspiciously.

"Can I help you?" he asked curtly. "We are in the middle of a lesson."

The woman extended her hand toward Khalili who took it hesitantly.

"I'm sorry. My name is Dimity Barrett. I'm a reporter from Network 10. I was hoping that you might agree to…"

"No!" Khalili was on his feet instantly and moved to stand in front of Ruby. "How did you get in here? How did you find out?"

Despite being startled by Khalili's sudden action, Dimity remained composed and gently held her hands up.

"Look. There's been talk. This young girl has been attracting some attention…"

Dimity carefully gestured to the auditorium behind her and the modest audience that were gathered there.

"I'd just like an opportunity to talk to her, if I can. Her story would make a great good-news item for our bulletin."

Khalili shook his head forcefully.

"I won't allow it," he snapped. "My student is not an exhibit for public consumption. She is here to learn. That is all."

Khalili suddenly felt a tug at the back of his pants and he turned to find

Ruby peering around him at the reporter.

"I can be on TV?" she ventured hopefully with wide eyed wonder.

"No you can't," Khalili chided out of the corner of his mouth. "You are not here to perform for a camera."

Turning back to the reporter, Khalili found Dimity tapping a note into her cell phone and he gasped.

"Miss, I would ask that you kindly leave right now. This is not appropriate at all!"

Dimity ignored the professor and instead knelt slightly toward Ruby.

"So your name is Ruby, yes?"

Ruby nodded eagerly.

"Ruby Delfey," she said proudly, to the exasperation of Khalili beside her. "And I've been playing the violin since I was four years old. I'm eight now."

Khalili huffed indignantly as Ruby spilled forth a flurry of information to the reporter before he had a chance to interrupt them.

"Ruby! Enough of this!" he snapped angrily. "This is not at all appropriate!"

"But, sir—this could be a good thing," she retorted softly as the reporter. "I always wanted to be on TV."

Khalili shook his head and stepped in between the reporter and Ruby once more.

"That is it!" he growled, knocking over the music stand as he waved his arm angrily. "Miss, I must ask that you leave at once!"

As he put his hands up to shepherd the reporter away from Ruby, Khalili looked up to see a cameraman filming their entire exchange.

"Jesus Christ!" he thundered. "No, no, no!"

Those in the audience, who were muttering amongst themselves, suddenly went silent as Khalili's voice carried across the auditorium. At that moment, Russ appeared from the top of the stairs at the back of the auditorium and jogged down them, two by two, toward the stage.

"Thank goodness," Khalili said breathlessly. "Russ, will you please get these two out of here immediately?"

Dimity stood up and raised her hands again in an effort to defuse the professor.

"Okay, okay," she said. "We're going, we're leaving."

Leaning toward Ruby once more, Dimity winked at her.

"Thank you, sweetie," she mouthed, then she backed away and turned toward Blake who had shut off the camera and stuffed it back into his shoulder bag.

Russ gripped her elbow as she stepped down from the stage and met her eyes with his own. He grinned clandestinely at her, out of view of the professor.

"Good one, Russ," Dimity cracked caustically out of the corner of her mouth before glancing at Blake.

"Did you get it?"

Blake smiled triumphantly as they left the hall and went out into the gardens.

"All of it," he nodded.

Ruby watched the reporter and her companion until they disappeared from view then sat down on her chair, smiling to herself as the thought of being on the TV caused her a buzz of excitement.

She didn't immediately notice Khalili but, as she looked up she found him looking at her disapprovingly, his hands on his hips. He began pacing back and forth. Ruby knew he wasn't happy.

"What on earth was going through your head just now?" he snapped angrily at her. "Do you know how irresponsible that was?"

Ruby shrugged her shoulders and fiddled with her violin.

"What did I do wrong?" she asked.

Her question caught Khalili off guard then and he paused, realising that Ruby hadn't actually done anything wrong. But he maintained his posture for the moment as he stepped to his chair and slid it toward Ruby.

"Look," he said, sitting down and collecting his thoughts. "I don't want people to know what we are doing here just yet. Ruby, I don't want to see people taking advantage of your gift or of you. You will get to show your talent to people in time, but you need to be patient."

Ruby frowned at the professor, grinding her teeth.

"Patient for what?" she probed with frustration. "I mean…what am I doing here? What am I working toward? Am I just gonna keep playing for you like we are now?"

Again Khalili blinked and couldn't respond right away, having been caught by another prescient question.

"Look…" he began, thinking on the spot. "Th-there will be something—an opportunity—but for now, we need to focus on your technique," he paused, leaning in close to Ruby. "If this school knew what I was doing with you, they might take a very dim view of it. I do not wish to jeopardise our future together."

Ruby's eyes widened at the mention of 'an opportunity' but, at that moment, she understood the gravity of the professor's concern. Her expression coalesced into worry then embarrassment and then shame. She looked down at her violin, unsure of what to say next.

"I'm sorry, sir."

Khalili placed a gentle hand on her shoulder then and when she looked up, his warmth and impish smile had returned.

"I'm sorry too. It'll be alright, Ruby," he reassured her. "We'll deal with whatever comes of this together. But for now, let us just continue playing music. Okay?"

Ruby nodded slowly and managed a wan smile as Khalili stood and went over to the overturned music stand, the sheet music that was strewn across the stage. Rolling his shirt sleeves up he lifted the stand and returned the sheet music to it. He collected his leather bag and picked it up.

As he turned back to Ruby, he noticed that her eyes were focused on him, but not on his face.

They were focused instead, on his right arm.

Ruby had noticed a strange set of markings on the inside of the professor's right forearm.

"What's that?" she asked quizzically, pointing to the tattoo.

Following her gaze down, he turned his forearm over. Khalili glanced down and smiled wistfully at the numbers there. Returning to his chair, he sat down and extended his arm forward so that Ruby could get a closer look.

Placing her violin in her lap, Ruby leaned forward and brushed her fingers across a series of numbers that had been inked into his skin.

Though they were faded, she could clearly make them out.

B26354.

She glanced up into the professor's eyes, her curious expression having erased all of the awkwardness from before.

"An old marking, child…to remind me of whom I once was," Khalili explained cryptically.

Ruby frowned and tilted her head so she could see the numbers more closely.

"Well…who were you?" she questioned.

Khalili sighed and considered the tattoo thoughtfully.

"I was but one of a proud group of people who believed in their identity even when others didn't. We fought for that identity…and some of us died for it."

Ruby gazed at the professor's arm.

"Oh…" she said wistfully, sensing a sadness in the professor's voice.

A bolt of realisation hit Ruby then and she remembered the first piece of music she played for Khalili here in the hall and how he reacted to it. Ruby looked at the professor quizzically and tilted her head.

"That piece you wrote, was that about you?"

Khalili smiled softly and nodded.

"Sort of," he said. "Though I wasn't as young as he was. I wrote the piece…based upon what it felt like to be in that place."

Khalili's mind drifted, as memories flashed across his mind.

"So long ago…" he mused. "I was certainly a different person back then."

"Are you not the same now?" Ruby asked quizzically.

"Are any of us, child?

"I don't really know," Ruby shrugged. "Nana says that we change many times during our lifetime but we all have something within us that remains the same—that never changes," Ruby paused, trying to understand that oft-told piece of wisdom.

"Your grandmother sounds like a very wise woman."

CHAPTER 18

The man with the suit jacket stepped quietly toward the open door of the office ahead of him.

The office was cluttered but not untidy. It had a distinct order about its chaos. It was quite unlike the usual office environment one would expect of a teacher. Indeed, stepping into Professor Khalili's office was like entering into another realm, far removed from the bland, modern day office accoutrements that one would expect. It was a gloriously rich and cultured space.

A pair of wall units that stood under the window behind an antique mahogany desk carried ephemera from Khalili's many years of travel. There were small statues which had a definite Middle Eastern flavour. There were samples of stringed instruments of an indeterminate design but which had a distinctively tribal origin. There was a small bust of Beethoven in one corner and a bust of Mozart in another. The desk itself was yet another example of Khalili's eccentricity. It was cluttered with tools, more suited to an office of yesteryear. A small antique desk clock tick-tocked away, an ornate brass Rolodex stood open, a black Bakelite telephone with a rotary dial kept a silent watch, an ancient looking leather diary lay open with random scribblings in lead pencil all over the pages. The only modern convenience in evidence on the desk was a slim Mac-Book computer that stood open and was powered on.

Along one wall hung several violins which looked very old and had a design which suggested rarity. Their horse hair bows hung beside them. One looked as though it needed particular attention as its strands were unravelling from their previously taut position. Centred in between them was a much larger cello which was the worse for wear.

And on the wall opposite, closest the entrance, stood a book case. One could be at once fascinated by the ordered collection of books occupying the towering piece of furniture, while being completely flummoxed at how on Earth Khalili was able to get such a large item of furniture through the comparatively tiny doorway.

The man stood in the doorway to the office and marvelled at the scene before him. Though he had seen Khalili's office before—many times in fact—he never ceased to be struck by the sumptuous collection the old man had accumulated over the years. It was as though Khalili's entire life was laid out here in this office and one could not help but be impressed by it all.

Khalili was absent from the office, so the man indulged himself by stepping inside and inspecting the contents of his bookshelf. Along with hardcover musical textbooks, there was a plethora of biographies—not only of musicians and composers but of historical figures, political figures and literary figures. The man could not help but smile at the presence of a biography of the late singer Freddie Mercury and he thumbed its spine momentarily, taking a peek at the cover. Shaking his head, he pushed it back and moved on. There were a few works of fiction, too, and the man took a moment to extract a tattered paperback copy of Graham Greene's *The Quiet American* and flip through its pages.

"Charlie," a voice from behind sounded, causing him to jump reflexively and drop the book he was holding.

"Jesus," he hissed, before scrambling for the fallen book. He turned around as he stood up to find Khalili standing in the doorway and his expression immediately morphed into one of apology.

"I'm sorry, prof," Charlie Lynch offered, handling the book in his hand as if it were a hot potato.

Khalili dismissed him with a wave of his hand and chuckled as he stepped in, setting a freshly made cup of coffee down on his desk.

"You like Graham Greene?"

Lynch shrugged and nodded.

"I'm not sure; I saw the movie a while ago. I thought Michael Caine was brilliant. I've never read the book though."

"Take it," Khalili offered smiling. "It's a wonderfully paranoid piece of fiction and rather prescient of things geopolitically—both in the 1950s and now."

Khalili moved around his desk and sat down. He took his glasses from his shirt pocket and placed them on before casting a cursory glance at his computer screen.

"Thanks, prof," Lynch said gingerly.

Khalili gestured with an outstretched hand, offering Lynch the empty chair on the other side of the desk.

"You wanted to see me?"

"If you have a moment," Lynch ventured, sitting himself down and placing the book on the edge of the desk in front of him, beside a rather garish looking carved wooden mask that stared back at him from its vantage point.

"I noticed you in the hall the other day—and last week—and the week before that," Khalili said with a matter of fact but still mischievous tone. "Watching my lessons with the child. You're curious, yes?"

Lynch felt a twinge of embarrassment and offered an ironic half smile.

"Well—I am, actually—so are a few of the others in the faculty. We're just a little…*curious*…as to what you're hoping to achieve with this kid."

Khalili nodded slowly and leaned back in his chair, resting his hands in his lap.

"I'm just teaching her, Charlie. I'm offering her some tuition to hone her technique."

"Are you sure that's all you're doing?" Charlie ventured cautiously, creasing one of his eye brows down in a probing manner.

Khalili chuckled softly, sensing the other's desire for more information.

"There's been talk, Khalili," Charlie continued. "Word is that you want to get her onto the sheet for the Malley-Joyce recital."

"And what if I do?" Khalili challenged.

"Well—that's certainly your choice. We've fielded our required candidates for nomination in the final field but I know there is room for a couple of extra performers," Charlie paused, rubbing his chin with his thumb, considering his next question. "The faculty is concerned that there might be a conflict of interest. They just…."

Charlie paused, considering his words carefully.

"…Why her?"

Khalili smiled knowingly and took a sip from his coffee cup.

"Why not her?" he challenged gently. "You've seen her perform. You've seen how gifted she is. You tell me that she would not be a perfect candidate for the concert line up."

"She is talented, I'll grant you that," Charlie admitted. "But what's in it for you, Khalili, what do you get out of this?"

For the first time since Lynch had entered the office, Khalili's congenial demeanour faded and was replaced by an uncomfortable suspicion.

"I am not looking for anything, Charlie," he answered evenly. "What are you getting at?"

"Well," Charlie began, pausing to glance at the miniature mask on the desk once more. "We both know what she is, Khalili – a black kid from the ghetto. And you're the aged professor approaching retirement. Makes for a good story doesn't it? If you can get her up on the stage in front of a big audience—could be your one last chance for a little bit of glory."

Khalili's expression flickered between disbelief and anger but he held himself in check.

"Are you actually serious, Charlie?" he questioned shakily. "I can't believe what I'm hearing from you – you, of all people. Who put you up to this? Cargram? Anderson?"

Lynch shifted in his chair then and he looked away from Khalili's withering glower.

"You know how naturally gifted that child is. This has nothing – NOTHING – to do with whether she is black or white."

Without realising it, Khalili slammed his fist down on the desk before him with such force that he upended the coffee cup, spilling hot liquid across the surface of the desk. His action caused Lynch to jump in his seat.

Realising what he had done, Khalili whipped a handkerchief from his pocket and hurriedly began dabbing at the rapidly spreading puddle. Lynch also got to his feet and added his handkerchief to Khalili's own.

Lynch felt awkward and regretful in the face of Khalili's reaction and he knew that he had crossed the line.

"Look, prof…I'm sorr—"

Khalili whipped his head up and fixed Lynch with a glare that carried the strength of a hurtling bullet.

"That child transcends everything I have ever known about the violin," he said.

He left his handkerchief on the desk and looked at his hands impotently as he sank down in his chair.

"She can pick up a piece of music that she has never seen before, read it and play it fluently within a breath of studying it. Her ear—it is an exquisite ear. She can reproduce a note as perfectly as it was intended to be played."

Khalili paused; the tension he held in his shoulders and neck seemed to leave him all at once and the anger that he had spewed forth went with it. He swivelled in his chair and stared out through the window.

"I am nearly eighty, Charlie. In all my years I have never encountered such a pure practitioner. Everything about her style—how she learned, how she came to be this wonderful musician—it's like looking in a mirror."

Lynch immediately knew that Khalili was referring to his own experience of learning as a child in the concentration camps and he lowered his head.

Khalili turned back toward Lynch and met him with an expression of earnest determination.

"I don't care where she has come from. She deserves a chance to be discovered, Charlie; a chance to show just how talented she is. Otherwise…she may languish where she is and lose that gift forever. I will not allow that."

Khalili shook his head for effect.

"And *that* is my only motivation."

For the first time, Lynch nodded slowly, understanding where Khalili was coming from. He stepped back from the desk, suddenly feeling small, and he wished he'd never broached the subject with his colleague.

"I understand," he said softly. "I'll tell the faculty that you're doing this on your own time. I'll tell them there is no conflict."

Khalili seemed to let go of the vestiges of his hurt and the impish smile returned as Lynch prepared to turn and leave the office.

"Hey," Khalili called after him. Lynch turned in the doorway and leaned against the frame, his hands in his pockets.

"Don't forget your book, Charlie."

After Lynch had gone, Khalili turned to his MacBook and wiped his hand over his face. Though he'd gathered himself, he was stirred up by Lynch's concerns.

Bringing up a webpage on the screen, Khalili typed in an address and hit "enter."

Light from the screen reflected on his glasses as his eyes scanned the information that had flashed up and he considered it carefully. He then clicked through to an application form and printed it out, leaning down under the desk to retrieve the document from the printer.

He held it up before him and nodded slowly.

"Opportunity," he muttered.

RAIN FELL OUTSIDE Elder Hall, pattering on the roof far above, echoing distantly in Ruby's ears as she practised her scales before Khalili.

Jeremy watched quietly from a seat in the front row, occasionally yawning.

Despite her concentration, Ruby sensed that Khalili was pre-occupied by something, by the way he was fidgeting in his seat and absently chewing at the ends of his fingernails as he was listening—*if* he was even listening.

She had also noticed the small video camera he'd set up over by the piano and had fiddled with numerous times this afternoon. Occasionally he would take some footage of her then spend several minutes reviewing the footage before filming some more.

Ruby tried to ignore his odd behaviour until finally it became too much. She stopped in mid note and lowered the violin.

"Okay, sir, you've seriously got ants in your pants about something," Ruby snapped, glaring at him with a disapproving frown. "What's going on?"

Khalili blinked and chuckled from behind his up-raised hand. Unexpectedly, he comically spread his hand across his entire face, hiding behind it.

Ruby laughed in spite of herself and jabbed theatrically at him with her bow

"Stop it," she whined. "You're hiding something and I wanna know what it is right now."

Slowly drawing his hand away from his face, Khalili turned to his leather bag behind him and took out a folded piece of paper.

He held it in his hands, turning it over and over, which only annoyed Ruby more. Her eyes went wide in a parody of anger but she couldn't contain her smirk.

"Sir!" she said warningly.

"Okay, okay…" Khalili began. "I have been talking to a colleague of mine about you and…"

He paused, taking in a deep breath of air and scratching the back of his head.

"And…" Ruby echoed impatiently.

Jeremy sat forward in his seat now, watching in interest.

"And…I think there may be an opportunity for you to participate in a very special concert for youngsters like yourself—*gifted* youngsters."

Ruby bit the inside of her lip to stop herself from squealing and looked across at Jeremy with wide eyes, sensing that she knew what Khalili was going to say next.

He held out the piece of paper which Ruby eagerly snatched from him and she opened it up. It was an application form.

"As part of the upcoming concert season at the town hall, the opening event will feature a contest for young soloists like yourself. The soloists will compete for a scholarship prize—The…"

"…The Malley-Joyce Scholarship." Ruby finished for him, sitting upright from her seat. Jeremy came up on stage now and Ruby showed the form to him eagerly.

Khalili blinked and tilted his head backward slightly, clearly impressed. "You know of this?"

Ruby looked over the top of the piece of paper at Khalili with a less than impressed expression.

"Are you kidding—of course. It's a scholarship awarded to musicians of talent by The Lavery School here in Adelaide," Ruby explained. "It's one of the best schools for music in the city."

She paused, scanning through the application form, shaking her head slowly.

"Are you actually saying that she could qualify for a spot in this?" Jeremy ventured.

"W-well…" Khalili stammered. "I can put forward a compelling case to the organising committee. But it's not as simple as that. Before we can proceed, we shall need the permission of a parent or guardian. In which case, you'll need to talk it over with your grandmother and your aunt."

As soon as Ruby heard the words "your aunt," she felt her heart sink. Khalili raised a sympathetic brow, knowing what Ruby was thinking at that moment.

"Many of the decisions that are made within your family, particularly those relating to the children, are done so by the women," Khalili observed. "Aren't they?"

Ruby nodded slowly.

"And Aunty Belle is way strict when it comes to me," she replied sombrely. "She doesn't like me very much."

Khalili leaned forward, resting his arms on his knees.

"I'm sure that is not true, Ruby," he countered. "I sense that your aunt is just protective of you children…especially from outsiders."

"Well, I know she won't have a bar of this when I show it to her. She's already pissed off because of the attention I've been getting from them news people. She thinks all this is a big fat waste of time."

"Well…" Khalili ventured, ignoring Ruby's use of profanity. "There is your grandmother. I am sure she would be more favourable to this opportunity. Don't you think?"

Ruby shrugged her shoulders and held the form limply in her hand now. Her expression became increasingly down cast.

"Nana can't make the decisions about me the way she used to…"

"And yet she has allowed you to come here, even after you were discovered outside the window…as has your aunt for that matter."

"It's not the same," Ruby said softly.

Her eyes turned up toward Khalili's own; her expression was calculating.

"You could come with me and speak to Nana and Aunty Belle. You could talk them both into letting me enter."

Khalili stiffened and held both his hands up, palms out toward Ruby.

"I'm not sure that is such a good idea. My presence in your home may not be well received."

"Nana trusts you," Ruby pressed. "You said it yourself—she's lettin' me come here to get these lessons. She knows how good a teacher you are."

Khalili nodded, pursing his lips thoughtfully.

"That may be but if I come to your home, it could be perceived as me interfering or trying to place undue influence on your grandmother…and your aunt."

Ruby huffed in annoyance and stood, setting her violin down and pacing around her chair.

"I can't do this on my own. Aunty Belle will put her foot down if I show this to her."

She turned to face Khalili then and crossed her arms in a gesture of defiance.

"Besides—*you* brought this to me, which means that you're just as keen as I am for me to be a part of this."

Khalili appraised his student with a poker face. For her part, Ruby maintained her probing stare at him.

His shoulders sagged and he whistled a puff of air out through his teeth.

He knew she was right.

"Alright," he relented. "You win. We shall present the idea to them together."

THE KNOCK AT the door was loud enough, although it was somewhat hesitant. Unsure of who might answer, Khalili shifted nervously as he looked down at Ruby. He shook his head and feigned a half-hearted scowl.

The front door opened and Belle peered at him through the fly screen. Almost immediately, her scowl told Khalili just how impressed she was to see him.

"What do you want?" she growled, failing to see Ruby who had inched her way back behind him.

"I was hoping that I might speak with you. I have something I would like to discuss with you."

Belle remained unmoved where she stood, sizing up the professor with a look of barely concealed distaste.

"We didn't appreciate those bloody news people rockin' up on our door step, asking questions, wanting to know about Ruby. We don't like getting that sort of attention."

Khalili stifled a lump in his throat and tilted the corner of his hat.

"I am sorry about that," Khalili offered hesitantly. "I had no part in it, I promise you."

He paused, and frowned awkwardly as he felt Ruby nudging at the backs of his knees, pushing him toward the door. Belle herself looked around Khalili, catching a glimpse of Ruby's elbow.

"I won't take up too much of your time Mrs. Delfey. I will be brief… then I shall be on my way."

After a long moment, Belle unlatched the screen door and opened it, gesturing with a subtle tilt of her head for him to enter.

In the kitchen, Virginia sat at the table with Asher—both of them hunched over her school project. Minty was sitting on Asher's knee playing with a stuffed animal.

Virginia stood as Khalili entered, followed by Ruby and finally Belle. Virginia's expression registered surprise and reverence upon sighting the professor.

"Good evening, Mrs. Delfey," Khalili greeted respectfully, taking his hat off and offering his hand to Virginia. "I hope I am not inconveniencing you."

"No, no," Virginia stammered as she gestured toward a chair opposite. She quickly gestured to Asher to put the kettle on the stove. "Can I offer you a cup of tea?"

Khalili smiled graciously as he sat down and nodded. Asher immediately set about preparing a cup, while Minty dropped down to the floor.

"That would be lovely, Mrs. Delfey. Thank you."

Belle had leaned up against the side counter with her arms crossed over her chest and was watching Khalili with a suspicious glower.

"I was just telling him, we don't appreciate the attention we've been getting lately," Belle commented acidly. "…People knocking at all hours— wanting to get their story on *the little black kid* that can play the fiddle."

Virginia flashed a glare at her daughter in law as she resumed her seat and Ruby sat down beside her.

Belle's barb might have stung Khalili, but he gave no hint of it having done so. Instead, he pulled the form from his jacket pocket and set it down on the table.

"Mrs Delfey. I have come to see you both about an exciting opportunity for Ruby. I have been in discussions with the organising committee for the Lord Mayor's Winter Recital Concert at Adelaide's town hall. As part of the recital, there is a section competition known as the Malley-Joyce Prize. It's a scholarship which will allow the winner to attend The Lavery School. It's a school with a highly regarded music program."

Khalili paused as Virginia slowly reached out across the table and took a hold of the application form. Grasping the glasses that hung around her neck, she lifted them up and placed them on.

"Now, the committee has already expressed an interest in Ruby, having seen her play for me at the hall and I can *almost* guarantee that she will be able to qualify for a place in the competition."

Asher gasped and looked excitedly at Ruby, immediately coming over and squeezing her shoulders affectionately.

"All it would require is your permission…as her guardian, for her to register her entry."

Virginia scanned the application form from top to bottom while Asher, Ruby and even Minty watched her expectantly.

"What's in it for you?" Belle asked caustically.

Khalili turned in his seat to face Belle. He shook his head slowly.

"There is nothing in it for me, Mrs. Delfey. Ruby is an extremely talented young violinist. This could be an opportunity for her to receive an education in one of the finest music schools in the city—fully paid for."

"Nana?" Ruby ventured hopefully. "I really want to do this."

Virginia hesitated, her brow furrowing.

"I…I'm not sure Ruby," she said. "It seems like…"

"I don't like it," Belle interjected abruptly, rounding the table and peering over Virginia's shoulder. "Sounds to me like a chance for you to show off your little *experiment* to all your posh white fella mates. There's no guarantee that Ruby'll win this thing."

Khalili bit the inside of his lip and nodded slowly. He knew he had to tread carefully here, feeling the antipathy radiating from Belle.

Virginia, for her part, craned her neck around to glare up at Belle disapprovingly.

"There are no guarantees of anything in this life, Mrs. Delfey," Khalili said. "But I believe in Ruby."

Khalili levelled his gaze at Ruby and rested his hands together in front of him.

"How much do you love your music?" he asked her softly, but firmly.

Ruby sat straighter in her chair.

"I love it," Ruby replied hesitantly. "I love it more than anything."

"Would you do anything for it?" Khalili asked.

At that moment, Virginia felt something akin to a crackle of electricity through her body as Khalili's questions echoed in her mind.

They echoed and simultaneously metamorphosed into another, long forgotten voice. A voice from Virginia's past.

A woman's voice.

Memory flashes blossomed. The parlour. The sounds of the violin. The woman sitting in her chair, listening to Virginia play.

Khalili glanced between Belle and Virginia.

"Ruby's…gift, is one of a kind Mrs. Delfey. I have not seen anyone in my fifty years as teacher who can play with the kind of skill that Ruby has. She has the commitment and she has the will. I think she can do it."

Virginia's concentration appeared to be far from the present.

Belle nudged Virginia's shoulder.

"Ginnie? We gotta talk about this. I don't want Ruby gettin' mixed up in this white man's business."

Virginia didn't hear her.

All those long years ago, Virginia had been presented with a similar proposal. A proposal she had rejected out of fear, out of the belief that she herself would be rejected. It was a decision she had thought little about in the intervening years but here and now, Virginia felt a new and surprising emotion in recalling those old memories.

Regret.

Regret at not having explored the possibilities that Agatha Penschey had presented to her in the parlour.

Here and now, was a chance for that gift to be nurtured in Ruby. This was the chance she and Ruby together had been hoping for.

Slowly, Virginia reached out across the table to Asher's pencil case where she drew out a pen.

Belle's eyes widened and her jaw set hard.

"Mum, we need to…"

"Oh, shush up!" Virginia cut her off resolutely as she set the form down on the table and signed her name with a slight quiver at the bottom.

"Last time I looked, I was still legally responsible for her. I think I can decide what's good for my granddaughter."

Both Ruby and Asher shrieked with delight and hugged each other enthusiastically while Minty clapped his hands and giggled, not quite knowing what to make of all the fuss.

Virginia's spark had returned. She briskly slid the form back toward Khalili with a satisfied nod, then put her arm around Ruby.

"Let's give her that chance, Mr. Khalili," she said confidently.

Belle abruptly turned and left the kitchen and Khalili watched her go.

"Don't worry about her," Virginia reassured him. "We only need to worry about Ruby."

Ruby's face lit up and she smiled broadly at her grandmother and at Khalili who happily folded the form and tucked it safely into his shirt pocket.

"Very good," he beamed. "I will submit these forms first thing tomorrow along with the video recording I made of you."

"Then what?" Ruby asked expectantly.

"Then we wait," Khalili replied. "The committee are renowned for keeping everyone on tenterhooks whenever they are assessing an applicant but I am sure that we have as good a chance as any."

Ruby's expression became somewhat pained then, until Virginia dug her fingers gently into her ribs.

"Patience, young lady. All good things come to those who wait."

CHAPTER 19

THE HOUSE STOOD SOLITARY ON THE TOP of a hill overlooking a quiet stretch of Australian Pacific coastline. The sea rolled and undulated toward the sandy shore, coaxed along gently by an evening sea breeze. Down a sloping meadow to a secluded shore, small whitecaps broke on the sand, a softly spoken background song that lulled the crisp white weatherboard house and its occupants inside. Soft lights glowed in the large windows that looked out on the beach and the sea.

Those occupants were relaxing in the spacious, partially renovated living room of the house. A young couple, lying together on a leather sofa, were winding down after a particularly busy day. The pungent odours of Asian cooking wafted through from the kitchen. The glow from television bathed both their faces, but neither one were really concentrating on it. Rather, they were content just to be together.

Sonya Llewellyn reclined in the arms of her lover, her bare feet intertwined in his, luxuriating in the warmth from his body. Andrew DeVries held an open beer bottle in one paint flecked hand while gently caressing Sonya's auburn hair with the other, smiling softly, watching how the glow from the TV bathed her soft features. Sonya's eyes were closed and she was drifting in and out of sleep, but visibly happy, as evidenced by a faint smile that tugged at her lips.

Sonya Llewellyn was a lawyer in a sleepy seaside village where she had practised for several years. Having resurrected a moribund practise that had once belonged to her grandfather as well as retiring a mountain of debt left by him when he died, Sonya Llewellyn now served the wider rural district surrounding the town of Hambledown and had earned a reputation as a tough and determined litigator.

Her partner, her lover, Andrew DeVries was a renowned recording artist, a classical guitarist—an American who had moved to Australia, having met and fallen in love with Sonya during an international competition for up and coming classical guitarists in Melbourne a year ago. Having won that competition, Andy had become a celebrated musician both in Australia and in his native United States though he now called Hambledown his home.

On the floor at the foot of the couch lay a sleeping dog – a black and white cross breed cattle dog, himself completely tuckered out after a long and happy day with his companion Andy.

Sonya had been in court all day down in the nearby rural centre of Merimbula, an hour's drive south from Hambledown. It had been a gruelling day and she was thoroughly exhausted. She hadn't even changed out of her work clothes yet. Instead, she'd kicked off her heels upon arriving home, untucked her shirt and removed her bra. Meanwhile, Andy had spent his day working on the house, which they had spent the past year or so renovating. Armed with plaster filler and paint brushes, he'd nearly completed the walls of the once poky lounge room, which was now an open and spacious living area offering them an uninterrupted flow through from the kitchen to where they were relaxing presently.

Andy shifted on the sofa, causing Sonya to groan softly. He smiled, planting a kiss on the top of her head.

"I gotta check the stove," he said, preparing to get up.

"No," Sonya replied languidly. "Let me go. I need a refill."

She squeezed her eyes shut then craned her neck toward Andy and kissed him long on his lips. She got up, clutching at a half empty wine glass on an adjacent coffee table. Below her, the dog stirred and lifted his head momentarily then went back to sleep with an audible sigh.

Sonya rose to her feet and sauntered slowly past the dining table. Andy watched her go, then turned back to the TV. Picking up the remote, he thumbed the volume, casually watching the news bulletin even though much of it passed over him as he took another mouthful of beer.

Sonya leaned over the wok on the stove top and breathed in the aromas from it.

"Mmmm, this is gonna be good," she mused as she gave the contents a gentle stir.

"I hope so," Andy replied. "I haven't tried it before so we're taking a leap of faith."

A leap of faith.

Where had she heard that before?

Turning down the gas knob, Sonya decided that it could simmer for a few minutes more. Placing her wine glass down on the counter that looked out over the dining room table and the living room beyond, Sonya went to the fridge and took out an open bottle of white wine.

"To Adelaide now…" the news reader on the TV began. "And a story that will surely warm the heart of music lovers everywhere. An eight year old Aboriginal girl is causing a sensation this week after being discovered performing a near flawless rendition of a legendary violin concerto at Adelaide's Elder Hall. The previously unknown violinist, Ruby Delfey, has been nurtured by a celebrated music professor who, it has been reported, discovered the child practising her violin in a garden bed just outside a window of the historic auditorium."

As the image of the young girl performing flashed up on the screen, Sonya looked up and frowned curiously, tilting her head to one side.

"Andy…turn that up," she said, coming around the counter and into the living room glass in hand.

Her voice startled Andy, who had nodded off again. He blinked, fumbling with the remote in his hand until he found the volume button and was able to turn it up. He sat up, rubbing his eyes. The dog too awoke and looked up at Sonya wearily.

The news reader continued.

"She has since surprised everyone with her prodigious talent which has been described as a revelation by seasoned music critics. There is talk now that Miss Delfey may qualify to perform in the upcoming Lord Mayor's Malley-Joyce Scholarship concert at Adelaide's town hall. The concert, which will feature the Australian String Quartet, is set for Friday July 6th at the town hall."

On the screen, Sonya watched the pretty young girl as she played her violin in front of a sizable audience. The sound of the violin clearly had everyone entranced. Andy's eyes flicked from Sonya to the screen and back to Sonya again. She too, was clearly struck by the presence of the child but he sensed something more from Sonya. It was something akin to a flash of familiarity in her expression.

"What is it, honey?" he pressed gently.

Sonya shook her head, as if unsure of how to answer.

"Hit record," she said finally.

Suddenly she marched toward the front door of the house as if gripped by a sense of urgency.

Andy complied, looking down at the dog who whimpered softly at the front door. Andy shrugged his shoulders in confusion.

"What's with her, fella?" he quipped breathlessly.

Andy clambered up from the sofa now and set his beer bottle down on the coffee table.

"Come on, Simon," he said. "Let's go see what's gotten into Momma."

Outside, both Andy and Simon looked up the driveway that snaked down from the main road to see a glow coming from the garage. They found Sonya in there, just out of view behind the Volkswagen sedan that sat in the middle of the garage, rummaging furiously through some boxes in an old wardrobe. Rounding the vehicle, Andy came up beside her.

"Sonya, what is it? What's wrong?"

"N…nothing." She winced as she struggled with a recalcitrant plastic storage crate. "I've…just gotta find something."

Andy watched her with mounting concern. She seemed possessed.

Abandoning the floor of the wardrobe, Sonya stepped back and she looked up. Her eyes went wide and a laconic smile crossed her lips. On top of the old wardrobe she spied a battered leather suitcase, just peeking out from underneath an old travel blanket.

"There you are," she said, then nudged Andy. "Give me a hand will ya?"

Together they wrested the suitcase out from under the blanket. Andy was surprised at how heavy it was and he wondered what the hell was inside it. Lowering it to the floor, Sonya blew a puff of air. She looked at Andy with a grin and bent down once more to appraise the suitcase.

"Shall we get it inside the house?" Andy suggested, gesturing to the single light globe that hung over the car. It cast a barely adequate halo of light throughout the garage.

"Good idea, honey," she agreed with a distracted smile.

Together they ferried the suitcase down the path toward the house, negotiated the set of steps and eased it inside with Simon following close behind.

"What in God's name is in this thing?" Andy asked breathlessly as they set it down on the living room floor.

"Secrets," Sonya replied with a grin. "*Heavy* secrets."

Appraising the locks on the suitcase, Sonya was relieved to find a small key hanging by a length of fishing line from the tattered handle. She immediately snapped the line, freeing the key and tested it in the rusty locks. She had to jiggle it at first but eventually the key slipped home and both locks snapped free with a satisfying click.

Carefully, she opened the dusty leather suitcase and peered down to see inside.

There were a number of albums, photo albums that were full to bursting, along with a myriad of envelopes, papers, cards and photographs, even some army service medals. Many of the items had spread themselves

around inside the case over the years, having come loose from the per-
ished remnants of rubber bands that once held them secure.

"Sooo…do you want to fill me in on just what this is, sweetie?" Andy
queried, growing ever more curious about his lover's strange behaviour.

"This case…" Sonya began wistfully as she fingered gently through the
contents. "It belonged to my grandmother. It's been sitting around for
years, ever since Harold died."

"Her husband?" Andy said in acknowledgement. "Your grandfather."
Sonya nodded.

"I remember this case. When I was a little girl, I remember Grandma
putting all her precious things inside it and she used to show me all the
things she'd collected over the years."

As Sonya spoke, she pulled out first day issue envelopes with newly
released postage stamps on them. She shook her head slowly with wonderment as a flood of childhood memories washed over her.

"Agatha was a total bower bird. She loved to collect…things! I mean,
look at these."

Andy took one of the elaborately decorated envelopes and appraised
it with a smile.

"Anyway…" Sonya continued. "The thing I remember most, was that
she was an avid photographer – *prolific* you might say."

Andy raised a brow.

"Sounds as if she might have given Ruth Broadbent a run for her
money."

Sonya gathered up as many of the loose photographs as she could and
set them aside on the coffee table. Simon, sitting beside her now, gently
sniffed those photographs.

"There was a set of photographs though, I remember seeing…" Sonya's voice trailed off as she lifted one of the heavy albums out of the
case and set it aside. Underneath that, on the floor of the case, Sonya
spied a single larger document envelope, with a single word written in ink
on its front.

"Carbelrow"

Sonya knew right then she had found what she was looking for.

Lifting the bulky envelope out of the case and turning on her knees to
the coffee table, she set it down. Picking up the remote, Sonya navigated
the DVR recording of the news bulletin backward until the footage of
the young violinist came up again. Looking for a particular moment on
screen, Sonya played the footage, then hit pause. She smiled at the freeze

frame of the girl playing as she was looking directly at the camera.

Opening the envelope, Sonya took out a bundle of old black and white photographs that had been secured with a thick ribbon of paper. Both Andy and Simon watched her intrigued, as she loosened the photographs and thumbed through them, handing them over to Andy one by one. She was looking for something in particular.

Andy studied each photograph in turn. There was an old farmhouse, flanked by two tall palm trees in the middle of some sort of wheat field; a pair of horses being held by their bridles by two women riders; a group of shearers hard at work in a shed shearing sheep; a pair of Aboriginal girls working in a flower garden. Andy paused momentarily at that particular photograph and flicked his eyes upward at the TV screen but was distracted when Sonya handed him another photograph, tapping it with her finger as he took it.

The faded sepia photograph was old but the image on it was still clear enough for him to discern the face of the child in it.

It was a young Aboriginal girl, taken in close up, holding a violin in her arms. Her raven hair was clipped neatly to one side and had a shine to it that, even in the old photograph, was brilliant. Her soft, angelic face was turned toward the camera so that her deep, large eyes looked directly at Andy. Her gaze was affecting. There was untold wisdom in those eyes but they were characterised by a silent sadness that echoed across time and touched Andy here and now.

He held the photograph up and out in front of him, comparing it to the frozen image on the TV screen. The same hair clipped to one side, the same soft face, the same deep and worldly eyes.

They were almost identical.

"Okay…" he ventured. "You have my interest. Who is this?"

The light from the TV hit the back of the photograph creating a hint of transparency in which Andy could just see something written on the back of the image from the front of it.

He flipped the photograph over and read the single inscription there.

"Virginia."

"I'm not entirely sure who she is," Sonya admitted. "Grandma hardly ever spoke about her…or the farm. All I do know is, she was married once—before Harold—and whenever she did begin to speak about that place, she became very upset. I only ever saw that photograph once or twice. Grandma especially became inconsolable whenever I asked her about the girl."

She looked down into the suitcase again and gently nudged another photo album aside to reveal a leather bound book underneath. Gently lifting it from its resting place, Sonya brushed aside a fine layer of dust. On the cover, embossed in gold lettering, were the words "Diary."

Underneath that, was a name: "Agatha Liesel Penschey"

Opening the dusty journal, Sonya carefully turned the pages, gazing down upon a flowing cursive handwriting. Sonya was familiar with her grandmother's handwriting and her love of journaling, recording her thoughts and memories. After she died, Sonya had been given a number of Agatha's diaries which charted an otherwise happy life with her grandfather Harold. It was only after Agatha had died that Harold Llewellyn seemed to lose his grip on the bottle and fall apart in a destructive miasma of alcoholism.

Clutching the journal, Sonya got to her feet and transferred to the sofa where she sat cross legged next to Andy.

This was a diary Sonya had never seen before. And the tone of the entries contained herein were altogether different. There was happiness and wonderment recorded in the earlier pages—the musings of a young woman who saw the world as her oyster. There were photographs too—the Eiffel Tower in winter, sprawling vineyards in the south of France, soaring snow-capped mountains in Austria, a group of young men and women—couples posing leisurely by the sea—the men in soldiers' uniforms, the women in swimming costumes.

In all of the photographs, a young Agatha posed happily alongside a handsome young man—one of the soldiers from the seaside photograph. Sonya had never seen this man before and deduced, both from the photographs themselves and the entries in her diary, that this was Agatha's first husband.

Flipping forward several pages, Sonya saw a definite change to the tone. Her eyes crossed over the words *"Cherbourg," "A long sea journey to Australia," "the dust and the isolation of this place."* The photographs too captured an altogether different Agatha. Gone was the carefree young woman portrayed earlier. Agatha had always been a beautiful woman with a radiance and smile that affected across time. Here, in the place described as Carbelrow, her smile was absent or barely there.

Turning a page, Sonya's eyes fell across a photograph of her grandmother sitting on the ground under a tree next to the same Aboriginal child featured in the photograph Andy held. It was an increasingly rare image among all the others—one where Agatha's smile radiated as did the smile of the young girl sitting beside her. Again, the violin featured in the photograph and was resting in the lap of the child.

Andy, meanwhile, was shuffling the DVR recording of the news item back and forth, looking for a close up of the child in the footage on screen. Holding the photograph up in his hand so that he could compare, Andy slowly shook his head.

"It's like…looking at a ghost," he mused softly.

Sonya nodded without looking up from the journal.

"It's too much of a coincidence…don't you think?"

Andy played the footage and zeroed in on the instrument the young girl held in her hand. Switching to the photograph, he compared the two violins. His eyes drifted across the upper bout of the violin, where the finger board sat over the timber.

In the photograph, he spotted a shallow indentation in the wood high up on the right hand side of the instrument. Referring back to the DVR, he moved the footage forward frame by frame, until he paused on a clear image of the violin.

"Look," he said, nudging Sonya's arm gently and handing her the photograph.

In the footage on the screen and the photograph Sonya held, the violin featured the same shallow indentation.

It was unmistakable.

Andy and Sonya exchanged a smile.

LATE INTO THE night, in the soft light of her bedside lamp, Sonya sat huddled in the bed with her grandmother's journal in her lap, while Andy slept beside her and Simon lay curled up in his basket at the foot of the bed. The curtains billowed from the breeze that filtered through the open window.

Holding her glasses between her teeth, Sonya wiped tears from her eyes then placed her glasses back on. She had carefully and meticulously read the journal from cover to cover with a practised eye and was now reading it a second time.

Sonya was convinced that no one in her family had ever been privy to this journal—not even her grandfather Harold. The recollections contained within the leather bound volume traversed almost fifteen years of Agatha Penschey's life and they were indeed a stunning contrast to the life Agatha had recorded in the years following.

Despite her having consumed every minute detail of her grandmother's life during that period, Sonya still felt shell shocked. She didn't quite know how to process it all.

Sonya leaned over and checked her iPhone. It was well after one in the morning. Closing the journal and resting a hand on its cover, Sonya rubbed her eyes under her glasses with her free hand.

She shook her head and snatched up the phone, opened a note taking app, then quickly keyed in a line of text.

Crammond-F-ARCH-2102.

Closing down her smart phone and setting the journal down on her bedside table, Sonya lay herself down in the bed and ran her hand softly along Andy's arm.

"Looks like I get to finish what you started, Grandma," Sonya whispered softly into the night.

CHAPTER 20

RUBY ARRIVED OUTSIDE ELDER HALL, HAVING RUN all the way from the train with Jeremy in tow. She stopped on the lawn and clutched at her chest, completely breathless.

She was desperate to find out if the application Khalili had submitted had been accepted. Jeremy had endured her incessant fidgeting and the constant checking of his watch and he knew no amount of trying to hold her back now was going to prevent Ruby from sprinting as fast as her legs would carry her. All Jeremy could do was lope along behind and make sure she didn't get bowled over in the afternoon traffic.

Ruby had thought of nothing else the entire day. Her teacher had become exasperated with her because she could not sit still in class.

As Ruby kicked up a carpet of leaves near the statue of Sir Walter Hughes, she abruptly skidded to a stop, suddenly gripped by a paralysing knot of fear that overwhelmed her.

What if the application isn't accepted? What if I'm not good enough? What if I do get accepted?

Ruby's thoughts played on her, rising to an almost intolerable crescendo when a familiar voice intoned above her, silencing the cacophony.

"You've the weight of the world on your shoulders again, child? What is troubling you?"

Blinking, Ruby glanced up at Sir Walter's imposing visage and tried to calm her breathing down.

"Sir Wally," she began breathlessly. "I find out today if I'm going to play for the Malley-Joyce Scholarship."

"Ahhh—The Malley-Joyce," Sir Walter said, clearly impressed. "A most prestigious recital. The professor must think very highly of you if he has registered you."

Ruby shrugged as she sat down at the base of the statue. Jeremy, having finally caught up to her, stopped a few feet away, sensing that she was 'in conversation' again.

"He does," Ruby nodded. "But I'm worried. What if they think I'm not good enough to be a part of it? What happens to me then?"

"Those are quite normal fears to have, Ruby. But you mustn't panic yet. You don't even know the result. I've no doubts that your teacher would have presented your application in the most favourable light."

Ruby nodded.

"This is something I never dreamed of before. No one has ever taken a chance on me like this."

"A chance you say?" Sir Walter questioned. "What makes you believe this has all been left to chance?"

Ruby craned her neck upward.

"You are here because you alone have pursued your love and crafted the opportunity where there might have been none. You proved yourself to your teacher and he has recognised your talent. You were always deserving. This was due to your determination."

Ruby looked across the lawn in front of Elder Hall then to the hall itself.

"Your teacher believes in you Ruby. Your cousin, over there, believes in you. So does your grandmother."

Ruby looked down at her hands pensively.

"What if I don't get in? I'll have disappointed everyone."

"You're so sure of that?"

Ruby shook her head.

"No, sir."

"Well then…?"

Ruby knew that there was only one way to conquer her fear and that was to march into the hall and find out.

She stood, having caught her breath once more, and prepared to walk across the boulevard to where Jeremy was waiting.

"Ruby."

Ruby turned around and looked up Sir Walter.

"I believe in you," he said.

RUBY AND JEREMY found Khalili talking with a group of students over by the stage. Together, they sat in the front row and waited patiently until Khalili had finished, then watched as the students dispersed. Some of them passed Ruby and Jeremy and some even whispered, "Good luck," softly to her. Ruby's cheeks flushed pink as Khalili waved them over.

His expression was neutral as he crossed to the piano and began shuffling through a pile of sheet music, doing everything he could to avoid looking at Ruby and Jeremy. They exchanged worried glances with one another.

It was Jeremy who finally grabbed the back of his shirt at the waist and yanked on it a couple of times to get his attention. Khalili turned and looked at him, then across at Ruby, giving nothing away.

"Well?" Jeremy probed in an exasperated tone.

Khalili lifted his hand to his forehead and rubbed it distractedly, squeezing his eyes shut and turning away from them both without response.

Both children were flabbergasted. Ruby hopped nervously from one foot to the other and felt her stomach plunge.

The application had been rejected, she was sure of it.

Taking a piece of paper from the pile on top of the piano, Khalili turned back to the children.

When he did so, he revealed to them a huge smile.

He handed the paper to Ruby.

"You have been accepted," he said.

Ruby's expression melted into one of shock and then joy as she jumped high on the spot and squealed with delight, her voice echoing around the auditorium. She flung herself at Jeremy who barely caught her and together they danced around in a circle, relishing the excitement of the moment until Khalili gestured for them both to calm down.

"Okay, okay," he implored, chuckling.

Several curious onlookers were studying the commotion.

"Calm yourselves, both of you. You're going to get us into trouble."

Jeremy and Ruby acquiesced as Khalili directed them to fetch a pair of chairs.

"I can't believe it," Ruby whispered excitedly to Jeremy, bringing their chairs over to the piano.

"You deserve it, Rube," Jeremy nodded proudly.

"You do indeed," Khalili agreed, hearing Jeremy's words as he opened a folder in his lap.

Together they sat down before the professor and he presented a folder to her.

"But now, the *real* work begins," Khalili said. "Since I first met you, I have been testing you—to see if you would be up to the standard required for this competition. I have no doubts that you are."

Ruby nodded attentively.

"But," he continued. "This won't be like anything you've ever experienced before. You will be performing in front of an audience for the first time, and you will be competing against students who have received years of structured education—who have spent hours every day honing their craft."

Ruby gulped softly and glanced at Jeremy.

"But you, Ruby," Khalili said, levelling his gaze at her. "You are just as capable—perhaps more so. Because not only do you have what is required in here…"

Khalili tapped her chest over her heart then, slowly, drew his finger up to his own temple.

"You also have what is required up here. It is what makes you special. You have a rare ability to think quickly with your mind and adapt accordingly. Your photographic memory is the key. What we need to do is hone that, through intense practise in order to ready you for the performances."

Khalili turned some pages over and gestured for Jeremy to come closer.

"The recital consists of three rounds: an initial qualifying round, a semi-final and a final round. There'll be eight performers in the first round. Four will progress to the second round and, from that, two will be selected for the final," Khalili paused, making sure that Ruby was following.

"We will need a repertoire for the three rounds that feature either a movement from a major sonata for violin and piano—to be performed with the string quartet at the recital and a pianist of your choice. Also, you are required to perform a short virtuosic work from a nineteenth- or twentieth-century composer and a solo piece of your own choosing. Each must be no longer than ten minutes in length."

"Sounds like a lot of work," Jeremy commented, crossing his arms.

"Perhaps," Khalili said, tilting his head from one side to the other. "But, I believe we can have you in a strong position by the time of the concert."

Ruby scanned through the information on the sheets in front of her.

"So…what would you like to include?"

"Mendelssohn," Ruby answered confidently, almost straight away. "I think I should perform Mendelssohn—a portion from the *Concerto in E Minor*, perhaps the second or third movement…and I want you to accompany me."

Khalili chuckled then and fixed her with a lopsided grin.

"Wouldn't you rather have the guest pianist perform with you? I fear I may be a little rusty."

Ruby shook her head firmly.

"We should perform together. We've done this piece enough times now. I know your style and I know your cues. If I were to partner with somebody else…it wouldn't feel…*right*."

Khalili considered Ruby's words when a male voice sounded from the rear of the auditorium.

"Looks like you've fashioned a formidable young student, Khalili."

Jeremy, Khalili and Ruby turned in the direction of the voice to see Charlie Lynch walking down the aisle toward the stage.

Stepping up, Lynch offered his hand to Ruby and she took it gingerly.

"Charlie Lynch," he greeted. "You must be Ruby."

Ruby nodded evenly.

"Yes, sir," she responded politely.

"Sounds like our esteemed professor here might be a little jumpy at the idea of performing again," Lynch clucked, smiling at Khalili. "This is the thing about being such a celebrated teacher—one invests so much in it that they forget why it was they got into it in the first place. Complacency will do that to a person."

Khalili levelled a disapproving glower at Lynch.

"What is this?" he snapped with a note of humour. "I think you are all ganging up on me."

"Maybe…" Lynch ventured, placing his hands in his pockets. "She makes a compelling case. You have developed the kind of musical partnership that many can only dream of. I think a return to the stage for a seasoned performer such as yourself, is long past due."

Lynch cheekily stepped up in front of Khalili and leaned in close.

"The kid has got it in one. You've gotten lazy."

Ruby crossed her arms and tilted her head expectantly, waiting for Khalili's response.

Khalili smiled caustically and nodded slowly.

"Definitely ganging up," he said, then he took a breath. "Alright. I'll do it."

Ruby clapped her hands softly and grinned broadly.

"Okay," he said, scribbling in a small notebook. "What about a solo piece?"

"Well…" Ruby began, thinking carefully about all the music she and Khalili had explored over the past couple of months. "…I'd like to perform *'L'Chaim.'* I know it better than any other solo piece. It qualifies as a composition, yes?"

Khalili nodded with a wistful smile.

"It does," he paused, a curious frown furrowing his brow. "Although, it is not a *known* composition."

Ruby considered the professor a moment before nodding her head confidently.

"I can do it," she said confidently. "I think it qualifies and I want to play it."

Khalili looked over at Jeremy who shrugged his shoulders.

"She's pretty good at it. Even I don't mind it."

Khalili nodded evenly and glanced at Lynch who smiled, clearly impressed by Ruby's conviction.

"Okay then," Khalili responded. "We shall add it and work it up for the recital. We still need a third piece however."

Ruby searched her internal catalogue of music and thought about it for several moments. As she did so, Ruby was aware of the distant sound of a mobile phone beeping beside her and she shook herself from her thoughts.

Looking over at Jeremy, she saw him surreptitiously reach into his pants pocket to silence his phone, his brow furrowing in embarrassment.

"There's so many," she said finally, a note of apprehension in her voice. "I might need to speak to Nana about this. Do I have time?"

Khalili nodded, his eyes flickering between Jeremy and Ruby, sensing a fleeting tension between them.

"You have time. Talk to your grandmother and we can submit the final repertoire—so long as you don't fuss too much."

Khalili stood as Lynch stepped toward Ruby, offering his hand once more.

"It seems some of us have underestimated your talent," he offered sincerely. "Good luck, Ruby. I have enjoyed listening to you play and I hope I can hear much more from you."

"Thank you," Ruby said.

Khalili went across to the piano and took out both the Mendelssohn piece and his own from his music book. He returned to his seat and took a pencil from his pocket.

"We have a month until the recital and much work to do. How do you feel about additional rehearsal sessions here in the next few weeks? Do you think you can make it?"

Ruby looked toward Jeremy who, surprisingly, nodded confidently.

"I'll make sure she gets here," he said.

"Good," Khalili beamed. "Let's get cracking then."

For the next hour, Ruby and Khalili talked about both pieces of music, setting the sheet music down on the floor so they could mark areas in the music that they needed to work on. Jeremy watched from his usual vantage point in the front row, silently marvelling at how Khalili and Ruby worked together. As Lynch had suggested earlier, theirs was a partnership quite unlike anything he'd witnessed. In the professor's presence, Ruby became a different person entirely—confident and focused. The timid eight year old he'd known all of his life was nowhere to be seen here. She was instead, someone much older and much wiser.

Khalili and Ruby progressed to working through the Mendelssohn piece together, practising the Andante from the original thirty minute concerto. Ruby felt a sense of comfort knowing that Jeremy was there, looking on.

Khalili too grew more comfortable in his own playing as they refined the piece together, adding their own flourishes to their performance in order to make it flow naturally from within them both. With *"L'Chaim,"* Khalili made subtle changes to the composition, which he had not touched in over fifty years, in order to enhance Ruby's interpretation of it.

And during the following weeks, as Ruby practised at the auditorium, she grew increasingly confident that Jeremy's commitment to her was genuine. He never missed her rehearsals. He always made sure that he picked her up from school on time and caught the train into the city in order to have as much quality practise with Khalili as she could.

At night, at home, both he and Asher and Minty listened along with Virginia in the granny flat as Ruby practised to a recording of the Mendelssohn piece, each time growing more comfortable in her performance as she refined it and made it her own.

All the while, Ruby sensed that something was troubling Jeremy. It had caught her attention in the way that he kept looking at his mobile phone and switching it off whenever they were in the auditorium or on the train commuting both to and from the city. She worried it was those boys again but kept her concerns to herself.

As Jeremy and Ruby crossed over the lawn in front of Elder Hall after a Friday night rehearsal, his phone rang in his pocket.

Finally, Ruby could stand it no more.

"Jeremy, what's going on with those fellas who keep messaging you?"

Jeremy looked away from her as he ignored yet another text message from Mickey.

"It's nothing you need to worry about," he replied as casually as he could.

"I *am* worried, Jeremy," Ruby protested. "I'm scared something bad is gonna happen and you'll get in trouble—*big* trouble."

Jeremy stopped underneath Sir Walter Hughes' statue and put his hands gently on her shoulders.

"Look Ruby, you have to worry about yourself, okay? You've got a chance to get out…to get away from Mum and Dad and all the trouble around us. Concentrate on that and don't worry about me. I'll be okay."

"And what if you're not okay?" Ruby challenged.

Jeremy didn't respond. He couldn't—because, deep down, he knew Ruby's question rang true.

CHAPTER 21

VIRGINIA STOOD AT THE KITCHEN SINK, PEELING potatoes one by one and handing them over to Asher who sliced them up and placed them into a baking pan in readiness for a new dish she was trying out.

Virginia glanced through the kitchen window into the back yard. Several men, including Rex were cloistered around a pair of upturned forty-four gallon drums which served as a makeshift bar, upon which sat several opened bottles of beer. The men drank and chattered boisterously in competition with loud music that blared from a stereo system. Belle herself was hosting several women who were laughing and chatting among themselves near a bar-b-que and table—a clear indication that this gathering wasn't going to slow down any time soon.

Virginia frowned darkly. Already several of the men were drunk. The flow of beer and conversation was quickly spiralling out of control. Being a week night—when the children should only have to deal with homework and prepare for school – such a gathering was patently inappropriate. Suffice to say, Virginia had forbidden Minty and Asher from going outside. The very least she could do was to contribute some food in a vain hope that the adults would eat and not totally obliterate themselves with alcohol.

While Asher and Virginia continued to prepare their dish, Minty sat at the table, quietly colouring in an activity book with a crayon, engrossed in his task—so much so that he didn't notice when his mother came in from outside and immediately made for the packet of cigarettes that sat on the countertop.

"I hope that racket out there isn't going to go on until all hours," Virginia said without looking up from her work. "You know the kids have got school tomorrow."

Ignoring her, Belle fished out a cigarette, lit it and took a long draw. She then reached down into one of the cupboards, took out a pair of salad bowls and set them down on the table.

"Rex is already shit-faced," Belle grumbled bitterly. "He won't listen to me or to anyone."

Virginia shook her head slowly.

"Davo's out there," Belle continued, mumbling through lips that were secured around the end of the cigarette. "He hasn't had anything, so there's no need worrying."

Belle leaned up against the edge of the counter and folded her arms. She narrowed her eyes and looked at Virginia.

Asher could sense the tension from her mother. She could also sense, from the slur in her voice, that she had been drinking. Asher's nervous sideways glance at Virginia was met by a reassuring wink from her grandmother.

"Mum," Belle began caustically, taking another puff. "What's goin' on with Ruby and the professor bloke down in the city?"

Virginia set the potato peeler down and wiped her hands on her apron. She had anticipated this but didn't think Belle would choose to confront her with the children present. Wearily, she turned to face her daughter in law.

"They are working toward the concert," Virginia explained cautiously. "He and I have discussed her having extra lessons in the lead up to it and I gave it my blessing. I want to make sure that she has the best chance possible."

Belle snorted smoke from both her nostrils and smirked bitterly at Virginia.

"I don't like him," she shot back. "And I don't think *he* should be sticking his nose in where it doesn't belong."

"What makes you think he's not welcome here?" Virginia challenged, stepping toward the table and gently patting the back of Minty's head. She rested her hands on the back of one of the chairs. Asher watched the exchange, feeling increasingly nervous and wishing she was somewhere else.

Belle crossed her arms over her chest defiantly.

"He doesn't belong here, Mum!" she said angrily. "He's not one of us. People are talking, you know."

Belle gestured with a sideways nod to the gathering outside, in the yard.

"Hell, you hardly even know him yourself, yet you're sending Ruby off to see him without any thought to the risks or the consequences."

Virginia shook her head. She turned away from Belle and resumed peeling the potatoes, handing them to Asher.

"I don't want to argue with you, Belle," she said sadly. "You don't need to concern yourself with Ruby."

Whether it was Virginia's act of turning away from Belle or that last statement, Virginia couldn't be sure, but the anger in Belle surged suddenly and without warning, she pounded her fist on the kitchen table before her. Minty jumped in his seat, scattering the crayons across the table.

"Don't you dare keep me out of this Mum! I care for Ruby's welfare as much as you do. I worry about her just as much as I do the other children. Do you think I don't see what's going on!?"

"And what is that, Belle?" Virginia sighed.

"She's getting mixed up in white man's business and it's not a good look. I don't like these do-gooding bastards thinkin' they can come into our lives and save us!"

Virginia appraised her with a sadness, a pity.

"Belle, go back outside. You've been drinking too much."

Ignoring Virginia again, Belle's angry facade began to crack and, unexpectedly, her voice started shaking with emotion.

"Th-they do it time and time again, Mum. Waltzing in, making all these big promises, then fuck off when the polish fades or when they bugger it up. That's how it was w-with…*Aggy*."

The mention of that name struck Virginia like a knife through her heart and she felt her knees buckle where she stood. No one had dared speak it in years. Not only had they made a pact as a family not to do so—for Ruby's sake—but they were also bound by traditional Aboriginal custom where the mention of a departed person cursed their soul and kept them from moving on to the next life. For Belle to speak the name of Ruby's mother now, was a grave offense.

Belle however, was unrepentant.

"They're all the same, Mum!" she raged, pausing only to drag back heavily on the cigarette. "How many of them came out of the wood work, with all those promises to help Aggy when she was hooked on the drugs and the sex, but then they didn't act? When Rex and I spent all those hours walking the streets, trying to find her—trying to bring her home. All those promises—and they just laughed in our faces in the end, when it was too late to save her."

Belle wiped at her moistening eyes.

"This *white fella* has got no interest in Ruby—whether she's talented or not. He just wants to use her to big note himself. And what's gonna happen when he too loses interest? He'll cast her aside and forget about the poor little black kid from the shit house."

Virginia seethed and she whirled around, stabbing her finger directly at Belle.

"NO!" she roared, chucking the potato peeler to the floor, which caused Asher, Minty and Belle to jump simultaneously. "This has got nothing to do with colour nor has it anything to do with Aggy – NONE OF IT!"

Virginia rounded the kitchen table, her nostrils flaring. Asher immediately went to Minty and lifted him from the seat into her arms while Belle stood back, fearing that Virginia might actually strike out at her.

"Professor Khalili doesn't give a damn about her colour!" Virginia hissed through her clenched teeth. "He sees what I see! Ruby's gift. He sees only what she is capable of. This is a chance for her to go on to greater things—*a brighter future*—away from here, away from this—all this shit!"

Virginia threw her hands up in the air and gestured all around the kitchen, the drab and draughty government housing in which they lived. Then she pointed an accusatory finger out through the kitchen window, to the back yard, to the men drinking heavily, getting louder and more obnoxious.

"The violin is everything to Ruby!"

Virginia kept her glare upon Belle while Belle stood fast, the corner of her lips quivering in anger.

"Is it everything to her?" she probed bitterly. "Or is it everything to *you?*"

Before Virginia had the chance to counter, Belle abruptly turned on her heel and strode outside, slamming the wire door behind her.

Virginia looked across at the children huddled together and went to them, gathering them into her embrace and smiling reassuringly.

"I'm sorry children," she soothed shakily. "You shouldn't have had to see that."

Asher stifled back a tear.

"Why is she doing this Nana? Mum is so angry at Ruby—all the time. It's not fair."

Virginia slowly nodded and stroked her hair.

"She's not angry at Ruby," she said softly. "There's a lot of things that your mother blames herself for—including what happened to Ruby's mother. Your Mum sees things—*people*—differently. Doesn't excuse her from yelling like a banshee, mind you."

Virginia added just enough theatrics to that last sentence that she elicited smiles from both Asher and Minty.

"What did happen to Ruby's mum?" Asher ventured hesitantly.

Virginia's good eye glazed over and she shook her head slowly, remembering.

"Your aunty was a very troubled young woman," Virginia said softly. "So troubled in fact that nobody knew how to fix her - least of all me."

"Why not?" Asher pressed, sensing pain in her grandmother's face.

"Well, let's just say that I was very sick for a long time," she paused, tapping her forehead with her finger for effect. "Sick in my mind and I couldn't help your aunty when she needed me the most. What happened to Ruby's mother—well—that was my fault."

Virginia went very quiet and Asher felt awkward, uncomfortable. She did not continue her questioning.

"Come on," she said, rising to her full height. "Let's get this food ready. Hopefully, they'll all settle down once they've got a bit of food in them."

THE NIGHT WORE on—and it became clear that the party was getting louder and more raucous. Despite Virginia's best efforts to encourage everyone to leave, she could not get them to acquiesce. The beer continued to flow, the music became louder and Rex's behaviour, predictably, became more unbalanced.

During all of this, Ruby and Jeremy arrived home from the city, approaching the house from the street and hearing the commotion well before they could see it.

They stopped by the gate and listened to the commotion, neither one of them certain whether to try and slip inside the house through the front door or instead brave the gathering out the back.

Jeremy glanced at Ruby who noticed his frown and his lower jaw grinding.

"Dad'll be wasted again," he grumbled nervously. "Any money says he'll start something in front of everyone."

"Maybe we could try and sneak inside without any of them seeing us," Ruby suggested.

Jeremy stepped up to the front door. A quick check of the handle confirmed that it was locked. He cursed aloud, checking his pockets.

"I haven't got my bloody keys," he said as Ruby came up beside him. "No one'll hear us knocking with that racket going on."

There was no avoiding it, Jeremy realised. They would have to take their chances and just hope that his father would be too busy with his drunken friends to notice them.

Jeremy lead Ruby around and unlatched the gate.

The dual spotlight perched on the corner of Virginia's granny flat shone into the yard as well as into the driveway, preventing Jeremy and Ruby from using the shadow of the house.

Peeking around the corner, Jeremy was confronted by a large group of men and women who had clearly been drinking. He spied his father in the centre, waving his arms as he engaged in a heated discussion with several of his companions, including Davo who, by contrast, appeared the most sober of the bunch.

Ruby gripped Jeremy's hand tightly as he gingerly stepped around the edge of the house, making a beeline toward the back steps.

They were almost at the back door when Rex turned in mid conversation and his eyes locked onto both if the children.

"Ehhhhh!" he crowed drunkenly, causing both Jeremy and Ruby to freeze where they stood. "Well, well—w-whadda we have here?"

Rex stumbled around one of the drums and staggered toward the children.

"Hey you lot! Have a look at at th-this. Here's o-our little show pony comin' home."

Rex unexpectedly brushed past Jeremy and shepherded Ruby roughly away from him, toward the group.

Ruby gulped, clutching her school bag to her chest and resisting her uncle, though she was too frightened to protest. Davo put his bottle down on one of the drums while Jeremy started forward but he hesitated, not wanting to inflame the situation.

Belle, who was sitting and drinking with Davo's wife Cherie, glanced in the direction of her husband and Ruby but didn't react.

Rex stood in front of Ruby and prodded her sharply in the shoulder.

"C'mon!" he slurred. "Give us a show. Let's see what you been doin' with that professor bloke."

Ruby blinked at the men standing all around her, watching her expectantly. She shook her head and backed away.

"N-no, Uncle. I don't want to."

Rex gave an exaggerated frown and he jerked his head back in mock surprise.

"Whadda ya mean you don't wanna?"

He lunged forward, tearing Ruby's school bag away from her and grabbing at the violin case inside it. He tossed the school bag aside and turned the case over in his hands recklessly, examining it. He flung it at Ruby like a football and she had to catch it reflexively to prevent herself from being hit.

Jeremy himself flinched and stepped forward once more.

"Dad…"

Rex stabbed a finger at his son and snarled.

"Stay out of this!"

A pall of fear knotted in Ruby's stomach as she clutched the case in her arms. Without realising it, she had begun to shake.

Rex towered over her, slapping away the violin case angrily. His glare bored into her and she felt herself wilting underneath.

"C'mon. What's a matter with ya?" he growled, spittle flying from his mouth. "Haven't you been learnin' how ta play it? Gonna become some sorta big time thing? Or—have you been doing *something else* with that teacher friend of yours, hey?"

Ruby couldn't have known what her uncle meant but those assembled around the drums, including Davo, certainly did. Belle too, staggered to her feet and pushed her way past a pair of revellers as the level of tumult dropped away. Extinguishing the music, Davo came up beside Rex.

"Hey," he countered, placing a hand on Rex's shoulder. "Steady up there mate. That's going too far."

Rex immediately shrugged Davo's hand away and flashed him a malevolent glare.

"Fuck off," he snarled. "This ain't none of your business."

Turning back to Ruby, Rex poked her hard in the shoulder once more.

"What *have* you been gettin' up to down there, eh?" he probed, causing her to drop the violin case and back away from him. She tripped on the edge of the grass where it met the concrete and she fell in a heap on the path.

She could feel her tears gathering and falling down. All Ruby could do was prop herself up on her hands as Rex stood over her, swaying back and forth. Jeremy stood ashen faced, unable to comprehend his father's disgusting behaviour yet unable to move out of fear of what he might do.

"You haven't been learnin' no music," Rex hissed. "I'll bet you've been making that professor *very* happy, haven't you…*you little slut!*"

"Rex!!"

Rex, Davo, Ruby and everyone present flinched at the sound of Virginia's voice and turned in her direction. She stood at the back door, hands on hips, glaring down at her son, eyes full of fury. Asher stood beside her, her own eyes reddened, her jaw set. Evidently, the two of them had been there for several minutes and had witnessed the appalling exchange.

Virginia descended to the patio, her glare remaining firmly fixed upon her drunken son.

"Get back from her now!" she ordered threateningly. She turned to the others who were watching silently. "All of you! Get out of here right now before I call the police on the lot of you!"

No one made any attempt to move.

"NOW!" Virginia bellowed.

Everyone reacted and without another word they gathered up their belongings and began filing out of the back yard. Virginia watched them pass by her, their heads hung low, nervous murmuring rippling through them. Beside her, Asher ignored the steady procession and, instead, kept her own eyes on her father. Her emotions were fracturing and quickly coalescing into a white hot hatred.

In less than a minute, only Davo and Cherie remained behind. Belle, too fearful of moving toward her husband, was being supported by Cherie.

Rex threw his beer bottle to the ground where it shattered on the concrete, mere inches from where Ruby lay.

"What did you go fucking do that for, Ma?"

"What the *hell* do you think you're doing, Rex?" Virginia demanded ignoring him.

"What do you think *you're doing*?" he retorted. "Allowing her to go to that teacher, to spend time with him. She can't be trusted you know."

Virginia thrust her hand up to silence him.

"Don't you dare! Don't you bloody dare…"

Rex shook his head and staggered on the spot. He glared down at Ruby and without warning, he spat at her.

"Little mongrel…just like her mother. And you lot," he paused mid-sentence, to jab a finger at both Jeremy and Asher. "You make me sick—for going along with it."

He began to turn away, when suddenly an inhuman scream erupted.

Without warning, Asher launched herself from the top of the stairs and sprinted across the concrete patio her arms flailing.

Rex could barely comprehend what was happening as his daughter suddenly launched herself at him, balling her hands into fists and thrusting them with as much force as she could muster into her father's face. They went crashing to the ground.

Asher straddled him as he hit the grass and then she unleashed her pent up fury. Pummelling his face with an unrelenting salvo, she punched and tore and scratched and slapped him as hard as she could, over and over and over again, screaming at the top of her lungs.

"I hate you, I Hate You, *I HATE YOU!!*"

All the long years of watching her father torment his family through his alcoholism, using it as a weapon and a shield to physically and mentally abuse them. All the horrible screaming and fighting between himself and their mother. All of his constant taunting of Ruby, belittling her because of the circumstances of her birth, of her parentage. All of the fear and the anger and the despair…

All of it came crashing forth like a tsunami, through Asher's tears and her fists and her screams.

Rex was unable to counter it.

He tried to shield his face from but it was useless. Through the soupy, panicked haze of his lop-sided consciousness, he heard a loud snapping sound and his fractured mind recognised the sound of his own nose breaking. Fountains of red billowed up over his line of sight and he actually smiled at the visual, even as several of his teeth shattered and flew in different directions. The blood spatters were obliterated instantly by his daughter's fists as they rained their destructive power down upon him. A jagged cut opened up above his left eye. Asher's fingernails carved deep gashes into his right cheek and instantly welled with blood. His nose was pushed over to one side as cartilage popped. Asher sunk her teeth into his skin, gnashing at it, ripping it apart.

And somewhere in the fog, Rex could hear the disembodied echo of his daughter's screams piercing his mind like a clanging bell, further unbalancing him where he lay, causing him to feel as though he were falling, even though he knew he was on solid ground.

The collective shockwave that traversed Virginia, Jeremy, Belle, Davo, Cherie and Ruby rendered them impotent to react to Asher's sudden and violent explosion.

It was Jeremy who blinked first.

Springing forth, he wrapped his arms around his sister, pinning her arms to her sides. Asher thrashed and screamed with even more violence and her arms broke free. She bucked and kicked in Jeremy's embrace, unleashing a fresh assault in his direction, forcing him to duck and weave as quickly as he could. Several blows caught him just under his cheek, causing a cut that bled.

Davo clutched at Rex's shoulders, desperately trying to avoid getting struck as he yanked on Rex's inert form, pulling him out from under Asher while Jeremy struggled to gain purchase.

Looking on, her face a mask of horror, Belle's mouth fell open and she dropped to her knees. She knelt on the ground, rocking back and forth. She made no effort to speak. Part of her did not want the violence to stop, even though it was spewing forth from her beloved daughter. Of all the children, Asher was the most unassuming. Belle never expected this of her.

No one did.

Virginia grabbed Ruby and shepherded her out of the way while Jeremy, ignoring the blossoming pain in his cheek, finally secured Asher in a bear hug. He pulled her from his father at the same time as Davo dragged Rex free from her legs.

Jeremy whispered in Asher's ear as he held her tight, trying to calm her. And then, all at once, her screams stopped. She went limp in her brother's arms and the fight went from her. Her eyes became vacant and unfocused.

Rex's visage was unrecognisable. It was as if he had been mauled by a wild animal. Thrashing weakly on the ground, he lolled in and out of consciousness, coughing and spluttering blood and kicking his legs, wiping at his face and staring at his blood-stained hands, cackling maniacally.

Virginia turned Ruby in the direction of the house.

"Quickly—upstairs now," she whispered. "Go and get your pee-jays on."

The sound of a police siren became audible from the front of the house and within seconds, two uniformed police officers appeared from the shadows of the driveway. Both of them shone torches into the yard, despite the spotlight above the granny flat.

Davo got to his feet and approached the police man and woman cautiously.

"We've received a call reporting a disturbance at this address," the woman officer said forcefully, her eyes falling across Rex's inert form, lying on the ground, then Jeremy who was still holding Asher. Her eyes went wide as she shone her torch back across Davo's face. "What has happened here?"

"I-it's…under control, boss," Davo stammered pathetically. "It's just a family beef."

The officer turned to her colleague with alarm.

"Call an ambulance, right away."

With Davo and Cherie's help, Virginia was able to get Asher inside the house, while Jeremy ran the bath. She was unable to to move or speak.

After the ambulance arrived and had ferried Rex away to the hospital with Belle attending to him, Virginia spoke at length with the police who took down all the details of the incident. She managed to convince them not to question Asher right then, but they warned Virginia that they would have to follow up later. Thankfully, for now, they were happy to leave well enough alone.

Virginia saw them off and then came inside the house to find that Cherie and Ruby were helping to bathe Asher, while Davo was speaking quietly to Jeremy in the kitchen.

Both he and Jeremy stood as Virginia walked in.

She smiled wanly and patted his arm.

"Thank you," she said simply, passing by him and going over to the kettle and switching it on. "I don't know what we would have done if you hadn't stayed."

"I'm so sorry, Virgie," Davo offered weakly.

Virginia brushed his apology aside.

"You can't be responsible for Rex. I know you've been forced to, in the past. This was going to happen eventually…" she paused, feeling her emotions threaten. "I just never thought it would be Asher who would be the one to confront him."

"Will she be alright?"

Virginia shrugged.

"We'll see what happens come morning. Not having her father in the house will probably help but…" her voice trailed off and an uncomfortable silence settled between the two of them.

Davo looked across at Jeremy.

"What about you mate? How are you holding up?"

Jeremy shrugged.

"I'm okay. I've copped worse from him. It's no big deal."

Cherie appeared in the doorway of the kitchen.

"Virgie, Asher's asking for you."

Virginia got to her feet and made her way through to the bathroom, with Jeremy, Davo and Cherie trooping behind her.

There she found Asher sitting on the edge of the bath, wrapped in her towel, being supported by Ruby. She was shaking gently, looking at her outstretched hand to see bruising that was already beginning to show on her knuckles.

"What is it, darling?" Virginia asked, sitting down beside her. "What's up?"

"Where's Dad?" Asher asked in a voice so soft, Virginia could barely hear it.

"He's gone to the hospital, Asher. He's getting checked out by the doctor. Your mum is with him."

"The doctor," Asher echoed vacantly. "Is he alright?"

Virginia looked up at Jeremy who'd stepped into view around the door, then she nodded, biting the inside of her lip.

"He's going to be alright," Virginia said reassuringly.

Asher broke down then and held both her hands out in front of her.

"I didn't mean to Nana," she wept. "I didn't mean to hurt him so bad."

Ruby gulped and instinctively rubbed Asher's back in an effort to soothe her.

Davo gently tapped Jeremy's elbow, signalling him into the hall. Cherie was wiping her eyes with a tissue.

"We'll head home, mate. Leave you to settle the girls in peace."

Jeremy nodded slowly.

"Thanks, Davo," he said simply.

Walking them both to the door, Jeremy stood on the step as they began to leave.

Davo turned around as he stepped out onto the path in front of the house.

"You look after them, mate," he said. "You're the man of this house, for now."

Jeremy felt his cheeks flush at the compliment and waved them away, then returned to the bathroom to find Virginia and Ruby helping Asher into her pyjamas.

She was still crying softly but was lifting her arms and legs to help herself and Jeremy felt relief that Asher was somehow functioning.

As Virginia worked her fingers to do up the buttons of her top, Asher looked up at her grand-mother. She went silent all of a sudden and tilted her head curiously.

She reached out toward Virginia's artificial eye and touched her cheek.

"Nana," she ventured. "What happened? What happened to your eye?"

Virginia raised her brow in mild surprise at the question and stopped what she was doing.

"You don't want to know about that," she said awkwardly.

"Please," Asher insisted. "I've always wondered about it. Won't you tell me?"

Virginia cast a concerned glance at Jeremy who actually shrugged his shoulders in a manner that said—*'it can't hurt.'*

Virginia considered it. A diversion from what had happened this evening would probably help and it was indeed something none of the children knew about—a long forgotten memory from another time.

Virginia hesitated, then continued to button Asher's top and dry her hair.

"Let's get you to bed first—and perhaps we'll talk about it."

CHAPTER 22

1959

VIRGINIA TOILED AWAY IN THE STABLES, TENDING to Agatha Penschey's chestnut mare and finishing up the last of her chores. She was rushing, having fallen behind in her work, due to a dust storm that had blown in from the north during the morning and sent everyone scrambling for cover. It was to be Virginia's weekly lesson that afternoon and, as always, she wanted to be finished in time so she could have the uninterrupted couple of hours that she so looked forward to while the Pastoralist was away.

She had missed her lessons over the past three weeks, due to the shearing season being in full swing. The entire station had become focused on the sizable flock of sheep, whose wool needed to be collected for market. All of Virginia's time had been taken up with assisting Mrs. Finchner in the kitchen, preparing meals for the shearers, serving them to the workforce, washing up and cleaning the accommodations provided to the shearers while they were employed on the farm. Her working day often finished after midnight and the few precious hours of down time she had were strictly devoted to sleep.

As such, Virginia desperately missed her practise as well as the freedom to play in the presence of her teacher, unencumbered by her duties and safe from the presence of the Pastoralist.

After brushing down the mare, feeding her hay and ensuring the bridle and saddle were squared away, Virginia and Simon kept a watch from the stable doors for the Pastoralist to come into view. The shining green Holden utility, that he'd only newly purchased, was standing at the side of the homestead in wait for the routine journey into the town so that the Pastoralist could attend his weekly business.

Through her anxiousness, Virginia quietly marvelled at the shining new vehicle which, it was rumoured, was kitted out with luxurious leather seats and a device called climate control. And while she was wondering at what sitting inside such a vehicle might feel like, a curious realisation came to her: that, in the all the years that Virginia had been here, she still didn't know just what that weekly business the Pastoralist attended to, actually entailed.

Shaking those random thoughts away, Virginia glanced over her shoulder at the large clock high up on the wall above the stalls of the stable and frowned.

It was already well past two PM.

"What is taking him so long?" she hissed.

Sitting beside her with his tall ears pointed forward, Simon whimpered softly and looked up at Virginia with eyes that shared her concern and eagerness to get indoors.

Finally, the Pastoralist emerged from the rear of the house, striding down the steps whilst rushing to put his jacket on. Mrs. Finchner trailed after him, holding a leather satchel. Virginia watched as the pair walked hurriedly to his utility, the Pastoralist still struggling with his jacket. He took the leather satchel, slinging it into the cabin then climbed in, slamming the door and starting the engine. With dust kicking up from the rear, the utility was off, rolling the through the gates of the farm.

Virginia wasted no time.

"C'mon Simon," she snapped, patting her hand to her thigh. "We're going."

They crossed over the compound. Virginia tried not to break into a run as they made for the homestead. Mrs. Finchner, who stood watching after the utility with her hand shielding her eyes caught sight of Virginia as she approached and smirked ironically without looking in her direction.

"Slow down," she chided humorously, out of the corner of her mouth. "Collect Agatha's tea from Marjorie on your way in and *don't* drop it."

Mrs. Finchner fell in behind Virginia as she skipped through the gate and up the garden path.

"Now, I hope you've managed to solve that Mendelssohn composition you were struggling with," Mrs. Finchner added as they entered the house.

"We'll soon find out," Virginia replied, picking up Mrs. Penschey's tea tray from Marjorie, who'd just set it down on the kitchen bench. She smiled at Virginia.

"I've been practising as much as I can, but it's never the same as playing for real," Virginia continued.

Simon scooted through Virginia's legs without missing a step and headed through into the hall as she followed after him. Mrs. Finchner hissed at the dog but smiled and shook her head as she picked up a tea towel and wiped her hands.

"Come on Marjorie," she quipped. "Put the kettle on. Let's take a break and enjoy some music, shall we?"

Outside, in the compound across from the homestead, the young farm hand stepped out of the shadows of the stable's entrance and studied the homestead. An oily sneer creased his mouth and he nodded as a feeling of satisfaction flowed through him.

Kicking at a stone on the ground, he turned and whispered to himself. "Gotcha."

Then he disappeared inside.

Virginia was greeted by Agatha's serene smile as she opened the door to the parlour and stepped through after Simon, deftly balancing the tea tray in her hands.

"Virginia," Agatha greeted warmly, coming across to the table where Virginia had set the tray down and began pouring them both a cup of tea. "I've been so looking forward to this. It feels like an age since we last sat down together."

"Yes, missus," Virginia agreed robustly. "I'm worried I've forgotten everything. The shearing season has taken so much of my concentration."

"Don't you fear," Agatha assured her, handing her a cup. "It takes a lot more to rob one of a gift such as yours than a few weeks away from it."

Virginia sat down on the sofa and sipped her tea, casting a furtive glance out through the front window.

"Will Boss still be away long enough for us to play? He was running late today."

In the past, it wasn't uncommon for the Pastoralist to return to the homestead on time or even earlier than usual, despite being late in leaving for town.

Agatha shook her head, dismissing Virginia's concern.

"It will be alright. He's going to be busy with the accountant today, so he will more than likely be later than usual. We'll have plenty of time."

Agatha's words were just enough for Virginia to feel the tension leave her and she relaxed just a little.

"Has there been any word?" she ventured, changing the subject.

Agatha knew what Virginia was asking and shook her head sadly.

"I'm afraid not," she replied. "I have written to the Office of the Protectorate in Adelaide as well as the Army Records Office and neither one has been very helpful to date. I did make contact with a woman in the

Adelaide Hills however—a woman who runs a haberdashery?"

Virginia's eyes widened at the mention of the haberdashery and she sat straighter in her chair.

"My mother worked at a haberdashery!"

Agatha nodded cautiously.

"It appears she knew your mother..." she began. "But, I'm afraid it seems that your mother no longer lives or works there."

Virginia expression of hope faded instantly and her shoulders sagged.

"Your mother apparently left the district several years ago," Agatha continued. "I'm afraid the woman I spoke to was reluctant to elaborate on where she might have gone."

Virginia bowed her head and Agatha reached forward, squeezing Virginia's hand encouragingly.

"Don't lose hope," she offered. "I'll continue to make inquiries—I *promise* you."

Virginia nodded and feigned a wan smile but she sensed, deep down, that there was very little chance of Agatha ever finding her mother or father.

Agatha Penschey had been true to her word and had written letters every fortnight. But the lack of any response from either department over the past year spoke volumes of the priority to which they had given Agatha's letters.

Virginia knew that they would regard any request for any information about Aborigines with little importance.

Pushing her feelings aside, she stood and went over to the violin on the table, regarding it sadly. Agatha followed her with her eyes. Her heart was breaking for Virginia.

"W-what would you like to work on today?" Agatha ventured, hoping to divert Virginia's thoughts away from her sadness.

Virginia allowed herself to smile over the top of her teacup and she flicked her eyes across to the door of the parlour.

"Mrs. Finchner's keen for me to play Mendelssohn again," she answered, keeping her voice deliberately low. "She knows I've been working on it."

Agatha smiled knowingly and opened a large leather bound volume of sheet music she had beside her.

"I sensed that's what you had in mind. Let's start with that and see where it takes us. We just need to ease back into the music like we did before."

Virginia lifted the instrument out while Agatha selected the correct recording from her collection of gramophone records. Setting the disk down on the player and lining the needle up, she nodded at Virginia to ensure she was ready.

Virginia luxuriated in the familiar feel of the instrument. How she had longed to hold the violin once more after so long being denied such a simple pleasure. For a moment, the sadness left her and she closed her eyes, in preparation to begin playing once more.

In the kitchen, Marjorie was pouring both herself and Mrs. Finchner a cup of tea to accompany the slices of fruit cake she'd placed on the table when the lovely sound of Virginia's playing filtered through into the kitchen from the hallway.

The *Concerto*, a favourite of both women, stopped them in their tracks and Mrs. Finchner gestured to the seat opposite, silently encouraging Marjorie to sit down.

The accompaniment from the recording of the orchestra married so perfectly with Virginia's performance, both women felt as though there was a real concert being performed in this very house.

Lifting her tea cup, Mrs. Finchner relaxed back in her seat and smiled. Marjorie shared a knowing grin. Evidently, they too had been looking forward to these afternoons once more after the frenetic activity of the shearing season.

Agatha closed her eyes and listened as Virginia negotiated the lofty composition. Soon, they were lost in the sound of the violin, the accompaniment of the orchestra, the grandeur of the music.

Out in the field in front of the homestead, a lone tractor paused. Its driver, one of the older farm hands, heard the music drift across the pasture and he stopped, resting his hands on the steering wheel for a moment to enjoy the music. He smiled, knowing that Virginia was playing once again and he was thankful to hear her music.

The senior horseman, riding along the perimeter fence on his stallion, also heard the music and he pulled his mount up so that he too, could listen. He smiled broadly, patting the side of the stallion's neck. After those long weeks without it, hearing the violin now was like a tonic.

After several minutes, something caught his eye away to the west. Looking up and adjusting his hat, the horseman looked out towards the road leading away from the farm and saw a plume of dust rising in the near distance. A vehicle was approaching. Squinting in the brightness of the sun, he cocked his head to one side, curious as to who it might be.

As the vehicle drew closer and he recognised its familiar shape, his curiosity melded into confusion. The utility was coming hard and trailing behind it was a motor bike.

Simon lifted his head from the floor where he lay in the parlour and tilted it, his ears flickering at a newly arriving sound that only he could hear at this moment. Agatha remained transported by Virginia's performance—so much so, that neither she, nor Virginia heard the sound of the engine, or the sound of tyres skidding on the dusty ground of the compound, or the car door slamming shut loudly.

Mrs. Finchner jumped in her seat and sent her tea cup spinning across the table at the bellowing voice of the Pastoralist as he stormed up the steps and burst through the kitchen door.

"AGATHA!"

He didn't acknowledge his housekeeper or her assistant as he barged through the kitchen, nearly knocking Mrs. Finchner from her chair. His eyes were filled with a satanic rage. Veins bulged on the sides of his neck. His nostrils flared—as though the music from the parlour was the most evil thing he had ever heard.

Mrs. Finchner could barely collect herself as she slowly realised what was happening. Her tea cup continued its inexorable roll across the table towards the edge where it fell, shattering into dozens of pieces on the tiled kitchen floor.

"Oh, Jesus, no," she heaved, exchanging a panicked look at Marjorie.

The Pastoralist stormed down the hallway towards the parlour, his footfalls on the boards now overpowering the music from the gramophone. Simon was on his feet now, quivering with alertness and looking towards the door while Agatha and Virginia exchanged looks of blind fear with one another.

Neither one was able to react when the door to the parlour exploded inward and the Pastoralist swept into the room, his fury tightening his features.

Paralysed where she stood, Virginia looked up into the eyes of the Pastoralist. Her jaw fell open and her arms dropped to her sides, releasing their grip on the violin and bow which clattered noisily to the floor. Time slowed to a crawl and all of the sounds around her became muffled and distant in her ears.

He lunged forward, his hand reaching out towards Virginia, while the disembodied echo of a dog's barking and yelp and a woman's shrieks barely penetrated her consciousness. She just stood there, waiting for all the terrible things to come.

The hand of the Pastoralist closed around her throat like a vice and before she knew it, he'd lifted her off the floor with a single muscular arm that fairly bulged as she grabbed impotently onto it with her own two hands. Her eyes went wide with panic, feeling the air to her lungs dissipate and her throat began spasming in a futile response to his crushing grip.

As she struggled, Virginia's consciousness began to tilt sideways. She sensed Agatha nearby who had sprung to her feet and pushed past the stand on which the gramophone sat, knocking it over as she made for her husband, her arms outstretched, her distant screams reverberating through Virginia's soupy mind.

"*Noooo!*"

Virginia blinked in terror as the Pastoralist lashed out with his free arm and landed a closed fist into the side of Agatha's cheek which wheeled her around like a top and sent her sprawling.

The Pastoralist glared into Virginia's unfocused eyes and released his grip just slightly.

"What do you think you're doing in my house, you little slut!"

Virginia shook her head in panic, trying to work her jaw to utter something—anything—in response. But she couldn't.

He whirled around on his heel with Virginia's comparatively small frame still in his vice-like grip and stormed past Mrs. Finchner and Marjorie.

Agatha fumbled about on the floor, trying to overcome the stinging pain in her cheek as well as the sense of dread that cut through her. Forcing herself to think, she scrambled to her feet and staggered after her husband. Mrs. Finchner rushed to her side and made a vain effort to support her, but Agatha slapped her away, crashing through the doorway in desperate pursuit.

The Pastoralist had thrown open the front door of the homestead and was now out on the verandah with Virginia struggling with less and less effort in his grip.

"I'll give you one more chance to answer me!!" he screamed into her ear, his lips mere inches from the side of her head. "What did you think you were doing? You're not a part of this place! You're not even a human being! YOU ARE NOTHING!"

Her consciousness was slipping and the cruel tirade barely reached her. Through Virginia's mind, the sound of her own heartbeat thumped like a church bell. Her vision blurred. Flashes of darkness erupted across her field of view.

And out of the corner of her eyes, she could just make out the blurry figures of Agatha, Mrs. Finchner and Marjorie bursting out onto the verandah, arms outstretched in desperation, screaming in disembodied unison.

The Pastoralist was unmoved.

There was no point in answering him, no point in defending herself. That which Virginia had always feared—the discovery of her gift by the Pastoralist—had finally come to pass.

Deep down, she knew it always would. Her eyes flicked to her left and she saw, standing there at the foot of the verandah with his hands in his pockets, the young farm-hand who had sodomised her so many times, a bitter and sardonic grin on his face. And in that last terrible moment the only thing Virginia could do was to smile at the irony of it.

The Pastoralist's eyes nearly bulged out of his head at the expression on the Aborigine's face and his white hot rage surged. He leaned back and flung Virginia from his grip directly at the verandah post in front of him, upon which hung a hurricane lantern. She crashed, face first into the post, shattering the glass of the lantern and sending glittering shards flying in every direction.

Virginia vaguely sensed glass slicing through the delicate skin of her left cheek, puncturing through her left eye and feeling warm liquid pouring down over her face. Virginia's last thought, as she finally succumbed to the darkness, was the strange observation that she felt no pain.

Agatha Penschey's horror was absolute.

She watched Virginia crumple to the deck of the verandah. She saw blood spatter on the timber of the verandah post and she saw the shattered lantern pitch from its hook and clatter to the deck several feet away. Agatha fell to her knees and cried out in anguish, while Mrs. Finchner placed a hand on her shoulder, lifting her other hand to her mouth in shock. Even the young farm hand, at the bottom of the stairs, lost his self satisfied grin and just stared dumbfounded, unable to comprehend what he'd just witnessed.

"Get this piece of shit off my property!" the Pastoralist bellowed, shaking the farm hand out of his stupor. The boy looked up, then back at Virginia's inert form, unsure of what to do.

"NOW!" thundered the Pastoralist, before turning to face Mrs. Finchner and his grief stricken wife. Without hesitating he started forward. "Get its things. I want it off my land in five minutes."

His last sentence struck Agatha and choked off her wracking sobs. She struggled to her feet and wiped at her eyes.

"Wha…what do you mean?! You can't send her away. Look at her!"

The Pastoralist was unmoved.

"That thing is mine! I own it…I can do what I want with it!"

He stepped forward, preparing to stride off the verandah when Agatha threw herself at him.

"You can't do this!!" she screamed, clawing at his chest with her hands.

The Pastoralist simply grabbed Agatha's wrists and flung them away.

"This has got nothing to do with you, woman. You meddled in things you shouldn't have. These blacks aren't people—they're bloody animals."

Realising that the farm hand still hadn't moved from where he stood, the Pastoralist shoved an angry finger at him.

"What the bloody hell are you doing?! Get her in the truck before I shoot you!"

Without another word, the Pastoralist turned and walked off the verandah.

By this time, the commotion had drawn the attention of the workmen from the tractor in the field in front of the homestead and they approached the homestead now, their expressions bearing a collective shock.

Agatha rushed to Virginia's side and dropped down, scared to turn her or place her hands upon her. Her tears flowed freely, seeing Virginia's ruined face. A mighty shard of glass protruded from her left eye socket and the socket itself was a mess of congealed blood and a jelly like substance.

Mrs. Finchner crouched beside her and stifled an urge to gasp.

"Agatha—let's get her to the hospital in town. She needs that eye seen to as soon as possible. I'll get Bob to take her in."

"What about Ver…?"

"Don't you worry about him," Mrs. Finchner cut in immediately. "I'll deal with him. Let's just get Virginia to a doctor as soon as possible."

Agatha managed a simple nod and Mrs. Finchner immediately looked up and down to the driver of the tractor.

"Bob. Bring the truck around right away. We have to get the child to the hospital."

The young farm hand was about to protest but was cut short when Mrs. Finchner suddenly sprang to her feet and stormed down the steps of the homestead toward him.

She didn't speak. Instead, she swung her arm with all the power she could muster and struck him in the jaw, knocking him out cold.

VIRGINIA LAY IN the tray of the utility, her head cradled in Marjorie's lap, a makeshift bandage now covering her head.

Her head throbbed and the pain from her eye made her feel so sick that she could barely move or speak so she stayed as still as she could.

The truck was idling and she was aware of people milling about but Marjorie kept Virginia's attention focused on her as she gently stroked her hair and whispered softly to her, words of encouragement that were shaken by her own tears and grief for her friend.

"Everything will be alright, Ginnie. Just hang in there, okay," Marjorie said over and over, her voice shaking uncontrollably.

The driver, Bob, eventually turned from the group behind the truck and walked toward the tray nodding at Marjorie.

"Is she all set?" he asked with an awkward empathy in his voice.

Marjorie nodded.

Nodding, Bob climbed into the cabin and turned the key. The engine of the truck turned over and spluttered to life. Virginia remained still in Marjorie's lap as the vibration settled back as the truck began to idle.

Over the sound of the idling engine, Marjorie heard a voice from the homestead and she looked up to see Mrs. Penschey running down the steps toward the truck, waving her arms and shouting. Marjorie noted with some confusion that she held an object in her hands.

Agatha crossed the path and climbed up into the tray of the truck falling to her knees and gently scooping up Virginia's limp form in her arms. Tears streamed down her face as she wiped a few strands of hair away from Virginia's good eye.

"Can you hear me, Ginnie?" Agatha stammered, her voice choking with emotion.

Virginia managed to nod.

"I'm sorry, my child. I am so, so sorry."

Marjorie bit her lip as she felt the warm moisture of her own tears stain her cheeks and she sat back to allow Agatha to cradle Virginia more gently.

"I promise you, Virginia," Agatha continued. "I will find your people. I will find them and return you to them. *I promise.*"

Virginia began to cry softly as she acknowledged Agatha silently.

Then she felt a familiar bulk being pressed into her hand and she looked down to see the violin case—Agatha Penschey's violin case—laying there. She began to protest, but Agatha pressed a finger to her lips and shook her head—*No.*

"Remember this, Ginnie," Agatha whispered through her tears. "You are from the Peramangk—that is your country. Don't let anyone take that away from you. They are a proud people. Remember!"

Virginia opened her eye and looked up at Agatha with an intensity that struck her like a bolt of lightning.

"Come now," Mrs Finchner urged, appearing beside Agatha and placing a hand on her shoulder. "They have to go."

Agatha nodded and leaned down, planting a final kiss onto Virginia's forehead.

She stepped back and climbed down from the truck. Virginia closed her eye again and allowed herself to drift as she clutched the violin case close to her. Marjorie held her once more and continued stroking her forehead softly.

The truck jerked forward and began rolling toward the front gate of the farm and in that moment, grief overwhelmed Virginia and she sobbed silently. From behind the stone out house that had been Virginia's only refuge, a limping Simon appeared and sprinted across the compound, barking as loudly as he could. He leaped across the cattle grate at the entrance to the farm and took off after the truck as it accelerated away, chasing it for several hundred yards until it disappeared over a rise and out of view.

The dog skidded to a stop in the middle of the dusty track and sat on his haunches, whimpering as he watched the dust trail from the truck slowly shrink in the distance.

His ears pricked forward, Simon lifted his head and let out a long mournful howl that carried over the meadow.

Watching the truck go, Agatha too succumbed once more and sobbed and sobbed as Mrs. Finchner held her close in a vain effort to comfort her.

For the second time in her life, Virginia Crammond felt herself being pulled away from everything she had come to know and in that moment of grief, the realisation dawned upon her that she would never, ever see this place again.

CHAPTER 23

1964

Dark grey skies. Steadily falling rain. Drab concrete paths lead to and fro with wisps of steam that rose from their surfaces. It was warm despite the rain—a November shower that came almost unexpectedly and saturated the earth…

…And the orphanage.

Imposing red brick walls rose out of the earth toward the sky to stand watchful, oppressive. They were silent overseers of those who visited and left the building to which those walls belonged. To any outsider, the orphanage was merely a large, grand building nestled in leafy park lands, adjacent to a main road that fairly bustled with traffic.

To anyone intimately familiar with the goings on inside this place, the orphanage was something else entirely.

The rain had sent everyone scurrying indoors. The gardens outside the main building of the orphanage were empty. The arches on either side of the main entrance were vacant. It was almost as if the place were abandoned.

And then…

A slight figure appeared in the window of one the large doors at the entrance to the building. Those doors opened slowly allowing the person to step out into the rain.

In the shadow of the great building, she appeared tiny as she stepped forward onto the steps, then darted sideways to seek shelter under the verandah. Lifting a hand, the young woman shielded her eyes which were concealed behind a pair of large sunglasses. She prepared to brave the weather, spying a bus shelter beyond the front gate but hesitated as the rain became heavier. She decided to wait, drawing up the collar of her raincoat and taking off her hat.

With no sign that the rain was going to stop any time, the young woman set down her single small suitcase and waited.

Reaching into the pocket of her rain coat, Virginia Crammond felt for the small flat bulk of the booklet there and took it out. Thumbing her exemption certificate open, she moved aside a piece of paper containing the address of a nearby boarding house, then looked down upon the small black and white photograph of herself. Her details, including her name and status as a half caste Aborigine had been typed next to it.

21 years old.

Virginia had reached the age where, by law, she was required to be released from the orphanage. She was no longer a ward of the state, nor was she a subject of the Aborigines Protectorate Office.

For all intents and purposes, Virginia Crammond was now considered an adult. But she had yet to understand what that meant.

All they'd told her was that she was required to carry her certificate with her at all times and produce it whenever she was instructed to do so. Without it, Virginia would not be able to seek employment, travel freely about the city or even enter certain buildings. Though it granted her privileges, the card felt like a noose around her neck.

She shook her head slowly and returned the certificate to her pocket.

Looking down at her suitcase, Virginia decided to sit for a moment and watch the driving rain as its noise rose in intensity.

Lifting her hand, she removed her sunglasses and set them down in her lap. A mighty scar traversed the socket of her ruined left eye from forehead to cheek, crossing over the eyelid itself which was now fixed in a permanently closed position. With her thumb and fore finger, Virginia massaged a knot of tension from her brow and looked out across the forecourt toward the street beyond.

The rain sounded so different here in the city.

Despite her relative youth, one could be forgiven for mistaking Virginia for someone much older. As she sat quietly, her body was hunched over, her shoulders were slumped, her head hung down. There was a weariness to her presence, as though she were subject to a constant, crushing weight.

Virginia gazed into the rain with her one remaining eye, an eye which had also been robbed of life, of vigour. Her young face, though still pretty despite its stark deformity, was a visage without expressiveness or vitality. Instead, it was a face that had carried the burden of decades of suffering and pain, rather than the carefree joy of childhood and adolescence. It was barren, lifeless—devoid of emotion. Her smile had been lost long ago.

The years Virginia had spent in the orphanage had completed the destruction of the child she had been. Rather than prepare her for the life she was now expected to assimilate into, it had instead robbed Virginia of her soul and left her empty.

Since coming here, she had endured years of cruelty, humiliation and pain. Years of being treated as less than a person. And now those perpetrators were showing her the door—discarding her as if she had never been.

It was never meant to be like this.

Virginia never returned to the farm. Upon being told that the eye could not be salvaged, the Pastoralist had refused to take Virginia back. In his mind she was an invalid—unfit for work; unfit to be productive. And, just like that he had gotten rid of her, as if she had never been.

In an instant, Virginia had been dispatched by train to Adelaide and taken to this place, where she had suffered at the hands of the Sisters who meted out even more misery than the Pastoralist had.

In the beginning, as she had when she had been first taken from her mother, Virginia had railed against her internment and escaped numerous times only to be brought back by the police and caned for her infractions. The Sisters punished her by working Virginia harder than she had ever worked before until her fingers bled and she was asleep on her feet from exhaustion. And then, in those situations—if she was caught napping— the Sisters would punish her even further by the hand of the cane, the revoking of privileges, anything to compound her misery.

They succeeded. They broke her. Virginia's resistance to them collapsed. She withdrew and did their bidding without protest. Once more she became silent and in time, no one could reach her—not even those few who offered her kindness or empathy. It was just how Virginia preferred it.

And now, after five long years, it was done. Virginia was released from the custody of this place and expected to make her own way in the world—a world that still rejected her kind as less than human.

Where she was supposed to go, she did not know. The case upon which she sat contained all that she owned. She had little money and no one to go to.

The sound of a bus tooting its horn shook Virginia from her reverie and she looked out across the gardens to see it standing in front of the bus shelter.

It was leaving.

Virginia stood, grabbed the handle of her case and fumbled with her sunglasses but, by the time she was ready to brave the weather and traverse the path toward the gate, the bus had pulled out and away and was disappearing into the flow of traffic.

Virginia cursed silently as she watched it go.

What am I going to do now?

She didn't know when another bus would be coming, if there would be one at all. They were notoriously erratic around here, or so she'd been told.

Virginia looked out at the sky once more and saw a couple of breaks in the weather approaching.

Perhaps, I could walk in the rain, she thought.

Just as she was about to step out from the arch, a voice called out from behind her.

"Virginia!"

Virginia turned to see a young nun running toward her from the entrance, waving with one arm, whilst holding a rectangular object in the other.

It was a case—a violin case.

The nun skidded to a stop underneath the arch, a few feet away from Virginia. She was out of breath and took a moment to catch it once more before holding the case out toward Virginia.

Virginia blinked at the young nun, who was only a couple of years older than her. Sister Joyce was one of the few nuns at the orphanage who'd treated Virginia with any sort of compassion, though she had never broken through Virginia's shell.

"I almost forgot to sign this out for you," the nun wheezed breathlessly. "I remembered it at the last moment. Thank goodness I caught you before you left."

Virginia looked down at the case in the nun's hand as though it were some foreign object she'd never seen before. She made no move to take it—she couldn't.

Inside, Virginia felt her emotions cascade at the sight of the violin case and the memories that it triggered.

She hadn't seen the case in years—not since she had arrived at the orphanage and it was snatched from her by the Sisters, to be locked away until she was released from their care.

Subsequently, Virginia hadn't played her instrument nor heard its sound in what felt like an eternity.

Sister Joyce gestured to Virginia to take it and was puzzled by her reluctance to do so.

"Take it," she said encouragingly. "It belongs to you. I made sure it was kept safe."

Slowly, Virginia extended her hands toward the case, allowing the Sister to place it onto them. For a long moment, Virginia could only look down at it. She didn't move or speak. She ran a single hand over the leather surface.

As she did so, Sister Joyce noticed a single tear well up in Virginia's eye which trickled down over her cheek.

"Oh, my dear," Sister Joyce stepped forth and placed a gentle hand on Virginia's arm. "Are you alright?"

Memories bubbled from a place where she thought she had buried them deep and they threatened to overwhelm Virginia. The discovery of Agatha's music, the beauty of the violin, the lessons in the parlour they had shared and nurtured each other with. And with those memories came the pain—a deep, emotional pain.

The promise Agatha Penschey had made to Virginia—to find her mother and her father, never materialised.

Virginia never heard from Agatha Penschey again. That one and only friendship, that which had sustained Virginia throughout her years as a domestic servant on the farm had been destroyed in an instant.

The Sisters had refused to allow Virginia to make contact with Agatha, telling her that Mrs. Penschey had been made aware that Virginia had repeatedly fraternised with the farm hands, thus disgracing herself. Agatha Penschey did not wish to see or hear from Virginia ever again.

Virginia had cried herself to sleep every night, refusing to believe that horrible revelation. She remembered the last words that Agatha had said to her on the truck, reciting them over and over in her mind, until those words too faded from her memory, crushed by the oppressiveness of this place.

They became too painful.

Virginia held the case in her hands now, weeping softly, shaking uncontrollably.

The young nun continued to hold Virginia's arm with a look of concern.

"Miss Crammond?" she ventured once more. "Please. Will you be alright?"

Virginia slowly collected herself and looked up at Sister Joyce, wiping away the tears with her hand.

She nodded and set the violin case down on top of her suitcase.

Looking out at the rain, Virginia's brow furrowed with worry.

"What am I supposed to do now?" Virginia said, her voice barely above a whisper.

"Well—you have the address of the boarding house, yes?" Sister Joyce replied.

Virginia nodded, patting the pocket of her jacket.

"Start there then. Get yourself settled. You'll be on your way in no time."

For the first time, Virginia looked up at the nun. Her frown was unmistakable.

"Do you honestly believe that?" Virginia challenged her. "Look at me."

Sister Joyce looked at Virginia's face. The colour of her skin alone was an impediment in itself but to add the visible scars that Virginia bore—both of them knew that the obstacles she faced were considerable.

The young nun tried to avoid looking at Virginia's eye until Virginia caught herself and quickly put her sunglasses back on. Sister Joyce hesitated, then glanced furtively over her shoulder, as though to ensure that no one was watching.

Reaching into her robes she took out a small rectangle of card and held it out to Virginia.

"Take it," she urged in a whisper.

Virginia took the card from Sister Joyce and studied it cautiously.

'E.J. Delfey & Son'

"It's a carpentry business," Sister Joyce said. "On the northern side of town. I know for a fact that they are in need of assistance with their bookkeeping. You can read and write and are good with numbers."

Virginia considered the card for a long moment, then deposited it into her jacket pocket.

She heaved a sigh and turned around to her suitcase and the violin case, picking them up in each hand then she faced Sister Joyce once more.

"Good luck," Sister Joyce offered sadly.

Virginia simply nodded.

The rain hadn't eased but Virginia no longer cared. She stepped out into the weather, armed with everything she owned and crossed the gardens to the gate.

Sister Joyce watched her go, feeling a sadness settle in her heart. She would pray for Virginia, as she did for all the children who came and went from this place. But the seeds of doubt for the welfare of Virginia

Crammond were undeniable. She could only hope that her prayers were answered in some small way.

Turning toward the entrance of the orphanage, Sister Joyce climbed the steps. She looked back one final time to see Virginia's small form disappear into the mist of the rain until she was gone from view.

CHAPTER 24

R AIN FELL OUTSIDE, PATTERING SOFTLY ON THE roof of the granny flat—
a soothing sound that brought Virginia comfort. Closing her eyes, she
listened, smiling inwardly at the subtle music the rain made.

The rain sounds so different here…

Closing and locking the sliding door, Virginia peered out through the
curtain one last time then drew it over. A distant siren wailed and she
chuckled bitterly under her breath. It seemed as though there were always
sirens here.

In the solitude of her little flat, Virginia shuffled slowly through to her
bedroom and gingerly sat down on the edge of her bed, placing her hands
on her knees.

In the soft glow from her bedside lamp, her eye glistened with the
moistness of tears. She held onto them though, refusing to let them go as
the weight of grief threatened to bear down. She felt a weariness unlike
anything she had ever felt before—the energy she had expended in breaking up the terrible confrontation between her son and Asher had sapped
her of her strength. A maelstrom of thought rushed through her mind
and with it, strong emotions that fed into her despair; the dysfunction of
her family, the violence of her son, her struggle to protect the children to
ensure they were safe.

So much violence. So much damage. Virginia carried the guilt of it all.
She herself had failed just as much as her late husband and her son. She
was so tired of it. She shook her head in a vain effort to rid herself of
the guilt.

An old and familiar pain throbbed at the back of her ruined eye and she
lifted her hand, resting the pads of her finger tips against her left brow,
cupping her hand like a shield over that side of her face. The warmth
from her hand soothed the ache for a moment and she sighed, allowing
the tension in her shoulders to release.

Looking up and letting her good eye drift across the room, Virginia
noticed the violin case sitting on her dresser. She regarded it with a curi-

ous frown.

"What are you doing there?" she asked audibly of the case.

Forgetting her eye, Virginia dropped her hand and gazed at the case. Recalling the events from earlier, she remembered picking the case up off the ground after everyone had cleared the back yard.

Slowly, she rose to her feet and shuffled across to the dresser, picking it up and returning to the bed with it.

Virginia's mind was flooded with a procession of new images; memories from another time and place.

Rolling bald hills stretching away to a distant horizon. A parlour room, filled with sumptuous furniture, warm timbers. A woman's hands—fine and delicate, gently placing her own small fingers onto the bridge of a violin. The woman's smile—warm and comforting and full of encouragement.

They visited Virginia from time to time but she usually pushed them away before they could linger and churn her emotions. This time however, Virginia allowed them to stay and push the trauma of the evening here and now away.

Resting it in her lap, Virginia slowly ran her hands over the leather case and smiled, feeling the rough surface with its many scratches, ripples and indentations that had accumulated over the years. She felt the tarnished locks, neglected but still functional. The stitching in the seams on the edges, frayed and hanging in places, had allowed the leather veneer to lift and separate.

Old and tired, Virginia mused to herself with a wan smile.

Virginia felt a long forgotten pull toward it, which startled her and she prepared to return the case to her dresser.

Virginia took a step forward, but she hesitated and she sat herself down. Turning the case around to face her, she frowned as one would frown at a recalcitrant child.

Still it beckoned to her.

Virginia pressed her thumbs to each of the mechanisms and released the latches with a satisfying snap.

Gently, she opened the case to reveal the violin inside—still intact, despite the reprehensible actions of her son, earlier.

The instrument, as always, was pristine. She had taught her granddaughter well in the care and handling of such a violin. There was a shine to the surface that almost reflected Virginia's features and she smiled.

She lifted the violin out along with the bow and set the case to one side.

Virginia instinctively began leaning her head from side to side, loosening the muscles in her neck. Holding the violin by the neck in her right hand, she flexed her arthritic fingers around it, managing to execute a progression of silent fingerings, then drew the violin up. She nodded to herself, almost surprised by the familiar feel of the violin under her chin.

She lifted the bow and extended and retracted her forearm a few times, loosening her limb as best she could.

Virginia closed her eyes and began to breathe. She focused on the sound of her breathing, excluding everything else. Then she lowered the bow onto the bridge of the violin and drew out a long note.

It was a ballad called *Prayer for the Children*, a hymn that Virginia's late husband introduced to her many years ago, when she had briefly flirted with taking up the instrument again.

Her husband.

Her dear companion who had salvaged so much of her life and dignity after leaving the orphanage. They'd met after she had gained employment in his father's cabinet-making business. Despite his best efforts, Virginia's fragile mental health would not permit her to return to the instrument she had once loved so much. But the hymn had remained with her, throughout her life—right up until Anders Delfey's death. Aggy had sung it in tribute to him at his funeral when she was still a young girl—before her descent into darkness.

The beginnings of a tune filled the flat with a soft refrain that was vital and pure, despite her advancing years and her tired fingers.

Can you hear the prayer of the children
on bended knee, in the shadow of an unknown room?
Empty eyes with no more tears to cry
turning heavenward toward the light.
Crying, "Jesus, help me
to see the morning light of one more day,
but if I should die before I wake,
I pray my soul to take."

The hymn often visited her, just before Virginia drifted off to sleep and it had become a sort of prayer of her own that she said for Jeremy, Asher, Ruby and Minty each night. Here and now, Virginia negotiated the tune with hands that shook ever so slightly as her fingers traversed the strings. Her concentration, her focus was finely attuned to the music and though the effort was supreme, Virginia did not falter.

Can you feel the hearts of the children
aching for home, for something of their very own.

Reaching hands with nothing to hold onto
but hope for a better day, a better day.
Crying, "Jesus, help me
to feel the love again in my own land,
but if unknown roads lead away from home,
give me loving arms, away from harm."

Tears trickled from her closed eye and though she wept, Virginia held her poise, maintaining her performance as she progressed toward the finale, refusing to allow the pall of grief to assail her.

Can you hear the voice of the children
softly pleading for silence in their shattered world?
Angry guns preach a gospel full of hate,
blood of the innocent on their hands.
Crying, "Jesus, help me
to feel the sun again upon my face?
For when darkness clears, I know you're near,
bringing peace again."

And then it ended. Virginia sat on the edge of the bed as the silence returned, holding the violin, breathing softly. Then, slowly, Virginia lowered it and the bow and held them in her hands.

Too moved to think. Too moved to act, Virginia just sat with her eyes closed and lingered.

CHAPTER 25

THE SCHOOL'S ATHLETICS FIELD WAS ABUZZ WITH students and teachers who had descended on it for the school athletics trials—a precursor to the annual event that was to be held in a week's time. Traditional field events were taking place inside the white lines of the running track, while qualifying races were being conducted for the track events. Presently, a group of boys from the younger year levels of the high school were being put through their paces as they competed for a spot in the intermediate 100 metre sprint events.

Students, teachers and parents lined the perimeter, a few feet back from the outside lane. The majority of them were watching in earnest, cheering and clapping, while other students mingled in groups a little way off, sitting on the grass and sunning themselves, chatting and laughing, happy to be out of the classroom for the day. They weren't so much focused on the events on the track as they were on the sun which shone brightly above them. It was a perfect day.

Jeremy, Wayne and a group of boys were roughhousing with each other further back still, content to be kicking a football back and forth. The senior events weren't scheduled until much later and, aside from Jeremy and a couple of the other boys, the majority of the group weren't participating at all. None of them were particularly interested in participating—neither in the events themselves nor mixing with the larger student body—that much was clear. Despite repeated efforts by several teachers—including Miss Glasson—to get them to join in with the rest of the school, the boys had thus far resisted and the teachers eventually relented, reasoning that, so long as they weren't causing trouble, their recreation could be tolerated.

Mr. Baxter was patrolling the perimeter of the track, armed with a clipboard and a whistle, supervising the heats. Occasionally, he would throw a malevolent glare in the boys' direction—clearly unimpressed with their lack of consideration—but they dismissed him with smart-alec pejoratives that he couldn't hear.

Jeremy, despite being outwardly dismissive of the athletics trials, was secretly looking forward to the senior 400 metre event in which he was entered. Occasionally, he would take a break from the others to watch the trials before being pulled back into the group. The others invariably engaged in rough play whilst kicking the football and Jeremy did his best to avoid getting into the middle so that he didn't injure himself. Consequently, the other boys gave him a hard time, laughing at him in a manner that was mostly insincere.

Everything he'd endured since his father and Asher's violent outburst had weighed heavily on him. The diversion of the athletics trials, strangely, proved welcome in taking his mind off of his circumstance.

That was until he heard a rumble of a familiar car's engine behind him. Jeremy turned and scanned the boundary of the school's sports field, until his eyes locked onto the familiar burgundy coupe that had pulled up into a vacant parking space and idled for a moment before its driver killed the engine.

Jeremy felt his stomach plunge.

He had continued to ignore Mickey's frequent text messages that hit his phone relentlessly at all hours. He'd tried to keep his association with the gang secret from his school mates.

What the hell are they doing here? his mind screamed.

In the coupe itself, Gavin and Mickey merely sat back in their seats and watched the group of boys in silence as they continued to kick the football.

Jeremy continued to study the vehicle discreetly. The occupants made no move to exit which probably meant that they were just going to watch.

Eventually, Jeremy decided that he'd had enough with the boys and he left them to wander over to the track where he sat down on the grass and fished through his school bag for his lunch box.

"You've had enough of being paid out, huh?"

Jeremy turned where he sat to see Wayne sauntering towards him.

"They're being a bunch of dick-heads," Jeremy mumbled nervously through a mouthful of sandwich.

Wayne sat down beside him and scanned the sports field, shielding his eyes from the sun.

"Maybe you're the dick-head," Wayne sneered, digging Jeremy in the ribs causing him to flinch and slap Wayne's hand away.

"The guys reckon you're gonna go into Miss Glasson's retard class. They'll be calling you worse than dick-head then."

Jeremy flashed Wayne an angry glower and turned away from him.

"That's none of their business…" he hissed. "…Or yours, arse-hole, so shut your mouth."

Wayne held up his hands mock defensively then and clucked noisily.

"Hey—I'm on your side mate. If that's what you feel you need to do to get by. There's no shame in admitting you have a problem."

This time, Jeremy balled his injured hand into a fist and shook it warningly at Wayne.

"You're really pushing it."

Wayne chuckled softly and nudged Jeremy again, less aggressively this time. When he spoke, his tone became uncharacteristically sincere.

"I'm just messing with ya. Look, I'd rather be in a class with Miss Glasson than Baxter any day. He's nothing but an up-himself prick. Has anything more happened since he kicked you out of class?"

Jeremy shook his head and tossed the remaining portion of his sandwich aside.

"Nope. I think Miss Glasson might have said something to get me off the hook. She's a pain in the arse sometimes but…she's a bit of alright."

Both boys paused as the crack of a starter's pistol sounded nearby and another group of sprinters—girls this time—broke away from the blocks.

Wayne nodded slowly as the boys followed the girls with their eyes as the girls sprinted away.

"Well, I think you should do it. Miss Glasson is pretty good and she tries real hard. I reckon it's an awesome class to be in."

Jeremy turned toward Wayne then and studied him curiously.

"*What?*" Wayne retorted with dramatic indignity. "You think I got to be a smart arse on my own? Shit mate, if I hadn't done time in her class last year, I would have been in a much worse position than you are now. It's not only you shady bastards that need a leg up."

Jeremy smiled wanly for the first time and regarded Wayne with a nod that suggested a sort of respect.

"So…" Wayne began, pointing limply at the dressing on Jeremy's injured hand. "Anyone called you out on that yet?"

Jeremy's smile instantly faded and he pulled his hand down out of view.

"No. Why?"

Again, Wayne held his hands up in front of him.

"Hey, I was just aski…"

"Yeah…well don't ask," Jeremy hissed. "And don't be going and mouthing off to anyone about what you think you might know. Because you don't know anything—alright?"

An uncomfortable tension settled between them and Wayne feared that Jeremy might actually lash out at him. He began to offer Jeremy an apology when, without warning, the group of boys recklessly crashed into both of them from behind, pinning Jeremy and Wayne to the ground underneath a scrum.

Jeremy's head was slammed into the earth so hard that he saw stars and a wave of nausea fountained up inside him. He cried out in pain. His anger at Wayne forgotten, it had instead blossomed into a fury at the callous act by the group, but he couldn't move underneath the writhing mass.

Struggling to free himself, Jeremy flailed with one free hand, trying to gain some purchase on one of the individuals on top of him in order to push them away. As soon as the bodies fell away from him, Jeremy's entire body spasmed and he sprang to his feet like a crazed animal, spitting and swinging his arms. A knifing pain between his temples continued to fuel his anger.

Jeremy singled out the ring leader, a tall and muscular teen named Chad who was laughing sarcastically as the boys began picking themselves up off the ground. Chad had been needling Jeremy all morning and leading the others in doing so.

Jeremy launched at him with his arm outstretched and caught him directly across his wind pipe. Chad's eyes bulged out of his head as he felt the air being sucked from his lungs. He crashed to the ground, hitting his head in a similar fashion as Jeremy had before. As the stars began swirling before the boy's eyes, Jeremy scrambled to his feet and prepared to pounce. At the last moment however, Jeremy was grabbed by Wayne and another boy who dragged him backward in attempt to calm him down.

"Man, we was just mucking 'round. It's alright, man!" the other boy pleaded frantically as the others assisted Chad up off the grass.

Jeremy struggled, trying to tear himself from them. He let out a guttural scream as he broke an arm free and swung around, slamming the fist of his injured hand into the cheek of the boy and sending him reeling. Wayne let go and backed away as quickly as he could to avoid getting struck himself.

As Jeremy prepared to hone in on Chad once more, a hand slapped down hard on his shoulder and spun Jeremy like a top. Jeremy looked up into the eyes of Mr. Baxter.

"What the bloody hell is going on here!" Baxter bellowed furiously.

Jeremy was too stunned and breathless to speak.

"S...sir," Wayne began desperately. "Jeremy wasn't doi..."

"I don't wanna hear from you, Robinson!" Baxter barked savagely, his hand still clasped like a vice on Jeremy's shoulder. "I was talking to Delfey here."

Baxter shoved Jeremy like a rag doll and stepped toward him. The crowd of students, teachers and parents in their immediate vicinity went silent as they turned their attention toward the evolving confrontation. One of those present was Miss Glasson.

Over by the fence of the sports field, Gavin sat forward in his seat and peered through the windshield at the sudden turn of events. He reached out and nudged Mickey, who was dozing beside him. Mickey sat bolt upright and blinked the sleep away as Gavin silently pointed out at the sport field.

"You've been screwing around all morning out here," Baxter continued. "…And now you're causing fights, disrupting everyone else's enjoyment through your own selfishness!"

Jeremy stumbled where he stood, shaking his head breathlessly and trying to respond. But the dizziness and the pain in his head prevented him from doing so. The other boys around him were backing away, all of them sensing that things were about to get nasty.

"Sir…" Wayne interjected again, more forcefully this time. He stepped towards Baxter and Jeremy. "Jeremy wasn't doing anything wrong. He wa—"

Without warning, Baxter lunged toward Wayne and pushed him, causing him to lose his balance and fall to the ground. Jeremy flinched in shock, as did the others.

"I told you to shut up, you little black bastard!" Baxter yelled satanically. A collective gasp rippled through those watching nearby, including Miss Glasson who stepped forward and grabbed onto Baxter's wrist.

"What the hell do you think you're doing, Stephen?!" she whispered angrily, trying to get herself in between Jeremy and Baxter.

"Butt out of this, Louisa," Baxter hissed in reply, pulling his hand away. He pushed past her and strode up to Jeremy.

Stunned, Miss Glasson turned around angrily.

"Stephen! If you do this, I'll have no choice but to report it," she implored.

Baxter paused momentarily, but didn't look back at her.

"You've already crossed the line," she added, hoping to stop him.

Baxter simply shook his head and glared at Jeremy.

"I've had enough of your bullshit, Delfey," he seethed, grabbing Jeremy's shirt front and holding it tight. "You are a constant disruption to this school and you have no future here. I'm going to make sure of that."

Jeremy's face went rigid. The fear in his expression was suddenly replaced by anger and he steeled himself where he stood.

"I didn't do anything wrong!" he shouted suddenly. He lunged forward and shoved his elbow into Baxter's stomach as hard as he could, causing Baxter to double over and clutch at his abdomen. He staggered back, tearing Jeremy's T-shirt in the process.

Jeremy stood before his teacher, stunned. His heart was racing. He stared in disbelief then looked at everyone around him, all of whom were staring back at him. Miss Glasson stepped forward, her arm outstretched, her expression sympathetic, pleading.

Jeremy stepped back, hesitated, then turned and ran. Tears began streaming from his eyes as his emotions overtook him.

"Jeremy!" Miss Glasson called after him.

Jeremy made it to the perimeter of the ground and leaped over the railing, catching himself on a loose piece of wire which caused him to fall in a heap on the other side. Ignoring the pain, Jeremy got to his feet, spun around and found himself face to face with a compact BMW sports car.

Mr. Baxter's BMW sports car.

His anger surged once more. He shot a glance behind him to see Baxter striding toward him from the track, yelling and shaking his fist in the air.

Jeremy turned towards the coupe where he saw both Gavin and Mickey looking at him from inside. Their expressions were expectant—encouraging almost.

Jeremy didn't hesitate.

He struck out, kicking the front passenger side headlight as hard as he could, shattering the glass and crumpling a section of the bonnet immediately above it.

Then he stormed off out of the car park, out of the school, disappearing down the street.

Gavin and Mickey exchanged glances as they watched Jeremy disappear from view. As Mickey kept his attention on the sports car just three spaces across from them, Gavin's attention had turned toward the arrogant-looking teacher storming toward the fence, followed by a woman and a group of students.

As he tilted his head slightly to one side, a curious smile formed at the edge of his lips and his mind began to work over an idea that had seeded itself there.

CHAPTER 26

HE WAS VAGUELY AWARE OF THE DOOR to his hospital room opening, but he did not immediately register his awareness of her.

A mighty bandage covered one side of Rex's face, obscuring his right eye and cheek bone which, so he had been told, had been fractured as a result of the assault wrought upon him by his daughter. His nasal passages were filled with wadding and covered with additional plaster to hold it in place, making it nearly impossible to breath.

My own daughter has done this.

Even now, days later, Rex could hardly believe it.

Slowly, he blinked his good eye and winced at the sharp pain from his injured one. In his misery, he had a flash of irony that he probably looked just like his mother had when her own eye had been damaged. He focused on Belle momentarily as she shut the door behind her, then he turned away as she stood at a distance from his bed.

He could see in his peripheral vision that her expression was stony; her eyes, though glassy and red rimmed from lack of sleep, still bored into his like a drill with an intensity that was immediately unsettling.

In that instance, he turned his head further away from her, unable to meet her gaze.

When she spoke, Belle's voice was ice cold.

"Do you have any idea what you did the other night?" she began.

Rex just shook his head slowly, wearily, immediately wishing she would leave the room.

"You've nearly destroyed Asher—not to mention what you've done to Ruby. The girls—they won't eat, they can't sleep. Asher is wetting her bed – she's twelve years old for Christ's sake! Jeremy won't talk to me. I'm scared we've lost him."

Belle immediately plucked a tissue from her hand bag. She never thought that she would shed so many tears as she had over the past four days. The enormity of what she faced both here in the hospital room and at home was overwhelming. It was crushing her. She had spent hours—

days even—preparing for this confrontation with her husband. Now she was here, Belle could feel her resolve collapsing already.

"What do you expect me to do about it?" he rasped, before holding his hands out toward her.

"Nothing," Belle responded bitterly. "There is absolutely *bugger all* you can do about it, Rex. I just wanted you to know just how much *damage* you've caused. I wanted to make sure that you understand how you've crushed those children."

Belle paused, steeling herself to deliver the ultimatum she had built herself up to deliver.

"When they release you from here, don't you even think about coming home. Do you hear me? Do you understand me?"

Rex remained silent, brooding. The air in the room became thick with tension and Belle's emotions see-sawed between grief and fury the longer he said nothing.

"You've got nothing to say to me?" she interrogated incredulously.

Rex squeezed his good eye shut, feeling needles of pain pepper his injured eye once more as a result of his action.

"You've said your piece," Rex whispered shakily. "Now go away – leave me alone."

Without warning, Belle pounced at the bed and grabbed her husband's face in her hands, pulling his head roughly in her direction.

"I haven't *nearly* said my piece, you miserable bastard!" she growled with an intensity that caught him off guard. "Ever since Mum and Ruby came to live with us, you've been so angry and so destructive, wiping yourself out night after night and taking it out on all of us. Why do you do that, Rex? Why do you hate us all so much that you're willing to tear us all apart?"

For the first time, Belle saw something in her husband's face that she hadn't seen in a very long time—if, in fact, she had ever seen it.

It was fear.

"What is it, Rex?" she pressed, harder this time, subconsciously capitalising on his faltering demeanour. "*Tell me.* I know you're keeping something from me and I want to know what it is. What's this hatred that drives you? Is it me? Is it the children? Is it your mum?"

His cheeks flushed then and his lip began to quiver.

"I-I don't hate you," he stammered impotently, retreating into his pillow as much as her grip would allow.

"Who do you hate then—and why!?" Belle yelled grabbing the neck of his T-shirt in her hands, her knuckles turning white. "Is it Ruby!? Damn you, Rex. Tell me!"

Rex began to shake and, without warning, he let out an anguished cry that caused Belle to stagger back in shock.

Rex dropped his head and his arms fell to his sides as he began to cry and sob uncontrollably.

Collecting herself, Belle stared across at her husband, caught completely by surprise.

"Stop!" he pleaded, choking back tears that fell over his uninjured cheek and stained red the bandage covering his right eye.

"Every time I see that child…in our house…" Rex managed through choking sobs. "All I can s-see…is her—all I can see is Aggy!"

The name of Rex's dead sister stung Belle in much the same way that she guessed it had struck her mother in law. In that terrible moment, Belle realised she hadn't heard Rex speak her name since Ruby was born.

Putting a hand up to his bandages, Rex held his head in a vain effort to splint his head against the pain but also, to hold himself up against the onslaught of his grief.

"I c-can't stop it!" he wept openly. "I can't stop the memories, Belle—of finding Aggy in that alley—after all those weeks of searching. She was—*bleeding from everywhere*. All those holes in her—all over her and…"

Rex gasped. His eyes went wide and he felt bile collect in the back of his throat as long dormant memories assaulted him all at once—memories he had blocked for so long from all those long years of drinking, of trying to forget.

Waves of nausea washed over him so powerful, he vomited into his lap.

"…and the b-baby!" he cried, kicking the soiled bed covers as far away from him as he could manage.

Belle stared stonily at her husband but inside, she felt her heart drop and shatter as though it were made of glass.

Dormant memories that, like Rex, she had buried deep down were now bubbling towards the surface and she had no way of shielding herself from them.

She had loved Rex's dear sister from the moment they had met but from that very first meeting, Belle knew that she was deeply troubled.

Aggy Delfey had struggled in her relationship with her mother. Virginia's mental illness in the years after leaving the orphanage took its toll on their family and, while her husband and son were able to cope with the years of mental pain and suffering Virginia endured, Aggy railed against it.

She railed against her mother; as a result, their relationship had fractured.

With their focus upon Virginia's internal emotional battle, both Rex and his father failed to notice Aggy drifting further and further away from them.

Rebelling against her family, Aggy had fallen into a netherworld of drugs and prostitution, going missing for days at a time before being brought home either by friends or the police.

And then, one day she didn't come home. Night after night, Rex had walked the streets of the city, searching for his sister. He'd watched Aggy Delfey's downward spiral for months as she became entrapped in this world, forsaking herself from everything she knew to a posse of low-lives and scum, until it was too late.

Aggy Delfey's final destruction came at the hands of the man who had raped her; the man with whom she had unwittingly conceived a child—a child that no one, not even she, knew of.

The man was a 'regular' of Aggy's, a dealer who had ensnared her in the world to which she had surrendered.

Her addiction ensured that he could use her for sex whenever he wanted while he could drip feed her a tantalizing but fractured supply of drugs. He raped her repeatedly and without conscience and Aggy endured it for fear that he would cut off her access to the drugs.

As time wore on, Aggy began to protest the violence she endured at his hand.

It culminated in a drug-fuelled argument in a city nightclub that had spilled out into the street and into the nearby alleyway. As the blade of the flick knife stabbed into her body over and over again, it triggered the premature labour of the child she unknowingly carried.

Had he been just a few moments earlier, Rex might have prevented the disaster that had befallen his sister.

"She didn't even know," Rex sobbed, holding up his arms in a parody of cradling a baby. "I scooped that kid up off that filthy pavement and held it up to her so she could see…and s-she didn't even know!"

His eye drifted to a spot on the wall in front of his bed and glazed over, his memories becoming lost in a maelstrom.

Belle was stunned, her jaw slack. Horror flooded through her as she struggled to process the words her husband had spoken—things he had never spoken of until this very moment.

She was unable to speak. She didn't know what to say. There was nothing she could say.

Her own memories of that night flashed before her.

She had arrived at the hospital to find her husband sitting alone in the waiting area of the Emergency Department, holding his head in his blood-stained hands, rocking back and forth.

As she sat down beside him and put her arm around his shoulders, he shook uncontrollably, unable to look up at her. Through his grief-stricken sobs, the only words he was able to utter were, "She's gone… It's over there…"

Belle looked to an area of the Emergency Room where several people were gathered around a small, wheeled cart, frantically attending to a tiny infant. So tiny, it wasn't even crying…

Belle snapped herself back to the present and immediately felt the walls of the hospital room begin to close in on her. Her heartbeat began to quicken, her breathing became shallow. A sense of claustrophobia overwhelmed her. She glanced at her sobbing, pathetic husband in his hospital bed.

Belle backed away toward the door and exited hurriedly, almost crashing into a nurse who had come to see what all the commotion was about.

Before she could allow herself to collapse, Belle turned and ran away down the hall.

RUBY SAT HUDDLED on her bed, staring at the violin case that lay just beyond her feet.

It had been days since she'd opened it. She couldn't bring herself to. To do so would be to invite all those terrible memories of her uncle's appalling behaviour to visit her and she couldn't bear the thought of reliving them again.

Her grandmother had set the violin at the end of her bed in the hope Ruby might pick it up and begin playing but not even that could cajole her from her trauma. The last thing Ruby could think of was music. All she could see and feel was pain, the broken pieces of their lives.

She hadn't seen Khalili in over a week. In the immediate aftermath of Asher's explosion, Ruby had taken the train into the city on her own and she'd approached Elder Hall from across the lawn. But something snapped inside of her. It was as if all the music she had learned and performed had suddenly left her. Her music was gone and she had panicked. She turned and ran away, even ignoring Sir Walter Hughes' statue.

She hadn't gone back.

Ruby was aware that Khalili had phoned the house and spoken to Virginia in the days following. Virginia had covered for Ruby by saying she was too sick to rehearse. He'd apparently accepted this explanation on the first occasion and the next—and the next. But as time wore on Ruby knew that both Khalili and her grandmother were growing increasingly concerned. The Malley-Joyce recital was fast approaching and Ruby was unprepared.

She knew she could only use the illness as a cover for so long.

But she wasn't sure if she even cared any more.

Ruby had watched Asher withdraw further and further. She stayed in her bed, refusing to eat or drink, shower or even toilet herself. As much as Virginia and Belle tried to coax her back to some semblance of activity, Asher stayed mute and her apparent catatonia was beginning to take its toll on all of them.

Jeremy had begun to disappear after school for hours at a time, coming home long after dark while everyone else was asleep. He too had withdrawn, had broken his promises to Ruby yet again. Ruby knew those boys who were taking him over.

Again, she wasn't sure if she cared.

About her music, about her future. She began to accept that, after all, she was destined to remain trapped in this fractured family forever.

KHALILI SAT AT his desk, gazing out through the window, lost in thought. Frustration gnawed at him and he felt powerless to do anything. His repeated telephone calls to Ruby's house had yielded little information to explain her sudden absence.

The recital was only two weeks away and there was still so much to do.

Hearing a knock, Khalili turned in his chair to see Lynch standing in the door way to his office.

Khalili gestured him in with a limp wave of his hand.

"Still no word?" Lynch ventured with an expression of sympathy.

Khalili threw his hands up in the air in exasperation and he shook his head.

"I haven't a clue," he responded. "Just like that, with no explanation, she stopped coming. Her grandmother says she is sick but…I fear something terrible has happened."

Lynch tilted his head slightly.

"Do you think that her grandmother might simply be telling the truth?"

Khalili shook his head.

"No. I could sense it in Mrs. Delfey's voice. She is covering for her.

Ruby is in trouble somehow. This is more than just an illness."

Khalili steepled his hands in front of his mouth and unconsciously began nibbling at his fingers.

"You could go out there," Lynch ventured helpfully.

"I don't know," Khalili sighed. "I am rarely a welcome sight at their home—as far as Ruby's aunt and uncle are concerned. They see me as a something of an intrusion—a troublemaker. I'm not welcome in their world."

Lynch reclined in his chair and crossed one leg over the other. Khalili noted with some annoyance his colleague's conspiratorial grin.

"When has that ever stopped you?"

BELLE WAS ASLEEP in her armchair in the living room when a loud knock at the door woke her abruptly. Minty, who sitting on the floor at her feet watching Sesame Street on TV, jumped at the sound and turned to his mother. She struggled to her feet, knocking over a beer glass in the process, before she made it to the front door. Cursing under her breath Belle unlatched the door and swung it open to find Khalili standing on the step. His face was filled with concern.

"Mrs. Delfey," he greeted nervously. "I am sorry to trouble you. Is Ruby or her grandmother at home? It's just...I am very concerned about her. It's been over a week and we haven't had any rehearsal."

Belle hung her head wearily and shook it slowly.

"Look...Mr. Khalili," she began, choosing her words. "Virginia and Ruby have appreciated everything you've tried to do but...Ruby isn't getting better very fast. I doubt she'll be able to be in this concert thing of yours."

Khalili huffed and puffed in barely concealed exasperation. He couldn't believe it had come to this.

"Mrs. Delfey, is there anything I can do? I just can't accept that Ruby is so unwe—"

"She's not well and that's that!" Belle cut him off angrily. "None of the children are. But it's our problem to deal with and nobody else's."

Belle opened the screen door and stepped out on the porch.

"Go back to your school, professor," she whispered in a tone that was mildly threatening. "Go back to your students and worry about things you *can* fix."

She waited a moment as Khalili desperately searched for the words to respond, then decided not to respond at all.

"You can't fix us, don't you understand? You never could."

She closed the door in his face without another word.

CHAPTER 27

GAVIN AND MICKEY APPROACHED JEREMY ON FOOT, having prudently decided to leave their car parked on the street, out of view of the school grounds.

They stood, watching Jeremy mingle with a group of his school friends on the quadrangle in front of the main building, until they caught his attention and he broke away from the group and jogged across the grass toward them. It had been several days since they'd witnessed Jeremy's act of vandalism on his teacher's expensive sports car.

When he came to within a few feet of them, Gavin and Mickey abruptly turned their backs to him and began walking.

"Come for a walk," Gavin instructed out of the corner of his mouth as they did so.

Jeremy blinked and shook his head subtly before falling into a brisk walk behind them.

Making sure they kept out of view of the school buildings, Gavin and Mickey made their way to the car park where most of the teaching staff's vehicles were parked. Once there, they began strolling leisurely in between each of the cars, as though they were customers checking out a car yard, peering in the windows of some of the vehicles, casually kicking the tyres of others.

Jeremy languished a few feet behind them, watching with a nervous expression.

Gavin came to Baxter's sleek BMW coupe. He stopped, then slowly rounded the car, running a gentle finger along the polished Duco, admiring it with a malevolent smile. He paused at the still damaged headlight, shaking his head but saying nothing.

Mickey, meanwhile, walked across to a nearby fence and leaned against it, hands in the pockets of his hoodie.

Jeremy shifted his glance between Mickey and Gavin, hesitantly joining Mickey on the fence until Gavin had completed his inspection of the BMW, then he sauntered across to the others, nodding subtly to Mickey.

Rubbing his bottom lip between thumb and fore finger, Gavin tilted his head slightly towards Jeremy.

"Baner has called in a favour," he began curtly, his eyes narrowing. "And we feel we're in a position to...*facilitate*. We also feel, that the time has come to test you. It's time for you to step up."

Mickey paused for a moment, allowing his words to sink in. Then he continued.

"Baner is looking for...*stock*...a particular kind of stock that will attract a high price on the secondary market and we reckon we've found just the right piece that will interest him."

Mickey nodded toward the BMW, then looked at Jeremy with an intense gaze.

Jeremy felt his mouth begin to dry. He felt his heartbeat quicken as the implications of what Mickey was saying struck home.

"He hates you..." Gavin stated unexpectedly. "Doesn't he?"

Jeremy turned toward Gavin, his expression registering mild surprise. It was one of the few times that Gavin had ever spoken to Jeremy. His heightened anxiety halted momentarily, distracted by Gavin's enigmatic presence.

"He ridicules you in front of the others, singles you out. I'll bet he takes the piss out of you in class all the time. Doesn't he, Jeremy?"

Gavin stepped forward in front of Jeremy, blocking his view of the BMW.

"He treats you like shit because he thinks you're nothing but a dumb fuck coon, doesn't he?"

The pejorative stung Jeremy, but he knew that Gavin was right. He was surprised that Gavin could know about all the humiliation Jeremy had endured at the hands of Mr. Baxter, even though he knew he shouldn't be. Gavin was right about a lot of things. The memory of being humiliated in class and on the sports field the other day returned to Jeremy's thoughts and he met them with anger that was fuelled by Gavin's prescient words.

"This is *your* chance for some payback. Your chance to take from him, what he's taken from you, over and over again."

Mickey turned to face Jeremy now.

"We want to hit that prick and take his car from him. If we do, we're going to be first in line for quite a handy payday—all of us."

Mickey allowed Jeremy to take in what he was saying, before he continued.

"You know him, know his habits and his movements. We want you to help plan this and carry it out. It'll be quick, painless, nobody will get hurt—except for Mr. Prickface's pride and his wallet—and you, Jeremy, will have earned your status as an equal."

Mickey gently punched Jeremy on the arm, the adrenaline surge returning once more, though this time, it was a surge accompanied by feelings of excitement, of anticipation, the promise of power.

A smile slowly broke across Jeremy's lips as he thought about the prospects. That was until Gavin stepped right up close to Jeremy and fixed him with a menacing glower that immediately wilted those positive feelings.

He remained there, unmoving, silent for several long moments, his presence alone causing Jeremy to crumble underneath it.

Jeremy tried to meet Gavin's eyes but he couldn't. Instead, they involuntarily darted in every direction but Gavin's.

"This is your chance, right? Your *one and only* chance," Gavin rumbled malevolently. "If you fuck this up…there *will* be consequences. Understand?"

Jeremy stood as still as he could, trying not to cower. He nodded quickly, anxiously, praying that Gavin would back away from him.

Eventually, and in a manner that was sudden, Gavin did stand back. He relaxed and the anger seemed to dissipate from him all at once. He even managed a smile.

"Now…what do we know about your friend Mr. Stephen Baxter?" he asked.

OVER BY THE main building, that looked out onto the lawned area flanking it and across to the car park, Miss Glasson sauntered leisurely on yard monitoring duties, chatting with a group of students whilst eating an apple. As she laughed along with them and surveyed the grounds, her gaze drifted across the lawns towards the car park where she noticed three individuals standing.

Though they were a considerable distance away, Miss Glasson identified Jeremy. The other two looked unfamiliar. Her first thought was that it probably wasn't unusual since this school had a considerably large student population. However, something in the way they were standing, occasionally looking across and pointing to one of the cars—Baxter's car—made her stop, lift her hand to shield her eyes and study them more intently.

An uncomfortable feeling settled in the pit of her stomach.

"HE WORKS OUT," Jeremy was saying, looking down at the ground. "All the time—at a gym on Main North Road. In fact, he's like, a part owner of it or something. He's always bragging about it. He's there at least four nights a week until late."

Mickey nodded, impressed.

"Good. We'll follow him then, for a couple of nights, see what he does, check him out a bit and then we'll make our move."

"I'll word Baner and his crew up," Gavin added. "Get them into position close by after we hit him so they can take delivery quickly."

"We should be in and out of there before the dick-head even knows what's happened to him."

Gavin and Mickey exchanged satisfied looks with one another, the cogs turning in both their minds. Jeremy examined them both, a worried furrow creasing his brow.

"We aren't…like…gonna hurt him. Are we?"

Both young men glared incredulously at Jeremy. He shifted awkwardly on the spot, his cheeks flushing crimson.

"You just make sure you're ready for this," Mickey retorted warningly. "We start tonight."

Jeremy immediately felt his stomach drop. He was supposed to be accompanying Ruby to her lesson tonight. He couldn't go back on his promise to her yet again.

"G-guys…I can't tonight," he stammered. "I've gotta be s-somewhere."

Gavin fixed him with that withering glower once again.

"Are you fucking serious?"

Before he could respond, both Gavin and Mickey abruptly turned and walked away from him, heading out through the access gate. Mickey turned in mid-step and pointed his finger at Jeremy.

"No excuses!"

"Jeremy!"

Jeremy stopped in the main hallway at the sound of Miss Glasson's voice and turned to see her coming toward him.

The cacophony of silent noise that were his conflicted thoughts abruptly stopped and, for just a moment, he was thankful.

She gently touched her hand to his arm, gesturing for him to walk with her.

"I wanted to catch you to see if you'd given any more thought to my program."

She kept her voice low, so as not to embarrass him in front of anyone who might pass by.

Jeremy rolled his eyes and side stepped, creating a couple of feet of distance between them.

"Oh *come on,* Jeremy," she responded in a pleading tone. "Don't hold out on me. You're breaking me here."

Jeremy wasn't quite sure what to say. As much as he liked Miss Glasson, she really was beginning to be a pain.

"Look Miss…" he began.

Suddenly, Miss Glasson steered him into an empty classroom and stood in front of him.

Her expression coalesced into a worried mask.

"Jeremy…is everything alright?" she ventured cautiously. "I saw you out in the car park."

Jeremy lifted his head up and away, trying not to meet her eyes. His heart began to thump again, though this time, it was out of fear.

"Miss…" he began.

"Was that this Gavin mate of yours?"

Jeremy's eyes immediately fell upon hers. He didn't know what to say.

Miss Glasson let her shoulders relax and met his gaze with empathy rather than anger—something that he did not expect.

"Look…Jeremy. I don't know what you're mixed up with but I want you to know this…" she paused, pointing her finger at his chest, over his heart. "You could be anything you want to be. No matter what it is you're struggling with, there are people in your corner, Jeremy. People who will be there for you and help you—in the *right* way."

Jeremy stayed silent and he bowed his head. Try as he might to ignore what she was saying, Jeremy couldn't stop her words from cutting through. And in the pit of his stomach, churning among all those other emotions he was feeling right then, a new knot had begun to tighten. It was conflict.

"Baxter's not worth it, Jeremy," Miss Glasson said softly, knowingly. "He's in enough *shit* already without anyone else adding to it."

How could she know? Jeremy thought anxiously.

His phone beeped in his pocket then and he took advantage of the distraction to break away from her.

"I've gotta go, miss."

With that, he was out the door before Miss Glasson had a chance to speak again.

The feeling of dread returned to her then as she leaned over the empty desk at the front of the classroom.

She knew in her bones that Jeremy was about to go down a path from which he wouldn't be able to turn back and she felt powerless.

"Shit," she hissed, pounding the desktop with her fist.

CHAPTER 28

R UBY SAT IN THE HOSPITAL CORRIDOR ON a seat outside Uncle Rex's room, waiting nervously.

She attracted the attention of various passersby—nurses, doctors, patients and visitors—most of them smiling at her as they passed or offering her a sympathetic 'hello.' She was small and meek sitting on the chair.

She didn't know why she was here. Virginia had received a call from the hospital which seemed quite urgent, so she'd asked Davo if he could drive both herself and Ruby to the hospital. Ruby tried to listen through the door, while she waited. There was some sort of conversation going on in there and it sounded a little heated, but she was unable to hear what they were saying.

Davo appeared from a nearby toilet and came up to sit beside Ruby.

"Everything alright, love?" he asked as cheerily as he could.

"I don't know," Ruby replied softly, shrugging her shoulders.

Davo could sense Ruby's fear and he did his best to make her feel at ease.

"Don't you want to see him?"

Ruby shook her head defiantly.

"I don't understand why he'd want to see me," she replied quietly. "Never took any sort of interest in me before now."

A myriad of reasons had gone through Ruby's mind on the drive over, but she could make sense of none of them. As fearful as she was of her uncle, a small part of her was intrigued but Ruby felt her nerve slipping and, by the time they'd arrived, she very nearly didn't get out of the car.

Checking a clock on the wall, Davo sighed.

"Shouldn't be much longer," he said. "Look, I'm right here if you need me, okay? Nothing bad'll happen while I'm around."

Ruby smiled wanly.

The door beside Ruby clicked open softly and her grandmother appeared.

Virginia appeared tired but calm. Ruby couldn't be sure what to make of what had transpired inside the room.

"Ruby," Virginia said softly. "Come on inside."

Ruby stiffened and almost shook her head.

Davo leaned toward Ruby and nudged her softly.

"Don't forget mate, I'm right here."

Ruby hesitated, glancing between Davo, her grandmother and the door of her uncle's room.

"Come," Virginia said softly, reassuringly.

Finally she stood and stepped softly inside her uncle's hospital room and saw him in his bed by the window, looking out.

Upon hearing her, Rex turned toward Ruby as she entered and she had to stifle a gasp. He bore multiple dressings over the right side of his face. His nose had sticking plaster taped over it and his right eye was closed over, swollen and bruised.

Underneath his dressings, his expression was difficult to discern. It was a combination of awkwardness, guilt, of shame even. His eyes didn't meet Ruby's, though he seemed to be trying to look at her.

For her part, Ruby stood well back from the bed, staying close to her grandmother. She felt anxious and afraid.

Slowly, Rex turned to his bedside cabinet and opened the drawer. He took out his wallet and set it on his lap, unfolding it and struggling with its contents. Ruby could see that the index and middle finger of his left hand were taped together, which made small movements difficult.

Succeeding finally, Rex took out the small rectangle of a photograph from inside, held it up for a moment to look at it, then proffered it to Ruby in his outstretched hand.

Gingerly, Ruby approached the bed and took the photograph from her uncle.

She knew right away what it was.

The young woman in the photograph looked up at Ruby though eyes that were similar to Ruby's own. Her face too was familiar, and not just because Ruby had seen this image before, in the bathroom at home. Ruby sensed that she knew this woman.

"She liked music."

When Rex spoke, his voice was ragged. But there was something about it that struck her. There was no anger or hate in it.

"…Liked to sing—*loved* it actually. She was always happiest when she was singing."

Rex looked across at her grandmother, who had removed her dark sunglasses and was watching Ruby, her hand on her shoulder. Ruby's eyes remained fixed upon the photograph as her uncle continued.

"That's one of the things I miss the most about her, her singing voice."

Ruby listened to her uncle, unsure of what to say. She had never seen him like this. So calm. So softly spoken.

Rex looked down at his hands and nodded slowly. Then he looked at Ruby directly and for the first time, she returned his gaze.

"She…would have loved you…your mother," he said solemnly. "I know she would have been proud, seeing you now."

He nodded, more to himself than to Ruby, seemingly becoming lost in a tableaux of memories.

Then, all at once, Rex's shoulders slackened, his expression faded and he lay his head back on the pillow, turning his face away toward the window.

Ruby was unsure of what or how to feel. The little piece of her past she now held in her hand was undoubtedly a gift—something that she had never experienced before from him. A unprecedented kindness. But the moment was too much for Ruby to process. She gave the photograph to Virginia who placed it into her handbag.

Taking her cue, Virginia gently patted Ruby's shoulder and she replaced her glasses over her eyes.

"C'mon Ruby," she said softly. "We should go."

Together they turned and slipped quietly out of the hospital room.

As they exited the hospital and slowly made their way across to Davo's waiting car, Ruby looked up at Virginia.

"He blames himself," she said. "Doesn't he, Nana…for what happened."

Virginia squeezed her granddaughter's hand gently. She knew that Ruby was referring to her mother.

"He does," Virginia answered. "He's spent a lot of years punishing himself. But, in truth, he did as much as anyone could do in trying to save her."

Ruby looked down, feeling a pressure between her temples.

"It doesn't excuse his behaviour now though," Virginia added, hardening her voice slightly. "Your uncle has to make some very tough decisions about his future if he wants to salvage anything out of this."

Virginia stopped before the car and turned to face Ruby, putting her hands gently on Ruby's shoulders.

"Earning yours and the others' forgiveness is what he needs to do first.

You children deserve no less from him. Don't ever forget that."

Ruby nodded slowly. She looked back at the hospital and felt a confusing onslaught of emotions.

Things made even less sense to her now than ever.

RUBY LAY IN the darkness of her bedroom, her eyes trained upward, watching as a light source somewhere outside her window cast strange shadows on the ceiling above her. Her drifting mind twisted those shadows into imaginary creatures that danced and frolicked to random songs she played over and over in her head until the game became tiring and she gave it up.

Turning to the clock on her bedside table, Ruby craned her neck to see the time.

It was ten PM.

Ruby sighed. Unable to get to sleep, she had tossed and turned restlessly, growing more and more angry with herself the harder she tried to quiet herself.

But Ruby's thoughts tormented her. They kept coming back to her music and Khalili, to the guilt she felt over having abandoned him. Every time she'd tried to pick up her violin, Ruby was sucked back in time to her awful confrontation with Uncle Rex. It made her feel physically sick. And now, with his gesture toward her earlier, her uncle had only succeeded in confusing her more about her place in this family and the truth about her parentage.

Reaching across to the bedside table, Ruby picked up the photograph of her mother and held it up in the half light.

She was a stranger, a person who Ruby had never known beyond the feelings she used to associate with her. While they never mentioned her name, the stories they told of her were fanciful lies, created to protect Ruby, but she was unsure whether they had been more harmful than helpful. Ruby had known some semblance of the truth for longer than anyone actually knew. She'd just gone along with the lies—mainly to protect herself.

Placing the photograph down Ruby tried to steer her thoughts away from it.

She'd heard Aunty Belle head Khalili off at the door earlier that afternoon when he had arrived to see if she was okay. Listening from the doorway of her bedroom, Ruby wished she had run to the front door and seen him herself, but Aunty Belle had made it clear to him that he wasn't welcome and he'd left before she took the chance.

Ruby turned over and looked across at Asher who was sound asleep in her own bed.

Asher still hadn't said anything since that terrible night and it was clear she was getting worse. Aunty Belle had begun to give her sleeping pills to combat the nightmares that woke her in the middle of the night and had her screaming and scratching at her face with such force that it drew blood. Aunty Belle and Nana were at a loss as to what to do about Asher and there was a very real fear now that she might need to be hospitalised.

Jeremy still hadn't come home. It was going on three full days and he was nowhere to be found. Aunty Belle had tried to reach him on his mobile phone, only to discover that he hadn't even taken his phone with him. It was lying on the bedside table in his room.

Ruby felt as though her world were crumbling and that nothing would ever be the same again. The weight of sadness crushed down on her and she turned over and began to cry softly into her pillow.

"Ruby."

Ruby's sobs caught in the back of her throat at the sound of Asher's voice and, as she rolled over, Ruby jumped.

Asher was standing at the side of her bed.

Her eyes went wide and, quickly wiping away her tears, Ruby quickly threw back the blanket to allow Asher to climb into the bed with her.

Flicking her bedside lamp on, Ruby looked into Asher's dishevelled features and saw, for the first time in days, a semblance of life having returned to her sunken eyes.

"Asher?" Ruby gasped, not quite believing that her cousin was here beside her of her own volition.

Asher hugged Ruby close and nodded.

"What's happening?" she asked with a curious frown, rubbing her eyes. "I feel so tired."

"You've been...*away*," Ruby replied awkwardly. "Sort of asleep...but not really asleep."

"Oh," Asher replied softly. "Why were you crying?"

Ruby shook her head and shrugged her shoulders.

"Everything is a huge mess. Uncle Rex is still in the hospital. He's pretty banged up...and Jeremy's gone missing. No one's heard from him in days."

Asher sat up straighter in the bed and Ruby slipped her pillow across a little so that she could rest back on it.

"Days," Asher echoed with a hint of alarm. "W-what about your rehearsals? He's supposed to be taking you to the city."

"I'm not going any more," Ruby replied downcast.

Asher gasped.

"Not going!? Why not?"

"I-I can't," Ruby stammered. "You've been sick. Uncle Rex hasn't come home. Aunty Belle and Nana have been worried sick about Jeremy and everything. The last thing anyone is thinking about is my bloody violin."

"But th-the recital," Asher's voice quivered worriedly. "How far away is it?"

"I'm not doing the recital any more," Ruby said, looking away from Asher. "I can't—not when things are so bad."

Asher shifted her body toward Ruby and put her hand on Ruby's shoulder.

"But you *have* to do the recital," Asher protested forcefully. "You can't let it all go to nothing. Not after all the effort you've put in."

Ruby blinked, overwhelmed by her cousin's sudden passion after having been so debilitated by her catatonia.

"B-but…what about you?"

"*What about me?* I'll be okay—I am okay. You're this family's hope, Ruby. You're the one who can show everybody that we're worth something. No matter what—you have to do it!"

Ruby sank back into the pillow.

"What if I can't? Your mum scared Mr. Khalili away. He's probably given up on me."

"I don't believe that," Asher retorted gently. "And I don't think you believe that either."

The girls were interrupted at that moment when the bedroom door clicked open and Minty poked his head in through the gap.

Asher and Ruby glanced over as he crept inside and stood before them, grasping his teddy bear by the leg and biting nervously on the finger of his free hand.

"Can't sleep," he squeaked under his breath. "*Jem* isn't here."

Ruby's churning stomach intensified at the mention of Jeremy's name and her mind swirled with fresh worry for him.

Asher coaxed Minty over and he darted straight for her, clambering up onto the bed and snuggling down in between the girls.

Minty looked up at Asher and smiled wanly.

"Are you awake now?"

Asher smiled wearily and nodded at her baby brother.

"Yeah Minty, I'm awake now."

CHAPTER 29

JEREMY PACED BACK AND FORTH IN THE car park of the football ground, his breath visible under the spotlights that bathed a bright light across the oval, even though he himself was cast in shadow. He was dressed entirely in black, just as Mickey had instructed. Black hoodie, black jeans and black sneakers. Jeremy felt that he stood out like a sore thumb and though there was no one who could see him from this distance, he feared being discovered eventually.

He checked his watch. Acid fountained in the back of his throat.

He had told himself over and over that he was ready. He had gone over the scenario in his mind, remembering the reconnaissance they'd conducted. They had watched Baxter. They had tracked his movements from the gym, to a twenty-four hour grocery store that he frequented every Thursday night on his way home and finally to Baxter's home itself—a smart, suburban town house in a fashionable estate. He was nothing if not a creature of habit. Predictable and thus foolish.

Gavin, Mickey, Spider, Jabba and Jeremy discussed their plan at length. They decided upon using an armed hold-up on the grocery store itself as a cover. They would take Baxter's keys and steal his precious BMW. Jeremy as part of his test would accompany Spider and execute the hold up. Gavin and Jabba would stand by in the Monaro and Mickey would be the one to drive the BMW. Members of Baner's gang would be positioned in an industrial estate near the deli and ready to take possession of the car. The hit would be fast, casualty-free and remunerative.

The BMW's value was considerable—so Jeremy understood—and the financial reward they were set to receive was lucrative.

It all sounded so simple. Hit and fade quickly.

So why did Jeremy feel so sick?

This was the moment he had been waiting for—the chance to prove himself by being the one to take the leading role in a job. All these long months of waiting were about to be rewarded…

…But other thoughts intruded on these ones.

Thoughts of his fractured family taunted Jeremy from the edges, knocking him off balance and feeding his conflict.

There were images of Ruby, betrayed yet again by his broken promise, especially now that she was on the cusp of participating in something that could shape her future.

He was tormented by images of Asher. Dear, sweet Asher who, of all of them, had suffered the most because of their father and had been broken because of him. She too had depended on Jeremy to protect her from their father so many times.

And his brother Minty—too young yet to understand the violence he routinely witnessed all around him. His fragile innocence could only withstand so much of the hurt before he also fell victim to it and became as damaged as he and Asher were.

All of these images and feelings and thoughts swirled around in Jeremy's mind forming a vortex that clashed with his desire to ascend in Gavin's gang.

And then...

The familiar rumble of the engine. The headlights that stabbed through the darkness of the car park. The familiar shape of the muscle car.

Gavin's Monaro rolled up to where Jeremy was standing, stopping mere inches from him.

Jeremy squinted in the headlights, unable to detect any movement from inside. As he rounded to the passenger side, the door snapped open and Mickey stepped out, greeting Jeremy with a blank stare. Jeremy stepped forward. Mickey handed him a black woollen ski mask then shifted the passenger seat forward.

Jeremy entered the car and settled in beside Jabba who, as usual, scowled at him disgustedly. They were all similarly attired in black clothing. The air in the Monaro was thick with tension. No one acknowledged him as Gavin gunned the engine and drove out onto the street. Before long they were motoring down the highway toward the gymnasium, toward Baxter, toward Jeremy's fate—whatever that was.

Jabba handed Jeremy a bulky object wrapped in black cloth. A shiver of electricity passed through him, immediately sensing what it was. His stomach plunged as his hands clasped the cold metal of the handgun and as he unwrapped the cloth, he gulped at the semi automatic berretta.

Jabba abruptly slapped his arm down and snarled at him.

"Don't point that thing at me, idiot! Jesus Christ."

Gavin craned his neck around, momentarily taking his eyes off the road to glower maniacally at Jeremy.

Jeremy's mouth went dry.

"Y-you never said anything about guns," he croaked.

Both Jabba, Gavin and Spider, who had leaned forward from his position beside Jabba and in doing so revealed the barrel of a sawn off shotgun, blinked at Jeremy incredulously.

"What'd you think we were gonna hold up the all nighter with? Fucking tooth brushes?" Jabba spat harshly, slapping Jeremy in the side of his head with his elbow hard enough that Jeremy saw stars.

Jabba shook his head.

"Gav—this turd isn't up for this. He's gonna screw it royally the minute we get there".

"He won't," Gavin responded malevolently. "He knows what will happen if this all goes south."

"I don't trust him, Gav," Jabba retorted. "He's a douche, a stupid douche and he's gonna sink us."

"I don't either," Spider added then. "I told you he hasn't got the balls for this."

"Right!" Gavin thundered, causing everyone to jump in their seats. "Everyone just shut the fuck up and get your shit together. Everyone knows what they've gotta do alright?"

He whirled his head around to face Jeremy again.

"And by Christ, you especially better have your shit together you little fuck, because if this does go wrong, I will feed you to the pigs myself. Understand?"

Jeremy sank back in his seat, trying to create space between him and Jabba which was virtually impossible.

The feeling in the Monaro was darker than Jeremy had ever anticipated. His conflict returned and, this time, Jeremy could not push it away. Everything felt as if were spinning out of control. Their animosity toward him was clear.

Up ahead, Mickey pointed to a line of brightly lit shop fronts, situated just off the main highway. One of them, a building that stood out from the others, was a gymnasium.

"Here we are boys," he announced.

Gavin slowed down and turned into the busy complex, idling along past a line of cars as he and Mickey scanned them all for Baxter's sleek navy BMW convertible, which they expected to be parked in front of the gym.

Mickey extended his finger silently, touching it to the glass. Following its line, Gavin squinted through the windshield until his eyes fell across the familiar shape of the BMW Z3 Roadster.

They'd timed it perfectly.

"Okay, boys," he said, checking his watch and pulling the Monaro into a newly vacant parking space. "We're live."

They didn't have long to wait. A mere five minutes passed before Stephen Baxter emerged from the entrance to the brightly lit fitness centre and crossed the thoroughfare, unlocking the car with his remote.

"Here we go."

Gavin started the engine and edged the Monaro forward, waiting for Baxter to start his own car and reverse out. They all watched as the BMW idled slowly towards the exit of the shopping centre and once Gavin was satisfied there was enough distance between them, he too pulled out into the traffic.

Jeremy watched as Mickey and Gavin kept scanning the traffic around them, making sure they didn't get caught behind another vehicle and lose Baxter. Jabba shuffled his huge frame in the middle while Spider, as usual, was dozing.

Entering onto the highway, they kept Baxter's car in sight, hanging back just enough so as not to be detected by Baxter.

"First turn up ahead," Mickey said, acting as Gavin's guide, even though he didn't need it.

Predictably, Baxter signalled his intention to turn left and Gavin followed suit.

Abruptly, Jabba reached over and snatched the handgun away from Jeremy. Inspecting it, he checked the magazine and the chamber, then held it up in front of Jeremy, pointing at the safety.

"Safe… Ready," he grunted, moving the switch back and forth. "Understand?"

Jeremy nodded hastily as Jabba shoved it back into his palm.

"Five minutes," Mickey announced stonily, gesturing to Jabba to nudge Spider.

Jabba elbowed him and Spider instantly snapped to attention, shaking his head and readying the shotgun in his arms.

Jeremy watched as all four of them pulled their ski masks down and massaged them into position. Suddenly, they had taken on a dark and menacing presence which turned Jeremy's blood cold. Fresh beads of sweat broke across his forehead. His heart thumped loudly. Looking down at the weapon in his hands, Jeremy felt those hands begin to shake.

Jabba looked over at Jeremy and shook his head in disgust.

"Pull your ski mask *down!*" he snarled.

Fear began to pulse through Jeremy and an awful realisation began to dawn on him.

They all hated him.

He would never gain an equal standing in this gang. He'd struggled for months for a place among them and, in all likelihood, he would always struggle. They'd used him before. They were using him now. Using him to carry out this brazen attack and, if push came to shove, they would hang him out to dry.

The words of his grandmother echoed somewhere in the deep recesses of his mind.

'You are the kuyeta—the first-born son of this family.' She'd balled her fist and tapped it to her chest, over her heart.

Images of his father obliterated Virginia's words momentarily as his leering face pushed itself into the centre of his mind's eye, cackling at him, filling him with hatred. The turmoil threatened to engulf him and he grappled desperately to focus on something that would keep him from losing his grip. Jeremy held his father's face there, using it to fuel his own hatred of him, while Virginia's voice continued to cut through.

'You will always have a place…you will never be alone.'

Up ahead the lights of a smaller complex of shops came into view and both Gavin and Mickey held their collective breaths as they watched for Baxter's indicator light to flash.

Time slowed to a crawl as they watched.

The right hand indicator light of the BMW flashed orange and Baxter turned into the complex.

"Game faces boys," Gavin grunted.

The Monaro slowed. Jeremy pulled the ski mask down over his face, feeling the wetness of his tears smudge his cheeks before they were absorbed into the wool.

The Monaro swung right and bounced into the complex, issuing sparks as metal struck concrete. Gavin braked alongside the BMW directly in front of the all night grocery store and threw open his door while Mickey did the same.

Jeremy leaped from the vehicle, the handgun raised in a two-handed grip as he fell in behind Spider, who had the menacing sawn off shotgun angled down in his right hand, only bringing it up as he stormed through the entrance to the store.

Virginia's voice echoed once more.

You belong boy…

Spider flicked his head to his right as he entered, scoping the checkout that was manned by a teen-aged girl who was barely fifteen years old. Pointing the shotgun directly at her, he scanned the small shop, identifying three customers, including Baxter, who was standing near the dairy fridge along the rear wall of the store. The others were spread out in different aisles, which only rose as high as their chests.

Jabbing his finger outward to give Jeremy a bead on each of them, Spider lurched toward the panicked checkout girl, flicking his eyes up and identifying the security camera above her head. Shotgun raised, he promptly blew it apart with a single shot which boomed throughout the store.

Baxter and the others panicked and instantly dropped to the floor as Spider screamed at the checkout girl to open the register, flinging a bag at her. The girl, whimpering in unadulterated terror, stepped forward, reaching for the panic switch under the counter when Spider fired a second shot a few feet from her shoulder, the pellets peppering the wall behind her.

"Open that fucking register now!"

Jeremy rounded the aisle closest to him making a bee line for Baxter, who lay prone on the floor, his hands spread out beside him, breathing fast and shallow.

Jeremy's heart pounded so loudly, that Spider's screams came to him as a disembodied echo. He felt so nauseous that he thought he would vomit.

Images continued flashing at him, tormenting him and he struggled to contain his tears.

His father, his mother, Asher, Minty…

Furiously wiping at his eyes, Jeremy stepped over a terrified elderly Asian woman who screamed. Raising the berretta in his hands, Jeremy pointed it at Baxter's head.

Baxter blinked at the black clad figure who approached him, the muzzle of the weapon aimed directly at him.

"Keys!" Jeremy rasped, disguising his voice as best he could.

Baxter's eyes narrowed in confusion. He remained still.

"*Keys!*" Jeremy screamed again, stopping just a few feet from Baxter and shifting on the spot, agitated.

Baxter craned his neck slightly, trying to get a better look at his assailant when Jeremy lurched forward, slamming the muzzle of the gun into the side of Baxter's face. He leaned in close, close enough that Baxter could feel his breath on his stinging cheek.

"G-give me your fucking keys!"

Slowly, Baxter moved his hand down toward the pocket of his gym shorts, pausing as he fished around inside for the BMW keys.

"You do this and you're dead," Baxter hissed shakily, his jaw stinging against the cold steel of the weapon as he turned his head defiantly, looking into the eyes the thug hovering over him. "You realise that, don't you?"

His grandmother's wise old eyes. Ruby's face, filled with hurt...

Though he did not recognise Jeremy under the ski mask, Baxter could see that, whoever it was, the youth was an Aboriginal.

Baxter sneered as he tossed the keys in front of Jeremy.

"You useless black fuck."

Spider glared incredulously in Jeremy's direction and howled.

"What are you doing?! Get the fucking keys!!"

At that moment, something snapped inside of Jeremy; he felt himself shatter like a pane of glass. The images he'd fought so hard to hold back surged forth like a torrent from a broken dam and his mind collapsed underneath. A single realisation cut through the maelstrom.

Whenever there had been conflict within his family, whenever his father had wrought his destruction upon them, Jeremy had stepped in and taken the brunt of it to shield Asher and Ruby and Minty from worst of it. Time and time again, Jeremy had put himself in harm's way for them and he had, for better or worse, prevailed. He had protected them. And maybe that was what he was always meant to do. That was his role, his identity.

To be a protector.

Calmly pocketing the keys, Jeremy leaned in close to Baxter again and whispered quietly in his ear.

"Stay down. Don't move."

His eyes filling with hatred, Jeremy rose, lifting the gun and aiming it directly at Spider.

"What the fuck..."

As Spider lifted the shotgun, he felt himself lifted off his feet and thrust backward like a rag doll as Jeremy fired two shots in quick succession. One of them slammed into Spider's left shoulder, spraying a large spatter of blood across the wall behind him. The other projectile buried itself deep into his upper thigh, glancing off the side of his bone, causing it to split in two.

As Spider crumpled to the floor, screaming in pain, Jeremy barked at the terrorised checkout.

"Call the police now!"

Kicking the shotgun away from Spider, Jeremy strode toward the exit and burst from the doorway.

Inside the Monaro Gavin and Jabba's eyes bugged out at exactly the same time. Mickey, who was waiting beside the BMW, dove for cover as Jeremy raised the gun and fired directly into the windshield. Over and over again, he squeezed the trigger, shattering the glass, raining bullets over Gavin's head, who'd barely managed to duck down out of the line of fire. Jabba wasn't so lucky. A bullet passed neatly through his earlobe, obliterating it in an instant before shattering the rear windshield behind him.

Squealing like a stuck pig, Jabba grabbed at his bloodied ear while Gavin desperately started the car, flipped it into reverse and stomped on the accelerator pedal. The Monaro fish tailed, careening backward and smashing through the darkened shop front of a hair dresser behind it.

Jeremy, stepped around the front of the BMW, finding Mickey cowering against the door.

Mickey looked up at Jeremy with an expression that registered something akin to shock and he raised his hands desperately.

"Don't do it," he rasped.

Jeremy just stood there, silent and unmoving.

Mickey backed away slowly, and sensing that Jeremy was faltering, he turned and bolted toward the Monaro as it jumped forward, tyres squealing as it retreated from the car park.

Mickey scratched desperately at the door of the Monaro, screaming to be let in as it tore away from him leaving him stranded in the middle of the street.

A siren wailed in the distance, drawing closer. Several dogs barked from the yards of nearby houses.

Jeremy watched as Mickey disappeared from view into the night. He turned and marched back into the store.

Spider was writhing on the floor, screaming in pain, an ever widening pool of blood fanning out underneath his ruined leg.

"What the fuck! WHAT THE FUCK?!" he wailed.

Jeremy walked up and stood over the top of Spider, gazing dispassionately down on him for a long moment as he screamed and clawed impotently at his injuries. Without warning, Jeremy struck out with his foot kicking Spider hard in the side of his head, instantly rendering him unconscious and bringing quiet to the store.

The distant siren grew ever closer.

Wiping the handgun quickly with the material of his hoodie, Jeremy dropped it into Spider's outstretched hand.

Ignoring the girl who was cowering behind the checkout, Jeremy walked over to where Baxter still lay on the floor. He took the car keys from his pocket and dropped them on the floor, mere inches from Baxter's face.

"Police are coming; just stay calm until they get here."

Outside, Baxter heard the screeching of tyres as patrol cars converged on the grocery store. As relief flooded through him, he saw the familiar blue and red glow flashing in the periphery of his vision.

He turned his head and opened his mouth to speak but the assailant was no longer there.

As police officers flooded through the entrance, Baxter risked lifting his head off the floor and scanned his immediate surroundings but he realised he was alone.

The assailant had disappeared.

CHAPTER 30

IN THE DEPTHS OF THE NIGHT RUBY shuddered and woke, disturbed by the sound of something scratching at the back door.

Scrambling into a sitting position and drawing the covers up around herself, Asher and Minty, Ruby shook away her sleep and listened intently, her heart thumping loudly. Rain fell softly on the roof above but there was definitely something else.

Footfalls on the steps. The jiggling of a door handle.

Someone was trying to break in!

Cowering down, Ruby quivered. The bedroom door was open and she desperately wanted to shut it but she was too frightened.

She heard the back door click, heard the squeak of the hinges as the door swung open.

The intruder was inside!

Footsteps on the creaking boards in the hall now. A shadow appeared, just outside the bedroom door. Ruby shrank as far down in the bed as she could but peeked over the edge of her blanket. She was utterly terrified.

And then…

A hand pushed on the door to reveal a familiar form.

Ruby frowned quizzically and then her eyes went wide. Reaching across to her bedside lamp, she flicked the switch to reveal Jeremy standing there in the soft light.

She gasped.

He looked completely dishevelled. His clothes were wet, soaked through from the rain. His hair was matted and droplets of water fell down over his face. His colour was ashen; his eyes were reddened and swollen and he shook from the cold and the wet that had seeped through his clothes and into his skin—into his bones.

"Jeremy!" she wheezed, throwing back the covers and scrambling across the bed to him.

Jeremy fell to his knees and then into her embrace as Ruby wrapped her arms around him, ignoring his sodden clothing.

He was here. He was alright.

"Where have you been? What happened to you?"

Jeremy drew himself back and looked up into Ruby's face.

"I-I couldn't d-do it," he stammered, his teeth chattering. "I…I…"

He dropped his head as tears welled up in his eyes.

"You couldn't do what?" Ruby pressed him worriedly. "What is it, Jeremy?"

Behind them, Asher stirred and sat up, rubbing the sleep from her eyes.

"Wh-what's going on?" she whispered.

Jeremy snapped his head up at the sound of his sister's voice and glanced around Ruby.

"Asher?" he whispered, blinking in surprise.

Overwhelmed by the sight of his sister awake, he shuffled on his knees across to the bedside and reached out to her, embracing her. He was sobbing freely now. Asher embraced him in return, the warmth of her arms radiating through him.

Jeremy looked up at his sister and at Ruby.

"I…turned on them. *All of them*," he said shakily. "They wanted me to do something real bad and…I couldn't do it."

Ruby put her arm around Jeremy and squeezed him gently.

"I'm done…" he said, his voice barely a whisper. "…With them. No more."

For the first time in what seemed like an eternity, Ruby felt a warmth inside her at the sound of Jeremy's words. Whatever had happened to him tonight, none of it mattered. Whatever the disappointment—the hurt and the pain that they had suffered and endured—none of it mattered. Because in that moment, in the darkness of their little room, Ruby knew that Jeremy spoke the truth. In that moment, despite his tears, she saw a strength in Jeremy that she had never seen before.

Asher leaned forward and touched her forehead to his and he smiled faintly.

"Everything will be okay," she whispered to him.

VIRGINIA CROSSED THE lawn from the granny flat, buttoning her dressing gown and blinking the sleep from her eyes. She had slept poorly and her back ached from having tossed and turned throughout the night.

A trio of birds chirped happily on the power lines nearby as they greeted the dawn and the rising sun. Virginia cast a cursory glance up at them and watched as they took flight, soaring over the yard before peeling away into the distance.

An old memory of a Mingka bird came to her.

The old dog lay at the bottom of the steps of the house. He lifted his head as Virginia approached and she dropped her hand to him, allowing him to lick her fingers. She climbed up to the back door and quietly slipped inside.

Upon entering the house, Virginia sensed that something was amiss. Glancing to her left, Virginia noted that the door to the boys' bedroom was open. Peering through and into the room, she noticed that Minty wasn't in his bed. Frowning, she turned and listened for the television in the living room, but there was silence. The whole house was silent.

A chill went through her and she shuffled hastily through the hallway to the door of Ruby and Asher's bedroom. She cocked her ear to listen for any sound, then gently turned the handle, opening the door as softly as she could.

In the half light, Virginia saw the children—all of the children—huddled together in Ruby's bed. Asher, Minty and Ruby were under the covers while Jeremy was curled up in his T-shirt and pyjama bottoms at the end of the bed, hugging his pillow.

Virginia stood in silence, her mouth agape, not quite believing what she saw in front of her. Her heart leaped and she pressed her hand to her her chest.

The children were here. They were all together.

Ruby stirred and woke, blinking her eyes and peering over the blanket at her grandmother.

Virginia smiled warmly, stepping into the bedroom and coming over to the bed.

Ruby watched her grandmother as she took in each of the children in turn. Asher sleeping softly, cradling Minty in her arms. Jeremy, curled up and fast asleep—safe in the company of his siblings. Ruby, smiling back at her.

Virginia's lip quivered and a tear welled in her eye.

Asher stirred then, and her eyes fluttered open. She turned to see Virginia standing there. Minty also woke and sat up in the middle of the girls rubbing the sleep from his eyes, clutching his teddy bear. Finally Jeremy awoke, stretched and yawned and looked up into Virginia's face. There was no malice there. No sense of anger or disapproval at what she surely must have sensed in him. There was only love.

Virginia sat down on the side of the bed as the children surrounded her and embraced her warmly, with hugs and kisses.

It no longer mattered—all that, which had come before. Neither the struggle or the hardship of Virginia's own life nor the trauma and heartache of the children's lives now. Because, in that moment, here in their little sanctuary, they were all together, bound by something greater than anything that sought to tear them apart.

Their love for one another.

DAVO STOOD IN the hall, waiting patiently as Jeremy, Belle, Virginia and the children sat at the kitchen table, speaking quietly.

The worry was clearly etched into Belle's features as she listened to Jeremy. Virginia, on the other hand, was peaceful, serene even.

Jeremy sat with his hands intertwined in front of him.

"Are you sure this is what you want to do?" Belle said, her brow furrowing even more. "The police aren't good to us people. You know that. They'll throw you to the wolves if they feel like it and they won't give it another thought."

Virginia touched her hand to Belle's shoulder and shook her head softly.

"Nothing of the sort is going to happen, Belle."

She glanced up at Davo.

"Davo's got a couple of good contacts within the force, haven't you Davo. He'll make sure Jeremy is okay."

Davo nodded and entered into the kitchen, coming up to stand beside Jeremy.

Jeremy was staring at the table, considering what he was about to do.

"This is the right thing to do, Mum. I don't care about what happens to them afterwards. I just know that I can live with it."

"Jeremy's information is gonna expose a lot of bad people in a lot of bad places," Davo added sagely. "I reckon the police will pin a bloody medal on him once he fills 'em in on all of this."

"But…what about us? Won't we be in danger?" Belle pressed.

Davo shook his head confidently and grinned mischievously.

"Don't you bloody bet on it. It'll all be handled."

Jeremy stood and looked around the table at his family. He touched his hand to Asher's cheek and she smiled sheepishly, if a little nervously.

"Let's go, Davo," he said.

Davo followed him as Jeremy went to his bedroom and gathered up his wallet and his mobile phone from his bedside table. Virginia, Belle, Minty and the girls gathered in the living room, waiting for him to emerge.

Jeremy exited his bedroom and looked up at Davo, taking a deep breath in.

"You'll be alright, mate," Davo reassured him, squeezing his shoulder.

Jeremy stepped into the hall and came toward the living room when, suddenly, he paused in mid-step and turned his head to the left as if something had caught his eye.

Ruby and Asher exchanged puzzled looks at one another as Jeremy disappeared into the girls' bedroom, emerging moments later carrying something in his hand.

He stopped in front of Ruby, holding the violin case out toward her.

"If I do this Rube…then you've gotta promise you'll do the recital."

Ruby took the case and held it, glancing from Jeremy to Asher—who nodded—and to Virginia.

"Deal?" Jeremy asked hopefully.

Ruby looked down at the case, running her hand across the aged leather. She nodded slowly.

"Deal," she whispered softly.

Jeremy smiled.

"I'll be home in time to take you to your rehearsal."

Opening the front door, Jeremy stepped out into the daylight and walked across to the car accompanied by Davo. He turned once more toward the house before climbing in and he nodded once at Ruby.

"Deal," he mouthed silently.

RUBY STOOD QUIETLY before the statue of Sir Walter Hughes, holding her violin case in her hands.

She did not speak. For once, she just wanted to be. A breeze wafted softly through the boughs of the surrounding jacarandas and kicked up some leaves on the pavement causing them to skitter around her noisily.

There was music in those leaves.

No matter where she was or what the sound or combination of sounds, Ruby could extract music from almost anything she heard. It was another of her grandmother's lessons, one which she had carried with her almost from the time she had begun under Virginia's tutelage.

And no matter what the music, Ruby found peace within it. Here and now, it was no different.

"Are you ready?" Sir Walter's voice intoned softly, floating down from above her.

With her eyes closed, Ruby nodded.

"I think so…I just hope Khalili will forgive me."

"To forgive, young Ruby, is to achieve a state of grace. I think you already know that."

Ruby turned around to see both Jeremy and Asher waiting patiently over by the steps to the art gallery building. She smiled knowingly.

"I know it," she replied. "I hope I can catch up in time."

"I have no doubts," Sir Walter said. "Now come on…stop loitering around here and get yourself in there…on the stage…where you belong."

Ruby nodded formally at Sir Walter and turned away once more.

"Ready?" Jeremy asked, taking his hands from his hoodie and putting an arm around her shoulder. Asher smiled warmly as she took Ruby's hand in hers.

"As I'll ever be," Ruby replied.

Together, they crossed the lawn once more and opened the door to the hall.

Inside, the auditorium was utterly silent and empty. Every single chair was empty.

As they crept inside and looked around, neither one of them could see anyone up on the stage. The piano there sat idle, its lid closed.

"I'm too late," Ruby whispered worriedly to Asher.

From somewhere behind the stage, the three children could hear the faint sound of a flushing toilet, then the sound of footfalls on the stairs.

From the rear of the stage, under the mighty pipe organ, Jeremy spied a figure who appeared there and he immediately pointed in the figure's direction.

Ruby's eyes widened hopefully, then she smiled as she recognised Khalili approaching the piano.

He sat down at it and took out a piece of sheet music from his familiar leather bag then placed it on the holder in front of him.

Jeremy, Asher and Ruby approached quietly and climbed onto the stage.

Jeremy looked down at her and nudged her gently.

"Go on," he whispered. "Go and speak to him."

Ruby flashed a worried look at Jeremy then at Asher and clutched her violin case tighter.

"Go on," Asher urged. "He's not gonna bite you."

Ruby stepped forward, approaching the professor cautiously.

Khalili lifted his head from the piano and slowly turned in his seat until his eyes fell across Ruby.

Ruby shuddered and stopped.

Khalili's expression was blank as he studied her up and down, then tilted his head to see Jeremy and his sister standing behind her.

Slowly, as though he were watching a flower bloom, Khalili's mouth parted and then turned upward in a warm smile. He tilted his glasses so he could see over them.

"I was beginning to think you would never get here," he quipped mischievously.

He gestured with his head for her to come closer and he reached down into his bag once more, pulling out a different sheet of music and placing it over the top of the one he already had in place.

Ruby gingerly set her case down on the edge of the piano and snapped it open, taking out the violin.

As she did so, she failed to see that Khalili was stifling a lump in his throat whilst at the same time, wiping away a tear.

Jeremy took up his usual seat at the front of the stage and motioned Asher to the seat beside him.

"Mendelssohn?" Khalili asked, lifting his hands to the keys of the piano.

Ruby nodded.

"Mendelssohn."

Together they picked up where they'd left off and it was as if no time had passed at all.

CHAPTER 31

ARRIVING HOME FROM SCHOOL, RUBY MARCHED STRAIGHT to her bedroom, tossed her bag on the bed and flopped down on the floor.

She felt impatient and had fidgeted for most of the day—not so much from nervousness but from frustration. The Malley-Joyce recital was now less than twenty-four hours away and, on the advice of both Khalili and her grandmother, Ruby had been encouraged not to pick up her violin to practise at all. Their reasoning was, that by taking a complete break from it in those final hours, she could relax and thus, approach the following day with a clear mind.

Right now though, Ruby felt anything but relaxed.

She and Khalili had rehearsed every day and she had thrived spending every waking moment thinking about and practising the pieces for the recital. She'd sat up in her bed, long into the night, going over the compositions in her head, practising the fingerings on her violin without the bow, repeating them over and over again until she was sure they were imprinted onto her consciousness.

Her performances had improved exponentially over the past two weeks. The Mendelssohn piece, in particular, with Khalili's piano accompaniment was flawless and Ruby had grown significantly in her confidence.

Being forced to rest like this now was maddening. It felt like someone had amputated her arm and no amount of diversion could assuage her frustration.

Asher trooped into the bedroom behind Ruby, set her bag down at the end of her own bed and sat down opposite Ruby. She fixed her cousin with a sympathetic expression.

"I know it must be tough," Asher ventured. "But the professor and Nana wouldn't tell you to rest if they didn't think it was the right thing to do. We've just gotta find something to take your mind off tomorrow."

Ruby looked at Asher with gritted teeth and threw her arms up in exasperation.

"Yeah, but what? This is killing me, all this waitin'."

"I dunno…maybe we could watch a movie or something?"

Ruby screwed up her face.

"That's *not* gonna work. Besides, I hate movies."

Asher shrugged her shoulders and fidgeted nervously, which Ruby picked up on and immediately felt a pang of guilt.

"Sorry, Ash," she offered.

Though Asher was much better, she still exhibited signs of discomfort whenever there was any hint of conflict or anger from anyone around her. Recognising this, Ruby, Jeremy and the rest of the family had resolved to make her home environment a much calmer place and it had helped her immensely. She had only just returned to school in the past few days. She was jittery but coping.

Asher smiled reassuringly at Ruby.

"It's okay. We'll think of something."

The front door clicked open and both the girls turned their heads at the sound of Virginia's voice calling out.

"Ruby? Are you home? Come up the front here. We've got something to show you."

Ruby and Asher scrunched their faces at each other, mouthing the word *We'* in unison, before scrambling to their feet and making their way through to the living room where they found both Virginia and Belle with Minty squirming in Belle's arms. Virginia set a large white box down on the coffee table and stood back, gesturing at it with both hands.

"Well? Come and have a look. Don't just stand there."

Ruby rounded the arm chair hesitantly and knelt before the box. She looked up at both Virginia and Belle.

"Open it," Virginia urged her.

Lifting the top off the box Ruby set it aside and looked down on a navy and cream coloured, handmade, cotton dress.

Ruby's eyes went wide as she gently lifted the delicate dress. It had a rounded neck with an understated frill bordering it, short sleeves and a gathered cream skirt that fell gracefully down before her.

"It's beautiful," Asher beamed excitedly, kneeling down beside an awestruck Ruby and squeezing her gently.

"Well?" Virginia pressed her granddaughter incredulously. "What do you think?"

"H-how?" Ruby answered softly.

Lifting a pair of shining leather shoes out from inside the box and setting them down on the coffee table, Virginia lifted the dress from Ruby's grasp and held it up so she could see it in more detail.

"Aunty Belle found the dress in a second hand shop and Cherie and I have spent the past week making some alterations to it," Virginia explained.

"And I bought the shoes over at the mall just the other day," Belle added, setting a wriggling Minty down on the floor.

Ruby looked up at her aunt with an expression of genuine surprise.

"We can't have you goin' off to the recital looking like a ruffian now can we? I've seen how you're expected to present yourself."

"I-I don't know what to say," Ruby stammered, overwhelmed.

For what seemed like the first time ever, her aunt looked at Ruby with an expression of genuine warmth.

"You don't have to say anything. Just play your violin…the way you've always played it. Show them white fellas how good you are."

"Thank you," Ruby whispered, feeling her emotions bubbling up at her aunt's show of kindness.

"Let's get some dinner on then," Virginia declared robustly. "We all need a good meal in our bellies for tomorrow. It's gonna be a big day."

JEREMY MADE HIS way down the near-empty hall of the school, toward an exit. Outside, he crossed over a large quadrangle heading in the direction of a smaller portable building that had an almost informal look to it in comparison to the larger buildings of the school. It was flanked on one side by a vibrant vegetable garden that was filled with a variety of seasonal vegetables that were close to harvest. On the other, was an attractive landscaped garden with a pretty arbour and a number of rose bushes that been recently pruned back for the winter in preparation for their spring blooms.

This was Miss Glasson's classroom and office, though it was less like a rigid classroom environment and more like a club room.

Stopping at the steps in front of the entrance, Jeremy put one hand on the railing and took a deep breath. Everything was changing and he felt himself changing along with it. There was no reason to fear it—he knew that—but he felt the butterflies nonetheless.

No reason to be afraid any more.

He had faced down those who'd sought to destroy him and had been fortunate enough to be given the opportunity to make a fresh start.

He intended to make good on that opportunity.

Entering the building, Jeremy gingerly glanced around the door and saw Miss Glasson sitting at her desk working at her laptop.

She looked up from her work and smiled warmly.

"Jeremy. Come in. I was just finishing up."

Her eyes narrowed as he approached the desk.

"You're hanging around a little late aren't you?"

Jeremy nodded bashfully.

"I had to…finish up some other stuff before I was allowed to leave."

Miss Glasson gestured to a chair opposite her, but Jeremy declined wordlessly.

"I ahh…wanted to talk to you about…your program."

Miss Glasson nodded, her eyes widening over the tops of her glasses.

"Yes," she ventured, waiting as Jeremy fidgeted where he stood.

"Well…I wanted to know…if your offer is still, you know—available?"

Miss Glasson studied Jeremy closely, her expression giving nothing away.

It didn't last. Her facade cracked, her smile returned and she stood from her seat, coming around to stand before Jeremy.

"I would love to have you join the program," she beamed. "I will get you in as soon as possible."

Jeremy's brow furrowed and his features flickered with a mixture of relief and embarrassment. As always, Miss Glasson was quick to pick up on his nonverbal cues.

"You've made the right decision, Jeremy," she said reassuringly. "If you work hard, we could have you back up to speed in no time. You're bright—you always have been. You just needed to believe in yourself."

Jeremy nodded, he bowed his head slightly and stifled a lump in his throat.

"How are things?" Miss Glasson asked him.

"They're okay…different. D-Dad's still in the hospital. He got an infection and they had to operate on his nose again. The police raided Gavin's house and arrested him and the others. They've given me immu…immune…"

"Immunity?" Miss Glasson ventured helpfully, to which Jeremy smiled and nodded.

"Immunity," he repeated. "My information has caused a lot of damage."

"Things are going to take a while to settle," Miss Glasson observed. "But they will settle."

Jeremy nodded again and looked at Miss Glasson.

"They will. Mum won't let Dad back home until he gets himself together good and proper, so I'm sort of the man of the house."

He smiled wanly.

"It's not too bad actually."

Jeremy's smile faded almost as quickly and he began to turn away.

"I worry about us, miss. I worry about what's gonna happen when he does want to come home."

Miss Glasson tilted her head and smiled with empathy.

"You'll work it out. You've worked a lot of things out lately and they've served you well. Just keep thinking about what the right thing is for you and for your family. You won't ever go wrong."

Jeremy nodded respectfully and turned to leave.

"Baxter's gone," Miss Glasson said. "For now, at least. He's on leave until they decide how to discipline him."

Jeremy turned back and looked at Miss Glasson.

"But you didn't hear that from me," she grinned.

JEREMY UNLOCKED THE door to the house and quietly stepped inside, hearing a commotion of sorts coming from the kitchen. For a fleeting moment, he felt panicked, as if there was yet another conflict going on, however the sound of raucous laughter and the chattering of his family confused him and he frowned in the direction of the kitchen.

Setting his schoolbag down in the hall, Jeremy stopped in the kitchen doorway to find his family bustling around in the kitchen preparing dinner. Asher and Virginia were at the stove, checking on a roast in the oven while Ruby, Minty and Belle washed and dried dishes and Davo and Cherie along with Professor Khalili set the dinner table.

The scene was comforting. Jeremy hadn't seen anything like this in a very long time. They were all happy, laughing and chatting away—so much so that none of them even saw Jeremy initially.

It was Belle who finally caught sight of him and smiled warmly.

"Jeremy," she greeted with surprise in her voice.

Jeremy noted her flicking her eyes up to the wall clock and couldn't help but grin slightly at the irony. It was rare for him to be home this early—if at all.

Belle embraced her son then shepherded him into the kitchen and gave him a stack of plates to set out on the table.

"We're having a little celebration tonight, son," she said. "For a change."

Jeremy glanced across at Ruby who met his eyes with a querying expression.

'Well?' she mouthed silently.

Jeremy simply nodded and Ruby smiled broadly, knowing he'd finally done it and had gone to see Miss Glasson.

Her exchange was swallowed up by Davo who plucked Ruby from her stool by the sink and set her down at the table.

"You've done enough work for the moment. Take a break while we get this tea on for ya. After all, you're the lady of the moment."

Ruby's cheeks flushed.

"How are you feeling?" Cherie asked her. "Not too nervous?"

"I don't know," Ruby answered truthfully, casting a quick glance at Khalili. "Never been in anything like this before so I guess I'll have to let you know when it happens."

"You'll be alright, Rube," Jeremy assured her, squeezing her shoulder as he sat down beside her. "I've seen you perform and I reckon it sounds awesome."

"Me too," Asher added for good measure. "You'll be superb."

"Now, now," Virginia interjected. "Let's not go whipping her up too much. You'll have her quaking before she even steps up onto the stage."

Setting the roasted lamb down on the table in the centre, she took up her seat while Asher and Belle placed the vegetables beside the lamb and Jeremy put Minty down on his knee.

Virginia took Ruby's hand and held it.

"All you have to do tomorrow is play the way you've always played. Remember all the things you put into your music—the pictures, the feelings, the sounds that you hear and forget about everything else. We'll all be there for you but just concentrate on you and what you've always done in your music."

Ruby nodded and smiled softly. She glanced again at Khalili who was himself smiling. He'd obviously appreciated Virginia's sentiments.

Looking around the table, Ruby's eyes finally settled on Jeremy and he returned a smile to her.

CHAPTER 32

RUBY SAT AT THE BASE OF SIR Walter Hughes' statue, her violin case resting in her lap, her eyes closed in quiet meditation.

She was dressed in her concert dress and had paired it with crisp white stockings. Her new shoes had been polished to a high sheen by Jeremy who had employed a similar technique to which he shined his football boots. Asher and Virginia spent the morning washing, combing and styling her hair. They'd tied it back and secured it with a beautiful butterfly clip that had once belonged to Virginia.

Ruby had attracted the attention of various passersby, some of whom stopped to compliment her on how lovely she looked and though outwardly, she baulked at their attentions, appearing self-conscious in her showy outfit, she felt very much a young lady. The dress fitted perfectly, billowing out daintily and her shoes were just the right size and fit that she felt comfortable in them.

Sitting here now, with the recital mere hours away, Ruby felt calm. There was the occasional twinge of nervousness while she was getting prepared at home but those feelings had drifted away on the drive into Adelaide in Davo's car. They spent the ride down singing songs with raucous enthusiasm, an attempt Ruby figured to further calm her nerves.

While Belle, Cherie and Asher parked the car nearby, Jeremy stood with Virginia under the arches of the art gallery, waiting.

Jeremy had dressed smartly in a pair of trousers and a crisp white shirt while Virginia wore a smart blouse and skirt that she hadn't worn in years. She'd matched her outfit with a lovely hat and smart shoes and looked so much different than usual. Both of them did. In fact, Jeremy couldn't remember ever having seen his grandmother look so formal. He himself couldn't remember the last time he dressed up for any sort of occasion. Despite this, he noted with amusement that Virginia was shifting her feet; the shoes she wore were clearly stiff and new and were uncomfortable.

Virginia was looking across the pavement to where Ruby sat at the large base of the statue. Her brow was furrowed in a worried frown.

"What on Earth is that child doing?" she whispered impatiently. "We'll be late at this rate."

"She talks…" Jeremy replied, motioning to the imposing gentleman sitting atop the marble base. "To him. He's like her imaginary friend or something. I never know exactly what they talk about but…"

Virginia turned her head and glared over the top of her sunglasses at Jeremy.

"How long has she been doing that for?"

Jeremy shrugged.

"I dunno…for as long as we've been coming here. It's like this little ritual for her. She talks to him before practise, kind of like a pep talk. If she doesn't do it, she says she doesn't feel right. Ready—or something."

Forgetting her shoes for a moment, a curious smile formed at the edges of Virginia's lips then and nodded once.

The young girl and the dog, her faithful companion to which she confided all of her secret hopes and fears…

Jeremy noticed his grandmother's expression and nudged her gently.

"What is it, Nan?"

"Oh nothing," Virginia replied wistfully. "Just remembering. I had a similar 'friend' when I was Ruby's age, though mine was flesh and blood, rather than a big piece of bronze."

Now it was Jeremy's turn to frown and Virginia chuckled at him.

"He was a dog—*a mongrel*—the kind you normally wouldn't pay too much attention to. Except that there was something about him—an intelligence, *a knowing*. He wouldn't leave me alone. I talked to him in much the same way. He was by my side practically from the moment I first met him. Until…"

Her voice drifted away and they continued to watch Ruby in silence. Jeremy sensed that he knew what she meant by her 'until.'

"Those sorts of friends can be vital," Virginia added softly. "Especially if you feel alone."

Jeremy nodded in understanding and felt a familiar twinge of guilt assail him before Virginia squeezed his arm reassuringly.

"She's not alone—thank the Lord. None of us are…really."

Virginia checked her watch and shook her head.

"But she might be if she doesn't *hurry it up*."

Ruby listened to the breeze as it gently rustled through the boughs of the surrounding jacarandas. She practised her breathing exercises and ran through the imagery of each of the compositions in her head once more.

"You look lovely in your dress," Sir Walter remarked from above her. "Your grandmother has helped you, I take it."

"Yes…and Jeremy and Asher—even Aunty Belle. She bought the dress."

"Well that is something. It appears this journey of yours has brought your family together in ways not expected."

Opening her eyes, Ruby looked across to where her grandmother and Jeremy stood.

"I guess it has," she mused.

"It is a fine thing. Regardless of what happens today, in a way, you have already won. Your gift has sustained you and your family—given them hope. It's given *you* hope…don't you think?"

Ruby nodded as a realisation came to her.

All of the people in her life who mattered were here with her today. They were her family, her people and in that moment, a feeling struck her—a sense of family, of belonging that she hadn't felt before—*ever*—and it made her feel good. It no longer mattered what came before, what she or they had endured or suffered or battled. They were, for all of their experiences, a family, they were together and they were happy—perhaps for the first time in a long time.

From that powerful realisation, Ruby felt strength flow through her that rose like a wave for several moments before settling back, as her focus turned toward the recital. From somewhere nearby, the sound of a clock chimed across the boulevard and Ruby began to feel a twinge of nervousness. It was midday—an hour until her first performance of the recital.

"There's still a long way to go," she muttered.

"I've no doubts that you will prevail, child."

Ruby craned her neck up at Sir Walter's figure and squinted.

"You love using those big words all the time, Sir Wally," she said.

"How many times have I asked you not to call me that?"

Ruby giggled under her breath and stood from the base of the statue.

"You like it," she quipped daintily. "You know you do."

Ruby turned to face Sir Walter and, from out of the corner of her eye, she saw a familiar figure approaching from across the lawn in front of Elder Hall.

It was Khalili.

Dressed in a suit and sporting a ruby red rose in his lapel, Khalili had spied Ruby before she'd noticed him and he was smiling as he approached.

Jeremy and Virginia stepped out onto the pavement and joined Ruby at the base of the statue.

"I thought I'd find you here," Khalili quipped as he stopped before Ruby and studied her proudly. "Well, well—look at you. You look every inch the young performer."

Ruby grinned bashfully and acknowledged her grandmother and Jeremy.

"Shall we walk together to the Town Hall?"

"That would be great," Ruby nodded.

"We better get a move on," Virginia said, tapping her watch yet again.

"Indeed," Khalili agreed. "We'll need to register and make sure we've submitted everything—and you've still not told me what that third piece is yet."

Ruby smiled conspiratorially and pursed her lips tightly.

"I'm *not* saying—I told you that already. You'll just have to wait."

Belle, Cherie and Asher appeared from across North Terrace and joined up with the others by the statue. Asher looked lovely in a floral print dress and slip on shoes; her hair was braided to one side and tied with a ribbon.

She smiled warmly at Ruby, clearly excited for her.

"Let us go then, shall we?" Khalili said, gesturing toward a nearby pedestrian crossing.

Together the little group began to walk from the statue when, suddenly, a high pitched chirping cause Virginia to stop and turn back.

From the trees above, a little bird flitted down and landed on the statue's shoulder, pausing there and singing cheerily.

Ruby too, stopped and looked back at the bird, going over to stand by Virginia, who seemed entranced by the bird's song.

It was light, happy, a pleasant sound that made Virginia smile.

"What is it, Nana?" Ruby asked inquisitively.

"A Mingka bird," Virginia answered sweetly. "It's a messaging bird. One that brings news."

"What news has it got right now?"

Virginia closed her eyes and listened closely to the little bird as it fanned out its tail.

"Hard to say exactly," she responded. "But my guess is that the news is good."

Virginia opened her eyes and gazed down at her granddaughter with a comforting smile.

"Let's go and see you play."

Ruby nodded and turned away once more.

Virginia lingered for a moment longer, until the bird flapped its wings and took flight again, disappearing above the boughs of the trees.

Finally, she walked slowly from the statue. As she did so, a voice—soft but strong—sounded.

"Good luck."

Virginia turned, but all she could see was the statue there, standing solitary under the mighty Moreton Bay fig. Her eyes narrowed and she looked up into the face of Sir Walter Hughes.

Shaking her head, confused, she turned away for a final time.

ADELAIDE'S TOWN HALL was already filling with people when Ruby arrived, accompanied by her family. Passing under the tall arches of the building's entrance and filing in to the resplendent foyer, Ruby felt her heart jump as she took in her surroundings. It was like Elder Hall in some ways, but in others it was a much more imposing environment.

With Khalili guiding them though the foyer, Ruby took Virginia's hand and squeezed it gently as they headed through a pair of large doors. Ruby was awestruck by the cavernous auditorium they had entered into. High above her head, the cream ceiling of the concert auditorium was lit by three huge chandeliers that hung from ornate ceiling roses. On either side of the auditorium stood huge, marbled columns that flanked high arches bathed in warm light. The stage before her was larger than Elder Hall's and, like the hall, the centrepiece of this stage was yet another massive pipe organ that towered above her. An orchestra was setting themselves up on the stage and familiar sounds of tuning instruments filtered through the auditorium. Upon closer inspection, Ruby recognised the four musicians of the string quartet positioned in front of the modified chamber orchestra.

Ruby turned to Khalili, her eyes wide.

"Are they for us?"

Khalili smiled and nodded.

"They are indeed, Ruby. They will play *L'Chaim* with you and our Mendelssohn duet—as well as that…*other composition.*"

Ruby grinned mischievously, in spite of herself, once more.

"Don't worry…besides, I might not get to play it yet."

Khalili met her with a disapproving glower.

"*Ruby.* Don't you be so quick to sabotage yourself. Remember just how formidable you are."

The seating around Ruby was both ornate and luxurious. Over 1,100 people could be accommodated here and, already, it appeared a capacity crowd was guaranteed. All around her, people, officials and families and children and musicians moved to and fro—many of whom seemed to know one another and were chatting in groups while Ruby's coterie made their way through the throng.

Virginia was equally impressed by their surroundings and perhaps a little daunted, although she didn't show it to Ruby.

"Would you look at this carpet," Virginia marvelled. "You could sink up to your knees in it."

Ruby managed a nervous smile at her grandmother as Khalili led them toward the front of the stage where, off to the side a registration table stood along with a group of official looking people.

Belle nudged Virginia discreetly.

"Mum, we might go and find a seat. Looks like they've got some reserved for us over behind."

Virginia nodded as Belle, Cherie, Jeremy and Asher crowded around Ruby and gave her encouraging hugs and kisses.

"Good luck, kiddo," Jeremy said warmly. "Give us your best, hey?"

Jeremy and Asher planted kisses on Ruby's cheeks and stood back. Ruby noticed Asher's eyes welling.

"We're so proud, Rube," she said softly. "No matter what."

Ruby waved them away before she could allow herself to become emotional. She turned to the table where Khalili was speaking to a very tall woman with close cropped, bleached blonde hair and gold rimmed glasses. The woman scanned Ruby up and down over the tops of those glasses, then to Virginia beside her. Her expression was blank. Ruby felt herself shrinking under her piercing eyes. Then, all of a sudden, the woman's demeanour melted into a warm and welcoming smile and she immediately stepped around the table with her hand outstretched.

"Good afternoon and welcome," she greeted breezily. "My name is Juliette and I shall be taking care of the performers today. Professor Khalili has told me so much about you, Miss Delfey."

Juliette then offered her hand to Virginia.

"And you Mrs. Delfey, I understand that you have been Ruby's teacher for her career thus far."

Virginia nodded hastily and gulped.

"I have," she said simply.

"Well come, come and let us get you organised," Juliette said, taking a pen from behind her ear and turning to the table behind her where she picked up a green folder and opened it. "Now there are eight soloists this afternoon, including Ruby, for the first performance. Four performers will proceed to the late afternoon second recital and then two will progress to the final evening performance. Our judging panel will be watching each of you and will score each soloist based on the criteria you would have read about in your own material."

Ruby nodded in understanding and watched as Juliette took out a name card and stooped down to attach it to Ruby's dress, just over her heart. Ruby looked at the card and noted that it had the number seven on it.

"I'll be seventh to perform, yes?"

Juliette nodded and smiled again as she stood.

"That's right, dear. Now, we must take you around to the rear of the stage where you can meet with the others and prepare yourself. The recital will be starting very soon."

Ruby glanced at Virginia. A worried expression crossed over her face.

Virginia took both her hands and leaned forward as best she could.

"Now don't you worry about a thing, Ruby," she said solemnly. "I'm going to go and take my seat. Just remember everything you've learned. This is your time now. Take your *palti* and give it to your audience."

"My *palti*," Ruby echoed. "My song…"

She gazed up at her grandmother and cocked her head.

"Nana… where do all these words come from? I know them because you taught me them, but…"

She paused, remembering her grandmother's first encounter with Khalili.

"You mentioned something to Mr. Khalili when you first met – about the *Pira-mank*."

Virginia chuckled softly and leaned in close to Ruby.

"The *Peramangk,* Ruby—the Peramangk. That is where your ancestors come from. It's where I was born. You carry their *palti* with you, where ever you go, their story. It is who you are."

Ruby gulped and nodded quickly as Virginia planted a kiss on her forehead.

"Go now."

"I will, Nana."

Khalili gestured to Ruby and she stood back from Virginia then turned and walked with Khalili to the stage. She kept her eyes on Virginia who waited there at the foot of the stage until Khalili ushered her through to the rear of the stage.

Ruby was confronted by a bustling backstage area where a throng of people were milling about. She could see the seven other performers she would be competing against. Of the eight, there were three boys and five girls—including herself.

As Khalili accompanied her, groups of eyes turned toward her. Ruby noted the other performers among them and some of them smiled, while others just looked on ambivalently or were practising with their own instruments, too busy to notice her. A couple of the performers had family members with them who studied Ruby intensely.

Khalili motioned toward a pair of empty seats before a lighted mirror which had been set aside for them both and together they made their way over and sat down.

Ruby immediately set her violin case down in front of the mirror and took her instrument out along with her bow and cleaning cloth.

From the front of the stage, she could hear the sound of applause from the audience as an announcer stepped up onto the stage and began to introduce the performance.

This was it. The recital was about to begin.

Khalili sat before her, watching Ruby as she went through her oft practised routine of wiping her violin with her cloth, making sure that the string tension was correct, checking and adjusting the fibres of her bow. He smiled proudly as she worked. Despite her youth, Ruby performed these little tasks with the hand of someone much older and wiser.

"How do you feel?" he ventured.

"Good," Ruby lied meekly. "I need to pee but, other than that, I'm okay."

Khalili chuckled softly.

"Do you think those other people are looking at me? Wondering what I'm doing here? They've probably never seen someone like me before."

Khalili frowned, glancing over his shoulder at the other performers and their accompanying teachers and families.

"Not at all," he chided gently. "You are equal among them, Ruby. There is no greater leveller than a recital such as this. I can guarantee you, they are probably just as nervous."

Ruby continued checking her violin, making some final adjustments to the pegs. Then she set it down on the counter top.

One of the young performers, a Japanese girl about Ruby's own age, approached her from across the carpet.

"Hello," the girl greeted gingerly. "I saw you as you came in and I just wanted to say hi and…you know, to say good luck…for today."

Ruby smiled sheepishly at the girl and offered her hand.

"My name's Ruby," she said.

The girl took Ruby's hand and nodded respectfully.

"I'm Meisa. This is my first recital. What about you?"

Ruby nodded.

"Mine too."

Meisa smiled in apparent relief and lingered for a moment, unsure of what to say next.

Ruby gestured to a nearby chair and glanced sideways at Khalili.

"Do you want to sit down for a bit?" she offered.

Meisa beamed and immediately retrieved the chair.

"How long have you been playing?" she asked, settling in beside Ruby.

"Since I was four," Ruby answered. "My nana has taught me since then but Mr. Khalili here has been my teacher for the past few months."

Meisa seemed genuinely impressed.

"I started when I was four too," she said. "That's *so cool*."

She leaned in close to Ruby.

"You're so lucky to have Professor Khalili. He is one of the best teachers in the country."

Ruby turned her head toward Khalili with an expression of suspicion and incredulity.

"You never told me that," she jibed.

"Well, you never asked," Khalili shot back jokingly.

He pointed to a big screen TV that was showing a live feed from the stage.

"They're about to start," he said. "Do you want to watch or would you rather not?"

"No, I can watch."

The recital began with one of the young boys taking the stage first. His performance of a concerto by Debussy immediately caught her attention and gave Ruby her first look at the company she was in.

As each soloist went up, it was clear that they were all so polished. Their were some clear distinctions between each soloist too. Each had a very individual style. A couple of them were technically brilliant, staying rigidly true to each of their chosen compositions' structure as it was set down on the page, while the other soloists displayed a more emotive approach, adding a touch of theatre to their performances.

One performer in particular, who was fourth on the program, proved to be the most exceptional Ruby had seen thus far. She wielded her violin through an impassioned rendition of a Bruch concerto, capturing the attention of many who were assembled in the back stage area.

"Who's that?" Ruby whispered to Meisa.

"Her name is Isobel Barrie. She's been described as one of the most promising talents this year. Everyone knows who she is."

"I've never heard of her," Ruby shrugged.

Meisa gulped subtly and nodded.

"She's an amazing soloist."

Ruby frowned at Meisa who stood as her teacher beckoned from over by the access to the stage. She straightened her dress and took a deep breath in.

"Good luck," Ruby offered.

Meisa smiled.

"Thank you."

Ruby watched her go then sat back in her chair.

Unconsciously, she began to bite at her fingernails as Meisa took to the stage. She could feel herself growing more apprehensive as the time for her own performance approached.

Khalili noticed her demeanour and he offered her a bottle of water.

"They're all so good," she commented from behind her upraised hand. "Better than I ever thought. I'm not gonna even come close to them."

Khalili reached across, took her hand and placed the water bottle into it.

"What makes you so certain?" he questioned.

Khalili turned toward Ruby and took her hand.

"When you get out there, notice where you are, take it in for a moment, then go within yourself. Put everything else out of your mind and remember that it is just you, the piece and your imagination. Make this piece your own, Ruby, and show them."

Khalili paused and took Ruby's violin in his hands. He brushed his hand over its shining surface.

"You and your violin, Ruby. Nothing else."

Ruby drank from her bottle, then set it aside and took her violin from the professor.

"Make it my own," she echoed softly with curious half smile.

Juliette approached Khalili and Ruby, and Ruby stiffened in her seat.

"Are you ready, Ruby?"

It was time.

All her training had come down to this. From that first discovery of her grandmother's forgotten violin in that dusty garage, to all those nights learning and practising under her tutelage as well as the countless excursions to the city and the window outside Elder Hall, to this very moment.

She stood and turned to Khalili who handed her the bow. He tapped the side of his head one final time for good measure.

"Show them."

Ruby stepped toward Juliette as the applause from the auditorium signalled her cue to take the stage.

Juliette guided her to the entrance where Ruby could see the chamber orchestra waiting in readiness.

"Please welcome our next soloist to the stage," the Master of Ceremonies announced. "Performing an original composition...Miss Ruby Delfey."

The applause struck up once more and, taking a deep breath, Ruby walked out onto the stage.

CHAPTER 33

THE LIGHTS SHONE BRIGHTLY AS RUBY TOOK in the capacity audience. Taking up her position beside the conductor Ruby stood perfectly still, straightening her back just the way Khalili had shown her and she held her instrument ready as the applause died away. The auditorium became utterly silent.

Her heart beat loudly as the musicians behind her lifted their instruments at the signal of the conductor, readying themselves.

This was her moment.

Ruby watched the conductor as he acknowledged her with an encouraging nod. Then he brought his baton down and the orchestra began to play—a single harmonic note that rose from nothingness and into being, giving life to Khalili's composition for the very first time.

Closing her eyes, Ruby entered into her familiar state of concentration, slowing her heart beat, listening as the gentle refrains from the accompanying strings lifted behind her, feeling a satisfying surge of adrenaline which carried her aloft. She could not have dreamed of a more beautiful sound. Ruby counted silently to herself and when she was eight beats from her starting position, she lifted her violin in one swift motion, settled her chin onto the rest and flicked her bow into the ready position.

Her first note was flawless, a strong and effortless refrain that carried through the auditorium with such clarity, that many in the audience were visibly stunned. She touched down and entered into her performance of *L'Chaim* relaxing back into perfect synchronicity with the accompanying musicians, leading them forward as she drew from their sound.

Her mind returned to the imagery of the concentration camp. Ruby saw the faces of the men, women and children once again. She tapped into their raw emotions—their fear, their torment, their desolation. She returned to the innocence of the child, who defied the prisoners' collective terror to stand apart from them and greet the towering shadow that brought down the walls of their prison.

Standing off stage to her right, Khalili leaned against the wall, his legs suddenly feeling like jelly. In all the years that had passed since he'd first composed *L'Chaim* in that very camp—in that very torment—he had only ever dreamed of it sounding as it did now. He felt himself teetering on the verge of tears.

His own memories sprang forth as the piece entered its darker phase. He remembered the child who had inspired the piece, the smiling orphan who he'd taken under his wing and kept safe during those years in the camp. It was that smiling face which had sustained Khalili himself and given him the motivation to survive, to endure and to write music when there seemed little point in doing so.

In truth, that very life which he had resolved to protect during their imprisonment, had been cruelly torn from Khalili. The monster, represented so benevolently in his composition, was in fact their Nazi captors. Rather than deliver them from their bondage to the verdant field beyond the wire fences of the camp, that monster had, in reality, taken the boy and delivered him to the gas chamber. Were it not for the Allied Forces' liberation of the camp soon after, Khalili felt certain he would have met a similar fate. The composition was, as a result, a tribute to this child whom Khalili could not save—the life that had been sacrificed so that many others could be saved.

Steadying himself, Khalili peered out from a gap in the stage curtain, gazing out upon the audience and the expressions on their faces. They too, were spellbound by this diminutive soloist. It was as though the imagery that he had conceived in his mind all those years ago—that which Ruby interpreted so vividly—had been delivered to every single soul in the concert hall here and now, so that they were seeing what she saw and feeling what she felt.

Asher slowly reached across for Virginia's hand and took it, feeling her grandmother squeeze it gently in return. They exchanged glances with one another and smiled knowingly.

Virginia closed her eyes and tuned into Ruby's violin. It had strength and confidence, with not an ounce of hesitation. Ruby arrived at each long note beautifully, drawing her bow with the grace of a dancer, lifting her audience up with her. She negotiated the more complex sequences effortlessly, moving fluidly, leaning into her violin when it was required and producing depth and emotion. Virginia knew that the audience was witnessing something special, something beautiful.

All sense of time fell away. The music was the only thing that mattered—feeling it and translating it. She felt nothing but peace within the performance.

And then, it was finishing. Approaching the finale with the dawning sun rising on the liberated prisoners in the meadow, Ruby lead the orchestra to the end of *L'Chaim*.

The audience erupted into appreciative applause. Jeremy and Asher, Belle and Cherie cheered, whooped and whistled above the rest of the crowd, turning to the people around them and patting them on the back and shoulders, making it known that they were with the young girl up on the stage. Asher leaned down to hug Virginia who sat in her seat, straight and tall, a dignified but beaming smile across her face.

Ruby stood on the stage, her violin by her side, overwhelmed by the attention, but smiling broadly. She felt exhilarated. She bowed low once, then twice, then looked across to the side of the stage to see Khalili clapping reverently, with tears of joy streaming down his cheeks.

Even before the first round had ended, Ruby knew she had made it through.

VIRGINIA SAT WITH Ruby back stage as both she and Khalili prepared for the second composition—the Mendelssohn piece.

Ruby had given the violin to Virginia to check and clean for her while she studied the sheet music for the Mendelssohn *Andante*.

Despite the field of contestants having been halved, there seemed to be more people milling about back stage now than there were when Ruby had first arrived. The other soloists were readying themselves and were surrounded by family members, assorted friends and their music teachers. Ruby could detect that a couple of them, including Meisa, were a little nervous.

She acknowledged Meisa with a nod from across the room now and Meisa smiled in return.

Ruby herself was much more nervous. She realised that she hadn't expected to make it through, so to be sitting here now felt strange, almost wrong. It didn't feel real.

Khalili had changed out of his earlier dress and into an expensive looking dinner suit, complete with a colourful bow tie. He was leaning down in front of the mirror presently, adjusting the tie and Virginia noticed beads of sweat on his forehead.

"You're not nervous are you?" she commented wryly as she elbowed Ruby gently in the ribs.

"No, not at all," Khalili replied, struggling to get the bow just right.

He eventually caused it to unravel completely. "Just never could...*tie* this damned thing."

Virginia stood from her chair and hobbled over to him, leaning down and taking the two ends of the bow tie in her hands.

"Let me have a look at it," she grumbled humorously.

Turning the ends over Virginia quickly and deftly tied the bow perfectly, much to the surprise of Khalili and the delight of Ruby.

Checking her efforts, Virginia stood back and nodded in satisfaction, noticing Khalili's expression.

"What? You think I've never tied a bow before?" she probed with mock indignation, before winking at Ruby. "Your grandfather often liked to wear a bow tie. Finicky dashed things they were."

Khalili dabbed at his brow with a handkerchief and craned his neck, testing the tension of his bow tie. He smiled with satisfaction.

"I'll bet you are nervous," Virginia challenged him. "You're preening yourself like you've got ants in your pants."

"I assure you, I'm not nervous," Khalili protested again, before his eyes flickered away from Virginia. "Well...maybe I am, just a little."

Ruby glanced up from her sheet music and at the professor.

"Really?"

Khalili smiled impishly and patted Ruby's leg reassuringly.

"Even seasoned performers are prone to the occasional jitters. Especially when we have the responsibility of a young charge in our hands."

Somehow, his admission put Ruby at ease and she returned his smile with her own.

"Look around you, Ruby," Khalili went on, gesturing discreetly to the other contestants. "All of them...so serious, so focused and all their people fussing around them as though they are as fragile as porcelain. But do you know what is missing?"

Ruby followed his gaze around the room, observing the other performers and the way they were interacting with their teachers and parents. Her eyes met Meisa's across the room once again, until Meisa's father scolded her in front of her group of supporters.

Ruby sensed that she knew what it was Khalili was getting at.

"There's a lot of...tension. They don't seem happy," she remarked.

"A very good observation," Khalili commended. He held his hands out in front of him, gesturing to their surroundings. "Look at where we are Ruby—where you are. You are performing in one of the most well known concert halls in the land. It should be an experience to remember for the rest of your days. This isn't an endurance event, a trial. You and I should have fun—first and foremost. Remember—this is what we love. When we go up there together, let us *love it*—yes?"

Ruby understood what Khalili meant and she took a deep, relaxing breath in and out.

Virginia, beside her, put an arm around Ruby and set the violin down in her lap. She gestured with a finger at Khalili.

"He's a wise fella," Virginia whispered softly. "You listen to him, eh?"

Juliette approached Khalili and Ruby and both teacher and student sat straighter in their seats.

"It's time, professor," Juliette said smiling. "You and Miss Delfey will be performing in a few moments."

Virginia leaned in and kissed Ruby's forehead.

"Good luck, sweetheart."

Together, Ruby and Khalili walked across the carpet and through the doorway that led onto the stage. The applause rose for them both. Khalili acknowledged the audience with a bow of his head while Ruby smiled. It was clear that they appreciated the presence of the celebrated musician and teacher and Ruby felt a warm sense of pride to have him here beside her.

A grand piano stood in the centre of the stage and the orchestra seating had been rearranged around it. The orchestra members themselves were standing and applauding along with the audience and Ruby acknowledged them as Khalili seated himself at the piano while she took up her position in front of him and to the left of the conductor.

The applause tapered away, and the conductor tapped his baton twice on the lectern.

Once again, Ruby began her breathing and straightened her shoulders, just as Virginia had taught her. The lights came down and the orchestra began.

A single bassoon heralded the beginning of the *Andante* and the orchestra gently joined it. Khalili lifted his glasses into place, turned the sheet music over and stretched his hands and fingers in readiness for his own entry into the piece. Although it was not usual for a piano to accompany an orchestra for this Concerto, when his fingers touched down onto the keys, the sound felt completely natural. His technique was gentle, assured and he looked up to see Ruby looking back at him smiling appreciatively.

As the opening melody moved toward her cue, Ruby lifted her violin once more, nestled her chin onto the rest and raised her bow.

She felt safe and assured in Khalili's presence and as her bow glanced the bridge of the violin, the resultant sound floated up across the auditorium, crisp and pure.

Settling into her seat, Virginia closed her eyes and listened to the beauty of the *Andante*, enchanted by the union of orchestra, piano and Ruby's violin.

And as she listened, her mind drifted up and away from the present and far into the past, to another time and place.

To the parlour room and the gramophone. To the child she had once been and the tentative first steps she herself had taken with this very same concerto, with that very same violin. The love she had for it and the music had first blossomed from Mendelssohn.

The scratchiness of the gramophone record, the tinniness of the sound from the speaker as she remembered melted away as the beauty of the orchestra here and now took its place in her consciousness, filling her heart, satisfying her soul.

Ruby once again became one with her violin, her hands moving fluidly. Khalili too, displayed vitality and emotion in his own performance, complementing Ruby's sound. They were in harmony with one another.

As she approached the central portion of the *Andante*, Ruby shifted her position slightly in order to prepare herself to take up both the melody and the accompaniment of the piece simultaneously in a complex display of fingering that was the highlight of this particular Mendelssohn composition.

Manoeuvring her fingers on the bridge, she stumbled ever so slightly and she felt a sharp twinge of panic, fearing she had lost her place. But she quickly gathered herself, stealing the briefest of glimpses at the audience. If they had detected her slip up, they gave no indication.

Virginia had heard Ruby's fumbling entry into the solo and felt the same twinge. It happened too quickly for many to notice but Virginia was sure the judging panel would have picked up on it.

Ruby then executed the tremulous accompaniment that required such nimble dexterity from her fingers. It took every ounce of her concentration as she traversed it, skipping across the complex section of the piece as though she were jumping across a fast flowing river, skipping from rock to rock, the threat of unbalancing and falling ever present. It was an exhilarating display, which was greeted with murmurs of appreciation from members of the audience in Virginia's immediate vicinity. Then, without any further hiccups, Ruby made it through and together, she and Khalili lead the orchestra towards the serene conclusion.

Once more, Ruby was greeted by an enthusiastic applause that rolled through the auditorium. Khalili stood from the piano, coming over to stand beside Ruby and together, they bowed and smiled warmly at one another.

In the audience, Virginia subtly made the sign of the cross over her chest and nodded to Belle.

"She did very well," Virginia said. "She did good."

Both Asher and Jeremy noted a hint of hesitation in Virginia's voice, but they said nothing and instead took in the enthusiasm of the audience, who seemed completely besotted with Ruby.

Several rows back from Virginia and the others, another set of eyes were focused on the diminutive performer up on the stage who bowed once more then turned with her teacher and made their way off as the next soloist was introduced.

Sonya Llewellyn held her program open to the page that featured Ruby's picture. Secured to that page with a paper clip, was the aged and weathered sepia photograph of the child who bore a remarkable resemblance to Ruby.

Beside Sonya, Andy kept up his applause as he scanned the audience in front of him, keeping an eye on the elderly Aboriginal lady he'd seen returning to her seat just as Ruby's performance was beginning.

As Sonya folded the program and lay it down in her lap, she looked over at Andy.

"Do you really think it's her?" she asked. "You really think she's still alive?"

"Well, who else could it be? It makes perfect sense."

Sonya frowned and coiled her arm inside Andy's as the house lights went down and the orchestra began their next performance.

"Keep an eye out then," she said. "I don't want to lose them in the crowd when they leave."

Andy leaned over and kissed Sonya's temple.

"Don't worry. We won't lose them."

CHAPTER 34

A LOW MURMURING CARRIED THROUGH THE AUDIENCE as all eyes looked to the stage, waiting for the MC to appear and announce which two performers would progress to the final round.

Asher and Jeremy craned their necks, trying to see over the audience in front of them. Asher squinted at the program in her lap, confirming that the announcement would indeed take place shortly.

"What's taking them so long?" she hissed in, squirming in her seat. Unknown to her, she was attracting the unwanted attention of those behind her, who scowled at hers and Jeremy's constant head bobbing.

"It's probably just so they can keep up the excitement," Jeremy responded. "But they're doing a bloody good job of it."

"Pipe down you two," Virginia snapped, glancing behind her, seeing a row of disapproving glares. "Just be patient."

As if on cue, the stage lights came up and the Master of Ceremonies strode out onto the stage and stepped up to the podium.

"Oh—finally," Asher said excitedly. "Here they are."

Following the MC from the right of the stage were the four semi finalists led by the young boy. Ruby followed behind him and behind her was Isobel Barrie. Meisa brought up the rear. Together, they stood in front of the chamber orchestra, taking in the applause. Ruby felt a lump rise in her throat as she looked out across the auditorium, so moved was she by the audience and their apparent appreciation. She felt very proud.

At the signal of the MC, the applause finally died down and he adjusted the microphone in front of him.

"Thank you," he announced, gesturing to the four children beside him. "Before we announce tonight's final two performers, I would like to congratulate this wonderful group of musicians who've taken part in this year's Malley-Joyce Recital. I'm sure you'll agree that they have performed splendidly here today."

Another round of applause carried through the auditorium as Jeremy glanced at Asher who rolled her eyes impatiently.

"Can they just get on with it?" she mouthed.

The MC signalled to one member of the judging panel who stepped up onto the stage and handed him an envelope. The applause dropped away quickly.

Asher instinctively clutched Jeremy's arm as the MC held the envelope up and opened it, taking out a card from inside.

"Tonight's two finalists have earned their place to decide the winner of the Malley-Joyce Scholarship and admission to The Lavery School."

He indulged a further pause as he read the names on the card.

"And the first finalist is…Miss Isobel Barrie!"

The young girl beamed proudly as she stepped forward and bowed low, acknowledging her coterie of supporters who sat in the front row, slightly to her left.

"And now…" the MC began, trying to quell the audience's continued applause. "The second finalist for the evening…Miss Ruby Delfey!"

Ruby's expression registered shock and she gasped, bringing her hands up to her mouth as she stepped forward. She looked across at Meisa beside her who grinned excitedly and encouraged her to stand forward, nudging her gently.

Jeremy and Asher were on their feet clapping and cheering, much to the dismay of Virginia who tried to quell their enthusiasm, urging them to sit down. But she herself couldn't stifle her own smile as the impact of hearing her granddaughter's name registered. She clasped her hands together and squeezed them with excitement.

Ruby's shocked expression remained as she stood beside Isobel Barrie, who politely took her hand as the MC gestured to both girls, clapping his own congratulations.

"Now," he continued above the applause. "Both contestants have submitted their pieces to the panel and the orchestra and they will be ready to perform for you in just a few moments. To Andrew and Meisa, well done on your performances this year. You have both done yourselves very proud."

At his signal, the two semi finalists bowed once then exited the stage. Isobel and Ruby followed behind them.

Khalili greeted Ruby once she stepped down and he immediately embraced her.

"Well done, child, well done," he congratulated, unconcerned about displaying his excitement. "This is unprecedented. No first-time entrant has ever proceeded to the final of a Malley-Joyce recital. How do you feel?"

Ruby looked up at Khalili through glazed eyes and bit her lip.

"Honestly?" she ventured with an awkward grin. "I'm shittin' bricks."

Khalili fixed her with a theatrical frown and tweaked her cheek gently.

"Come now. That's no way to talk. Let us sit down and go through your piece one final time."

Ruby shook her head defiantly and she stood back from Khalili.

"No," she said, her eyes narrowing in determination. "I'm not gonna let you in on this one. I have to play this on my own—no help."

"But Ruby…" Khalili protested, before he was cut off by a wave of her hand.

"I'm sorry," she said, unmoved. "But you said it yourself—we each have one piece of music that must come from us alone. I have that piece—but it is one you can't guide me through, professor."

Khalili stood, hands on hips, studying her. Then he relaxed his shoulders and shrugged, realising that she would not be swayed.

"Are you sure…" he began.

"I'm ready, Professor Khalili," Ruby said, without hesitation. "I know I am."

Khalili nodded and smiled, knowing her conviction.

"You are formidable, young Ruby…I knew that about you right from the beginning."

Khalili sat down and looked toward the television screen as Isobel took the stage and prepared to deliver her final performance.

He patted the chair next to him.

"Come, my friend. Sit and let us watch this last performance together."

Ruby caught Meisa out of the corner of her eye across the room. She was gathered with her parents and family. Their eyes met and Ruby waved to her. Meisa smiled broadly and crossed her fingers, mouthing 'good luck' as they were ushered through a side door by an official.

The applause from the audience sounded distant as Khalili gestured to the TV screen. Ruby turned her eyes toward it seeing Isobel taking up her position. The house lights dimmed and she began her performance.

Isobel Barrie played with consummate skill, proving that she was a formidable talent.

Having chosen the second movement from Ravel's String Quartet, she lead the orchestra confidently and assuredly from the spirited beginning, through the complex and theatrical composition, infusing it with a passion that left no one—least of all Ruby—in any doubt that she was going to be hard to beat.

Ruby studied her closely, watching how she moved with the piece. Isobel had changed into a vivid blue evening dress for the final, that heightened her presence on stage and drew the audience to her. Ruby noted her flawless technique—it was almost clinical and her concentration was precise. Ruby felt a knot of nervousness.

As the performance progressed however, Isobel made some slight errors in her transitions that, to the casual observer, might have gone unnoticed, but Ruby spotted them almost as soon as they occurred. Khalili did too, and they exchanged a surprised glance at one another. Suddenly, it seemed that they were affecting Isobel. For the first time, the indomitable mystique that surrounded Isobel Barrie was beginning to crack. Though she might have tried to deny it, Ruby took comfort in those errors. Isobel Barrie was suddenly just as fallible as any of them might have been.

Khalili turned to Ruby and indulged her with a knowing grin.

A subtle tension began building in Isobel as the pressure of her moment began to tell on her features. Her technique took on just the slightest hint of desperation as she fought to maintain control of her performance. Though it remained powerful, Ruby could see that Isobel had lost her emotional connection to the piece.

Finally, as if time had passed in an instant, Isobel Barrie reached the finale and she entered into it as strongly as she had begun. She had strengthened her grip once more and, with a final pluck of her strings, Isobel finished her performance and the audience struck up with enthusiastic applause.

Ruby breathed deeply and prepared to stand when Khalili placed his arm around her and gently squeezed.

"This is your moment. Make it your own. You can do this, Ruby."

"Are you gonna be here?"

Khalili nodded and smiled.

"I'm going to join your grandmother for this one—out there. I shall be with you."

He gently nudged her to stand up.

"Go. Your audience is waiting."

Ruby cradled her violin and bow in her arm and walked slowly to the stage entrance. The nervousness surged on a wave of adrenaline but Ruby began going inside herself, controlling her emotions so that they became a distant thrum.

Isobel appeared from the stage and stepped down. Ruby nodded but

Isobel kept her eyes forward and her expression stony as she brushed past her. Ruby blinked and watched her go but before she could react, the MC announced her name. Smoothing her dress one final time, Ruby pushed Isobel from her mind. She appeared from behind the curtain and made her way over to her spot in front of the orchestra.

Her heart began to thump. Her mouth went dry and she felt sweat on her brow, but she ignored them, returning to her breathing and finding her centre once more.

On cue, the quartet members and the orchestra turned over their sheet music in readiness and, as Ruby took up her position, the cellist winked encouragingly at her.

Ruby managed a smile as the house lights dimmed, the applause died away and the orchestra lifted their instruments.

Khalili crouched low as he quickly made his way to the empty seat beside Virginia and sat down.

"So?" Belle pressed immediately. "Did she tell you?"

Khalili frowned and shook his head.

"She is determined to keep it a surprise," he answered in a gruff whisper. "She's stubborn—no doubt about it."

Virginia smiled knowingly for a fleeting moment then she rubbed her brow with thumb and fore finger.

"Let's just hope she knows what she's doing, eh?"

The quartet began—introducing a soft harmony that carried across the audience with a warmth and ethereal serenity.

Ruby closed her eyes and began to count time in her head, synchronising her breathing and concentrating on the quartet's sound. She was centred now, calm and peaceful. This was it.

'Make it your moment.'

The quartet approached a subtle pause and Ruby lifted her bow, waiting until the music trailed off to nothingness for the briefest of moments, heralding her cue. Ruby bowed her head.

From the moment that Ruby drew the first plaintive refrain from her strings, Virginia knew what her granddaughter had chosen as her final piece. A shiver of recognition passed through her at the opening notes of the hymn.

Ruby swayed gently on the stage, rising gently on the balls of her feet entering into the composition—that which Virginia had secretly cherished for years—the one piece that her tired fingers could still negotiate across the bridge of the violin.

It was *Prayer For The Children.*

Virginia gripped the arms of her seat as Ruby held the bow precisely, producing the silken notes of the song with a gentleness and clarity that struck the entire audience dumb.

The sound was beautiful, more beautiful than Virginia could ever have dreamed of. Virginia knew Ruby had captured her audience. The auditorium around her was entranced and enthralled by her violin's song. And as she approached the end of the first passage of the hymn, the orchestra softly joined in with her, adding a unifying harmonic to her solo.

In Rex's hospital room, Davo sat quietly beside Rex, watching the concert on the television. Rex had been dozing on and off but at that moment, when Ruby began her solo, his eyes fluttered open and he turned his head towards the television. He recognized the hymn right away and, like the audience watching, he was captured by it.

Quietly, Rex began to cry and Davo reached over and squeezed his friend's shoulder gently.

It was the hymn of his sister, the hymn of Ruby's mother. From across time, the bitter years since her death, Aggy Delfey's beautiful voice returned to him and he rejoiced in it. Quite unconsciously, Rex raised his hand and placed it over Davo's and smiled through his tears.

Beside Virginia, Khalili sat in reverence of his young student. He knew this hymn well—though he was accustomed to hearing it performed *acapella* by a choir, rather than as an instrumental piece. Here and now, the beauty of Ruby's symphonic interpretation was undeniable and she commanded it.

In her mind, Ruby tapped into the memories of that terrible night— when Uncle Rex had confronted her in the back yard and Asher had in turn attacked him in Ruby's defence—and she poured it into her performance now.

After everyone had left and Uncle Rex had been taken away in the ambulance, Ruby had snuck out of the house and huddled in the rain, under the window of her grandmother's granny flat.

And, peering through the window into Virginia's little bedroom, Ruby witnessed her grandmother play her violin for the first time—the only time she had ever seen her grandmother do so. All that time that Virginia had taught Ruby since the discovery of the violin in that old car, Virginia had never actually played it in Ruby's presence.

In that moment, out there in the rain under her grandmother's window, Ruby knew that this was what she wanted to play.

Her eyes opened and she saw Jeremy and Asher in the audience—both of them were visibly moved. They had endured so much more than any child should, but together, they had prevailed through their love for one another. It had given them hope. In her own prayers, Ruby had asked for strength for all of them. Somehow, those prayers had been answered.

Virginia's eyes had welled with tears as long-forgotten memories bubbled up from deep inside her and flashed before her now.

Of her childhood, before she had been taken—her happy and carefree life in the Adelaide Hills. The faces of her mother and father, as vivid as if she had seen them yesterday; riding tall on her father's shoulders as they walked across the meadows near home, holding her mother's nurturing hand. Of the water hole where she had frolicked with her friends, so many years ago. Those friends—so full of soul and life, their bond seemingly unbreakable—until the people who came to take her away crushed it, robbing her of her youth. Her innocence.

Virginia had, long ago, abandoned the notion of prayer—or a belief that would deliver her from the life she had been forced into. Any hope of being returned to her mother had been cruelly snatched away from the moment the Pastoralist threw her against the verandah post on that wretched farm.

Yet, somehow, Virginia had found hope amidst her tragedy.

Ruby's performance weaved its way through the tapestry of Virginia's memories, bringing forth more of her past.

She remembered the dog, her unfailing companion who had been at her side as she'd worked from dawn until dusk, in the heat and the dust, the cold and the rain. The dog who had lain at the end of her bed as she huddled under her threadbare sheets, crying late into the night in the little stone out house. The dog who had become her protector against those who harmed her and sought to rob her of her dignity.

And she remembered all those countless afternoons with Agatha Penschey in the parlour of the homestead, where music had become her salvation, empowering her with a unique and special gift. The gift she had buried for so long. The gift that now lived on in her precious granddaughter.

Khalili noticed Virginia's tears and hesitated, wondering if he should comfort her or offer his hand to hers. But, for the first time, Virginia Delfey sat taller in her seat, she held her head high and proud and in that moment, Khalili realised that those were tears of joy rather than sadness. Belle leaned forward and acknowledged the professor silently, with a nod of respect, of gratitude.

Ruby continued on, absorbed in the hymn, complete in her performance. She was aware of nothing but herself and the music. Her fingers felt lighter than air. They hit their marks and she wielded her bow with the grace of a dancer. The beauty of the hymn was undeniable. Somewhere in her awareness she knew that she had never played like this before.

She arrived at the final bars of the hymn with a melding of the Orchestra's strings that produced a pure, perfect harmony. Then she rose up, lifting her violin's last notes above the Orchestra where she finished alone—as though the sound had been liberated and had taken flight.

It was done.

The crowd rose unanimously to a standing ovation. Their applause was electric, their appreciation unmistakable. Ruby lowered her violin and looked out into the auditorium, smiling politely—overwhelmed by the moment. She curtsied once, just as Asher had taught her, then turned to the Orchestra and curtsied again. The members of the quartet in front, those who had witnessed her first performance in front of the professor at Elder Hall, stood from their seats and clapped wholeheartedly, their eyes red with emotion.

She searched the faces of the audience once more and found both her nana and Khalili among them. His smile was just like the one he'd worn after that very first performance in his presence. It was simple, respectful but in his eyes, she knew, that his pride in her was complete.

Ruby bowed her head to him, then turned and walked from the stage.

CHAPTER 35

Isobel and Ruby walked onto the stage together for the last time, greeted once more by a standing ovation from the audience. The MC gestured to them both with an outstretched hand as they stood beside him, at the same moment as a representative from the judging panel stepped up with the envelope that held the final result.

Ruby watched as the MC took it and whispered something into the ear of the representative. She nodded once then returned to her seat.

"Ladies and gentlemen," the MC announced as the applause died away. "I have the results here which have been gathered from the four members of the judging panel. Each judge has scored both finalists independently, using the set criteria and no panelist has conferred with any other during the recital tonight."

"The winner of the Malley-Joyce Scholarship will receive full tuition and residency at The Lavery School, which will secure their continued education and music tuition throughout their entire academic career. I'm sure you'll agree this represents a once in a life time opportunity for one of these wonderful young performers here."

The MC peeled back the flap of the envelope and took out the card from inside.

Asher took Virginia's hand and squeezed it tightly. Jeremy leaned forward, listening expectantly. Virginia glanced at Khalili and smiled nervously.

The MC blinked at the card in front of him and he gulped in what appeared to be surprise.

"We...we h-have a tie," he announced.

A collective gasp issued from the audience followed by a low murmuring that rippled throughout the Concert Hall. Ruby glanced across the audience at Virginia, then at Isobel beside her, who appeared equally confused.

The MC conferred with the representative from the judging panel once more, nodding as she explained the situation to him, out of range of the microphone. Once they had discussed the scenario, he stepped back to the lectern and adjusted the microphone.

"Ladies and gentlemen," he began, holding his hands out, palms down, gesturing for quiet. "I have been informed that in this situation, a count back scenario comes into play. The judging panel are now reviewing their results for each candidate from each round, to determine the winner."

Ruby's mouth went dry as she clasped her hands behind her back. She held her posture as best she could, as she watched the judges look over their scoring sheets and relay their scores for both Ruby and Isobel from the previous rounds to their representative.

Several agonising minutes passed during which the level of tumult in the audience rose and fell.

"What's happening?" Belle whispered to Virginia. "Why are they taking so long?"

"I'm not sure," Virginia answered, shaking her head. "I guess they're making sure they've got their numbers right."

Belle glanced nervously at Cherie and Jeremy.

"They love to keep everyone hanging, don't they?"

The judging panel studied the compiled scores one final time between them and once the last member nodded in the affirmative, they all followed suit.

The representative stood once more and walked up to the stage.

"Alright," the MC announced with renewed vigour as the representative handed him the sheet. "The count back has been checked and confirmed. I will now read the results for both girls from each round."

The audience fell silent once more as the MC placed the sheet on his lectern.

"For the final, both candidates scored an equal 75 out of a possible 80."

The audience applauded appreciatively for both girls and Ruby looked over at Isobel who nodded respectfully in return, adding a smile.

"For Round 1," the MC continued. "Miss Ruby Delfey scored 76 out of 80. Miss Isobel Barrie—78 out of 80."

The audience uttered a long procession of "ooh"s and followed with another round of clapping which faded quickly at the gestured command of the MC.

"Okay—now the next scores I read will determine the winner of this year's scholarship," he said earnestly.

Virginia steeled herself in her seat once again and reached over to place her hand on Khalili's.

"Round 2. Miss Ruby Delfey—78 out of 80. Miss Isobel Barrie—80 out of 80!"

The applause came up before the MC could finish, but he continued over the cheers and the whistling.

"Ladies and gentlemen, Miss Isobel Barrie is this year's winner of the Malley-Joyce Scholarship. Please join together in congratulating her."

Virginia felt her heart plunge at that moment but she gave no hint of her emotions. Instead she sat proudly in her seat, her eyes forward as she held up her hands and applauded her granddaughter on the stage, who embraced Isobel warmly and congratulated her.

"You were amazing," Isobel offered with genuine admiration.

Ruby nodded in thanks then stepped back and clapped along with the audience, the orchestra and the officials, smiling graciously.

Jeremy and Asher were applauding their cousin as fervently as they could and Virginia noted that both of them had tears in their eyes even though they, too were smiling.

The MC stepped across to Isobel first, handing her a scholarship certificate and taking her hand in congratulations. She stepped forward, visibly overwhelmed, to bow to the audience and her supporters in the front row who stood and cheered. Juliette appeared from the side of the stage armed with two bouquets of flowers and presented one to Isobel, leaning down to kiss her cheek. Then she turned to Ruby and presented her with the second bouquet. She stooped down and kissed Ruby's cheek.

"Well done, my dear, well done," she said into Ruby's ear, above the din. "You have won a lot of hearts here tonight."

Ruby blushed and smiled in gratitude, feeling a warmth flow through her.

"Thank you," she mouthed.

"Ladies and gentlemen, please continue your applause for Miss Ruby Delfey," the MC announced. "This recital has been her very first public performance and I'm sure you'll agree she has shown herself to be a tremendous talent, worthy of a bright future."

The MC gently encouraged Ruby to step forward and she stifled a gasp of surprise when the audience responded enthusiastically by remaining on their feet in a standing ovation.

And in that moment, even though she had lost, Ruby felt overjoyed. For she was here. Her dream had indeed come true. It had always been her dream, from the very moment she had discovered that newspaper article in her classroom, to achieve all that she had achieved right here. She had done it, regardless of the outcome.

Ruby searched for Virginia in the crowd and found her beaming face, her exuberant smile and her tear stained eye.

Virginia side stepped out into the aisle and hobbled toward the stage. Ruby reflexively started forward. She leapt down from the stage and ran into her grandmother's outstretched arms which closed around her and held her, the embrace secure, safe and filled with love. Together they stood at the foot of the stage and held each other close while the applause continued.

Ruby looked up from Virginia and saw Khalili, his smile and his own misting eyes, large with pride.

THEY HAD GATHERED backstage, all of Ruby's family, where they were watching as a throng of people were mingling with the other performers and laughing and chatting.

Ruby continued to receive warm congratulations from a myriad of people, adults and children. So overwhelmed by all the attention was she, that it all seemed to blur. She couldn't quite comprehend it. Though she delighted in the flattery, Ruby soon felt the creeping tendrils of exhaustion begin to take hold.

A sizable group of media representatives were also there, including the reporter that Ruby saw at Elder Hall. Each had taken their turn in interviewing Ruby, this time, with the blessing of Khalili who himself, had answered a number of questions willingly.

Ruby was glad when the crowds of people began to peter out and she could spend a few uninterrupted moments with her family. She was marvelling at the runner up prize she had received—a hand crafted Graham Caldersmith violin. She had also received a cheque for $1,000, which she hadn't expected at all.

Asher sat beside Ruby, her arm around her, a broad smile lighting her face.

"Everyone was so impressed, Rube. They're all talking about you."

Ruby's cheeks flushed pink and she squirmed in her seat.

"I didn't even win but I feel like I did. I don't really get it."

"You were marvellous, darling," Virginia said proudly.

Ruby glanced at Khalili.

"What will I do now?" she asked with a hint of worry in her voice. "Is that it for me?"

Khalili sat back with an expression of mock indignation and shook his head.

"Most certainly not," he said gruffly. "We are a partnership, you and I. A good partnership can never be broken. This is just the beginning."

Ruby smiled, reassured, then considered the cheque in her hand. If that was the case, Ruby thought, then she should begin to honour his assurance right now. She thrust the cheque out toward Khalili.

"Take this," she said firmly. "This is for everything you've done."

Khalili chuckled and gently pushed her hand back, glancing bashfully at Virginia.

"No, no. You put that in a safe place and keep it. You have earned your prize. It is for you to savour."

"But…" Ruby began to protest.

"We should start an account for you," Belle suggested, interrupting. "And place it in there so you can save it."

Ruby nodded hesitantly, setting aside the new violin and placing the cheque in her own violin case, snapping the lid shut securely.

At that moment, Juliette approached them and smiled warmly.

"There is a reception for everyone next door in the banqueting room. Why don't you all come through and have something to eat and drink."

The mention of food caused both Ruby and Asher to sit up straight in their seats.

"I'm up for that," Asher quipped enthusiastically. "I could eat the leg off a horse."

Together, they all stood and gathered up Ruby's and Khalili's belongings. Ruby handed her violin case to Jeremy and patted it.

"Hold this for me," she said quietly, motioning toward the stage entrance. "I just want to have one last look."

Jeremy nodded and watched her skip across to the stage entrance and disappear up the stairs.

The orchestra was packing up their instruments and various stage hands were assisting while a slowly dwindling contingent in the audience were filing from the auditorium itself.

The lighted auditorium seemed so much larger now without the presence of so many people there. Ruby stepped down from the stage and walked down the central aisle, taking it all in without the pressure of competition weighing on her.

The stage before her, even now with all its myriad attendants packing up and leaving, still looked like the most wonderful place. A place where she had felt right at home.

She had been here. Up on that stage, doing what she loved.

Had it really happened?

Virginia, accompanied by Jeremy, Asher, Belle and Cherie appeared from the side door. She slowly made her way across to her granddaughter.

"There's nothing quite like it, is there?" she quipped. "The stage."

"No," Ruby responded softly. "I love it there, Nana."

"Once it's in you, it never leaves. Music has been so very much a part of our people."

Virginia followed Ruby's gaze toward the stage, silent memories lingering within her. She turned toward her granddaughter.

"Come on," she said, putting her arm around Ruby. "Let's go and get you something to eat."

Ruby nodded, and together, they began to make their way from the auditorium when a voice from behind them called out.

"Mrs. Delfey?"

Virginia stopped, turned around and felt herself grow lightheaded as she looked into the eyes of the young woman standing there. They were vivid eyes—familiar eyes.

Virginia blinked.

"Agatha?"

All at once the colour drained from her face, she staggered where she stood, forcing Ruby to react quickly by supporting Virginia under her arm.

"Nana?!" she exclaimed as quietly as she could. "Are you alright?"

With an equally concerned expression, the young woman stepped forward from the handsome man who accompanied her as Virginia fought to regain her composure. Ruby held tightly to Virginia's hand, concern etched into her features as her eyes darted from Virginia to the stranger and back again.

"I'm fine, I'm fine," Virginia whispered breathlessly, patting Ruby's arm to reassure her. She stood straighter, gripping her walking stick a little tighter as Jeremy and Asher came across.

"I'm very sorry, Mrs. Delfey," the young woman offered, extending her hand toward Virginia. "I didn't mean to startle you."

Virginia nodded quickly, her lip quivering.

"It's alright," she said in a whisper.

Sonya managed to smile down at Ruby and she offered her hand.

"You played beautifully tonight, Ruby. I was really hoping you'd win the scholarship."

Ruby nodded politely and smiled.

"It's okay. I'm just glad I was able to play," Ruby began, eyeing Jeremy and Asher, then turning to the stranger questioningly. "Nana…"

"I'm alright," Virginia repeated, more forcefully this time.

Reaching into her purse, Sonya took out the small rectangle of a photograph and offered it to Virginia, who took it slowly.

Gazing down at image of her childhood self, Virginia felt her emotions overwhelm her and she lifted her hand to cover her mouth.

"My name is Sonya Llewellyn," the young woman said as Virginia took her hand. "Agatha Penschey was my grandmother."

Ruby's head turned toward Sonya and her jaw fell open in shock—as did Belle's, Jeremy's and Asher's.

Sonya turned back to Virginia who bore a wistful smile and in that moment Sonya knew this woman was the same Virginia.

Ruby shook Virginia's hand and stood closer.

"Nana?"

Virginia smiled through burgeoning tears and squeezed Ruby's hand reassuringly.

She looked up at Sonya again, whose own eyes were beginning to mist.

"You…look so very much like her," Virginia said softly.

"Th-thank you," Sonya replied hesitantly, blushing.

Turning to Andy who was still standing patiently behind her, Sonya gestured for him to come forward.

"Mrs. Delfey, I'd like you to meet my partner, Andrew DeVries."

Andy came over and smiled, offering his hand to Virginia.

"Hello, Mrs. Delfey," he greeted.

"Call me Virginia," she said impishly.

"Um," Sonya ventured. "I'd like to talk to you if I could but perhaps now is not the best time."

Virginia hesitated momentarily and glanced at the children before nodding.

"We were planning on joining the others for the reception, before heading home. You can come with us if you like."

Sonya smiled and nodded.

"That would be lovely but I…What say we arrange to meet tomorrow instead? I have quite a lot to talk to you about."

So many questions…

Virginia considered Sonya's suggestion then nodded slowly.

"That would be good. I would like that very much."

Sonya handed Virginia a business card and she took it, gazing at the details on it. Jeremy quickly scribbled their home address down on Sonya's program in return.

"Is she…still alive?" Virginia ventured, a slight lilt of hope in her question.

Sonya shook her head slowly.

"I'm afraid not," she replied sadly. "Agatha died only a few years ago. It was very peaceful—slipped away in her sleep."

Virginia nodded, unsurprised.

"Come to my house tomorrow morning," she offered. "We'll talk then."

CHAPTER 36

PEERING THROUGH THE CURTAINS IN THE LIVING room, Ruby spied the compact black sports car pulling up outside the house, behind Khalili's blue Mercedes.

"They're here!" she called, running to the front door. Swiftly opening it, she skipped out onto the porch as Sonya and Andy stepped out of the vehicle and waved to Ruby who smiled.

Virginia looked up from the bathroom sink. She tilted her head at the sound of Ruby's voice and bristled with nerves—more nerves than the ones she'd experienced the previous evening. She had subsequently slept poorly. Her mind was racing as a result of the chance meeting with Agatha Penschey's granddaughter.

She inspected her features in the mirror and quickly splashed some more water on her face.

There was a knock at the door then and Belle's voice called to her.

"Mum," she hissed urgently. "Are you alright in there?"

"I'm coming, I'm coming," Virginia shot back hurriedly.

Outside, Ruby skipped across the lawn toward the front fence. She noticed a dog in the rear of the vehicle and she cocked her head curiously at the sight of it.

"Good morning," Sonya greeted as she stepped into the front garden.

"Is that your dog?" Ruby asked, pointing at the car.

Sonya turned back and nodded at the proud-looking cattle dog inside, its ears standing straight up, its long tongue lolling as Andy took a moment to lower the windows of the car.

"Yes he is," Sonya confirmed. "He's our baby—a big baby at that. We can't go anywhere without him."

Andy chuckled under his breath as Sonya winked knowingly at him.

Ruby noticed Sonya carrying a large briefcase and she wondered what on earth was in it. It fairly bulged to the point that Sonya almost couldn't manage it without holding it in both arms.

Virginia opened the screen door and stepped out into view. She smiled nervously and brushed down her dress quickly as Sonya and Andy approached.

"Look Nana," Ruby said. "They have a dog."

Looking over at the car, Virginia felt her heart skip at the familiar sight of the black and white cattle dog, peering out from the back seat.

"*Lantara*," she breathed.

A ghost.

Containing herself, Virginia flicked her eyes upward at the blue sky. The sun was out and it was quite pleasant.

"D-don't leave him trussed up in there," she quipped shakily. "Let him out and let him get some air."

"Are you sure?" Sonya questioned with concern. "I don't want to…"

Virginia interrupted her with a brush of her hand.

"Nonsense. Let him out. I'll get one of the kids to fetch him some water."

Sonya shrugged at Andy, who returned to the car and opened the door, allowing the sleek black and white dog out.

Simon instantly trotted inside the yard and stopped beside Sonya, sitting down, his tail wagging.

Virginia gazed at the dog, stifling a gasp. Her mind flickered back to the past, to the farm.

"My word," she whispered, leaning on her stick so she could bend down and greet the dog, who licked her hand happily.

"His name is…" Sonya began.

"Simon?" Virginia finished for her, scratching the dog's head gently.

Sonya's eyes widened in amazement as she turned to Andy.

"Y-yes, that's right."

"Your grandmother had a pup like this one," Virginia answered before tapping the familiar silver name tag that hung from the dog's neck. "He wore a tag just like that one too."

Sonya grinned knowingly at Andy.

"That's…actually the same tag, Mrs. Delfey. Agatha kept it and gave it to me when I was a child…as a sort of keepsake."

"Virginia. Call me Virginia," Virginia frowned as Asher arrived on the door step, armed with a bowl of water.

"Come on inside," Virginia said, ushering them indoors and into the kitchen where Khalili and Belle were preparing a tray of sandwiches with Minty's help. A pot of tea sat on the table that been covered in a chequered cloth.

Belle nodded her greeting while Khalili turned from the kitchen sink as they entered.

"We've made a sort of brunch…for you," Virginia said as Khalili greeted both Sonya and Andy, introducing himself to them. "I hope you're hungry."

"You're very kind," Sonya replied bashfully. "I-I must apologise again for arriving out of the blue like this, Virginia. When Andy and I saw Ruby on the TV, I took a chance on the possibility that she might be a relative of yours but I never dreamed that she would actually…lead me directly to you."

Virginia feigned a hurt expression momentarily, which she quickly replaced with a mischievous smile.

"I'm a tough old bird," she quipped. "It'd take a hell of a lot to do away with me. I—we—are pleased to have you."

Asher came up beside Virginia and whispered in her ear momentarily, to which Virginia nodded.

"Asher here is suggesting we might like to sit outside. She's prepared a table for us out the back."

Sonya and Andy exchanged glances, smiled and nodded.

THEY GATHERED AROUND the table in the backyard, which Asher had dutifully set up in hopeful anticipation of serving brunch there. Virginia sat at the head of the table. Belle sat beside her with Minty wriggling on her knee and Khalili sat next to Belle, opposite Sonya and Andy. Jeremy assisted Asher in bringing out the food and drink to the table while Ruby had retrieved Simon from the front of the house and introduced him to their dog. He sniffed around the older dog now on the grass nearby. Despite a few hesitant growls from the older animal, it seemed they were relatively comfortable with one another.

As cups of tea were poured along with glasses of lemonade for the children, Sonya reached down and opened her briefcase, lifting an aging manila folder out from inside and setting it down on the table between Virginia and herself.

"I don't quite know where to start with all of this. There is quite a lot to tell you."

Virginia smiled and offered both Sonya and Andy milk for their tea.

"Just start from the beginning," she said reassuringly. "Take your time, we've plenty of food."

Sonya smiled and nodded, taking a sip from her cup.

She opened the folder.

"Well…when I saw Ruby on the television, there was something about her that seemed familiar. She touched off a memory which lead me to the photograph of you. I found it among some old papers and journals that belonged to my grandmother—Agatha."

Virginia took the photograph of her childhood self from the pocket of her apron and set it down on the table. Both Ruby and Asher leaned in to examine it more closely as Sonya continued.

"I remember, as a little girl, snooping about in an old chest that Grandma used to keep all her precious things in—her journals, her papers and photographs. In particular, I remember the photographs of the child and I would ask Grandma about her. But she would always become very emotional and upset whenever I did. For the longest time, I didn't understand why."

Virginia picked up the photographs inside the folder in turn, examining them, shaking her head slowly. The Pastoralist's farm, the kindly stockman astride his horse, Agatha Penschey—leading her favourite mare—a photograph that Virginia herself had taken.

The sepia images took Virginia's breath away and her lip trembled.

"She loved photography…your Nan," Virginia said softly. "She loved to capture images of life. It made her happy."

Sonya paused, taking a breath in, considering her words carefully.

She gazed into Virginia's eyes.

"Agatha was heartbroken after you were sent away, Virginia. She couldn't forgive Vernon Penschey for what he'd done to you and it wasn't long before their marriage disintegrated. Agatha moved to Adelaide for a time until the settlement on the property came through and…"

"Settlement?" Virginia queried, interrupting Sonya.

Sonya slid an aging and fragile document out from the folder and put on her glasses.

"The property, *Carbelrow*, was in Agatha's name, according to the deed," she explained, reading from the document. "When she first came to live there, Vernon's family was in significant financial difficulty and Agatha, being from a wealthy family herself, poured a large sum of money into the farm in order to make it profitable. When the marriage broke down and she moved away, she…sold it out from under him."

Virginia's expression was one of stunned amazement at the revelation and she shook her head slowly.

"Agatha spent years," Sonya continued, "searching for you, exhausting every avenue she could. But it seems the authorities did their best to thwart her efforts. They took a dim view of her persistence."

Virginia bowed her head and closed her eyes fleetingly.

"I thought she'd...abandoned me," she said, her voice cracking. "At least—that's what they told me...at the orphanage."

Sonya looked up from her papers and gazed at Virginia, who was fighting to keep her emotions from overwhelming her.

"She never wanted to give up on you. She badgered the Protectorate Office—undertook her own investigation, but they wouldn't budge. Eventually, it seems, the bureaucracy won out."

Ruby watched on as Sonya turned over a few pages and traced her finger over the documents in front of her.

"Agatha also searched for your parents. She found the township where you grew up..."

"Totness..." Virginia said.

Belle and the children all looked at Virginia. This was the first time she had ever mentioned her childhood home.

Sonya nodded and continued.

"She spoke with people who knew them. After you were taken, your mother went to Adelaide in the hope that you might be reunited with her. Sylvia Crammond visited the hospital every week, hoping to take you home. She wrote letters to the Protectorate Office, begging...for you. But they refused every one of her submissions—that you be returned. Then...after you were sent away, Sylvia left Adelaide altogether. The last mention I have of her suggests she settled in western Victoria."

Sonya paused once more and breathed in before delivering her next piece of information.

"She died—a broken woman, some time in the 1960s."

The revelation assailed Virginia with an emotional force almost too much to bear. She brought her hand to her mouth and closed her eyes. Ruby went to her grandmother and put her arms around her as Virginia's hand began to shake.

Belle set Minty down so that she could reach across and take Virginia's hand. Virginia smiled at her, reassuring them silently that she was okay before looking back to Sonya.

"What about my father?" Virginia queried hopefully, her voice quivering.

Sonya raised her brow then and she held up her finger.

"It seems you had mentioned to Agatha once that your father was in the military," she said.

Virginia nodded slowly, as an old memory coalesced from deep within. She smiled absently at the face of her father.

"I did…" she remembered wistfully. "He served in Korea. But I never knew what happened to him."

Sonya lifted a new document out from the pile and offered it to Virginia.

It was an Army Service Record, complete with an accompanying photograph of a young, uniformed Aboriginal man with neatly groomed and parted hair, broad shoulders and handsome face.

Virginia felt the air being sucked from her lungs. At first, it seemed to be the face of a stranger but as she kept looking at it, the disparate memories of her father began to draw into focus—for the first time in decades.

A young girl, balancing on top of a man's shoulders. A strong, yet tender voice, telling her dream time stories from memory, singing an old Peramangk lullaby to her…

Virginia touched a finger to the cheek of the man in the photograph.

"Archibald Crammond," Sonya read from the service record. "Private in the Australian Expeditionary Force to Korea, 1951—your father."

Ruby craned to see the photograph in Virginia's hand and gently tilted the document so she could see it.

"He was part of the multinational defence of the Kapyong Valley when Chinese forces attempted to push into South Korea," Sonya continued. "Against considerable odds, the Australian troops, along with soldiers from the Canadian Infantry, managed to halt the Chinese advance and turned the tide of the battle in their favour. But—it wasn't without cost. 53 Australians were recorded as being wounded and there were…32 casualties…of which your father was one."

Andy reached down into the briefcase this time, lifting a small square box from inside and passing it to Sonya who placed it down in front of Virginia.

"Though Aboriginal personnel were generally not recognised for their service," Sonya explained. "Your father was singled out by the command for several acts of courage under fire during that battle. He saved the lives of several of his comrades before being fatally wounded by the Chinese. His commanding officer advocated on behalf of your father, that he should be recognised."

Sonya opened the box for Virginia, who gazed down upon two shining medals pinned side by side to a green fabric cushion underneath.

"Archie Crammond was cited for bravery and awarded a special citation posthumously. Agatha was able to obtain these medals with the support of your father's commanding officer, who was still alive in the mid 1970s—after she moved from Adelaide to Melbourne. That was where she met her second husband—my grandfather."

Virginia sat completely still. It was as though a thick veil had been lifted, a veil which had kept secrets for decades, everything that Virginia had ever known about where she had come from. Her very identity, her very being.

Ruby gazed in wonderment at the medals in the little case and a copy of the photograph of her great-grandfather that had been mounted inside the lid. Jeremy and Asher got up from their seats and crowded on either side of her and Khalili so they too could see the medals and photograph.

"He was a hero?" Jeremy asked.

"Yes," Sonya answered with a smile. "Very much so."

Virginia reached into her apron again, grasping a tissue and wiping at her good eye.

"We can take a moment if you like," Sonya offered with concern and turned to Andy who nodded in agreement.

"No, no," Virginia. "It's alright. I'm alright—please, go on."

Hesitating, Sonya closed over the service record and placed it to one side. She leaned forward slightly, steeping her fingers together in front of her as she considered her next words carefully.

"Now…there is something else which I've discovered only recently—since I saw Ruby on the television."

Reaching into the briefcase once more, Sonya lifted out another old folder and placed this new one on the table.

"My grandmother was an astute financial mind who made some very fortuitous investments during her lifetime," Sonya said, putting her glasses on once more. "Several years before Agatha left her first husband, during the period in which the farm prospered, she invested a small amount of money in a trust fund without her husband's knowledge."

Opening the folder, Sonya placed her finger on the first document there.

"This fund was designed to mature over the long term so once Agatha set it up, she filed all the documentation away and it was basically forgotten. It was never mentioned in her will, nor was my grandfather even aware of it. He never took much notice of Agatha's chest after she died, though it remained in his possession. When I opened the chest, the original documents for the trust fund were in there."

Lifting the document from the folder, Sonya glanced at Andy then turned it over and handed it to Virginia.

Virginia took it slowly and studied it carefully for several moments, scanning the document with her eyes, mouthing the words as she read them.

"Trust fund in the name of…Virginia Crammond," she murmured.

Virginia glanced over the top of the document at Sonya.

"I was able to retrieve the details from the institution where it is still held," Sonya said. "…Including its current value."

Virginia felt her heart quicken. Her mouth went dry and her hand began to shake more visibly than before. Beside her, Ruby listened intently. She had been sipping her lemonade but now she had stopped and was looking from Virginia to Sonya and back again.

"As at close of business today, there will be just short of $85,000 in the fund."

Belle, Ruby and Asher gasped in unison while Khalili put his hand to his mouth. Jeremy dropped his glass of lemonade, spilling it all over the table in front of him while Virginia sat perfectly still, her expression registering complete shock.

"It's yours, Virginia," Sonya said solemnly, her own voice now quivering with emotion. "Agatha Penschey was never able to reconcile her guilt in having been an accessory to your displacement and servitude. She wanted to provide for your future—to hopefully get you off the farm and into a boarding school that could give you the kind of musical education she so wished for you…as well as the opportunity for a better life."

Sonya's voice caught in her throat. Her eyes began to mist.

"Until the day she died, she never forgot—she remembered you, Virginia."

Virginia slumped back in her seat, trying to absorb the enormity of everything that Sonya had laid bare in such a short time. The missing pieces of Virginia's life that had been so cruelly taken away from her. Sonya Llewellyn, Agatha Penschey's granddaughter had returned them now—finishing the journey of the only true friend Virginia had ever known.

And now this gift, a gift she never could have dreamed of. Suddenly, she felt a wave of panic and she shook her head.

"I-I can't accept this," she said in a shaking whisper. "It's…too much. *This is far too much.*"

Sonya shook her head now, her eyes full of empathy. She reached across the table and took Virginia's hands in hers. In that moment, in Sonya's touch, Virginia felt the familiar hands of Agatha Penschey, reaching out across time, from the tranquillity of the parlour of the homestead.

The memory of those hands—which had taught her to hold the instrument, to play it and learn it…

"Virginia, it is her legacy. Her apology to you," Sonya said as Andy put his arm around her gently. "Agatha died carrying the burden of her failure. She wished she could have found you, given you back your past and provided for your future. I am here now to finish what she started."

Sonya placed the documents before Virginia and took a pen from her purse. Looking across at Ruby first, then Asher, Jeremy and Minty, Sonya nodded to them.

"You can give your grandchildren *that future*," Sonya ventured.

Virginia hesitated, blinking through her tears as she focused on the documents. Her hand hovered over the pen.

Belle squeezed Virginia gently, her own tears falling as she too looked lovingly across at the children.

"Do it, Mum," she whispered. "Do it for the children…for their future."

And then Virginia wept openly, letting the flood of memories and emotions spill forth. All the long years of trauma and hurt, the accumulated experience of her dislocation from her beloved Peramangk country, her ordeal at the hands of the Pastoralist and her feelings of abandonment by Agatha—the only person who ever mattered to her. The memories of her childhood were freed from the place deep inside where she had buried them in order to protect herself.

And finally, she was free.

Virginia lifted the pen and signed her name to the paper.

Ruby, Asher, Jeremy and Minty all gathered around her and enfolded her in their arms, squeezing her tight and planting kisses on her cheeks.

And through her tears of joy and love, Virginia reached out across the table and took Sonya's hand once again. They smiled at one another.

"Thank you," Virginia whispered silently.

Khalili's blue Mercedes pulled into the entrance of the grand, tree-lined boulevard and proceeded slowly inward toward a grand Victorian building that was surrounded by leafy trees.

Ruby craned her neck to see through the windscreen and take in the austere building whilst, behind her, Virginia herself scanned their surroundings reverentially.

The Lavery School was indeed as pretty as had been described in the prospectus but being here, in its presence, its beauty was something else entirely. Perfectly manicured lawns, pretty garden beds that were filled with colour. Students meandered casually on the lawns or sat in groups under the shade of the foliage. For a fleeting moment, Virginia was reminded of the orphanage, but the building they were approaching here and now held nothing of the sense of dread or oppression that Virginia associated with that other place. She could only sense warmth.

Khalili brought the car to a stop at the bottom of a set of stairs leading up to the administration building and turned off the engine. He looked across at Ruby who sat still, pensive in her crisp, new uniform. Sporting a burgundy blazer with the emblem of the school on its right breast pocket, a matching tartan skirt, shining leather shoes, Ruby looked very much the young lady, ready to face her new journey.

Yet he could see the worry etched into her face.

"Whatever is the matter, my child?" Khalili scolded gently, glancing over his shoulder at Virginia.

Ruby gulped and gripped the brim of her hat tightly.

"I dunno," she shrugged nervously. "Scared I guess."

Virginia leaned forward from her seat and placed her hand on Ruby's shoulder.

"You've got nothing to be scared of, love. This will be a wonderful experience for you—where you'll be able to do everything that you love and go farther than you've ever dreamed of."

Ruby peered out through the glass at the building again then looked down into her lap.

"But you won't be there, Nana…" she glanced at Khalili. "Or you, Prof."

Khalili smiled empathetically and patted her shoulder.

"Of course we'll be with you," he assured her. "We'll always be with you—at the end of the telephone, on weekend visits…any time you need us, we'll be here for you."

Ruby turned the corner of her lip upward and played with her hat in her hands.

"And we are with you in the gift you bring to this place," Virginia said impishly. "Take your *palti* in there and share it with them."

My *palti*, Ruby thought, smiling as she remembered what her grandmother had taught her.

"My song," she said quietly.

Ruby pushed down the handle of the car door and stepped out onto the pavement.

Khalili assisted Virginia to exit the car then retrieved Ruby's bags from the trunk.

Ruby went to Khalili and hugged him before he even had the chance to let go of her bags.

"Thank you, Professor Khalili…for everything," she said.

"You are…*most* welcome. And *thank you*—for giving me the gift of teaching…one last time."

Ruby stepped back from Khalili and wiped away fresh tears, before turning to Virginia.

Grandmother and granddaughter stood before one another now, too moved to speak. Both reached out and took each other's hands and held them.

"I'm…s-so very proud of you," Virginia said, gazing into her granddaughter's worldly eyes. "Go and catch your future now…okay?"

Ruby nodded, struggling to hold back her tears. She embraced Virginia and held her tightly, not wanting to let go.

"I love you, Nana," she wept.

Virginia smiled, a radiant smile.

"I love you too, my child of the Peramangk."

Ruby let the warmth of her grandmother's words nourish her for a long moment. Then, she stood back and stood tall, looking proudly upon Virginia and Khalili.

Placing her hat on her head, Ruby hefted her back pack onto one shoulder. Ensuring that her Vrassidaun violin was secure in the front pocket of her travelling case, she turned and climbed up the stairs, to the entrance of The Lavery School.

At the top, Ruby stopped and turned one final time to smile down at Virginia and Khalili.

And in that moment she felt the connection to her grandmother, as strong and as vital as it had always been.

And she knew she would never be alone.

EPILOGUE

12 YEARS LATER

A BREEZE WAFTED THROUGH THE BOUGHS OF a willow tree and touched the surface of the water hole, creating a rippling pattern that arced outward from its centre and dissipated gently upon the craggy shore.

Light from the sun danced over the water—a silent ballet of light that reflected in the eyes of the young woman who stood alone under the willow tree, quietly waiting.

She is tall, lithe and beautiful; with long raven hair that falls like silk half way down her back. Her flawless skin; the colour of coffee. Her eyes; filled with wisdom despite her relative youth. Her presence; confident and assured—yet she projects a calm serenity.

She stood in meditation, listening to the sounds all around her. The wind through the trees, the rippling of the water, the chirping of the birds somewhere in the sky above, the cattle in the field nearby. She closed her eyes and listened. To her, it was music—an opera in and of itself—a performance of nature that was for her and her alone to savour.

She was at home here in Peramangk country.

The sound of an approaching vehicle gently shakes her from her reverie and she opened her eyes slowly and turned to see the new arrival.

The blue and white police sedan slowed to a stop just down from the rise upon which she stood, under the canopy of the willow tree. It idled for a moment, then the driver extinguished the engine.

The front and back passenger side doors opened first revealing both a young woman dressed incongruously in the uniform of a chef and a teenaged boy dressed in a school uniform and blazer. Sighting the lone figure standing under the tree by the shore of the water hole, they smiled up at her.

"Ruby!" Minty called out, waving happily.

Setting down the small urn she was holding, Ruby turned and smiled warmly as her cousins skipped up the hillock and embraced her.

"Sorry we're late," Asher apologised before thumbing at the police car behind her. "Blame Jem. He was busy playing hero again."

Ruby planted a kiss on Minty's cheek and glanced over his shoulder as the driver's side door finally opened and Jeremy climbed out.

He smiled as he took off his hat. He was dressed in the crisp uniform of a police constable.

He was taller now, broad shouldered and carried a quiet air of confidence. So different to the boy he once had been.

Rising up to the top of the shore where Ruby stood now, he hugged her and kissed her cheek.

"How are you, Rube?"

"I'm good…better now you're here."

"You won't be late, will you?"

Checking her watch, Ruby shook her head.

"My flight's not until five, so I have a few hours yet."

Asher clapped her hands excitedly.

"Who would have thought, eh? London. You must be so thrilled."

Ruby smiled softly.

"Yeah. It's…I still can't quite believe it."

Jeremy glanced down at the urn beside Ruby's feet and regarded it with sadness.

"It's small," he said. "Smaller than I expected."

Ruby bent down and picked it up in her hands carefully. She held it out toward the others and they gathered around in a circle. Jeremy reached out and laid his hands over Ruby's. Asher followed suit and finally Minty.

They closed their eyes and fell silent, allowing the sounds of the water hole, the trees and the birds to take over for a moment.

"Nana said that this water hole was one of her favourite places," Ruby spoke softly. "She played with her friends. She fished here with her dad and she had picnics here with her mum. She said…she was happiest when she was here."

They all opened their eyes together and Ruby drew the urn back.

"This was her homeland—her *watta*. It is our homeland. This is Peramangk country…from where Nana was gifted to us."

Ruby carefully lifted the lid of the urn and stepped away from the others.

Looking up at the boughs of the willow, she waited for the right moment, then tipped the urn.

The ashes spilled forth and caught the breeze, blowing gently across the water hole.

Minty put his arm around Asher as she wiped tears away and Jeremy stood close by in quiet contemplation, watching as the mortal remains of their grandmother settled across the water hole, across the bank on the far side and further afield, until they disappeared from view.

Satisfied, Ruby turned and rejoined the others.

From the boughs of the willow above their heads, the breeze picked up again and in that moment, a sound akin to a satisfied sigh carried down and lingered among them.

SHE HEARD THE orchestra. She heard the audience. Standing in the wings, she stepped from left foot to right foot, a nervous excitement coursing through her. The luxurious red evening gown was so new that it felt starchy and uncomfortable. But it was undoubtedly beautiful. The heels, equally new, felt only marginally better—but only because she had worn them in for several hours. She held the violin in readiness as she ran through the mental exercise she had practised countless times over the years—her preparation to perform.

She was here…she almost couldn't believe it.

The applause trailed away as an announcer's voice sounded.

"Ladies and gentlemen. Would you please welcome to the stage, all the way from Australia—Miss Ruby Delfey."

Ruby lifted her head and stood tall as the applause struck up once more. She took in a deep, even breath and stepped out onto the stage, squinting in the powerful spotlights that trained themselves on her as she approached her mark in front of the orchestra.

Royal Albert Hall seemed vast—much more so than she had ever expected.

Looking out upon the audience before her, above her and around her, Ruby smiled politely, bowed her head then acknowledged the conductor beside her. He tapped his lectern and raised his hands to the orchestra.

Ruby raised her grandmother's violin to her chin and readied herself.

The conductor lowered his baton and the orchestra began.

Down in the audience, several rows back from the front of stage, a small and diminutive figure sat straighter in his seat.

And as his former student brought her bow down and began to play, Khalili closed his wizened eyes.

And he smiled.

L'Chaim

ACKNOWLEDGMENTS

To Steve Gilshenen, a Peramangk descendant, who unlocked the door to a beautiful language and a culture that has captivated and moved me.

To Molly Ringle, who became my sounding board and confidante during the writing of this novel. Your assistance and counsel was a diamond.

To Scott Taylor, who has been one of my strongest advocates and friends during this writing journey and whose encouragement and enthusiasm helped me no end at a really critical time.

To Chemda Khalili, who has taught me more about the value of identity in recent times than anyone I know and who allowed me to craft a character who is possessed of her beautiful spirit.

To Anne Akiko Meyers, Lisa Mazzucco and Rebecca Davis for their very kind consideration in the use of a beautiful photograph that truly captures what music means.

To the team at Central Avenue Publishing, namely Meghan Tobin-O'Drowsky and Jessica Peirce who polished this book like no-one else could.

Finally, my deepest love goes to my family - to Emily, Xavier and Lucy for giving me the greatest gift of all.